WHERE THE FIELDS GROW LIGHT

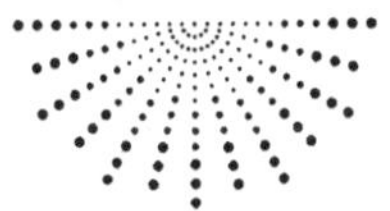

AARON DICK

First Edition

Book Cover Illustration by Léo Violet
Book Cover Design by oliviaprodesign

ISBN 978-0-473-52344-2

This novel is dedicated to Andrea,
for all the adventures she has taken me on,
including the one that led to this story.

PROLOGUE

Her earliest memory was the day that she had found her mother's light.

When she thought back on it, she would recall the pale blue milky glow. It filled her mind from edge to edge, but with no sense of a source or space around it. The light crept out from behind the edges of an old wooden door. By the time she was nearly twenty years old she had seen the door in her waking life many many times. But still, somehow, it was always a strange and unusual door in her memory, as though it had appeared into her life from some other world. Something about that feeling appealed to her. Her lips would smile and she would think on how many other wonderful new things there might be yet to see in the world.

It was the door in her mother's study. As she grew up she had become more and more familiar with the intricately carved whorls that covered its surface and the curled metal work that traced out from the corners and hinges, swirling up into a distinctly organic looking handle.

She could remember her hand reaching up, a

child's hand, tiny and delicate, stretching for that handle but not being able to quite stretch far enough. In the memory she would imagine that the door was slightly ajar. She had relished the rough wood beneath her fingers as she relived the moment that she had grabbed the side of the door and pulled it slowly open.

She had been young, perhaps only three years old, and she was not supposed to be in her mother's room. Normally they kept the door closed, to protect the small light from her curious stubby little fingers, but they must have forgotten on this occasion. It was a wall between her and something new and exhilarating.

In her memory, the hinges had creaked like the mysterious doors in all the best stories. Sometimes she wondered if it had creaked then in reality, or if the noise was something that she had added to her memories as she grew older. She did know that the door had never creaked since then as far she could remember. A creaking hinge didn't make sense, the door was well used and therefore well oiled. But still, in her dreams and memories, the hinges groaned.

Behind the door, the source of the light sat, growing timidly in its little terracotta pot on a table, beneath the glass panels of the cupboard-sized greenhouse that her mother had built to encourage it.

The plant was surprisingly small, considering how much light it gave off. It was only a few handwidths tall, and its stem and its vines were as thin and delicate as spider's-web. A few long, narrow, white petals curved around each other as softly as a summer's breeze. Two green leaves, as broad and thin as the surface of a pond, moved gently in the breeze of this small girl entering the greenhouse. The petals

shone with light and she stared until her parents discovered her and bustled her out of the room. She was
not supposed to go exploring, it could be dangerous.
In her dreams, she visited the tiny light, and then
swam into deeper blacker rest.

WHERE THE FIELDS GROW LIGHT

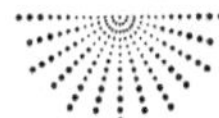

Shanti loved going to Temple in Graama, the small village she had lived in all her life. She cherished sitting with her family on the large red cushions that covered the floor and staring up at the spiral of candles that lined the circular walls of the hall then curled into the centre of the domed roof.

Every week her family would close their store and get dressed in their nicest clothes and then join most of the village in the large circular building, walking through its wide doors and greeting the priest Bratis as they entered. Bratis would always be found in his long white robe at the door while the villagers were entering, offering greetings and enquiring about everyone's health. Bratis noticed when someone was unable to attend.

She loved hearing him speak about the Masked God. The Masked God was always unknown, and could be anyone. It watched over everyone and manifested when one person took care of another. Shanti loved the stories that Bratis read from the Writ about times the Masked God had manifested most strongly.

After the stories, as the adults rose and stretched and chatted with their neighbours, the children would race out of the Temple and play in the fields and wood that lay behind it.

Taanin, her elder brother, was not good at making friends. He would stand at the side of the fields, watching as the other children ran backwards and forwards from the fence to the wall, shrieking in delight as they twisted to avoid the tag of the chasers.

Once Shanti had turned around, panting by the fence, one hand on the solid wood to keep herself upright, and watched her brother. He stood at the other side of the field with his skinny arms crossed and curls of his long hair draped over his face. He turned as if to leave, but then turned back and waited.

"Hey Galan!" she yelled. "Call Taanin to run!"

Galan was a stocky boy, almost a young man. His cheeks were dark from the effort of chasing the other children, but he turned to look at Shanti and then at her brother. He shrugged then nodded.

"Alright Taanin! You're the last one on that side. How fast can you go?" He called, beckoning Taanin into the grass.

Taanin uncrossed his arms and then clenched and unclenched his fists, as he tried to figure out what to do. Shanti thought he looked like a chicken, nervously looking first one way and then the other, with the same wide open eyes. Then, like a sparrow leaping away from a cat, he darted forward.

Taanin ran with an awkwardly long gait, and didn't move his arms as he ran, meaning that he didn't actually cover a lot of ground as he charged forward. He made one rudimentary attempt to dodge away from the tag of a small girl with a plait that nearly reached her hips before Galan sprinted up behind him and placed a solid tag squarely between his shoulders.

"Good effort," laughed the older boy. "Well done!"

Taanin smiled shyly, pushing his hair out of his face. "Thanks," he said, though Shanti could barely hear him.

"Well I'd say that makes it your turn," added Galan, gesturing to the children leaning on the wooden fence. "Which ones run now?"

Taanin caught Shanti's eye and grinned. "All the girls!"

Without waiting to see what the others did, Shanti leapt forward. She ran as hard as she could directly ahead, trying to get as close as possible to the safety of the far wall before she had to expend energy in avoiding the chasers. Galan had chosen someone else as his target, racing off to her left. Screams from behind her indicated that many of the chasers had chosen other prey as well.

Taanin was jogging towards her, still in his strangely upright way, and she swerved sharply to the right and twisted away from his outstretched hand. She heard him gasp in surprise. She straightened in her angle, feet pumping and arms swinging. Excitement had her heart pound even harder and she reached forward for the wall, slamming into it hard enough to drive the air from her lungs. Dazed, she turned around and raised an arm.

Cheers erupted from the boys at the fence, and they moved as one to begin their own charge across the field. Shanti looked sideways down the stones and saw the other successful girls lifting their own hands as well.

"Good work Shanti," laughed Taanin as he jogged up next to her. "I was nowhere near you after that dodge." His eyes were bright and happy.

She winked at him. "I'm not here to make things easier for you, you know."

He smiled again. "Of course not. Thank you."

The game continued under the heat of the midday sun.

As the children grew tired the game would inevitably break up and small groups would splinter away to other pastimes. Many would go home to tea with their families, some would leave to finish the chores that had been put on hold while Temple was in service. Fellbin had tapped Shanti on the shoulder.

"What is it, Fellbin?" Shanti's younger brother was too young to take part in the game on the field still, but she could see that he was chafing for a chance to do something now that the older children were splitting up.

"Can we go into the forest now?"

The forest around Graama was old and quiet and green. The thick trunks of the trees stood like pillars in a castle from a story, holding up the dark green leaves of the ceiling and permitting occasional columns of sunlight to pierce through. There wasn't much undergrowth and the paths were well worn. Shanti and Fellbin gathered Taanin with them and began walking towards their favourite place in the forest; the great statue.

Bratis spoke of the statue sometimes. He said that it was not mentioned in the Writ, but that the statue was so huge that it must have been built to honour the Masked God. The priest would pull his long hair back from his face and look at the children sitting on their cushions as he spoke.

"Many many years ago, probably even before your parents were children," he would begin, to the chuckles of the parents. "The people who lived in these lands decided to build a statue in honour of something very important that happened. From my research, I have discovered that there was a king who would travel through all of his lands every year, as he wanted to ensure that all his people were safe and well. When he came to these lands, he found that there was much hardship. So, he ordered wagons and wagons of food to be brought out here and distributed to all the families of Graama, and Baargu. In recognition of this wonderful representation of the Masked God's care for us all, the people of the villages spent years building a giant statue of him. When it was finished the villagers from both Graama and Baargu could see his face over the top of the forest.

Of course, that was a very long time ago," Bratis would finish. "In the years that followed there were storms that pushed at the statue and the hill it was built alongside suffered from slides, and eventually it fell over. But mark you young ones be respectful of that statue. It is a reminder of how we all should try to embody the will of the Masked God."

Shanti liked thinking about that story as she and her brother wove around the trees on their way to the statue. She loved hearing about the kindness that the Masked God inspired.

"Tag!" yelled Fellbin as he slapped Shanti on the back and then ran off between the trees.

"Uh oh!" yelped Taanin, before he too ran away from her in a different direction.

"Hey, that's not fair!"

The three of them ran backwards and forwards, weaving around the trees and leaping over fallen logs. Sometimes they would hide behind a trunk, holding their breath as they waited for a chaser to pass, then running away with a snapping of twigs and rustle of leaves.

As they got closer and closer to the clearing that held the statue, the game grew more difficult, as it always did. Instead of simply tagging each other, they would try to tackle their siblings to the ground. Shanti learned how to slide her foot into Fellbin's way when he lunged at her, turning his own momentum against him and sending him reeling to the ground. She would push Taanin's arms open when she was ensnared by him, breaking free before he could bear her down.

Shanti chased Taanin out of the shelter of the trees and into the longer grass of the clearing, grabbing his shoulders at the last moment and thrusting a leg amongst his ankles so that he fell. She landed on top of him, pressing his shoulders to the ground.

"Got you," she laughed.

Her brothers laughed too, Fellbin running over to them and helping them both to their feet.

The statue sat before them.

There was a hillside behind the statue and every winter the earth shifted and slid closer to the statue itself. Small mounds were beginning to rise around the waist and shoulder of the statue and one day it was possible that the entire carving would vanish beneath the soil. That would be a long time in the future though. In the meantime, the rock was worn down and smoothed by wind and rain, and birds nested in the higher crevices that remained. The small red flowers that bloomed in the spring like a rash across the statue's skin were absent now as winter approached, but the green lines of their vines still crisscrossed its surface.

It truly was gigantic. Although it no longer stood proudly as Bratis insisted it once had, the face was still mostly recognisable. It had large kind looking eyes, and a sharp nose over a bushy moustache. There was no crown on the head, which always made Shanti wonder if Bratis might be mistaken about it being a statue of a king.

Shanti wanted to believe him, but as she spent days playing on the statue with her brothers, she had to admit that she thought Bratis might be wrong. The statue wore no crown, and did not appear to be clothed or armoured in a way that would mean it was a king. It had been exposed to the weather so long that the lack of detail may simply have been caused by wind and rain smoothing the surface of the statue. Perhaps it had once worn finery suitable for such a figure. Shanti held on to the hope that the statue was a visitation of the Masked God though, built in recognition of the generosity that came from unknown faces and was such an important part of life.

It lay on an angle now, lying sideways in the ground, with most of its legs covered by the low grassy hill alongside it. One arm was lifted, though it was half buried now too. Together, the three siblings walked up and onto the half buried arm and began walking towards the head.

The head was massive. From where they stood, near the shoulder, the nose was easily twice as high as Taanin. They had to detour across the chest in order to climb higher, using the vines and grass that covered the statues as handholds, and the weathered cracks and crevices for their feet. Gravel shifted as they climbed, clattering to the ground below them.

Eventually they managed to manoeuvre their way to the top of the head, sitting down to examine the view.

The head was no longer visible to the villages over the trees, but the signs of life in them were visible from the statue. Smoke rose from distant chimneys, and birds were easy to spot circling the fields looking for food.

Shanti looked out over the trees, peering as far as

she could into the distance. Far far off to the east were the faint impressions of hills.

"What else do you think is out there?" she asked her brothers.

"What do you mean?" asked Taanin, his brow creasing.

"Who cares," chipped in Fellbin, before he began to clamber straight back down the statue. Taanin laughed and followed. Shanti looked out over the trees one more time before joining them. She couldn't see anything else but those hills, and the signs of the villages, no matter how she tried. Then she slowly made her way down the worn stone and dirt of the statue.

AFTER A SHORT GAME of hide and seek, Fellbin began to complain that he was getting hungry and so they started to follow the paths back towards Graama.

Halfway through the forest, they began to follow the banks of the stream, a small trickle of water that tinkled around smooth round stones. Fellbin kicked up water, trying to splash Taanin.

"Stop it!" snapped the older boy. Fellbin just laughed.

"You'll get your shoes and clothes wet. Just stop splashing would you?" asked Shanti.

Fellbin rolled his eyes, but refrained from splashing after that.

After they had been walking for about twenty minutes, another boy came strolling towards them through the tree trunks, whistling as he came and with a rabbit slung over his shoulder.

"Hello Ban," called Fellbin. Shanti wondered where her younger brother had met the other boy, known in Graama for his petty mindedness. "What have you got there?"

"Caught myself a rabbit." replied Ban with a smirk. "Now I was wondering what to do with it. Their feet are supposed to be lucky, maybe I'll take it home and chop one off!" He laughed horribly and shook the string that held the rabbit. Startled, it kicked and bucked against his back. "I might find out how well it jumps with only one." He grinned, pulling his lips back from his shining teeth.

Shanti blinked. "It's still alive?" she said.

"Well, yeah. I snared it back a ways" He jabbed a thumb back into the forest. "But I'll get around to killing it eventually. Might make stew." Ban shrugged. "Would have been easier if the snare had done a better job, but we live and learn."

Shanti found that she could not speak. Her thoughts were bound up with the rabbit, just as its legs were. She could only think of how scared it must be, and how cruel it was to carry the thing around and joke about cutting its feet off. Without making any decisions, she charged directly at Ban, burying her shoulder into his stomach and knocking him to the ground.

"What the-" he had yelled, before the impact drove all the breath from his lungs. As they sprawled across the ground, he let go of the string and the rabbit began to kick in its bindings. Shanti reached over and began to loosen the string. Just as she opened the knot enough to slip it back over the rabbit's heels, letting it bound away through the leaves and moss of the forest floor, Ban recovered and lunged at her.

"What do you think you're doing, you little-" He growled, tangling one hand in Shanti's hair and pulling her backwards.

From there, the fight escalated. Ban was strong, and his anger drove him to cruelty. His fists swung wildly. Taanin darted in and out, clearly knowing that he should get involved for the sake of his sister, but unable to decide how. Fellbin screamed and charged at the older boy and was elbowed in the face for his trouble. Shanti fought back, slapping at Ban and wriggling out of his grip, but never quite fast enough to completely escape. The heat of her anger faded, and she began to feel cold dread cover her skin in goosebumps.

Eventually she managed to push hard with her legs and roll the older boy onto his back, where she found herself lying across him. She spun slightly, then dug the long fingernails of her left hand into the soft flesh between his thumb and finger. Ban began to yell in pain and, as he did, she shoved the top of her head into his chin, closing his teeth with a sickening snap. Shanti leapt sideways, finally free of the boy's hands.

Ban stumbled upright, blood spluttering from his mouth as he clutched at his face with both hands.

"'At 'ave 'ou 'one, 'ou 'upid 'irl?" he snarled, before turning to run to the stream where he splashed handfuls of water on his face. The water fell in a red rain.

"Let's get out of here," exclaimed Shanti, grabbing Fellbin and beginning to run towards the village.

"Come on Taanin!" she yelled, finally sparking movement from her older brother. Together the three of them sprinted until their lungs were bursting and their legs were stinging. The path led at first straight alongside the stream, and so they ran alongside it, sometimes darting through it or across the round wet stones. A crash made Shanti spin around, wondering if Ban had caught up with them and was now punishing Taanin for his sister's actions. But it wasn't the young trapper. Taanin had slipped on an algae covered rock, spinning and falling awkwardly into the stream. His face had gone pale.

"Are you alright?" Shanti panted. She heard the sounds of Fellbin stop running and coming back to see what had happened.

"I… I…" Taanin was trying to speak. He lifted himself by his left arm, water streaming from his soaked clothes. Then he gritted his teeth and tried to raise his right arm. Shanti gasped. Taanin's arm had an extra corner in it, halfway along his forearm. It looked as though he had grown a new elbow.

"Can you get up?" asked Shanti, feeling her throat tighten.

Taanin opened his mouth, then groaned and rolled his eyes. He managed to nod though. Slowly, so slowly that Shanti was sure Ban would burst out of the trunks onto them any moment, Taanin stood up and moved out of the stream. He was breathing hard, and cradling his damaged arm.

"We still need to run," said Shanti. Again Taanin managed to nod. The three of them began to move, jogging at first to gauge how Taanin could cope, but stepping faster and faster if he kept up.

They didn't stop when they saw the red brick buildings of Graama from the edges of the forest, nor when they had run through the lanes between the fields, lined with low stone walls. They pounded through the main street until they were at home, safe, with the door slammed shut behind them.

"What on earth happened to you!" screamed their father, Neeran. He was a skinny man everywhere but his stomach, which popped forward like a small ball. He wore his black hair long, and maintained a small moustache and beard on his face. Right now that face was screwed up in horror.

"Taanin fell over," Shanti began, but found she was bustled aside without much attention. Neeran knelt down by Taanin, guiding him to a soft couch in the sitting room. Their father whistled softly.

"This is one awful break. What were you doing?"

"We were just..." Taanin swallowed, sweat beading on his forehead. "I mean, I was..."

"We were chasing each other," said Shanti. "And Taanin slipped on one of the rocks in the stream. Can you do anything?"

Neeran sighed and shook his head. "Not here, not me." He wiped his son's forehead and stood up, running a hand through his long hair. "We are going to have to get him to Baargu, and that trip is a couple of hours. Best try to get on our way now."

Baargu was the next village along the main road from Graama. There would be a doctor there, someone who was trained in ways to set this bone so that Taanin would be able to use it again in the future, who knew what herbs would bring down his pain and risk of infection. Nobody in Graama had such training, though everyone knew some folk remedies.

Normally the idea of a trip to Baargu would have excited Shanti. Ever since she had been a tiny babe, she had wanted to spend her days exploring distant places, discovering new things. Even Baargu, which was easy enough to visit and return from within a single day, offered some excitement and novelty. When Shanti had been younger, visitors from the next village would find themselves followed around their business in Graama by the tiny girl. But this time the trip would not bring her joy.

Fellbin had been standing in the doorway watching, but by the time Shanti turned to give him some instructions, the young boy had completely vanished.

Shanti was fairly sure that they would not see him before they returned. Instead, she raced upstairs to her small room and grabbed some essential items. "A blanket to keep him warm... New shoes, in case we have to walk a long way... A change of clothes for me." She spread the blanket out across her bed and then threw everything in the middle of it. She slipped next door to the boys' room and grabbed a change of clothes for Taanin also. Then, confident that she had everything that she might need, she picked up the corners of the blanket and tied them together, creating a bag of sorts.

As she walked back down the stairs, ready to call out to her father that she was ready to go, there was a sudden and extended banging at the front door.

Shanti stood on the stairs and watched as her father came out of the sitting room to answer the banging. His face was tight as he pulled the door open.

Vit was standing on the front step, blood soaked down the front of his shirt. His father Tareen stood behind him, one massive hand on his son's shoulder.

"What are you going to do about this, eh?" yelled the man. His face was curling up in anger. Neeran gaped and shook his head.

"What do you mean? What's going on? I have some problems to deal with myself right now and-"

"I bet you do Neeran, I bet you do! Those young rats must be a handful and a half!"

"Rats? I beg your pardon?" Neeran's voice was growing in volume and anger to match that of Tareen's. "You come banging on my door, only a few hours after Temple, to call my children rats?" His fingers tightened on the wood of the front door.

"What would you call someone who did this to your boy then?" And the man waved a hand at the blood on his son's front. Ban was holding a rag to his face and glaring at Shanti, who was still frozen in one spot on the stairs.

"You think one of my boys did that?"

"Not at all. It was her!" The finger stabbed directly towards her, holding firm and still in its accusation. Shanti stepped back up one stair.

"Shanti? You must be mistaken, Shanti is always taking care of everyone. She would never do something like this."

"Oh, he's sure, aren't you son?"

Ban nodded.

"But it took us long enough to figure out what he was trying to say. I think he's cracked some teeth, or broken his jaw, or mangled his tongue, or something. I'm going to have to take him to Baargu, no one here will be able to cope with this."

"Shanti?" Neeran turned and Shanti saw the confusion and hurt rising in her father's brown eyes. She wanted to melt away into the floor. She clutched her stomach with her hand and grimaced.

"I… I'm so sorry dad…" She bowed her head, hot tears building in the corners of her eyes.

"Well. I can see that we will have to have a very long conversation with our daughter when we get back tonight." Neeran turned away from her and spoke to Tareen. "Taanin has broken his arm, so we were just arranging to go to Baargu as well. Do you have a coach? It seems that we should share the transport. Perhaps we can sort this out on the way. Shanti, bring the bag."

He spoke her name shortly, clipping the sounds to a rapid conclusion. A tear dripped from the end of her nose, but she nodded and walked down the stairs.

"Fellbin, help your brother."

Before she knew it, Shanti found herself sitting wedged into the corner of a coach seat, pressed against the side of the compartment with only a slim view out the window. Ban sat opposite her, their knees almost touching. His eyes still glared into hers.

While the coach rattled along the road towards the next village, Neeran and Tareen discussed how they would deal with the consequences of the day. Neeran ended up agreeing to pay for Ban's care, an agreement that burned Shanti's ears and made her lower her head again.

Her side of the fight did come up eventually. She didn't trust herself to speak, sure that her father would think that she was only trying to make excuses for what had happened, but Fellbin was always happy to speak with no regards to the reaction, and he explained about the rabbit and the way Ban had spoken so cruelly of it. Tareen had grunted and pursed his lips, agreeing that his son should not have behaved in such a way. But then Neeran added that it was no excuse for Shanti's actions. She was to be restricted to the house unless she was in lessons, working at the family store, or attending Temple.

"For how long?" she murmured.

"Until I believe and trust that you won't push your feelings onto someone else," replied her father.

After the discussion, the trip lapsed into silence.

Over an hour passed before the coach rounded a corner and Baargu could be seen past the trees. Luckily the village doctor was not busy and she saw both children immediately. Ban was seen first, as the amount of blood loss worried the doctor.

Shanti sat in the next room, avoiding her father's eyes. "I'm sorry," she said.

He placed one hand on her shoulder. They waited.

Ban came out with bandages around his lower jaw.

"- regularly, and give him plenty of these herbs.

He will need to replace the lost blood and give his mouth time to heal." The doctor turned and smiled at Neeran. "Alright, now we will take your boy."

Shanti and Fellbin came in too, but there wasn't much excitement to be had in the doctor's private room. She examined Taanin's arm and then gave him something to bite down on while she pulled the pieces of the arm back into position. Taanin's skin paled and his eyes rolled, but he managed to hold on through the pain. Then she used some pieces of wood and cloth bandages to hold the arm still. Finally, she gave Neeran a clay pot filled with a paste made from herbs.

"Give him some of this to help with the pain. He'll need to come back to see me regularly, to make sure it is healing properly."

Neeran thanked her and made some arrangements to pay her for her time. Shanti wasn't very familiar with money, but it certainly sounded like a lot.

As the two families rode the coach home under a darkening twilight sky, Neeran and Ban's father discussed the difficulties of having to travel so far to get help for their injured children.

"We're just lucky that it wasn't any more serious," said Tareen. "And it was plenty serious!"

"I agree. We will have to get the council to ensure we have a doctor in Graama. I don't know how we will get them, but we need them."

When they got home, Shanti's mother Auga had arrived also. She looked worried, and bundled Taanin into her arms as the family walked inside.

"Where have you been, when I got home the house was dark and silent. It was as though you had all completely vanished!"

"I had to take Taanin to Baargu, he broke his arm this afternoon."

"Oh my poor sweet child." Auga cradled his head in her arms, kissing his hair.

"Yes. But we rode with Tareen and his boy Ban."

"Oh?"

"It appears that Shanti got into a fight with the boy over his treatment of a rabbit. She nearly broke his jaw, and severely damaged his tongue."

"What?" Auga turned her gaze onto Shanti, who tried to hide behind herself.

Neeran explained the whole story as they worked together to produce a simple dinner. Everyone ate quickly, and then Fellbin and Taanin were bundled into their beds. Shanti was told to wait for her parents to speak to her in the sitting room. She sat silently, with hands on her knees, and wondered what would happen to her. By the time they returned the darkness of the night outside was pressing against the curtains.

The conversation was serious, but brief. Auga and Neeran never shouted. They were not angry, just disappointed. It all made Shanti feel even worse.

"You have always been so good at taking care of your brothers," Auga explained. "You help keep an eye on Fellbin. You are so kind to Taanin. It just makes us sad when we see that you are not treating others that way."

"And we need your help," Neeran reminded her. "I have my hands full in the house most days, and your mother works so hard at the store. We rely on your help." His eyes were so large. Shanti nodded.

"I'll do better," she said.

"Good," said Auga, leaning over to hug her. "Now go to bed."

That night Shanti lay in the darkness for hours. She kept replaying the day in her head, wondering how she could have done anything differently. The rabbit's eyes had looked so scared. But her parents relied on her. They needed her to take care of her brothers, to help out. They need her to stop letting her feelings get in the way of that.

Shanti rolled over and pulled her blankets higher around her shoulders. She wouldn't let them down.

SHANTI GREW up making sure that she was helping. She began to come with Auga to the store from the time she was ten years old, and she made sure to keep an eye on Fellbin whenever her parents were busy. That was enough to fill anyone's days, but still she found more to do.

Soon after starting shifts at the store, Shanti volunteered to spend some time learning about lights keeping from the Village Gardener Sudru.

The woman lived in a small rundown shack on the edge of the village, but it was really only a place for the gardener to sleep. The rest of the time she spent carefully pruning and weeding around the few lights that bordered the signs of the village's businesses. The Tired Rabbit, the pub that sat in the middle of the village, had green vines that traced around the metal letters of its sign. The Mayor's house traditionally grew red lights around the front door, but since the mayor was voted on every few years, Sudru had to ensure that the lights were healthy enough to be transplanted if needed. Weeds threatened the delicate lights, and so she spent long hours plucking every dangerous shoot from the soil, or devising methods to remove insects from their stems.

Once a week, Shanti followed Sudru around for the morning, trying to learn as much as she could about the care of the lights. She wanted to bring her knowledge home to the small self-made greenhouse that was attached to the back of their house, to use it to help her mother encourage the tiny light that grew there into something even more magnificent. Over years, she slowly began to understand how to improve the soil, what sort of compost to build that would suit the specific variety of light that Auga was tending. The benefits were small, maybe a few centimetres more height, but every new leaf made Shanti's heart swell with pride.

Shanti spent one morning listening to Sudru lecture about the dangers of morning frosts. Lights were sensitive to temperature, and the coolness of morning could be the death of many species. Sudru described exactly how the frost would affect the plant, killing of the edges of its leaves, or blackening the tips of its shoots. She wouldn't allow Shanti to leave until the younger woman had been able to draw three versions of a leaf that Sudru held up, drawings to show the leaf when healthy, when affected by frost, and when affected by heat.

Now, allowing her mind to wander after its workout, Shanti walked to the edge of the village where its clustered red brick buildings stopped abruptly and were replaced by a low stone wall that encircled the village before breaking off into branches of stone that divided the fields beyond. Shanti could see her neighbours in many of those fields, working to gather the vegetable harvest before the winter began to settle in, and beginning repair-work to the walls that had been worn down by the last year's storms.

Taanin would be out there somewhere, developing his callouses. He had grown up insisting on taking part in the most laborious work he could find in Graama. Shanti hoped he was actually talking to some of the other labourers, but imagined he wasn't.

She would have to take him out with her again soon. She stood and enjoyed the view of the fields stretching off towards the hills beyond, dotted with clumps of low green trees.

"Entrancing sight, yes?"

Shanti blinked, the sudden closeness of the voice surprising her.

"I'm sorry?" She turned to see who had spoken to her. An older man with a narrow tuft of white hair protruding from his chin was smiling up at her. He stood arm in arm with an older woman, who wore a shawl wrapped around her head, with only a few small greying curls of hair poking down from her forehead.

"The view is quite beautiful," The man gestured towards the fields, bright and green in the sunlight, a gentle breeze rustling the plants and carrying smells of living things to them.

"Oh, I see, yes it is lovely," Shanti smiled at the couple.

"We have come out on a special trip," the old man began to explain. "This is my wife Dulku, and my own name is Darsat."

"It's a pleasure to meet you both, my name is Shanti." She shook their hands.

"Are you from this place?" asked Dulku.

"Yes, born and raised," admitted Shanti cheerfully.

"It is beautiful. We came here all the way from Gorduum because of Darsat's clever idea. He works at the University you know?"

"Oh, that sounds very important." Shanti was surprised to see people from the great city coming all the way to Graama. All the stories she had heard about Gorduum made it sound as though it was a magnificent place, with towering buildings and full of strange and delightful inventions. These people must be used to so much more overwhelming sights and sounds than a simple field, no matter how green it was. "What brings you so far away from there?" To her mind, there was no reason to ever come to such a small, quiet place as Graama.

"My Darsat, he has such a clever idea!"

Shanti nodded. "He must, to work at the University. I've heard that not even one in fifty of the cleverest people are able to find a space in the University."

Darsat lifted a hand to brush aside the compliment, but nodded and smiled at Shanti's remark. "Well, I suppose it is a very careful community." He ran a hand down his narrow beard. "In fact, I have heard that there is an impressive statue not far from this village! I believe that it may in fact be an ancient map of the stars in the sky at night!" He smiled even wider, his teeth gleaming in the sunlight, matching the twinkle in his eye.

Shanti tried not to frown, but she was confused. The statue to the north was huge and interesting, but it was also half-forgotten and falling apart, half buried in landslides down the hillside and overgrown with vines and bushes. How could it be in any way connected to the stars?

"That is a wonderful idea sir." Shanti paused as she considered what to say next. "How did you come up with it?"

"I should love to show you! Come, let us find a place to sit down!" Darsat and his wife turned to walk back into the town and Shanti followed them. They seemed friendly, and she had nothing to do until it was time for her shift at her mother's store later. Besides, they were from outside the village, they must have plenty of wonderful stories to share.

The trio walked back between the brick buildings

to the Tired Rabbit, where they sat and ordered a meal. Darsat spent the time they were waiting for their food by gesturing widely and explaining his theories about the statue.

"You see, in the engraving and sketches that have made it back to the University, it is clear, at least to me," and here he glanced down briefly, hinting at his humble nature. "Clear to me that the knobs and rounded edges of the statue's face and clothing have a correlation to the constellations." He dug a hand into his jacket pocket and drew out a worn and much-folded piece of paper. "Here." He unfolded it care-fully, and slid it across the table to Shanti. She could see where the paper was beginning to separate along the folds that had been made so often. On the paper itself she was surprised to see that it really was a faded sketch of the statue to the north, the outline of its shape quite clear, although the details looked smeared or fuzzy to her.

"I... I'm afraid I..."

"Here my dear," said Darsat, as he leaned over to point at the drawing. Dulku smiled encouragingly and thanked the maid who placed a platter of bread and cheeses down between them at the table.

"Can you see this cluster of wrinkles and ridges, near the chin?"

"Yes."

"Well, that must be the Mountains of the Sky, don't you think? The arrangement is so precise! Down to the millimetre! And, of course, that would mean that this part leading down from that is?" He left the sentence unfinished, hanging in the air as a question. Shanti found she wanted to have an answer for his curious eyes. Dulku chewed on her bread and cheese, emitting happy noises.

"I suppose it would be... The Archer?"

"Exactly!" Darsat fell back into his seat in triumph and reached over to pick up a piece of the hard pale cheese. "Well done my girl!"

Shanti looked at the drawing again. She could see how Darsat might find the shapes of the stars in the picture, but she didn't think it was very accurate. It was only a sketch of the statue, and she felt sure that its proportions were not precise.

"What do you mean 'down to the millimetre'?" she asked. "Surely the stars are far further apart than that?"

"Yes, yes." Darsat tried to cover his mouth as he answered, but a few stray crumbs spilled down to his beard. "I mean to say, they are within millimetres of the most well-regarded star charts."

"Oh." Shanti picked up some bread, and began to spoon some relish onto it. "And how would you measure that against the actual stars in the sky."

"I would… hmmm." Darsat chewed thoughtfully. Dulku laid a hand on his shoulder. "That's an interesting question. Certainly one I shall have to consider deeply, once this expedition is completed."

Shanti finished her lunch in lighter conversation with the couple, discussing their family and life in Gorduum. But she couldn't quell the voice in the back of her head that though this man must be very peculiar if he had never thought of looking at the stars to compare them to his drawing before.

They finished eating, and by then Darsat was too excited by their conversation to return to his and Dulku's stroll through the village. Instead, he insisted that all three of them head out into the forest to see if they could reach the statue before Shanti would have to turn back to go to work at her mother's store.

"I'm sure my mother wouldn't mind if I was a bit late anyway."

As they set out, Shanti shivered and pulled her shirt a bit higher around her neck.

"It's a good thing you came now," she commented as she arranged her clothes to protect against the chill breeze. "If you had been much later you would have risked the first snowfalls of winter."

Shanti realised that she was walking along the street alone. She turned around and saw Dulku stopped on the street with wide eyes and a stunned smile.

"Snow, really?" The couple started walking again and hurried to catch up with Shanti. "I had no idea! That's wonderful, we would have loved to see that!"

"Do you not have snow in Gorduum?"

"Not at all! I don't think I've ever seen snow in Gorduum, but I've heard so many stories! So bright and white. It must be absolutely beautiful!" Dulku was clutching her shawl around her shoulders and joy was leaking out of her skin.

"I mean, yes of course. But it would have made this walk quite difficult. The slush on the paths would have been very wet and mucky, and your clothes-"

"Slush? What do you mean?"

"As the snow melts, or people walk through it a lot, it makes the ground muddy and slushy." Shanti was finding conversation with these people rather confusing. Sometimes they were completely oblivious to the most obvious things! "The snow is beautiful but it would have made a walk through the woods to the statue really awkward."

"How peculiar!" exclaimed Darsat. "I've always thought of it like tufts of wool!"

THE WALK WAS A PLEASANT ONE, strolling beneath

branches that spread wide in the canopy above them. Many of the leaves were red and orange by now, and the occasional bright piece of foliage drifted down to the path like a feather in the breeze. Birds slipped from tree to tree, and their infrequent calls echoed through the wood. The smell of the leaves that coated the forest floor was musty but not overpowering. Before long they found the land beginning to rise as they approached the hill that Shanti knew had slipped to embrace the statue many generations earlier. No one in the village remembered a time when the statue hadn't been mostly covered by earth and flowers.

When they were about halfway to the statue, Shanti noticed an old log to the side of the path. It was half buried in a drift of fallen brown and black leaves. It looked like a perfect spot, she thought to herself. She walked over to pull back the bark of the log, revealing a whirling mass of tiny pale insects then leaned down to examine them.

"What is this?" asked Dulku.

"I think it might be termites," murmured Shanti as she inspected the small creatures. "They are perfectly ordinary out here in the forest, but they can be a nuisance in the village, and this log is not as deep into the forest as I would have liked." She stood up and looked back down the path, as though she could see the brick buildings of Graama through the trees. She pursed her lips. "I may need to get someone to come out here and kill this nest, it could easily spread into the village."

"You are a very observant person," Dulku complimented her as she took the younger woman's arm and continued their walk down the path. "I did not notice the log at all, nor that it had so many insects in it!"

"Insects get everywhere really," replied Shanti. "It's actually more interesting to discover where they are not!" She laughed. "I've been trying to learn a bit of how to take care of lights from the Gardener in Graama. Last week she had me learning how to identify the difference between a hundred potential pests that might kill our lights," she explained. "Termites were one that stood out when she described the sort of place they build their nest. I've been keeping a wary eye out to see if they are in the woods, and here I find that they are! Sudru would not be happy to know that there are some this close."

"Do you remember many other pests?"

"Oh sort of, I am still only learning after all." Shanti counted off examples on her fingers. "There are bugs that lay eggs on the lights, and their larvae eat through the stems and leaves. There are bugs that eat the roots from under the ground and some that eat the leaves. Aphids that suck the moisture from them, slowly starving the lights. And all of that is not to mention diseases and funguses that can damage them!"

"Hmmmm," said Dulku. "It certainly sounds like a lot of work. I must remember to look more closely at the Gardeners back in Gorduum when we return."

In front of them, Darsat walked along the path as though his tongue were directly connected to his feet, his words tripping out of his mouth with a similar metronomic regularity as his steps. Dulku supported his running descriptions of the forest with appropriate noises, encouraging and admiring. At some moments Darsat would finally allow himself to pause and simply walk in silence. It was then that Dulku would ask him curious and engaging questions, sending him off into his meandering stories again.

Shanti found that he wasn't really saying anything

very important most of the time and so she allowed her mind to wander as they walked, but every now and then a word or phrase would penetrate her own thoughts. Mostly he admired the nature around them, taking joy in the smallest things that Shanti would not have thought particularly exciting. Large black beetles slowly crossing the leaf-covered path would cause Darsat and Dulku to stop for minutes and coo, and they were thoroughly engaged by a vine that was growing up an ancient tree on their left at one stage.

The rest of the time he was expounding upon the theory that he had suggested, linking the carvings and images of the statue to the stars. He spoke about his studies, closely investigating the stars by colour and shape. Apparently he was something of a well-known name in scholarly star circles, and Dulku emphasised this by pointing out just how often people came to him to help solve their problems. According to his wife, Darsat's own studies must be interrupted at least three times a week by other scientists. Shanti made the appropriate sympathetic and impressed noises.

At one stage, Darsat mentioned another journey they had taken a year or two earlier.

"Do you know what a transit is my dear?"

"No." Shanti considered the word. "I don't think I've ever heard of a transit at all."

"Well, that isn't really surprising, it is a very special idea that we have come up with as astronomers." Darsat's smile beamed from beneath the white scruff of his beard. "The idea is, when a planet or moon passes in front of the sun, we can see its shadow."

Instinctively, Shanti raised her face to look towards the sun, flinching as she realised what she was doing.

"Obviously we must not look directly at the sun," laughed Darsat, as Dulku placed a hand on Shanti's shoulder to check if she was alright.

"Yes, I wasn't thinking," chuckled Shanti.

"It is okay. But, by using our instruments to carefully measure how big the shadow appears and how fast it moves across the sun, we can use mathematics to work out how far away so many things may be!"

"That sounds very complicated. You must be clever to work it all out."

"Thank you very much my dear. Well, it turns out that some time ago there was going to be such an event, although they are often very rare and hard to see. Luckily, I received funding and was able to travel further south, even to another country, where we were able to observe the transit very well."

"It was a beautiful trip," sighed Dulku. "The land looked so different, and the animals and plants were so strange. They were like things I had only read about in children's stories."

"What sort of things?" Shanti found that she could feel her blood pulsing stronger in her chest.

"At one time a giant animal walked past our lodge. It was taller than three men standing upon each other's shoulders, so tall! But mostly this was because it had such long and thin legs and a long and thin neck also. It was yellow and covered in brown splotches as though children had been throwing mud at it. It was so beautiful."

Shanti tried to imagine such an animal but found it difficult. "It sounds very exciting!" She wished that she could see it and looked out between the trees, trying to imagine that such a creature was walking between their trunks in the forest alongside them.

"Oh yes. Dulku did enjoy the wildlife. I myself found the plants quite interesting also, trees that looked to be growing upside down, and strangely solid leaves covered in spikes. Very engaging."

"Did their lights have new colours?"

Darsat and Dulku raised their eyebrows. "Oh, but they did not grow lights."

Shanti blinked. "Why not?"

"Lights are very temperamental and difficult to grow, as I am sure your Gardener in Graama must have told you."

Shanti nodded.

"We are very lucky to be able to grow them here," Darsat continued. "And I have not heard of many other countries that grow so many or so well as us."

"What do they do? How do they see in the streets in the evenings?"

"They use fire. Candles. Lamps. If they have money, they buy lights from us, and employ our gardeners in order to keep them alive as long as possible."

Shanti walked on in silence. She couldn't imagine a world without lights.

In due time, they walked up gently curving paths and slopes and emerged from beneath the canopy of trees into a large clearing with low scrubby bushes poking up from the long swaying grass. Before them lay the statue.

It was always shocking how large the statue was in person. Despite growing up by the statue, and visiting it often, she still found herself pausing to admire it whenever she entered this clearing. Darsat had his sketch, obviously, which had even included a small silhouette of a human to one side for comparison. But a drawing, no matter how well composed, was not the same as reality. Darsat paused at the edge of the clearing, patting at the pockets of his trousers and coat as though looking for something he had forgotten. Dulku squealed, though softly. Shanti smiled, enjoying the reaction of the travellers.

The head of the statue lay on the elbow of its arms, as though sleeping. A single shoulder rose nearly as high as the trees surrounding the clearing, before the angle of the statue's body slid towards the ground, making it appear as though the statue was sleeping and the earth were its blankets. If Shanti stretched herself to her full height, she could just curl her hand over the wind-worn nose. Some of the younger children in the village would leap as high as they could and use this handhold in order to pull themselves higher, clambering across the statue like wild animals.

Darsat and Dulku began circling the massive stonework, while Shanti made herself comfortable on the grass and watched them. The two were bubbling with excitement, clearly impressed. Dulku walked around to the rear of the statue, leaning over to place one hand flat on its weathered surface, the other holding on to the material of her shawl. She moved her eyes up the shape, admiring every measure.

In the meantime, Darsat was attempting to climb up the higher of the arms, barely able to reach around it, and struggling as his left leg didn't seem to be able to bend as far as a younger man's would have. Yet, his determination paid off and, eventually, red-faced and huffing the cool air heavily, he found himself standing atop the stone.

"Look at me my love!" he called out to Dulku, pulling a handkerchief from his breast pocket and waving it in the air over his head. "I am the king of the castle!" Dulku laughed and clapped.

Shanti found herself feeling envious that he was calling to Dulku, a realisation that shocked her. It took her a few moments of introspection before she thought she understood her feelings. It wasn't as though she was attracted to either of the older couple, and of course they were already married to each other! But as she watched them call and joke with each other, acting as though they were young children, teasing each other, glorious smiles beaming from their faces,

It reminded Shanti of the games she had played in this same clearing with Fellbin and Taanin, chasing each other amidst shrieks and laughter.

She would clamber as high as she could up the statue, and they would give chase, pulling her tumbling to the ground. She had grown up with many bruises from their games, but had learned to give just as well as she got. Once she had managed to turn a grab from Taanin back on him, spinning him off the edge of the statue's shoulder. He had lain winded on the ground for long minutes, gasping until he regained his breath.

She watched the older couple playing and smiled. She wished that she had someone whom she could play with in the same way. Someone to share in new joys with.

The face of a young man from Graama named Buan began to treacherously form itself in her mind. She frowned, wondering why her mind would turn to him when she was wishing for playful things. Buan's brow was stern, even when conjured up by her imagination, and although his eyes were deep and honest, there was no smile on that mouth. She couldn't picture herself laughing with him over something as inconsequential as the lopsided leaf that Dulku was giggling over with her husband.

"What a wonderful place," Darsat said to Shanti after he had managed to lower himself back down.

He wiped his forehead with his handkerchief before tucking it away again. "This is a very wonderful place," he repeated, as though he had to ensure that the world knew of his approval.

Dulku was still walking around the clearing, admiring the trees and examining the statue from different angles. Darsat opened up his satchel and drew out a large pad of paper, taking it over to his wife.

"Oh thank you my darling!" Dulku's eyes flashed with a smile and she took the pad quickly. She pulled something from a pocket and settled down with her back to a tree trunk on the side of the clearing. She held up the small object and then began moving her hand across the paper. Darsat returned to where Shanti was still standing.

"What did she pull out?"

"A piece of drawing charcoal," Darsat answered as he leaned down over the satchel again, his hands moving around in its depths. "She loves to draw, especially when we are in new places, so she carries some sketching materials with her at most times. Aha!"

He pulled out a cardboard folder with pieces of yellowing paper edging out from its sides, dog-eared and folded by its journey in the satchel. He unwound the brown string from the brass pin that held the folder closed and then knelt down to open it on the ground.

Shanti found herself looking at a bewildering pile of maps and diagrams, with mathematical lines and geometric shapes covering each sheet, small dots and points peppering them from top to bottom. "Are these more star charts?"

"Exactly, you are quite right!" Darsat was searching through the sheets, shaking his head occasionally and moving some of the sheets to the bottom of the pile. "I think this one," he murmured, handing one sheet up to Shanti before continuing to shuffle through the papers.

Shanti held it up and examined it more closely while he worked. There was a title, the officious sounding "Celestial Figures as visible from Northern Zamina during the Summer Equinox." It meant nothing to her.

"Yes, I am sure of it!" He moved off towards the statue, holding the star chart up in front of him, as though he was trying to see through the paper to the statue beyond, turning the paper to try and line up the markings of the chart with the statue. Dulku moved across the clearing and stood with him as they examined the massive stone figure, one of her arms around his waist.

Shanti stood up and moved closer, unsure if she was trespassing on a personal moment for them.

"... Maybe if you invert the chart?" she heard Dulku murmur to Darsat.

"Possibly, but if I invert it to match the Aqueduct to this brow line, then I wouldn't have a match for Arkheel the Hunter through the chin anymore."

"Are you sure that they should all be oriented the same? Perhaps each constellation is individual?"

"Is everything okay?" asked Shanti, stepping a little closer. Darsat and Dulku turned back to her, a large frown creasing Darsat's face, though his eyes never left his star chart. Dulku lifted a hand from his waist to his shoulder.

"It is okay. It is just that..." he paused and breathed deeply. "It appears that these charts do not match the statue's form nearly so well as I had imagined." He began to walk back towards his satchel. "I will come back tomorrow with more equipment. I will make some more detailed sketches and measurements, but…" He knelt down and tucked all his charts back into their folder, twisting the string around the knob that held the folder shut. "It does not look good."

"At least we have had a nice vacation from Gorduum, my love?" Dulku ran a hand through his hair, and Shanti again felt a flash of envy that these two had found someone who would care so much about the other's hopes.

"Indeed." He turned and looked up at his wife with glowing eyes and a small smile. He took his wife's fingers between his hands. "It is a beautiful place, so we will stay and enjoy being here for a few days before we return."

He stood and picked up his bag.

"I just wish this had looked more promising."

As THEY WALKED BACK through the forests to Graama, Darsat continued telling Shanti about Gorduum. Now that he had been disappointed by the lack of astronomical connection to the statue, he spent less time recounting tales of the far off lands that he and Dulku had visited during his studies, and instead he spent most of the walk explaining how glorious the large red brick buildings of his home were, how impressive the four story buildings of the University could be as they towered over mere students and professors. He could not say enough for the beauty of the terracotta tiles of the roofs, and was of course very proud of the ancient temples and statues that still filled Gorduum from its distant past as capital of a mighty empire.

Dulku added her details too, explaining that the streets were full of life and character, and how markets flooded the streets and that delicious food and wondrous clothes were around every corner. Shanti found her heart was beating faster, and she could not help but grin at the idea of visiting such a fantastic place.

"And of course, the lights are beautiful, growing along every building and illuminating the streets all night."

"Really? Every building has lights on it?" Shanti was amazed. Just as she couldn't imagine a country with no lights, having so many sounded overwhelming. Graama had few carefully tended lights, and each was precious.

"Very nearly, my dear. Of course, some of the poorer areas have fewer lights, but even there some donor has usually provided for a small bush to help keep the streets lit and safe." He coughed to clear his throat. "Recently, it seems as though there are less than there used to be." Dulku nodded.

"I think that it's all those scruffy types that are beginning to fill the streets," she said, frowning slightly. "There are just so many of them, and always in the areas that seem to be darker than they once were."

"Quite so my love." Darsat frowned also. He shook his head. "It is bright enough in most streets still. Perhaps you will come to visit us in Gorduum one day Shanti, and we can show you how beautiful it is."

"That would be wonderful. There are very few lights in Graama."

"Yes, we did notice that." Darsat brightened, looking up into the forest canopy as they walked, listening for bird calls. "But I must imagine that it is difficult to keep them alive out here. The climate probably doesn't suit them as much."

"No, I believe it is a little too cold to truly let them flourish. My mother keeps some in a greenhouse and

Sudru is working constantly all the time, to keep the few around the village alive."

"That is excellent to hear! We must keep the traditions alive if we are to maintain our reputation as the best gardeners of lights in the world." Darsat's eyes twinkled as he patted Shanti's shoulder. "You must congratulate your mother for her interest in the subject, and for stoking your own."

The trio left the forest and began to move through the fields towards the small village. Thin pillars of smoke were beginning to rise from their tall brick chimneys, lifting like strings that twisted around themselves in the still air. The sun was already very low on the horizon, though workers still moved through the fields, and would do until much later in the day. Children ran shrieking down the stone-walled lanes between fields, waving sticks at one another. Dulku laughed as she had to dart aside to allow one particularly loud young girl bolt by.

Suddenly a wave of the children burst from the fields and came charging in towards the village. Shanti saw four leap over the wall ahead of herself and into the same lane as them, before sprinting in towards the buildings, where flickering oil and candle light was beginning to glow in some windows. Another three came pounding along the dirt behind them.

"Hey, Gatik," called Shanti to one of the younger boys, reaching out a hand to slow him down before he passed them. "Why is everyone running back to the village all of a sudden?"

The small boy bounced up and down on his heels, trying to peer over and around Shanti as though he could see something wondrous just behind her. "I heard from Tarani that Saju overheard Mrs Tortor through the kitchen door and she said that she heard her saying that we would definitely be getting a huge display of lights for Festival!"

And, having managed to expel all the information he had as quickly as he could, Gatik bounced past Darsat and Dulku and began sprinting after his friends into the village.

"How exciting," Shanti said, before noticing that Darsat was trying to hide a small smile. "What?"

"I am just very amused to see all these children who are so excited over a rumour. It seems to me that there are no lights to be seen yet?" the older man answered.

"I suppose there couldn't be," admitted Shanti.

"Well then, why must they run into the village now?"

Shanti found herself smiling also. "Because it is so exciting sir! Don't you celebrate Festival in Gorduum?"

Darsat chuckled. "There are many many celebrations in Gorduum! But I don't know this particular event. Tell me, why is it so exciting?"

"It is mostly to celebrate the end of a successful year, and the hard work that goes into farming and harvest. We decorate the village with streamers and bunting, and if all goes well Sudru will bring out some of the more exotic lights and place them in the Tired Rabbit so we can admire them.

A few years ago we had a circus come to perform for us, and the mayor even arranged for all the children to go for free." She smiled at the memory of the acrobats, swinging through the air on their ropes, and climbing up a pile of chairs stacked haphazardly. They had been so strong, so controlled.

"That sounds wonderful. So, it is a farming thing?"

"Of course, we give thanks to the Masked God at

the same time, acknowledging the way he watches over us and provides support from unexpected places. Families come together for dinner, and there is dancing on the green in the evening."

Darsat nodded. "We have more of these sort of celebrations in Gorduum. Long serious parades, and serious songs to sing about the god. I must say, your Festival sounds much more entertaining!" Darsat laughed happily. "Well, we can find our way back to our rooms quite happily now. Perhaps you would like to go and celebrate this exciting news with your own family?"

"That's very kind. I'm sure I shall see you both again soon. I hope you enjoy your stay in Graama!"

SHANTI ARRIVED at the store to find her mother looking as harassed as a cat in an alley with a dog at the entrance.

"Ah, Shanti, finally you arrive!" Auga scurried back to the counter, where a line of customers waited patiently. Although, as Shanti looked closer, it was the sort of quiet patience that was coloured with tense mouths and dark eyes. These people hadn't been given cause to complain yet, but they were tired of waiting.

"I'm sorry mother, I didn't realise it was this busy," she said as she slipped behind the counter and began taking the next order. For the following hour, she found that she was constantly moving, smiling as best she could to her neighbours as they came through, and feeling a familiar ache in her shoulders and feet as she reached high on shelves and carried small but noticeable loads backwards and forwards through the shop. Although her mother was supposed to have gone home by now, off to the office in their house where she could check on the accounts, Shanti noticed that Auga stayed to help until finally there was a full ten minutes without a new customer entering the store.

"What happened? It's not usually that busy," asked Shanti, wiping her forehead and tucking her hair back behind her ears.

"I don't know," said her mother. "It seems like everyone suddenly wanted to buy something delicious for dinner or dessert tonight."

"Oh, I think I understand," said Shanti, nodding to herself.

"Why?" Auga looked at her with curiosity. "What have you discovered?" She removed her work apron and hung it up through a door behind the counter, out of the way of customers.

"The children are excited because they have heard a rumour that there will be a huge lights display for the Festival this year."

"Ah, and everyone believes them, and so there will be celebratory meals tonight." Auga nodded. "That does seem a likely cause of all this fuss. Well, it is quiet now. I'll leave you to it."

As she went to open the door and head home, it swung wide before she could even grasp the handle. Auga jumped back in surprise, which was just as well, as Gebis Tortor strode into the shop with barely a glance to check if there was anyone or anything in his path. The mayor of Graama was nearly as wide as he was tall and was accustomed to having things his own way. Shanti always thought it was amusing to see the man helping his wife run the Tired Rabbit. There he turned and ran to obey like any of the other staff when his wife called.

"Good afternoon," he bellowed, his voice making the shelves and jars tremble.

"Hello Gebis," said Auga. "I hope you are well."

"I will be, though someone has sabotaged my clothesline this afternoon." He glared meaningfully at Shanti before returning his attention to Auga. Shanti blinked at stepped back, unsure why he would look at her while making such a statement.

"That sounds very frustrating. I hope you catch whoever did it! However, I'm just heading off for the day, Shanti will see you are taken care of," said Auga.

"I'm sure she will, but stay awhile; I think you'll be pleased at my purpose here." He moved to the counter, his legs swinging like ponderous pendulums. "I would like to place an order." He winked at Shanti, then turned to lean on the counter, facing her mother. "For a great deal of lights!"

"Oh?" Auga raised an eyebrow. Shanti felt her heart flutter a little in excitement at the confirmation of the rumours.

"Yes! You shall need to send someone to Gorduum immediately! We have created a list of what we shall need, and we will fund the journey, by train due to the expedient nature of the order, and also their accommodation." Gebis' teeth shone from his grinning mouth and Shanti was overwhelmed by the list he laid down between them all.

AFTER THE BUSTLE and excitement of the day, with an expedition through the forest, meeting fascinating new people with fantastic stories to tell of faraway places, and then the announcement of a huge lights display for the village, Shanti could not help but grow restless during the rest of her shift in the store. She slouched behind the counter, uninterested in doing anything much as she waited until she could head home. She thought that she could hear the dust settling on the shelves as it drifted down in the late afternoon light.

The shop door's bell jangled and shook Shanti to attention. She straightened up behind the counter and lifted her head from her hand and rolled her shoulders.

Buan was standing in the aisles near her serving counter holding his fingers together and rubbing his hands over each other. A smile flickered across his face, like a mouse peeking from its burrow briefly before ducking back inside. "Good afternoon Shanti!"

"Good afternoon Buan. How are you today?" Shanti smiled as her friend moved into the store and looked around as though he had accidentally wandered in and was casually browsing through the stock. He picked up a large jar of nails and examined it closely.

"Oh, you know. Doing as well as one can." He caught her eye and smiled again before coughing and refocusing on his very important nails.

"I'm glad you are having such a fine day that you can find nothing to tell me about it." Shanti rested her elbows on the counter and supported her chin on her hands as Buan put the jar down and walked over to lean on the counter. He flushed slightly.

"You'd be bored by my stories. Today has been all about harvesting, and all that that means is that I've been pulling vegetables out of the mud all day."

"Is it really so muddy? I would have said it had been quite sunny and warm today."

"Yes, but the fields retain the water so that the plants can grow properly. At least, for this crop, you see-"

"I think you may have been right the first time," interrupted Shanti. "I think that I *am* bored by these stories." She grinned, to show that she was only teasing him.

"I did try to warn you!" Buan's eyes were wide and his voice sounded slightly panicked. Shanti took pity on him.

"So, if you are supposed to be harvesting, why are you here?"

Buan scratched at the stubble on his chin. Ever since he had been a young boy, he had been proud of any hint of his growing manliness. Likewise, ever since she had been just as young, Shanti had found his showing off to be amusing.

Once when they were about six or seven years old Buan had tried to show off by lifting heavy rocks that they found in nearby fields while running around with Taanin. Fellbin had been too young to join the games yet. Shanti had wrestled her brother off the mound they were each trying to claim, and Buan had blinked, uncertain how to attack. Then he had had his amazing idea to demonstrate just how strong he was, heaving and puffing until he had the large flat rock held high above his head, until he had yelped and twisted and dropped it on his foot. The accident forced him to lie in bed for nearly three months while it healed properly. The incident had helped Neeran and Tareen convince the council to arrange for a doctor to come to Graama, even though Buan's family were closer to Baargu anyway.

Despite the pain, inconvenience, and the disapproving tones of his parents, Buan had never grown out of this impulse to try and prove how grown up he was.

"To be honest, my dad did send me in to order some flour, apples, eggs and apricots." Buan recited the list carefully, mentally ticking off the items on his work-darkened fingers. "And mum wanted to check if you had any cloves at the moment? She wants to make some stuff for the Festival."

"That's quite an order," Shanti replied. She straightened up behind the counter, looking over Buan's head as she thought about the order, and missing the way he watched her face so closely. "I'm pretty sure we have everything, but I'll have to go and double check on the cloves."

Shanti turned to go into the back of the store, where the more expensive or fragile items were kept. She drew the key up from the chain that hung around her neck and used it to unlock and move through the solid wooden door that secured her mother's most valuable stock.

As she had been trained to do since she was ten, she judiciously locked the door behind her before setting off along the shelves. They were lit by wide short windows, set high in the walls. The light slid through in a fan of orange, the setting sun using the small angle to illuminate the room. Usually she or her family would only move through to check stock in this area early or late in the day, when less customers came by. Shanti leaned close to the boxes and barrels, squinting at the labels that her mother had scratched out and gummed to the sides. "Cinnamon.... Cutlery.... Ah, Cloves!"

Shanti opened the box and checked how many of the small, sweet-smelling buds were there. Satisfied, she turned to move back out of the storeroom.

She sighed as she moved back down the row of shelves, light flickering across her face as she moved. How much longer will I have to do this, she wondered. How many journeys back into this dark little room to look for little bits and pieces for my friends in this little village? She thought of her brothers. Neither of them were going to be able to take over the responsibilities of the store any time soon.

Taanin was probably going to just end up being an even less chatty version of Buan soon. He spent most of his days hard at work in the fields, trying to learn as much as he could about the rhythms of the farm. It was hard for him to learn, as their family had grown up in the buildings of Graama, not working in the fields, but he never complained and he worked as hard as any of the other men out there. Shanti was sure he favoured the arm he had broken when he was young, trying to prove to others that he was just as strong as anyone else. She sometimes wondered if he was trying to prove it to himself.

Whereas Fellbin was simply too young and untrustworthy still. He would be more likely to deliver rotten eggs to their customers as a joke than to take stock of the shelves and send out replenishment orders. If their mother and father were to ever have some peace and time to themselves, working in the store less often, then it was up to Shanti to keep the place running.

With well-practiced hands she unlocked and opened the door, stepped through and locked it again behind her, pulling her orange skirts through so they wouldn't get caught.

Buan was still waiting at the counter, leaning forward over it. He smiled broadly as she came back in, and she found herself smiling in return. *He does have a fascinating sparkle in those brown eyes,* she thought. *And maybe he smiles more than I thought.*

"Yup, we can handle all of that." She pulled over a small pad of paper and a roughly sharpened pencil. "So, tell me the list again?"

As Buan repeated the list and Shanti carefully wrote down the items and quantities his family needed, a bell rang and the store's door opened. Mr and Mrs Bolbol came in together, smiling and talking loudly about their preparations for the Festival in four weeks' time.

Buan warmly greeted the older couple, shaking Tebrin Bolbol firmly by the hand and giving Tamra Bolbol a small kiss on her cheek. They began discussing their families' plans for the festival, what clothes they would be wearing to Temple, which family members would be coming for dinner, or hosting their own dinner.

"Good afternoon Mr Bolbol, good afternoon Mrs Bolbol." Shanti gave a little wave from her side of the counter.

"Good afternoon dear," said Mrs Bolbol. "And what will you be doing for the festival?"

"Oh, my mother is planning a big dinner for us. And I think we will be inviting the Dopop cousins from Baargu as well."

The relations would make the journey in a few hours, probably longer than the usual trip thanks to younger cousins jumping off the cart and running up and down the narrow lanes that led from one village to the other. Farmers would wave from the fields, and the thought reminded Shanti that Buan's family land was actually closer to Baargu as well, though he had always spent much time with the children from Graama as he grew up. She considered this for a moment, while the three others spoke. Perhaps Buan and his family had more friends here than in Baargu.

Shanti's mother came from Baargu herself, and she still had a sister and brother-in-law who lived there, a leather-worker who specialised in shoes for the village, but also was willing to put together whatever the villagers asked for: from aprons to gloves and even leads for toddling babies. They had three young children whom Shanti loved to see when they had the chance, and a Festival dinner would be a perfect opportunity.

"Oh how fun! It will be great to hear some news from nearby."

"I'll be sure and pass on any gossip that is fit to tell," laughed Shanti.

"I hope so!" The older woman's eyes creased delightfully in the corners as she smiled. "Will you be coming to the town dance beforehand?

The Festival was traditionally a chance for all the musicians amongst the village to break out their voices and instruments and enjoy a get together in the commons by the pub. The village would gather there after the morning's Temple and spend most of the afternoon singing along and dancing, until they all headed back to their homes, families and celebratory dinners.

"I'm not sure, I think my mother was hoping I would stay home and help prepare the dinner this year. I know Taanin will be helping." For the last year or two, he had stayed in the house most of the day during the festivals, helping cook and clean more than socialise. Shanti knew that her father was wondering whether Taanin would ever make more friends and expand his circle. If Taanin ended up staying at home too long, he might get too used to it. Shanti was hoping that, if she stayed in the kitchen to help prepare meals, then Taanin would be forced to get out and interact with his peers.

Buan was standing behind the Bolbol's and so they couldn't see the way his eyes froze and his smile began to fall into a frown.

"Oh, I know it's good to help out, but surely you can spare an hour for some dancing? You know it's important to get out and see everybody on a day like this, right?" he said, speaking quickly.

Shanti tried not to giggle at Buan's sudden interest in her plans for the festival. As the Bolbols had not been able to see Buan's expression slip, so too could he not see their knowing glance to each other.

"Buan is quite right, my girl," said Tebrin Bolbol, rubbing the back of his forearm and using a deep serious tone of voice. "You should of course help your family wherever possible, and perhaps you could take a shift while ensuring your delightful mother gets a chance to come and enjoy a song or two!" He winked at her. "At the same time you must get out of the house for a while."

"Well, I shall have to see how much work there is to be done. I think you are right that I should let my mother out first."

Again, Buan's face grew stricken. Shanti was enjoying this.

"Well, I have your order all written down Buan. I will arrange the delivery before next week starts, alright?"

"Yes." Buan's throat bobbled as he tried to think of something else to say. "Yes, alright. Um…"

"Do you think your mother would prefer the delivery in a fortnight?"

Buan shook his head slightly. He started to reach out a hand towards Shanti and then shook his head, clearly changing his mind. "Alright. Um, I hope I see you at the Festival then? Maybe we could sit together at Temple if you are really busy?" He tried to make the question sound more like a statement, but it was no use.

"Yes, I hope so." Shanti didn't want to be cruel. She did enjoy Buan's company, and she did hope to come and enjoy some dances. The relief that flooded his cheeks was almost as amusing to watch as the panic from before.

She covered her mouth and chuckled after Buan left the store, while Mrs Bolbol laughed and laughed.

As the day drew to a close, Shanti's younger brother Fellbin came in to help her lock up.

"Thanks Fellbin. How have you been today?" Shanti asked as she brought the storeroom key up on its chain and passed it over to him.

"Oh, you know. Nothing too much going on. I hung out at the Tired Rabbit for a while."

"Oh, I didn't see you there. I took some visitors there for an early lunch."

"You probably went before I did then, I've been spending the whole morning chopping firewood for Bratis. That poor cold priest, how would he survive the winter without me?"

Shanti giggled.

"And despite my generosity, when I got to the pub I didn't have any money so old Gebis wouldn't give me even a sip of cider. What is to be the reward for my charity?"

"Oh, you poor boy. However did you cope?" Shanti raised an eyebrow at her little brother's complaint.

"No worries, I just loosened a knot on his laundry line out back" Fellbin hung the key around his own neck and grinned at her, his teeth appearing shocking bright in his face, beneath the messy black curls of his hair. "He'll find things go a bit sour if he tries to put too much on at once." Fellbin started giggling, pleased with his own tricks.

"Oh Fellbin, I do wish you'd learn to leave others alone." Shanti tried to admonish her brother, but found it difficult in this instance. Gebis Tortor was often stuffy and overbearing, especially with the children of the village. It was a tribute to the quality of the village youth that they all enjoyed spending time at the Tried Rabbit despite his lesser qualities and tendency to complain about the way they spilled their drinks. At least now she knew why he had glared at her earlier that afternoon. Everyone knew that she was the one responsible for keeping Fellbin settled down.

"Do you mind doing the final locks, I really want to get home and sit down."

"No worries," grinned Fellbin.

"I'll see you at home. Don't break anything!" Shanti began walking to the door.

"Would I ever do a thing like that?" Fellbin spread his arms wide in injured innocence, but his eyes glittered happily.

Shanti took a wide detour on her way home, visiting the Tired Rabbit to check on Gebis. As she had suspected, he was angry to have had an entire load of clean laundry dropped onto a muddy backyard, thanks to a loosened knot. Without actually giving Fellbin's name, Shanti tried to calm the Mayor and helped gather the laundry up to be rewashed. After spending half an hour cleaning the clothes and helping rehang them, making sure that all the knots were as secure as possible, she finally felt that she was able to continue home.

"Thanks for coming by Shanti," grumbled Mr Tortor. "I just wish that brother of yours could be as level headed as you."

She nodded, trying not to directly admit that Fellbin had caused the problem in the first place. As she continued home, she worried about her younger brother. He found it so easy to lie, and he caused so many annoyed frowns amongst the inhabitants of the village. If she ever did manage to leave, what would he do that she would not be around to undo?

Her worries gnawed at the back of her mind as she strolled through the dimming streets towards home.

THE GLOW from the small greenhouse behind their home outlined the narrow two-story building against the evening sky as though in a faint white mist. Shanti walked around the side of their small home to the left, as their neighbours home was part of the same building on the right. Here she was able to open a hatch on the outside of the greenhouse and lean inside. The small pale light grew happily inside, thin vines hanging in coils around its pot.

She and her mother had been trying to grow new lights for years, but none of them were sprouting in the soil of Graama. The greenhouse held a variety of pots filled with disappointing soil. Shanti examined a few of the newer pots in order to check for signs of growth but was not surprised to see no changes. Then she checked the temperature and humidity in the greenhouse was still suitable for the small light that they had been able to keep alive, and was satisfied that conditions were still good.

Having checked on the light for her mother, Shanti returned to the front of the house, opened the door and stepped in to discover heat and noise filling the hallway of her family's small home. The kitchen banged and rattled with pots and pans and the voice of her father. Delightful smells and steam filled the house.

"I'm home!" Shanti called out, wondering if anyone would reply to her.

"In here darling!" came her mother's voice from the sitting room.

Shanti walked in to see her mother lazily reclining in a sitting chair, with a book in her hands. Taanin was sitting in another of the chairs, massaging his hands.

"Go and help father," she told him.

He blinked as he looked up. "What?"

"Can't you hear him?" asked Shanti. As she spoke, there was a loud crash from the kitchen, followed by a string of curse words.

"Oh. What's he doing?" Her elder brother still didn't move.

"He's making dinner, and he could use some help." Shanti spoke slowly, as though each word had to have time to flutter through the air before it could land in Taanin's ears and crawl its way inside. "I know you've been working hard, but please go through and give him a hand. I need to speak to mother."

"Oh, you think I should help him." Taanin began to lift himself from the chair. "You should have said."

As Taanin loped out of the room, Shanti turned to see her mother's shoulders shaking as she giggled behind her book.

"Good evening mother. What are you reading?"

"Oh, just that new romantic thing that we picked up a month or two ago. Mrs Dutut finished it last week and said that she thoroughly enjoyed it and so I thought I would give it a try. How was the afternoon, my love?"

"Fine, if a bit slow." Shanti talked with her mother about some of the customers who had come through, and their orders if they had asked for something that stood out as unusual. She was casually mentioning Buan's order including cloves when her mother tilted her head to one side and asked, "How is that young man anyway?"

"Buan?" stumbled Shanti. "I'm sure he is fine. He looked very happy when I saw him."

"I bet he did, I bet he did." Shanti's mother waved her hand in the air, as though shovelling aside Shanti's words with the closed book she was holding. "But you wouldn't see him looking any other way. Did he say much about their family farm? What about his parents?"

Shanti passed on what little she could remember about Buan's recent life, although she did begin to realise that he hadn't told her a lot.

"Mmm. I think it would be good of you to spend more time with him. They should pull through just fine, as long as we all lend them a hand, but I have heard some stories to say that they might be having a bit of difficulty right now."

"He did seem to want to see me at the dance during the festival," murmured Shanti.

"Good, well see that you do give him a dance at some point." Shanti's mother nodded.

"And Mr and Mrs Bolbol wanted me to make sure you got a chance to come out and dance too."

"Me?" Shanti's mother gaped at the suggestion. "Whatever for!? I suppose I could, now that Taanin is getting so familiar with the kitchen." She winked at Shanti, then smoothed down the sides of her dress.

"Yes, I suppose I could go and kick my knees up at least once on the day."

Shanti settled onto another chair in the room, making a mental note to ensure Taanin actually did help out in the kitchen. He was getting better, but still needed so much reminding. It probably meant that she would need to spend a lot of the day in the kitchen herself, but it would be worth it to ensure their mother was able to enjoy the festival. They continued the conversation while the clatter of the kitchen washed over them.

There was a bang as the front door was flung open and Fellbin came bursting into the house.

"Good evening all," he bellowed as he strode into the sitting room and gave his mother two strong kisses on the cheeks. His mother laughed and kissed her son in return.

"Good evening Fellbin! Clearly you have had a great time of it today! What have you been doing?"

"I spent the afternoon with old Bratis, in the temple, getting some reading tuition from the Writ." Shanti was impressed. Fellbin's eyes never once even flickered in her direction slightly. His cheeks didn't grow flushed. He wasn't fidgeting or stammering. For a moment, Shanti wondered if he might actually be telling the truth this once, and his earlier tales of mischief at the Tired Rabbit were actually the lies. But no, Gebis had been angry, and his laundry had been in the mud. Was that not Fellbin's fault? Maybe he was talking about the morning, when he had told Shanti that he was chopping wood for the priest?

"That's wonderful Fellbin. Perhaps you will join me in reading some of these novels one day. We could spend the day together, just reading."

"Mother, obviously that sounds absolutely amazing," Fellbin began, before sighing and shaking his head, with a hand pressed to his chest. "But I am still learning. Priest Bratis said I was coming along well but I don't think I would be able to do your novels justice."

He sounded genuinely heartbroken at this confession. Their mother's eyes twinkled.

"Of course. And how did you spend the evening, that you rush in here now all dishevelled and panting?" She ran a hand across his head, stroking his short black curls.

"Helping the farmers on the other side of Goose Hill." Again, Fellbin spoke with absolute conviction. "They were trying to clear some scrub and low bush from their orchard, so I've been cutting and shifting the wood all afternoon. That's why I was late, I had to come so far to get home to my wonderful family."

Shanti began to giggle slightly. She had left him in the store not an hour earlier! There was no way that he had been over past Goose Hill before she saw him, and obviously it was impossible that he had gone there after she left and still made it home so quickly. Fellbin frowned at her, but their mother laughed openly and ruffled his hair.

"You are a monster!"

Shanti laughed too, but made another mental note to go and speak to the farmers near Goose Hill. If Fellbin was mentioning them so often, it was likely that he had done something over there and hidden eyes knew what she might have to do to make up for it. Their father came into the room, wiping his hands on a kitchen cloth, and looked around at the laughter and smiles.

"Oh I see. You're all having lots of fun without me or your brother, huh?"

"Just as usual I guess," laughed Shanti's mother. Shanti's father laughed too.

"Alright, well don't have too much fun, dinner will be ready very soon. Taanin is just letting the sauce simmer, and then we should be ready to sit and eat."

Indeed, it was only a few minutes later that Taanin poked his serious face through the door and invited the family to come into the dining room, where a large pot of rice was sitting next to a pot full of a thick delicious yellow creamy sauce and some tender beef. Shanti had to wait as the family squeezed into their seats, because the room was small and the table took up most of its space.

Mr Penpen brought through a plate of flat breads and everyone bowed their heads as he recited a small prayer of thanks to the Masked God over the food and then everyone began to fill their plates.

There wasn't a lot of discussion during dinner, everyone was very hungry. Soon Shanti was using the last crust of bread to scoop up a delicious mix of rice and sauce and then chewing on it, savouring the final morsels.

"That," she said slowly and with great deliberation. "Was delicious. Thanks dad."

"Yeah, thanks!" The rest of the table joined in as they began to rise, clearing away the plates into the kitchen and dunking them into the pot of water that was boiling over the oven.

As a group they scrubbed the plates and then dried them, tidying everything away and then moving back into the sitting room.

SHANTI'S MOTHER and father retrieved a deck of cards and moved back into the dining room, shuffling the cards as they went, ready for their usual evening of quiet games and gentle teasing.

Shanti gathered some sewing that needed to be done and settled onto a comfy chair in the living room. She let the warm sounds of her family wash over her as she began sewing some buttons back onto one of her favourite dresses. She had managed to pop them off while running around with the children of Graama a week earlier, playing a chasing game with them. Luckily it had only been a few buttons and she had not been left clinging her dress onto her shoulder. She was able to find suitable replacements in the household sewing basket, and found that the task was very handy for sitting quietly and allowing her ears to focus on the conversation that her mother and father were having in the next room.

Auga was speaking mostly, between calls from the game they were playing; trying to determine how they would best be able to manage someone going to Gorduum in order to find, pay for, and collect the lights that the Graama council had ordered. The list was very extensive and the council had already declared how much they were willing to spend for the festival. Auga sounded worried that there would not be enough left to fulfil the order, especially when the costs and risk of travel were considered.

"I mean, they've said they want 50 red loose blossoms, and those are always very fragile. I would expect at least a third to die on the trip, so we would actually have to buy about 65 of them in order to fulfil expectations."

"Ideally, yes, and that is difficult." Shanti's father replied in a much calmer tone of voice. He was always one to assume the best in any situation. "But we have good contacts, thanks to your brother. I'm sure we would be able to scrounge together enough for the order."

"Well, my brother is not the most reliable person, you know that. He's from Baargu remember."

"Not everyone from Baargu is trouble."

Shanti couldn't see her mother, being that they were talking in the other room and she had her back to the door, but the silence that followed that statement made her smile into her sewing. She could just picture the raised eyebrow of her mother, staring back at her father.

The inhabitants of both villages traded with and

entertained each other regularly. Shanti's uncle, her mother's brother, had left to take up an apprentice-ship there when he was very young. Shanti's memories of him were brief images of a tall dark man with a very ready smile visiting once or twice a year when she was younger. Now he had moved to Gorduum to follow business opportunities, and they hadn't seen him in three or four years.

"Okay, I know you have had some run-ins with some of them, but-"

Auga's snort echoed through the house.

"Well, he's still a connection."

"I suppose." A huge concession from Auga.

"And also, you have to remember that the Festival is not as big in Gorduum. For such a big city, it certainly sounds as though a large number of the people there barely know who the Masked God is. Dunin's letters have made that clear. So there should be plenty of lights available. And they grow so many down there!"

"I suppose. Although, maybe if the Festival is not as important, then they may not have as many cele-bratory blooms."

"Very well, the world may cave in, I must admit it!" Neeran laughed as he replied.

"In any case," Auga grumbled. "The order has been made and we shall have to do something. Which of us will go?"

This was it. This was the moment that Shanti had been listening for. She paused, with her needle poking halfway through the last button.

"Well, of course I had assumed I would go," said her father.

"Of course? Of course? And why did you expect that I would not be the best choice?" Auga didn't sound angry, but there was an undertone that suggested she was considering outrage as an option.

"It's just that you are so good running the store. I suppose I thought that I would be more disposable to our everyday lives? Shanti is very good at keeping the house, so you wouldn't end up having to do too much of the housework while I was gone. Fellbin would be a handful, but hopefully you would be able to have Taanin keep watch over him. And the neighbours would help."

"That is all true, but they all apply just as much to you. You can handle the store when you must, and the children and neighbours would all help. Shanti has been very useful in keeping stock and managing the accounts there also. She is shaping up into quite an accomplished young woman!"

"We're very lucky."

Shanti felt herself blush as she listened to her parents' compliments. Now is the perfect chance, she told herself. She took a deep breath and set the dress aside on the arm of her chair, then stood and walked through to the sitting room.

Her parents both turned to look at her as she walked in. Although she knew they loved her and weren't judging her, she still felt a small ball of ice begin to form in the base of her stomach.

"Hello dear. Did you need something?" Her father was sitting on the far side of the small table, with a fan of cards held in his hands. He barely glanced up from them as she walked in, pursing his lips slightly as he considered the game he was engaged in. Auga turned in her chair, closer to Shanti, placing her cards face down on the table in front of her. She tilted her head slightly as she watched for Shanti's response.

"Um. Yes." Shanti felt like her face must be about

to burst into flames from the heat that poured from her cheeks, but she dove forward regardless. "I thought that maybe I could go to Gorduum for you. I could make the order and bring the stock back. You both know that I'm ready."

Auga and Neeran looked at each other across the table, though Shanti could only really see her father's half of the exchange. Shanti wished she knew how to interpret the look, but it was the sort of communication that came from years of marriage. Maybe one day she would know someone that well.

"I don't know Shanti," began her father. He sniffed and frowned, placing his cards face down on the table too. "You're still very young."

"I would be with Uncle Dunin most of the time though, wouldn't I? He would make sure that I was okay."

Auga grunted. Neeran raised an eyebrow at his wife, and Shanti was surprised to see her mother look away.

"I suppose he would. I just worry that his priorities might not be the same as ours. He is a very busy man." Auga shrugged. "I just wouldn't be surprised if he intended to help you and watch out for you, but ended up not being able to, leaving you pretty much on your own."

"I think he would be okay." Shanti spoke with as much conviction as she could, but she did have to admit to herself that she didn't know her uncle very well whereas her mother did.

"Maybe."

"But then, what about the trip? You would have to travel through Baargu to Afestaa before you could even get on the train, and it is quite a long journey. Then there is the supervision of the lights on the return journey." Neeran shook his head slowly. "I don't think you are quite ready. It is a long trip for someone as young as you to undertake on their own."

"But what about-"

"I agree with your father Shanti." Auga stood up at her chair and stepped forward, with a soft, regretful, yet understanding smile. "Maybe in a year or two we will send you into Gorduum to fulfil some other order. But not yet."

"You are so kind to offer to help though," her father added.

"And I know how much you want to get out and see more of the world." Auga made it over to Shanti, placing hands on both her daughter's shoulders. "But I just need you to be patient a little longer. Alright?" She looked into Shanti's eyes.

Shanti was disappointed. She could feel tears pricking at the corners of her eyes, but she knew her parents were just trying to protect her. She felt good for asking, the ice had melted from her stomach almost immediately, but she knew she needed to get out of the house for a while so that she didn't appear too upset for her parents.

"Okay. Maybe in a year or two." She forced herself to smile and then left the sitting room.

Shanti left the sitting room and gathered her things from the living room. She didn't want to risk her brothers seeing how upset she was. Taanin would attempt to comfort her, but would not accept if she wanted to be left alone, whereas Fellbin would probably just make jokes at her expense. She left the living room on her way to the cupboard to place her sewing aside until later.

Just as she got to the front door, wondering what she would do, where she would go, there was a knock on it. Shanti pulled open the door. Standing by the doorstep, looking down the street and laughing at something out of sight, was one of the most beautiful men in Graama. His long black hair hung down around his shoulders in gentle waves that curled into ringlets at the very tips. Shanti had to resist the impulse to reach out and run her fingers through it. His rich brown eyes gleamed, even in the dim light of evening, and he wore a shirt and trousers that were just tight enough to make his strong arms and legs clear.

"Hello Fabrin," Shanti said to the young man.

"Oh hello Shanti!" Fabrin's smile burst out of the long beard that he wore. It was like a flash in the night sky, a shooting star. "It is you whom I was hoping to see. I was wondering if you wanted to come for an evening stroll?" He smiled again and offered her his elbow.

Shanti smiled but paused to think it through. She considered how she was feeling after the rejection, however logical it may have been, of her parents. She thought about Buan, and how clearly he had expressed that he was interested in her. She looked at how tall and strong Fabrin was, and wondered if he had ever wanted to get away from Graama.

"Oh alright," she said, sliding her arm into his and stepping out of the house.

He placed one hand on top of hers as it sat in his elbow, and they moved down the street.

OTHERS WERE ENJOYING the starry evening as well, older married couples strolling through the lanes and talking softly to one another. They would smile and greet each other as they passed, pausing at seats that allowed them to sit together and look at the stars. Some of Sudru's few lights grew in slow loops up posts by each seat, hardy blue ones, with thick vines and small solid leaves. The Gardener took pride in keeping these comfortable seats illuminated in all seasons, and spent much of her time checking on them. The night sky was particularly clear, although that meant that the cold was pressing in.

"So, how was your day today?" Fabrin asked.

"It was very interesting!" Shanti explained how she had met the older couple who had come from Gorduum in order to investigate the giant statue to the north. "Darsat theorised that the statue was connected to the constellations in some way. Isn't that a fascinating idea?" Shanti shook her head at the enormity of such an idea. "Although, even with a very quick look this afternoon, he didn't seem as convinced anymore."

"The statue is connected to the stars?" Fabrin's forehead creased. He snorted through his nose. "I don't quite... Do you mean that you can see certain stars from it? For example, perhaps one particular star rises over the elbow every night?"

"No, more that the shape of the statue is designed to match the shape of the constellations."

"How odd. Why would anyone have done that?" Fabrin frowned a little, as though the possible statue-maker had decided to do such a thing only to frustrate him.

Shanti squeezed his arm to soothe him, feeling the strength in his bicep as she did. "It may not be the case, but I thought it was a fascinating idea."

"I suppose."

Shanti went on to explain that her family had taken an order for a great variety of lights to be delivered for the Festival. This she did not talk about for long, as it made her heart feel solid and heavy.

"That sounds great!" Fabrin smiled again. "I'll very much enjoy seeing that!" He looked down at Shanti, the corners of his brown eyes creasing with amusement. "I'm sure your family will bring us something spectacular."

"I hope so." Shanti walked on in silence for a moment. "Would you want to travel to Gorduum to fulfil an order like that?"

"I don't work for your parents." Fabrin spoke almost without thinking, responding automatically to declare that such a thing couldn't happen. It was the same way one might say 'I cannot fly, I have no wings' or 'I don't paint portraits, I never trained'.

"No, but I meant if your work required you to go."

Fabrin blinked, light from a nearby upper window shining off his eyes. "I have enough leather here to work. And I can order more to come in." He licked his lips. "I usually order new tools to come in also. I don't know what might ever cause me to go in to Gorduum."

"But, just imagine? Say that something did?"

"I suppose I would go in. But I cannot think what for." Fabrin ran his fingers across hers where they sat on his arm as they walked. "Don't worry, I'm not planning on travelling away and leaving you all alone in Graama."

"Well, I wouldn't be alone exactly." Shanti tried to change the subject slightly, feeling a little disappointed by the way he simply didn't seem to have any understanding of her desire to go out and see more of the world. "After all, Buan is here. Maybe I could spend some time with him."

Fabrin smiled broadly and raised his eyebrows when he met her eyes. "Yes, I daresay you could! But does he smile like I do?"

Shanti smiled and looked down, feeling her cheeks blush. Even when Fabrin was not saying all the things she wanted to hear, he was still able to charm her with his presence.

As they walked on, they passed Darsat and Dulku sitting outside the Tired Rabbit and having an evening drink. The couple were laughing, though Shanti wondered how many of Darsat's theories had been disproved already. Dulku was happily chatting with some local women who were sitting outside also, and Darsat had found a pipe to puff on.

"Good evening child," he said.

"Fabrin, these are the people I told you about."

Fabrin stepped forward and shook Darsat's hand firmly.

"It's an absolute pleasure to meet you both," he said, charm radiating off him like heat from a flame. Shanti watched him and found herself judging him as though from outside herself. He was very polite, and confident, and he certainly looked very pretty. The idea of staying around Graama with him made her fingertips tremble. She bit her lower lip and looked away from the small crowd outside the pub.

Buan was watching her from the end of the street.

"Hello Buan! How are you this evening? Shouldn't you be home by now?"

Buan walked slowly closer, his eyes darting from Shanti to the people behind her. Shanti told herself not to turn around and check on Fabrin. That would only make matters worse. But why did she think matters were bad at all, it's not as though Buan had ever actually asked her out, they were not a couple at all. And even if they were, she was certainly allowed to have friends. She grasped the end of her long, thick plait and rolled the ends between her fingers nervously. This was a lot of emotions to process all of a moment.

"Hello Shanti, it's very agreeable to see you this

evening." Buan smiled at her as he approached, although she could see that his eyes were tight. "I was thinking of staying in the village tonight, just to catch up with some friends, but now I am wondering if perhaps I should start heading home."

Shanti looked up into the dark air of the evening. Stars shone back down on them.

"But it would take you hours to get home, and it's already so dark! Surely you should just stay. Would you like to come in and have a drink with me and my friends?"

Buan's smile wobbled a little, but then his eyes locked onto hers. "You know," he said, his voice gaining strength with each syllable, "I think I will. After all, you are right, it would take me so long to get home now, that I may as well."

Finally, as he stepped by her to walk into the pub, Shanti felt it was safe to turn around. Darsat and Fabrin were chatting as though they had known one another forever, although Fabrin had managed to move around the older man and sit on a bench that allowed him to watch Buan for her entire conversation with the other man. At the moment, his eyes were on Darsat and he appeared fully engrossed in their conversation, but he did flick his attention to Shanti and give her a small wink as she headed inside. She laid a hand on his shoulder as she passed.

"Would you like a drink?" she asked.

"Yes, thank you. I would love a cider please." Fabrin reached up to touch her hand on his shoulder momentarily, and then refocused on Darsat. Behind the men, Dulku was smiling as she took a sip from her own glass. She nodded at Shanti. Shanti didn't know how to respond, so she turned and went into the pub.

Buan was shaking hands and laughing with many

other men in the pub as Shanti entered. The oil lamps around the low walls filled the room with a deep orange flickering light. Laughter filled the air, along with the slightly sweet smell of spilled ale.

Shanti caught up with Buan just after he had placed an order with Menka, the girl behind the counter.

"So, are you still looking forward to the Festival?" Shanti asked loudly, leaning close to her friend so that he would be able to hear her over the hubbub of voices.

Buan nodded and allowed his eyes to roam over the crowd of people conversing behind them.

"Because I've been thinking that it will be really fun to have a night out dancing."

Buan nodded again. He leaned towards her, although he didn't quite meet her eyes.

"And a night to see some wonderful lights of course."

"Of course." Shanti wondered if he had understood her intention. So she decided to try again.

"And I haven't forgotten that I promised you at least one dance." She tried to accompany her words with a bright smile, although she felt self-conscious and wondered if the smile came across as fake. Buan looked at her now, and a small smile touched the corners of his mouth.

"Thank you, I will enjoy that." Menka returned with a tall glass of ale for him. He thanked her and took a sip.

Just as Shanti opened her mouth to order, Buan leaned across the counter.

"And how about you Menka, are you looking forward to the chance to have a dance at the Festival?"

The young woman glanced between him and Shanti, but grinned. "Absolutely! I never get much of a chance to let my hair down, I'm always stuck serving in here on the evenings! But Mr Tortor has said that he wants to make sure I enjoy the evening!"

Shanti was surprised. The landlord was usually so dour with the younger inhabitants of Graama. Maybe the Masked God was watching Menka through Gebis' eyes.

"Great, well I hope that I can get at least one dance with you."

"I'd love that!"

Shanti coughed and then leaned over to make her order, trying to keep her face under control. Was Buan just trying to make her jealous? He'd always been interested in her. Maybe she had misunderstood. And besides, she didn't think that she was interested in him, did she? He was just a farmer, and had no desire to be more than a farmer, while she wanted to go out and see something of the world. But why then did she have this small pain in the back of her head as she watched Menka and Buan smile and talk to one another.

Menka placed the glasses of cider in front of Shanti, barely even looking at her.

"I'll catch up with you again in a little while, okay?" Shanti asked Buan.

"Yes, I'll come back out in a moment," he answered without turning his head.

She picked up her two glasses and made her way between various older men and women to the door.

Outside, Fabrin and Darsat were discussing the aesthetic features of the statue in the north. Shanti arrived just in time to see Fabrin shaking his head.

"No, there's no way an artist would deliberately have disfigured the statue just to match some randomly chosen shape that suits your charts."

"You might say so young man, but I have seen a

great many cultures whose art does not look as ours does. I would not be surprised to find that a different standard of quality applied here."

"But it would make the statue completely out of proportion! Eyes, hands, fingers, they don't look like that!" Fabrin's voice was loud, but there was a laugh in it and he was smiling. Darsat was smiling too, though his short white beard hid some of it, and the fingers he stroked through it disguised the smile further.

"Here you are," said Shanti as she placed the drink by Fabrin.

"Thank you," answered Fabrin, before returning to his conversation. Shanti walked by and sat with Dulku, a little bit away from the men.

"How was the rest of your afternoon?" she asked the older woman.

"Oh it was fine dear." Dulku took a sip of her drink. She looked deep into Shanti's eyes with a knowing gleam. "How is your evening shaping up?"

"Um…" Shanti looked over at Fabrin, completely engrossed in his discussion of art and the impulse that drove people and societies to make it. She thought of Buan, inside in the warm, talking to Menka. She remembered the way her parents had effectively told her that they didn't trust her and she wasn't capable enough to handle a simple task, though they had said it with all the care and kindness in the world. She sniffed a little. "Not well I'm afraid."

Dulku reached over and patted the younger woman's hand.

THE EVENING DREW ON, chilly breezes pulling thin strands of clouds across the stars onwards to the distant hills in the east. The garden was illuminated by wide flat yellow leaves of light that spread over the awning of the pub. Laughter still spilled from inside as the door was pulled open and closed from time to time, and Shanti spent much of her time talking with Dulku. The older woman was trove of adventurous stories, telling Shanti all about travel to distant countries and staying in strange homes with peculiar people. Shanti drank it all in, hanging on Dulku's every word with glittering eyes. In between these tales, she would check in with Fabrin and make sure that she was spending time with him also, but he engaged in Dulku's stories only when there was some element of artistry or design involved.

"That sounds awfully intricate," he said after Dulku had described the beaded curtains that one of the lodgings she and Darsat had strayed in used instead of walls. "Were they interlaced, or each a single strand?"

"It's funny you ask, young man," answered Dulku. She leaned forward, using her free hand to gesture as though handling the beads in front of them. "It was mostly interlaced, in a kind of hexagonal pattern, ensuring that the walls stayed in position for most of the time. There was even a wooden runner along the base that these strings were connected to. However," she said with sharp emphasis, "There were a few areas that were only single strings with beads on, and those were easily pushed aside. Darsat and I used them as doorways, but I don't know if that was actually the purpose of them." She leaned back again.

"Wasn't it cold?" asked Shanti.

"No actually." Dulku took a sip from her glass. "In that part of the world, so far south of here, it is rather hot even at night. There were some breezes, and I would even say that it did get windy at one point, but it was never cold."

"What about privacy?" Shanti tried not to glance at Fabrin, though she was glad that they were sitting outside where the heat in her cheeks was unlikely to be noticed or commented upon.

"Yes, well." Dulku looked over at her husband and chuckled. "In theory the beads were supposed to obscure anyone on the far side from truly seeing in, but they could certainly hear. I know that when I went for a walk at one stage I was quite sure I knew what was going on on the other side of some walls!"

Fabrin cleared his throat and then asked a question about the size and shape of the beads, heading into a detailed discussion of the craft that must have gone into the making of the structure.

Shanti moved over to talk to Darsat, who was just finishing a wild story about striped horses that chased him and his guide in some other country. The others laughed heartily as he wrapped it up, but then all moved off to other conversations, leaving Shanti alone with the older man.

"How are you doing, my dear! You do have a sombre expression on your face, as you have all night. Is something amiss?"

"No, not really." Shanti ran a finger around the lip of her glass.

"Oh go on," he said, reaching over to pat her hand. "I don't mean to pry, but you were so much more cheerful earlier, and I wonder what must have changed for you. Is it something to do with your friend?" He tilted his head at Fabrin questioningly.

"No, it's not Fabrin! I just had some bad news at home this afternoon."

"Bad news? The way I have been hearing, you should be excited to see a beautiful display of lights in only a couple of weeks? All the others in town have been made quite joyous by the news!"

"Yes, I am excited for the display, it will be wonderful. But my parents run the store here in Graama, and they received the order to actually go and get the lights. I volunteered to go, so that I could help. They both really need to stay and run the business you see. But they said no."

"Oh I see. That is a disappointment." Darsat puffed on his small wooden pipe, looking up at the stars that twinkled in the sky above them. "Did they explain to you why they would not allow you to go? Are you too young?"

"They think that I'm not experienced enough to handle myself in Gorduum. They may have a point."

Shanti sighed. "Although I would love to go, I have never even been as far as Afestaa. I don't know if I would be able to handle myself in such a big new place."

"Oh, you seem very capable to me."

The compliment made Shanti smile.

"And besides, they say the god is always watching! But I can see why they might think Gorduum can be overwhelming. If you went alone for stock, you would have to undertake business dealing, yes?"

"Yes, but my uncle is a businessman there. We would hope that I could stay with him and ask him for advice or guidance while sorting out the business side of things."

"Well, it seems to me that you have most of the support you need." Darsat sat up a little straighter in his chair. "All you need is a companion to take you on the journey, in my opinion!" He pointed at her with the stem of his pipe.

"I suppose that might make them feel more comfortable. But who could do that?"

"Myself, obviously!" Darsat laughed loudly. "I will be returning to my post at the University shortly, as it seems that this statue is entirely unsuited to my theories. I could escort you back! I will be your watching eyes!"

"That's a wonderful idea!"

The two continued talking, discussing Darsat's post at the University as a professor of astronomical studies. He spent his time split between telling halls full of students about the stars and objects of the sky, and travelling across the world in order to get a proper and varied view of such objects. By the way he spoke, sometimes he managed to write the stories of his travels or what he saw into books, but this was the least of his concerns.

After a time, Buan came outside. His cheeks were flushed, and Shanti wondered whether that was due to the heat of the bodies pressed inside the small pub, or whether it was instead due to the number of drinks he'd had. Perhaps it was something else that had warmed him while he was inside. Or someone.

He was carrying a glass of dark brown ale out with him, and Shanti thought she noticed a slight stumble as he moved along the path. Maybe there was a loose stone?

Buan came up beside Fabrin and clapped a hand onto the other young man's shoulder. The sound echoed in the night air, and Fabrin's wide smile twitched.

"Hello Fabrin! How are you doing?"

Buan's voice rang louder than necessary. Shanti frowned and began to stand up, intending to tell him off for his rude interruption but Darsat shook his head.

"I think you'd do better to let them hash it out, dear," he said. "Young men can get quite headstrong. In the long run, it does them better to know where they stand."

Fabrin had turned his smile onto the newcomer, and lifted a hand to Buan's own shoulder. They appeared to be talking in a friendly manner, but Shanti could see that both of their eyes were flashing.

Dulku leaned forward and resumed whatever the conversation had been when Buan walked up. This drew both of their attention to her, and their hands returned to their pockets.

The conversation continued, although it was difficult for Shanti to be sure what was going on. Dulku was introducing them to another wondrous object that she and Darsat had seen in their travels. This one sounded like some sort of building, built of shining white and blue stone and rising high up into the sky as a series of domes and jutting spires.

Shanti leaned over to Darsat. "That sounds amazing!"

"It was! Why don't you go over and hear about it?"

Shanti nodded and stood to join the others.

As she came closer, she heard Fabrin asking if Dulku knew the dimensions of the main room of the building. It appeared to be central to the entire edifice, like some sort of gigantic hall.

"I would not know the precise numbers Fabrin, but I can tell you that it was at least as wide across as three or four train cars. Have you travelled by train?"

Fabrin grimaced and shook his head slightly. "No no, I've no real reason to get on a train. I mean," he shrugged. "I suppose that I wouldn't mind going along to see one in action one day. I've always been curious to discover exactly how the engine drives the wheels."

"I travelled by train once," blurted Buan, glancing at Shanti as she entered the conversation. She was surprised. Buan had never told her about any train journey before. Suddenly she found herself looking more closely at his face, wondering what other secrets he might be hiding from her.

"When was this?" she found herself asking, the surprise and curiosity clear in her voice.

"Oh uh," he blinked rapidly and smacked his lips. "A long time ago. I guess I must have been pretty young, I don't really remember much about it."

"I'd love to hear about what you do remember though."

"When I say that I haven't been on a train before," interrupted Fabrin, stepping slightly forward. "That was only to say that I have been quite busy here, building up a very successful business and developing some very fine skills in my leatherwork. Obviously, travel could only serve to introduce me to even more ideas and contacts, so I am sure I will expand in that manner sooner rather than later."

Shanti thought she caught Dulku smiling as the older woman took another sip from her glass.

"Now that you ask," said Buan, though he glared at Fabrin as he said it. "Perhaps I do remember more than I thought!" He swayed a little, rubbing his mouth and chin with one hand before seeming to gather his thoughts together. "I would have been about six years old, and my parents took me by train to visit an aunt in Prafee. I think she was sick, or dying, or something terrible like that, but I was so young that all I noticed was that we were staying in her house near the seaside."

"So, not to Gorduum then?" Shanti couldn't help but feel a little disappointed. "Just another village?"

"Well, it was by the seaside. There were boats and seagulls." Buan looked a little confused. "I went for a swim in the sea."

Shanti wondered why the thought of travelling to see the ocean was less exciting to her than travelling to the great city. It was said to grow lights bigger, brighter and more successfully than anywhere else in the world. Maybe she just wanted to learn more about them, having spent so much time with Sudru.

"Do you remember much about the train ride itself young man?" Dulku offered helpfully.

"Oh yes, it was a magnificent machine, so huge and made of shining black metal!" Buan burst with sudden enthusiasm, describing the train and its passenger cars in such detail that Shanti quickly lost focus.

"Isn't that incredible Shanti?" He said, twisting around to see what she thought.

"Oh, yes I suppose it is. I expect it would be quite interesting to travel by train."

The conversation continued.

EVENTUALLY, people began to drift out of the pub and head home. Shanti yawned and stretched, hoping that one of the others would notice that she was ready to go home. Fabrin stood quickly and moved over to be next to her.

"Getting late?" he asked.

"Yes, and I think I should get home before my parents begin to worry."

"I'll walk you home!" Buan stood so sharply that he nearly knocked over his chair.

"Actually, I thought I'd walk her home. After all, I'm the one who took her out in the first place."

"Thank you Buan, but I did come out with Fabrin, so I think it would be most appropriate if he walked me home."

Buan nodded, but his shoulders slumped as he did. "Maybe next time."

Fabrin offered Shanti his arm as they began to

walk down the street towards her house and she gratefully laid her hand on it. Her eyelids were beginning to droop as the evening rolled on.

"Thank you for coming out with me," said Fabrin.

"It was my pleasure. I was grateful for the chance to get out of the house this evening actually."

"Yes, it sounds like you had a disappointing afternoon. I hope the evening got more cheerful though?"

"It did indeed." Shanti looked across at Fabrin, who was watching her, his face close to hers. His smile was much smaller, though echoes of it remained in the tilt of his lips and a glint in his eyes. Before she knew it, they were by her front door.

"I really enjoyed your company tonight," he said, stepping in closer. He shifted his arms, so that she found herself holding one of his hands, and his other was reaching out to her side. His face moved closer to hers.

She found her thoughts flashing by, wondering whether he was really someone that she wanted to encourage. After all, he didn't seem to be very interested in leaving the village, and that was all she really wanted, even if she couldn't imagine when she would ever get the chance. But then his lips met hers and she found her thoughts vanishing.

It was a gentle kiss, though Fabrin's lips conveyed his confidence. Shanti reached one arm around his shoulder as warmth flowed through her. Then, she pushed him back and took a deep breath.

"I've enjoyed your company too." She stepped up to the front door and opened it. "Good night Fabrin."

"Good night Shanti," he returned, his smile back and wider than ever. "I'll see you again soon I hope!"

She smiled, but did not answer as she shut the door.

Her parents were still sitting up in the living room

as Shanti walked through. For a moment she worried that they were waiting up for her. However, they barely glanced at her as she came in.

"How was your night?" asked her father, not lifting his eyes from the small hardback book he was reading. Her mother continued sewing a repair to some of her brother's trousers.

"Excellent. Fabrin and I went to the pub and had a couple of drinks. I introduced him to Darsat and Dulku, those visitors that I met this morning."

"Sounds very nice. How is Fabrin doing?"

Shanti wondered if they could see into her head, and felt her cheeks beginning to grow warm.

"He's very well," Shanti answered, but something made her add, "although he does seem to be quite single minded about his leather working business here."

"Of course," said her mother. "He's a smart young man and he knows how to make the most of his talents."

"Yes, and I'm not saying that he isn't talented. It's just that…" Shanti trailed off. She didn't know how to tell her parents that she felt so strongly about going outside Graama and seeing the world. She knew that they were relying on her as the most dependable one in the family. Hadn't they been speaking earlier about the way that she was the only reason that one of them would even be able to go into Gorduum and collect the order for the Festival? She felt ashamed of how desperately she had sought news and stories of the world outside all through the night, and how eagerly she had listened to Dulku tell her about things that sounded so different to life here. Even though her parents didn't know that she had been talking about these things, she was worried that they would be hurt if they found out. They must think that she wanted to abandon them.

"Oh sweetheart." Her mother tilted her head and paused in her needlework. "You'll get a chance to go out into the world for a time, if you want. But just not now."

"That wasn't what I meant." But the red angry feeling that blossomed in the back of her head made Shanti wonder if maybe she had been hoping that her parents would have changed their mind in her absence. Perhaps she had been hoping that they would feel guilty for trapping her even longer in the small village, without a chance to get out into the world and see some of the wonders it held.

"We've decided that your father will go," said her mother, as Neeran nodded in his chair. He closed the book and placed it on his lap, with his thumb tucked between the pages so that he wouldn't lose his place.

"We thought that your mother would be more useful to be around the store if I were away."

"Can you imagine your father trying to run the store without me for a week?" Auga chuckled and shook her head, a smirk on her lips. Neeran pretended to frown at her, but Shanti could see that he found the idea amusing too.

"I get it. I really wasn't asking to go again, I was just saying that Fabrin may not be the man for me." Shanti was feeling flustered, unsure what she wanted to say to her parents. She didn't know what she wanted them to say to her either. "It's just that Darsat said that he would have gladly chaperoned me to Gorduum if you had changed your mind." Shanti found her voice caught in her tight throat as she spoke, so she finished quickly and swallowed thickly. Her eyes felt hot.

"Who is this Darsat again?" asked Neeran, his

forehead creased as he tried to summon more memories of what his daughter had said about the man.

"That was that professor you said you spoke to this morning, wasn't it?" said Auga.

Shanti nodded.

"Well, you did say his wife was with him." Auga pursed her lips. "And I suppose we'd be able to meet him first." She trailed off as she considered the idea. Shanti felt her breath flutter in her chest, and she had to hold one hand on her stomach to try and calm herself down.

Neeran had raised his eyebrows and was watching Auga closely, but she didn't seem to notice her husband at all. Finally, she shook her head.

"It's a very kind thought, and I'm sure having a chaperone to go with you would be a good idea for when you do end up going to Gorduum by yourself. But we've made our decision, and so we will stick to it. There's too much business to attend to. Maybe you can meet up with his wife and him for a holiday in the future, a tour of Gorduum."

The sudden vacuum in her throat as her mother spoke robbed Shanti of the ability to respond. She tried to smile and nod, acknowledging her parents' decision, then turned to return to her room.

How was it possible for so many emotions to boil through one young woman at once? She had been curious to hear about so many distant lands during the day, then excited to hear about the light display that would be displayed for the Festival. Then joy had preceded disappointment as her parents had discussed who would go on the journey. Then an evening of glee, guilt, satisfaction, and exasperation as Buan and Fabrin had let their mouths run away with themselves at the pub. Even an ecstatic high when Fabrin had kissed her. She considered the recent memory and relished the warmth that it brought to her. Yes, even if he wasn't the man for her in the long run, it had definitely felt good to be wanted; to be needed for who she was and not needed as a support for others. And now, just as she went into her room and got changed into her nightclothes, a sort of empty hole that gnawed at her stomach. As she lay in her bed, she wondered if tears would come. She wondered why it was so important to her, it was only a short trip. She wondered how Buan was feeling right now.

SHANTI WOKE in the morning feeling much better. The sun was beginning to peek past the curtain on her narrow window. The chill air of the night was beginning to fade. She felt warm and cosy beneath her blankets, but she knew that she would have to get out of them soon. She relished the feeling for a few moments more.

After forcing herself to climb out of bed, she washed and got dressed and went to the kitchen for breakfast. She found the rest of her family there, in various states of preparation for the day.

Auga and Neeran were sitting near each other and discussing their plans quietly. They sipped from steaming mugs of tea in between comments. If Shanti had wanted to, she would have been able to hear what they were saying easily enough, but from the simple and serious expressions on their faces, she assumed that they were working out details of the journey into Gorduum. Much as she understood their decision, she didn't want to know anything more about that.

Fellbin was spreading thick whorls of butter onto heavy slices of bread that he had toasted a little over the oven. As he sank his teeth into one, his eyes rolling in pleasure, he noticed Shanti entering the kitchen. Spraying crumbs, he asked, "What happened with Fabrin last night?"

Shanti could barely understand him through the food in his mouth.

"What do you mean?" she replied, sitting to slice herself a piece of bread.

"Well, he came to pick you up, you guys were out for ages. Are you sweet on him?" Fellbin waggled his eyebrows up and down meaningfully

Shanti tutted at him. "He's very good looking, but-"

"He is a very pretty man, all the girls talk about him. Apparently it's his forearms, they look very strong? Care to venture an opinion on that?"

"No!" Although Shanti remembered the feeling of his arms as they held her and turned her to face him, pulling her into his embrace. "I think he might be a little sweet on me, but I will need to spend a lot more time with him before I will know exactly how I feel about him." She spread some raspberry jam onto her slice.

Fellbin nodded and took another monstrous bite. "That's fair. Shakti asked me out, but she has this weird freckle on her forehead that used to make me uncomfortable, but now we've been hanging out a lot anyway and she's actually quite funny."

"How is that related to Fabrin?" Shanti took a much more reasonably sized bite of her bread.

"Well, it just goes to show, you never really know until you spend some time with a person. And also it shows that looks aren't everything. If you don't agree that he's pretty, he might turn out to be some sort of," and here Fellbin looked thoroughly out of his depth, waving one hand in a vague gesture, "Nice person?"

"I doubt anyone is suggesting that Fabrin isn't very pretty." Taanin spoke softly as he came back inside with buckets of water hanging from a pole across his shoulders. He began to transfer them into jugs to keep in the cool shade of the pantry. "His nose alone is-"

"I don't know if you're helping," Shanti told her older brother.

"Was I trying to?" Taanin's gentle voice belied the wit of his comeback, but he smiled as he said it to show that he intended no harm. "Anyway, Shanti is allowed to show interest, or to not show interest, in anyone at all."

"Thank you," said Shanti.

"Even if Buan has been pining over her for years and years, and hoping that she will finally open her eyes to him."

Shanti spluttered as she choked on some crumbs from her bread.

"Oh? I knew that Buan mooned over her, but is it really that serious?" Fellbin had finished his breakfast, but he was settling back into his chair as the conversation developed.

"Oh yes." Taanin spoke with certainty. Buan and he had grown up together, both with introverted natures that meant they drew together to observe while the other children had scampered backwards and forwards through the village streets. Maybe that was why Shanti still had trouble picturing Buan as a real possibility for her romantic future. He had grown up acting like an older brother to her.

"Now, I hardly think that's fair."

"Oh, I'm not accusing you of anything, you have no reason to feel guilty." The words alone made Shanti begin to feel so. "As I said, you are allowed to have your own feelings. It's just that he has tried so very hard to figure out what you are looking for."

"Well, I'm not completely sure I know what I am looking for just yet myself." Shanti could tell that her voice was rising, but she didn't seem to be able to bring it back under control.

"I know what you want," said Fellbin, putting both his hands behind his head. "You want to get away from here." He bit his lip and grinned mournfully. "Don't think Buan is gonna fit into that plan though."

Shanti had finished her breakfast and so, having had enough of her brothers' teasing, she bid them a good morning and retreated back into the living room with her parents.

Auga and Neeran had arisen and were tidying up the living room. Someone would need to go and open the store very soon, and it was going to be Auga today. She tied her shawl over the thick black waves of her hair and kissed her husband.

"I'll see you later my love," she said as she headed out the door. "And I'll expect you to join me later please Shanti," she smiled as she passed her daughter.

"Okay mother."

Neeran sighed and picked up his hardback novel. "None of you appreciate these. This was a fantastic story and I think you should all read it." He waved the green book at Shanti.

"Thank you, but I'd prefer to go and see the real world rather than allow someone to tell me about it." Part of Shanti hoped that the comment would needle her father, as punishment for his decision to keep her in Graama even longer. The greater part of her felt a little sick and hoped he hadn't noticed the barb.

"I thought you were enjoying the stories that professor was telling you, stories about this 'real world' that you find so interesting?"

"Yes, but at least he was telling me the stories in person. If I am talking to someone who has actually been to these places, then I can ask them questions, I can find out more. With a book, all that there is is what the author has decided to tell me." She shrugged. "It's not as good."

"But until you get to the places yourself, surely it's better than nothing?" Neeran placed one palm flat on the book's cover. "You could read it while I'm away in Gorduum?"

"Yes probably." Shanti tried not to sound curt, but hearing reconfirmation of her parents' decision stung like someone stabbing her with a pin right in her chest. "But still, I would like to go and see if I can speak with Darsat and Dulku again today before they decide to leave, and before I have to go into the store and help mother. So you may as well put that book away for now."

Neeran smiled and nodded. "Another time perhaps." He moved over to the wall with the shelf. The shelf was high up on the wall, and Shanti believed it was originally installed to hold keepsakes and treasures up high where they would be on display but not picked up very often. If a person were to reach up high, they could just manage to put something on it or take something down. However, Neeran was not a very tall man anyway, and he was getting quite fussy about the small collection of novels that he was beginning to build up. He had six already, and he reread them often while he saved up and sent away for new ones. Two of them had been lent out to his friends in the village, although he kept a scrupulously accurate notebook of who had which book and when they had said that they would ensure it was returned by. He even noted down any damage that the book had suffered, from dog-eared pages to small stains on the paper, so that he knew who to blame for each.

In order to place the book back on the shelf properly, he pulled a stool out from behind the sitting chair and set it below the shelf before stepping up and onto it. He placed the book into position, shifting one of the other books so that the correct order was maintained, and then pursed his lips as he considered whether he wanted to reread one of the other books and if he should get it down now.

Shanti felt like the next few seconds slowed down, as though time had become thick molasses, oozing from moment to moment. She watched as her father shifted his position on the stool, just slightly, adjusting his weight from one foot to the other. As he did, one of the thin wooden struts that connected the legs popped away from the thicker wood, and the stool tilted sharply. Neeran threw his arms out sideways, but grasped nothing, and he stepped forward onto the air, looking for any way to halt his fall. There was a loud crack as his foot hit the floor, and his face screwed up in shock and pain. Then he yelled.

Shanti ran over and grabbed her father by the shoulders "Are you okay?"

"No!" Neeran groaned and yelped, both hands grasping at his leg just above the ankle. "Get your mother! Get the doctor! Unseen eyes, this hurts!"

Shanti ran into the kitchen, nearly colliding with Taanin as he burst in to find out what the noise had been.

Shanti leaned on the counter of the store and sighed. Although she knew that this was the best way she could help her parents out while her brothers had carefully carried Neeran to see Tanama the village doctor, she did wish that she could have had some more time to talk to Darsat. And Dulku had promised to share more stories about the parts of their travels that Darsat had been uninterested in, but that Shanti found intriguing. Darsat was obsessed with astronomy and artworks, intently interested in finding patterns in the architecture and statues and paintings of different cultures, especially when there was a possibility that they could reveal some aspect of how those people viewed the stars above. However, when it came to homes, clothes, traditions and the way the people actually spoke and behaved, he sounded content to let them be.

So, Dulku had promised to explain what she had noticed about different festivals, different families, and the ways that these other people acted that sounded so strange to Shanti. There was so much that she could learn from them both!

There was a tingling noise as the shop's door opened and someone walked in. Shanti stood up straighter.

It was Fabrin.

"Well good morning to you, my sweetheart," he began, strolling up to the counter and leaning forward to take hold of Shanti's hands in his own. She blinked and found herself unsure of how to reply. That greeting was more familiar than she expected, but maybe she had misunderstood something about last night?

"How has your morning been? Missing me?" He lifted her hands to his lips, then turned his deep brown eyes on hers. They were as dark as a forest.

"Not really," she stammered. "I just saw you last night. It hasn't really been that long." Self-consciously, she removed her hand from his and placed it back on the counter. She found she had the feeling that she needed to wipe it clean, but she refrained from doing so. That would just be rude! "But my morning has been quite chaotic. My father fell off a stool and hurt his leg. That's why I'm here this morning, otherwise I wouldn't have been on."

"Poor man." Fabrin shook his head. "So, what shall we do this afternoon? I've got a few boots that I need repair today, but then I'm hoping to get out and look for inspiration this afternoon!"

"I wasn't really thinking that far ahead," Shanti said carefully, narrowing her eyes slightly. "I thought I might check in on my father though. After all," and she slowed down her speech, to ensure that the young man heard it clearly. "He might have broken his leg this morning. There was a loud, horrid cracking noise." She paused for a moment before continuing. "I watched it happen."

"Yes, dreadful, but there's not really anything you can do about it now. Why not go out and enjoy yourself as best you can?"

"If I felt inclined to go and enjoy myself, I think I would see where Darsat and Dulku are and see if they would mind telling me any more stories."

"He was a most gratifying man to talk with. He really appreciated the fine details of things, the craftsmanship that goes into a true work of art. Not like most of the people here." Fabrin turned to face away from Shanti, leaning his back against the shop counter and resting on his elbows, as though looking through the walls of the store to the village outside. "They don't really understand what quality hides in their midst."

Shanti was confused. Suddenly Fabrin was much less interesting than he had been the night before. Now she looked at the way his shirt pulled tight across his strong shoulders and could only think about how he probably wore clothes slightly too tight on purpose, just so he could show off his muscles. But that was a cruel thing to think of someone, and she put the thought aside. Instead, she decided to follow his statement and see if he could connect with her own hopes for the future.

"Maybe you should travel someday, so you can find people who really understand your work?"

"It's crossed my mind." Fabrin turned back around. "But you know that for people to really get it, you have to be in one place long enough for them to see the effort that it takes." It was his turn to sigh.

"Travelling might be good for inspiration and picking up a few techniques, but I'll need to come home if I want people to acknowledge my time and effort." Somehow his face gave off a feeling of heartbreak at the idea of his public never truly comprehending him.

"You could live somewhere else though, couldn't you?"

"Don't be silly." And that was all the thought that he gave to her suggestion. He didn't even have the courtesy to offer a justification or argument. Shanti felt a cold prickle on the backs of her neck and forearms.

"I have to check some of our stock levels, perhaps write up an order for some consumables. If you'll excuse me?"

"Oh, okay." Fabrin stood up straighter and ran a hand through his hair, though he looked confused. "So, shall I come by again later and we can spend the afternoon together?" He walked around the counter, coming close to Shanti and holding her by the shoulders.

"I don't think so, I really want to check on my father."

"Well, if that's what you want," he muttered, then leaned forward to kiss her. She turned her face so that he kissed her cheek. Again, the confused look crossed over his face, creasing his forehead. "I'll see you around!"

Shanti could see the confusion lift from his face by the time he left the store. He began walking away from her slowly, dragging his feet a little, but as he opened the door he was stepping lightly and almost whistling.

She shook her head. How could she have missed how self-centred Fabrin was? Had he always been this way, or was it something that had developed because of their kiss? Had her seeming interest in him made his ego grow out of scale?

Shanti barely had time to walk through the storage spaces in the back of the building before she heard the bell at the door ringing again. She dusted off her hands on her apron as she walked back through to the main shop, calling "I'm coming, just a moment!"

"There's no rush at all," came the soft and familiar reply.

Buan was standing awkwardly by the counter as she emerged. Shanti wondered if he had seen Fabrin leaving the shop just before. Then she wondered if that was why he had come in. Finally, she wondered if the tight feeling in her stomach was guilt or something else. She had no reason to feel guilty, so that didn't make sense. But it felt very similar to how she felt when she contemplated leaving her parents by themselves to run the store and manage her brothers without her.

"Oh, hello Buan. How are you feeling this morning?"

Buan grinned sheepishly and rubbed his chin, speckled with the dark stubble of a morning without shaving. "I've been better," he admitted. "I think I may have had a few more ales than was proper."

"Yes, I rather think you might have." Shanti arched an eyebrow and crossed her arms, but allowed a smirk to touch the corner of her mouth as she did so. "It did seem to allow you to talk about a great many things that you otherwise might not have."

"Yes. I'm sorry if I was embarrassing or offensive." Buan's face turned from shame to earnest worry so quickly that it was as though he had simply swapped between a pair of masks. The muscles of his face barely moved, simply snapping into new positions. "I would hate to think that I had upset you from my poor decisions."

"No, you didn't." Now Shanti grinned. "It was rather entertaining, and you did tell me all about your travels on a train when you were younger." She reached over to push his shoulder. "You'd never told me about your train expertise before! I saw a whole new side of you."

Buan straightened his shoulders and lifted his head a little higher. "That's wonderful! I'll tell you more about it sometime, if you really like. Are you free this afternoon?"

Shanti explained about her father, and how she would need to check in on him. Buan was shocked and enquired as to Neeran's condition, declaring that he would go to see Shanti's father himself later in the day. He even offered to bring around some ale from the pub. This time Shanti did feel slightly sad that she didn't have much free time in the afternoon.

"Well, maybe another day. I hope that your father is okay."

"Maybe we could plan a train journey of our own! You could show me the seaside."

"Yes, I could! But not this year. I've got to get the repairs to the house and barn finished, and then there's the planting season, and the animals." Buan shrugged. "But we could look at plans?"

"Yes, we should talk about plans." Shanti tried to hold onto the enthusiasm she had felt moments before, but the disappointment that slid through her muscles as he listed reasons that they could not go pulled her shoulders lower. For a fleeting second she had thought that Buan would help her go out and see something new, but his duties at the farm reined in those dreams, as her own responsibilities so often did too. "Maybe we can spend some time together tomorrow."

"Sounds perfect," smiled Buan.

NOT LONG AFTER NOON, Taanin arrived to take over for Shanti.

"How is he?"

"It's not too bad, but he will be out of action for quite a while. Tanama said that we probably should have left him where he was and asked her to come and see him there." Taanin and Fellbin had lifted their father carefully, putting his arms over their shoulders, and painstakingly hobbled across Graama to the small building that Tanama operated out of. From what Taanin said, Tanama was not impressed that Neeran would have been putting pressure on the damaged leg to get there, even if he had barely done so.

"Did he break something?"

"Yeah, we were sure of that before we even got him to the doctor."

Shanti untied her apron and lifted it over her head, hanging it on the peg behind the counter. "How come?"

"The way his ankle turned and twisted." Taanin grimaced at the memory "It wasn't at all natural."

"Ugh." Imagining her father's ankle twisting at odd angles made Shanti feel nauseous. "Is he at home now?"

"Yeah. She managed to pull it into position, but we had to hold him down and give him something to bite while she did. Now it's strapped up and bound and he'll need to use a crutch to walk. But he's not really supposed to walk at all."

"For how long?"

"Tanama didn't say, but she said she'd come and check on it periodically."

"Alright, well I'll go and see him."

Shanti got home as quickly as possible, and rushed over to her father in his chair, tumbling onto him in a huge hug.

"Yargh!" he squawked, lifting her slightly.

"Oh my gosh, I'm so sorry!" Shanti leapt off the chair again just as quickly. "I didn't think I would get your leg!"

"You didn't really, but even shifting my weight takes some planning right now." Neeran's face was pale, and his eyes looked dark, but he managed to smile at her. "How was your day, love?"

"Nothing compared to yours. Taanin let me know the updates when he took over. Are you feeling okay?"

"It's actually not too bad when I stay still." There must have been truth to this, because even as she watched, his colour improved and he breathed easier.

"It was dreadful when I fell, and it was a nightmare while Tanama was setting it into position, but now I just need to stay still as much as I can."

"You poor thing."

"Poor thing indeed." Shanti's mother strode into the living room with a mug of hot tea in her hand. She passed it over to her husband. "He's going to wallow in this, just you wait and see. Taking advantage already probably."

"You'll have time to reread all your books," teased Shanti.

"He might, but who'd get them down for him, death-trap as that stool is?"

Neeran chuckled and sipped at his tea.

"Well." Auga turned with her hands on her hips and stared at her daughter. "Are you going to go and pack or what?"

"Sorry?" Shanti was confused, lifting her hands to ward off her mother's glare.

"With your father wrecking his leg like this, there's no way that he can go on a trip into Gorduum and go gallivanting about the streets sorting out our orders. And I can't do it, leaving him here to somehow take care of the house AND the store at the same time, when he can't even make his own tea."

Auga pulled a cloth out of her pocket and began dusting all around her husband, aggressively pushing the faint traces of dust backwards and forwards, and occasionally punctuating her speech by flicking the cloth and creating an audible crack. "So it will have to be you. Is that professor still willing to chaperone you?"

Auga didn't meet her daughter's eyes, and at first Shanti thought that her mother was so angry that she couldn't even look at her. But then, as the words

Shanti had just heard sank in, her mother slowly managed to drag her eyes up to meet her daughter's.

Those eyes were creased with worry, and between them Auga's forehead was squeezing into tight furrows. There was a tension in her face, as though the skin was trying to pull back and away from whatever it was that she imagined was going to happen. Shanti looked into her mother's face and saw another way to interpret her anger. Auga was scared for her daughter.

"Do you mean it? That's wonderful!" Shanti ran over to her mother and grabbed her into a mighty hug.

"Thank you daughter, I'm glad my pain can bring you so much joy," said her father dryly. Auga shushed him without looking. Her arms clung to Shanti, the fingertips digging in slightly more than usual.

"You will have to be so, so careful," she said into Shanti's shoulder, the sound muffled.

"Of course."

"I will have to write you out some instructions and contacts. And we will have to hope that Dunin is able to accommodate you at such short notice. Your father or I would have been able to convince him, but I don't know what he will say to you."

"I'm sure he can find me a small space in a cupboard at the very least." Shanti's heart was racing and she could hear the blood pounding in her head. She felt giddy and shocked, all at the same time. She was going to Gorduum!

"And you," snapped Auga, turning back to face Neeran as she released Shanti. "This is all your fault! If anything happens to my girl, you are going to pay for it!"

Neeran blinked and his mouth gaped. "My dear, I'm concerned for her too, but she will be fine! She can bring the professor to meet us so that we are sure of her chaperone, and however much of a fool your brother has been, he will not put his niece in danger." He turned his gaze back to Shanti and sipped at his tea again. "Maybe the Masked God was watching you more than me this morning. You are going on an adventure love." He winked over the cup.

THE REST of the afternoon passed in a blur. Shanti had to find Darsat and Dulku as soon as possible, a task that involved tracking them down via the village's network of children, running down the streets and alleys in the fading red glow of the afternoon sun. Whoops and laughter echoed across the fields, and many of the village's inhabitants were nearly bowled over by racing children. Eventually she tracked the couple down. They were walking hand in hand around the perimeter of the village, having spent the morning back at the statue with more instruments and documents. Darsat was smiling, but Shanti could see that he was quite disappointed at how quickly he had proved his own theories wrong.

She spoke urgently with them, trying not to ignore what they had to say about their day in her rush. Although she wanted to drag them running through the streets back to her house, the two only laughed politely and took their time strolling along behind her. At multiple points she had to stand and wait for them to catch up to her, so fast was she walking. Her nerves were flittering, and she had to press her hands onto her legs to try and keep them still.

When they finally came in to meet her parents, Shanti dashed to her room and started gathering clothing and belongings on her bed. A hairbrush, a set of formal clothing so that she would look professional when meeting with business contacts, light casual clothes for any exploring she might get time for, a small circular mirror that she had been given for her birthday when she was twelve. The pile grew larger and larger.

She could hear the four of them chatting in the living room, a happy murmur with no recognisable words, and it sounded promising. She found a suitcase on top of a wardrobe and spent twenty minutes cleaning it of dust and spider webs, bringing the clasps back to a reasonable shine, before piling all her belongings into it. Lastly, she snatched up an old leather satchel that Fabrin had made. Her father had bought it for her when she was quite young, and she habitually kept whatever she wanted with her for longer days in it. The fact that Fabrin had made it slowed her down. She wondered if perhaps she should leave it behind. The thought spun out of her head quickly though, and she hurried downstairs with the satchel over her shoulder, banging on her hip.

She pulled the suitcase behind her into the living room, panting slightly, just in time to hear Neeran say "So there will be no trouble buying a ticket at the station in Afestaa then?" and to see Darsat shake his head in response. She brushed a wisp of hair off her forehead and back behind her ear. The others all laughed at her.

"In a hurry are you?" asked Dulku, holding a cup of tea between her hands.

"Of course." Shanti sniffed. "Aren't you?"

More peals of laughter broke out.

Shortly after this, Darsat and Dulku shook hands with Shanti's parents and told Shanti that they would meet her first thing in the morning outside their lodgings.

"There's no need to go charging off at night. We'll organise a coach, gather our things, and be ready to set out bright and early. Besides, we'll enjoy the journey much more during the day, and there will still be enough time for you to complete your business," explained Dulku.

Although she understood, Shanti was exasperated and had no way to release the energy she found building inside her. She was practically bouncing on her toes. Impatient for the morning to arrive, she ate her dinner with rapidity and then went to bed early, where she felt as though she stared at the ceiling for hours before finally getting to sleep.

IN THE MORNING she gathered her suitcase and hugged and kissed her parents. She held onto them for a long time, suddenly overwhelmed at the thought of leaving them. She felt tears rising from her chest, feeling heavy and hot.

"Are you sure it's okay?" she murmured into her mother's shoulder as they hugged, and felt her mother's hand stroke her hair comfortingly.

"It will be fine," replied Auga. She stepped back from her daughter, holding her by the shoulders and looking into her eyes. "These two are such kind people and they will get you to Gorduum with no problems I am sure. And once you are there, my brother will take care of you."

Shanti wished that she believed her mother. She could see creases of worry appearing around Auga's eyes again, and the thought that she was causing more problems for her mother brought tears bubbling up again.

Once she had composed herself enough, and then cried again as she knelt to hug her father where he sat in the chair in the living room, she stood. She had to try to put the guilt she felt at leaving him untended aside. She had to remember that her mother would obviously take great care of her own husband! But Shanti knew that Auga would be busy in the store, more so than usual without Shanti to take some shifts. Taanin would not be around to help as he would be in the fields, and who could rely on Fellbin? Her throat tightened as she lifted her satchel and turned to leave.

"Oh, you might need these!"

Shanti took the money and notes that her mother provided for the order and for Shanti to pay for food and transport, tucking them safely into her satchel. Then, Taanin kindly carried her suitcase for her and escorted her to the coach, where Darsat and Dulku were waiting. To her surprise, Buan was waiting there too.

"What are you doing here?" she asked him, walking over and greeting him with a large hug. As she stepped back, she felt his hand linger on the small of her back before falling to his sides.

"I heard that you would be leaving today." Buan smiled. "How could I let you leave without saying goodbye?"

"It's very kind of you to come. Shouldn't you have been back at the farm by now? You've been in the village for days now it seems!"

"I will have to rush back now," he admitted, lowering his eyes to the ground. Shanti felt bad for reminding him. He was such a dutiful boy and he probably felt guilty for not being at his family farm as often as he should have been. But it did also mean that she felt a small glow of pleasure as well, at the idea that she was so important to him that he would put himself in such a position.

"I'm sorry, I didn't mean to focus on that. Thank you so much for coming down."

"It's my pleasure."

Shanti became very aware that Dulku was standing only a few meters away, watching them both intently. She stepped back from Buan a little and looked over at the older couple.

"And thanks again to you both for agreeing to take me into Gorduum. You have no idea how much this means to me." She caught up Dulku's hands in her own, and the older woman beamed in response.

"It is absolutely our pleasure. Darsat wasn't going to have any more luck here. That much was obvious immediately."

"Indeed so," murmured Darsat sadly, shaking his head. He managed to smile as he said it though. "I had convinced myself that your statue would meet my hypothesis, I was so certain. The sketches and images that I had found in various records," he began firmly, lifting a pointed finger to emphasise his statement before glancing around the small group and coughing. "Well. You have all heard my theory. And you all know that it doesn't hold up. Such a shame."

"It is a shame sir, but I do appreciate your willingness to escort Shanti," said Taanin as he swung her suitcase over onto the coach. He opened the door as Dulku and then Darsat climbed on board. "I know our parents will sleep more soundly knowing that a fine couple such as yourselves are travelling with her."

"I'm sure it will be our pleasure," came the professor's voice from inside. Taanin turned to look at Shanti, still holding the door open. Shanti looked at Buan. He stood, rocking slightly on his heels as though a wind was pushing at him, though the morning air was still and crisp. His short dark hair was standing in tufts and spikes, and his clothes looked rumpled. She realised that he must have run out of the clean clothes that he brought with him.

"I'm really glad that you came," she said, stepping up to him again. She reached out and around his shoulders, pulling his head towards hers. The kiss was soft and sure, but she kept it brief, very conscious of her older brother watching. Still, the shock and happiness that passed over Buan's face made it worthwhile. "I hope to see you when I get back."

"I hope so too!" blurted Buan, holding onto her hand as she stepped away to the coach.

She climbed in past her brother, who lifted one eyebrow just slightly as she did so.

"What?" she grumbled before settling into the dim space beyond. She sat next to Dulku, straightened her skirts, and then looked straight across at the blank wall opposite her, trying to ignore the door as it closed, and refusing to look out of it. She didn't know why, but she felt like she had said and done everything that she needed to, and now she just wanted to move on, to travel away, and process her own thoughts and feelings. Thankfully she didn't have to wait long before she heard the driver calling on the horses, and they rattled into motion down the streets.

"Is he still there?" she whispered to Dulku, who had to lean closer to hear the words.

"Maybe child, but you don't have to look. You've done it now, you're leaving!"

She was leaving. After years of wishing and hoping and trying, she was leaving. It was only a short trip, she was due back within a week, but for now, she was heading beyond the reaches of anything she had done before. She grinned and looked at her new companion. "This is so exciting!"

"Isn't it though! Now," said Dulku, with a twinkle

in her eye. "Tell me all about these young men who are so drawn to your company."

Shanti blushed, but she spent the rest of the day answering questions and telling stories of her youth, detailing everything she could about her past. Dulku listened and questioned and occasionally passed on advice for the younger girl's future.

As they passed Baargu Shanti peered out the window excitedly. She didn't come here often, and she looked closely to see if she could spot buildings that had been repaired or renovated, scanning the people they passed to see if she spotted any familiar faces. Dulku chuckled to watch her.

Before she knew it, the village had rushed past the windows and the coach and rumbled into the forest on the far side of the village. All at once, Shanti was further from home than she had ever been before. She had to remind herself to breathe out.

After another hour or two, Afestaa appeared in the distance. This was more than a village, thought Shanti as she admired the large buildings that rose to either side of the coach. They were built in the same manner as those in Graama and Baargu, but here there were far more that were two stories tall. The number of people walking along the streets shocked Shanti. She turned to Dulku.

"It's huge!" she breathed.

Dulku opened her mouth and bobbed her head from one side to the other, then smiled. "I suppose it is a lot bigger than Graama, isn't it?"

They came to a stop at a strange building that looked like a long wooden deck with a shed at one end, manned by a worker from the train line who sat on the stool in the shed and smoked his pipe. As Shanti climbed out of the coach, the platform had looked like a gateway to the whole world, a stepping stone to wonders and delights that she had only heard of in stories.

"This is the train platform," Darsat explained, leading them to the shed and speaking with the man. The worker didn't even rise from his stool at first, but then moved into the shed and came out with some pieces of stiff cardboard that Darsat said were their tickets. Then the trio found a set of benches to sit on while they waited for the train.

Before she could lose herself in imagined adventures, the train arrived in a storm of noise and steam. Shanti stared at the gigantic black machine, like a massive rod of metal covered in wheels, and hissing worse than a frightened alley cat. It pulled huge rectangular coaches behind it, like some sort of mechanical centipede. It was one of the most incredible things Shanti had ever seen.

It had barely stopped before Darsat and Dulku had loaded all their luggage with the help of the worker from the shed, sat themselves in a carriage and watched the platform begin to fall behind them as the train set off once more.

As she had climbed aboard, Shanti had recklessly pushed past other travellers in a rush to claim her seat, next to a large window and well-padded so that she could enjoy the view as long as possible without shifting. Long afternoons chasing her brothers through the woods near Graama stood her in good stead. Her chaperones had called out that they would find other seats and she should come find them once the train was moving. Then she had left them behind.

She didn't feel too bad about leaving them in that moment, as they had spoken for so many hours during the coach ride. Though she was excited by the stories they told her, and she knew they had more to say, they were older, and clearly needed some time to rest. Whereas she needed to sit in a seat with a magnificent view of new fields and vistas as the train clattered through them.

She felt as though she was somehow letting down all those people back in Graama who had helped her come this far if she didn't absorb every sight, sound and sensation during the journey. However, frustratingly, the early part of the trip had been quite uneventful, containing mostly trains heading the opposite direction on a set of tracks running parallel to their own, and as many large flat fields as she might wish to see in a lifetime. She had watched Afestaa disappear behind them through the window from her carriage, a carriage that she thought was incredibly well made and luxurious.

The train had passed through another town almost immediately and it was the first of many sights that would open Shanti's eyes. The platform at this location had a tiled roof with carved lintels. There was no single shed at the end, as at Afestaa, but a long low building, with multiple vending windows, and even a small restaurant where she could see people buying sandwiches and hot tea before setting off again.

Shanti was impressed. Travelling by train must be extremely common for the inhabitants of this town. She became very aware that no trains even came close to her home in Graama. She felt very small as the train chugged past this platform.

Slowly twilight surrounded them, and Shanti found herself slipping to sleep on her padded leather seat, the rhythm and sounds of the engine ahead of her lulling her into dreams.

EARLY THE NEXT day Shanti and her chaperones arrived at a gigantic building of iron and glass. The railway exchange was at least three stories tall, full of empty space and rays of light. Shanti stopped to admire the sights as they changed trains, asking Darsat and Dulku about the magnificent edifice. Darsat admitted that it was quite an impressive piece of engineering, even to his well-travelled eyes and that there were some at the University who made trips out to this city simply to study the building and the methods that were used in its construction. As they spoke the dull hum of other travellers filled the air around them like a swarm of bees.

Shanti and her two companions waited in the massive railway exchange for two hours before following a steward to their next train. This one should carry them the rest of the way to Gorduum, explained Dulku. Shanti was pleased to discover just how much more luxurious it was than the first train they had travelled in. These seats were covered in thick plush velvet. Gold-tasselled rope hung from wooden blinds that lined the windows.

Given the distance of the journey to come, Dulku had arranged tickets that provided them with bunks in a sleeping carriage. Shanti's cabin was next to theirs, of course. Despite the luxury of the seats, her bunk was less impressive. Barely wide enough to fit herself and coming with only a thin, though finely embroidered, sheet to cover herself, Shanti was not looking forward to spending a night trying to sleep in it.

They spent most of the morning sitting by the windows and watching the countryside continue to pass bay. Hills were beginning to feature more often, and forests. Every feature fascinated Shanti, but the hours of sitting meant her legs were stiff and she ended up spending much of the day's travel walking along the carriages trying to loosen her muscles. Her neck felt sore from her sleep in the simple seats of the last train, and a headache kept nudging at her temples until the train stopped for afternoon tea in a little town called Duus. She purchased a scone and carried it to the small stream that meandered through the middle of the town.

Swans paddled along the stream and sunlight speckled the water. Shanti ate the scone slowly, breaking it into small pieces as she looked at the people that walked to and fro along the riverbank. Next to the river sat a wide round Temple. An elaborate mask was carved in stone above the main entrance, but when Shanti looked inside she found the hall too luxurious for her liking. There were benches carved into ornate plant-like styles, and large golden oil lamps hung in the corners. One of the things she always admired about Bratis' Temple was the simple furnishings of the hall. It was a place where anyone could feel welcome, she always thought. Although, Sudru did manage to keep a beautiful green vine of light growing around the edges of the roof, and that glow was much more beautiful than the low flames from the oil lamps that flickered through the door and windows here.

Before long, it was time to return to the train.

The afternoon slowly faded into evening, and Shanti trepidatiously climbed into her bunk.

After an hour of tossing and turning and trying to find an inch of comfort without success, she decided to stay awake awhile longer. Her eyes fought against this decision, and her brain felt as though it was sitting in a pile of wool, but she decided to go for a walk through the train.

She passed the cabin that held Darsat and Dulku in their more comfortable sleeping quarters. She glanced at the window, but the blind was drawn down and no light shone through from inside. Shanti followed the blue lights vine that grew wound around a thin metal rail in the corner of the roof, heading for the end of the carriage. After passing outside and stepping across, pulling her shawl close against the wind and chill of the night air, Shanti found herself in a regular passenger carriage. She sat down at a larger seat and looked out the window again, discovering that they had begun to travel through the light groves and fields. Spread out around the train tracks to the horizon, dots of coloured light ran in rows and patterns.

The train was approaching a bridge, the land beneath sloping up to meet the tracks, blacker than the depths of a coal mine in contrast to the lights that grew in patches and bushels over the hillside. Shanti peeked towards the sky and was rewarded by a strange reflection. The stars in the sky, scattered like a fine dust across an expensive black tablecloth were a remarkable mimic of the land spread below. In the distance the land rose to form the White Mountains, named for the snows that covered their peaks year round. The lights did not grow so high along their slopes, and the mountains blotted out the stars, so a band of jagged black divided the two groups of lights.

Shanti rode the train through fields of light, drifting in and out of sleep. Guilt kept pulling her tired eyelids open. After so many years of pleading with her mother, to finally be allowed on this journey to Gorduum meant that she did not want to allow herself to miss a moment. This trip was a once in a lifetime opportunity, and she knew her family and friends would want to listen to her pour out her experiences, so that they could see how clearly she appreciated the gift that she had received. And so, though sleep hammered against her, she kept watching.

She even resorted to holding her eyelids open with her hands, but found that the weight of her head would grow until it fell sideways, closer and closer to sleep. Eventually she gave in again, leaning against the cool glass of the window. The last thing she saw was a spiral of yellow lights in the distant darkness.

SHANTI GROANED as she shifted into another position. Her neck ached and she squeezed it in an attempt to soothe the muscles before she realised that there was a man sitting in the seat opposite her. Shanti glanced over him, wondering when he had arrived. He was well bundled up in a thick overcoat and a heavy woollen hat that he wore pulled low over his brow. His eyes were small and black and glared out from beneath the hat.

The man must have been a native of Gorduum, Shanti decided. He took no effort to enjoy the glorious fields of light that she could now see sliding past the windows and that made her think he had grown used to their beauty.

"Good morning," she ventured, feeling the words in her mouth awkwardly. She had barely spoken to anyone during this trip, even Darsat and Dulku, and she felt as though she was out of practice. The man focused on her for a moment and then glanced away again. He didn't even have the decency to grunt in response.

"So, where are you travelling to?"

The man withdrew into himself a little, like a flower closing its petals as the sun dipped below the horizon. Shanti tried to cover her confusion with a polite smile and turned back to the window, but she felt her stomach tighten. She felt as though she had intruded on something private, although she had been sitting at these seats for longer than the man. She used the reflection of the carriage in the window to look around. Most of the other seats had one or two travellers in them, though they were all lost in their own quiet worlds. The man in the seat across the aisle from Shanti and her silent companion cradled a bottle of wine in his arms and delicately held a small thin glass in front of him. Slowly he lifted the glass, inhaled through his nose and then took a long sip from it. Shanti watched his shoulders lift as he sighed in pleasure.

The train was passing over another short bridge at that moment, roughly ten meters over a small paddock of brilliant yellow ball-shaped lights. Their glow was soft and friendly, warming as a summer sun. A strict linear order appeared among the lights in the distance ahead of the train and she realised that those must be the first buildings of Gorduum.

The reflection in the window also allowed her to examine her neighbour. Though he gave the impression of being wrapped from head to toe, completely covered, in fact she was able to see his face quite clearly. His hard black eyes peered out from beneath a strong brow with thick black hair, and his nose was short and bulbous. His mouth was currently set in a firm line, and the creases in his cheeks coupled with the paleness of his thin lips to give Shanti the impression that he was deliberately pressing them together. Perhaps he was worried that he might accidentally smile or, unseen eyes, mistakenly offer a word of polite conversation. Shanti smirked at the idea.

Enough of him, Shanti admonished herself, thinking of Priest Bratis' oft repeated reminder "the Masked God sees through hidden eyes". Even such angry and hard eyes as this man may hide the god's generosity. She tried to think of something else. This journey has been longer than I knew and it has taken me to all those far away places I have dreamed of. I am surrounded by sights I may never get the chance to see again. I should enjoy them.

"Keep to your own side," muttered the dark man. Shanti shifted her legs so they no longer interfered with his long black umbrella, though she felt he was being very rude. The umbrella was coming unravelled along the edges and more than one thin metal spine was showing its unattached tip. Shanti looked away from the man and met the eyes of a young woman seated further down the train. Her eyes sparkled; clearly she had overheard the man's comment. Shanti glanced at the man to check that he had closed his eyes, then gave a nervous smile to the woman. Her shoulders shook delightfully as she laughed silently. She rose and nodded slightly in Shanti's direction and then turned to leave the carriage at the far end. Her skirts moved enticingly around her as she made her way to the door. Shanti ran a hand through her hair, pulling her plait across her shoulder as she fidgeted with the ends. Snores began to rumble up from the glutinous depths of her neighbour's throat.

Instead of spending the rest of the night obsessing with the rude man seated nearby, and not allowing herself to spend too long thinking about the sparkling eyes of the woman who had just left, Shanti turned back to the windows. Dulku had explained that the best time to come into Gorduum was at night, and that she had carefully considered which train they would leave by and which train to change to in Duus. She had been proven spectacularly correct. The hills were painted in streaks and dashes of colour, in multifarious hues.

Gorduum was the source of almost all the lights in the known world. The people grew the lights in fields that stretched for kilometres around the stone of the city buildings. Darsat had explained that the buildings were a poor reflection of the beauty that surrounded them, which was impressive when she realised how much her new friend clearly loved and admired constructions and stonework.

Her eyelids slid across her eyes, as dawn drew nearer, but she fought to keep watching for her first real sights of Gorduum itself, not just distant lights and shadows. The regular clatter of the train's wheels along the tracks rocked her gently towards sleep, as a babe in its cradle is rocked by a softly whispering mother. Her neck ached again and she squeezed it, feeling the pleasurable ache of weary muscles as she kneaded the flesh. She had to pull at her shawl so that she was able to follow the sore muscles closer to the base of her neck and down towards her shoulder blades. She rested her head against the shining metal of the windowsill and dozed once more, allowing the light fields to blur and flicker as she passed them by. The train continued to wind down the hills that bunched around the port of Gorduum, slipping through tunnels and trees as she grew ever closer.

She shook her head awake again, mindful that her reveries were allowing her mind to drift, and leaned forward, lifting the back of her head off the soft cushion of her seat. It was the comfort of the cushions that was luring her to sleep, she thought. She leaned her forehead on the cold glass of the window, hoping its chill surface would help her stay awake, and looked out into the dark night that rushed by.

Here she could see lines and tangles of light glowing from where they grew, out in the distance.

Beyond the window of the train, the fields where light grew stretched across the hills and valleys seemingly forever. It was as though the stars of the sky had fallen to the earth and now gently sat upon the grass and dirt emitting their soft glow; as though someone had trained thousands of fireflies or glow worms to sit patiently in rows and lines on the turf, in their multitudes of colours. Constellations of red, white and yellow drifted past the window as the train rushed onwards. Webs and galaxies trapped on this earth by the farmers who tended these light fields. It was a sight she would never forget, in all her days.

She sighed. As much as they might ask, she could hardly sit everyone she knew in Graama down one by one and describe every second of the journey to them when she returned. Still feeling guilt bubble in her stomach like a stew, Shanti leaned back into the soft embrace of the seat, and slept.

DAWN WAS JUST BEGINNING to seep into the sky when Shanti blinked and found herself sitting alone in the seats of the carriage that was now silent and still. Even the man with the wine bottle had already left, although he had left the bottle behind, empty beneath his seat. Shanti lifted herself with a grunt and had to stretch out all her muscles after an awkward sleep slumped at the end of the seat against the wall and window. Maybe the bunk would have been worthwhile, she considered ruefully. Her fingers cracked as she flexed them back and forth and she squeezed her toes inside her shoes. She let out a short yelp as she tried to stand and discovered that her left leg had gone to sleep and was suddenly flooded with stabbing sensations.

Shanti managed to make her way down the aisle back to her own carriage, where she found Darsat and Dulku wrestling with their luggage and heading to the door and off the train.

"Ah, there you are child," exclaimed Dulku as Shanti shuffled closer, rubbing the sleep from her eyes. "We were beginning to wonder."

"I couldn't sleep, so I went to a seat where I could see the countryside better."

"And, by the looks of your hair, you fell asleep anyway?" chuckled Darsat. Shanti just nodded, and yawned.

"Well, we are here. Get your luggage and help us get out."

Shanti did, pulling her suitcase to the exit behind the couple, then stepping down onto the concrete platform. Then she raised her eyes to see this entrance to one of the greatest cities in the world.

Around her stretched the long flat expanse of the platform. There was very little of the iron wroughtwork that she had expected, no swirls of metal that would show off the industrial commerce of this city. She had seen some of that in the fences and railings of the station in Duus, and around its windows. But here, instead, she saw gleaming marble columns and arches, carefully carved stonework that made the huge buildings look even more amazing. Shanti was sure that the entire Tired Rabbit run by Mrs Tortor would be able to fit beneath the wide roof. Massive circular windows lined the walls just below the pristine white arch of the ceiling. Further windows, long and thin like leaves, lined the ceiling. The entire effect was one of light and air, despite the solid obtuseness of the rocks that made up the building.

She was standing far beneath a mighty clock, hanging from strangely-thin iron girders that stretched overhead like a technological rainbow, a sign of humanity's skill and ingenuity. The clock itself had four faces, so that it could be read from any position inside the main concourse. Shanti didn't want to appear simple, but found that she kept looking up and simply watching the hands of the clock as they ticked slowly through the minutes. The movement hypnotised her, and she had to force herself to move. The clock told her that it was around a quarter past eight in the morning. After some careful study, she determined that the clock itself must have been only slightly smaller than her father's kitchen. Lights grew in twining rows along the girders and wound their way down the sturdy chains that held the clock aloft. Shanti found it hard not to stare. Some of the fiercest reds she had ever seen lit the clock faces from within.

Shanti was standing upon one of at least five platforms, long and flat and punctuated by thick columns that drifted into the heights and held up the ceiling. She could see figures bustling away to her right, clearly the other passengers of her train, having collected all their luggage and begun the task of moving off to the city. One or two uniformed conductors were strolling along outside the carriages, peering in through the windows and whistling to themselves. She imagined they were checking that everyone had left. Their inquiring gazes made her feel conspicuous and she straightened her back and smoothed her skirts.

Each of the other platforms had a train stopped to either side of it. Steam coiled and burst from beneath the engines, carried away in a gentle morning breeze and occasionally washing over the platforms themselves. People rushed around those trains too, just as she imagined they had around her own, picking up bags and trunks, scuttling off towards the exit. Shanti smiled to see people greeting their loved ones, a hug or perhaps even a quick kiss. Seeing people who needed each other was so beautiful. Shanti was very aware that she was standing on this platform alone. She pulled her scarf looser from her neck and then tighter across her shoulders. Though the morning air in Gorduum was already warmer than she was used to in the frost covered fields of Graama, she enjoyed pretending that the cloth was someone holding onto her shoulders.

Her low heeled shoes clacked against the smooth grey concrete as she made her way to the baggage carriage. One of the conductors grinned at her as she passed and found herself blushing as she smiled back. Pull yourself together, she admonished herself. You're not some petal headed fool, here in the big city to be lost in its charms. You have an important duty to perform. Still, she couldn't help glancing back over her shoulder to see if the man was looking at her again. It turned out that he was. Shanti began to walk a little faster.

Darsat and Dulku had managed to conscript a young boy wearing a tight buttoned up uniform and a strange small round hat that had to be held onto his head by a thin blue ribbon. He was pushing a low wooden trolley, and helping lift the older couple's cases onto it. Everyone else from her train must have already collected all their belongings and rushed off. She wondered if that was something she would have to get used to about Gorduum, people living at a greater speed than she did, always with something or someone important to see or do. It was of no real concern. She shouldn't be in Gorduum long enough for it to affect her.

As the boy struggled with Darsat's case, the professor came back to Shanti.

"Here you are. This is the place you've been wanting to go. Now, would you like to come and see the University, or have a cup of tea at our house? Perhaps we could go sightseeing?"

"No, thank you," replied Shanti. "I'm aware of how quickly my business must be conducted if I am to get the lights back to the village in time for the festival. I'll find my way to my uncle's immediately."

"Very sensible." Darsat stroked his goatee and nodded. "Well, what is his address? We will drop you off."

"That would be sensible too," began Shanti. "But I think I will take myself."

Darsat blinked and made a small spluttering noise. "I don't think that is wise. I did make promises to your mother and father, and I would hate for-"

"You did, and that was amazingly kind." Shanti reached out and held one of Darsat's hands between her own, pressing it affectionately. His skin was surprisingly tough. "Without your promises, I would not have been allowed to even come this far! But I want to prove to them that I am old enough and capable enough to do this."

Darsat sighed, his face turning sorrowful. "I really don't know about this."

"I promise, it will be okay." Shanti studied his face, wondering how she could convince him.

"But you've never been here before. You don't know what it is like or where anything is. The Masked God may be watching over us, but there are plenty of dangerous people in the city. You don't know anyone here!"

"I know you both, and you are both quite splendid."

Darsat spluttered at the compliment. Shanti felt a small shudder in her chest as she considered his warning, but felt a spark of stubbornness further within herself. She had been able to wrestle Fellbin to the ground at his most mischievous. She was certain she could protect herself if needed. And besides, the Masked God watched through hidden eyes.

Dulku came over to see what was going on.

"Shanti says that she wants to go on her own from here."

"Oh my dear, is that wise?"

"It may not be wise, but I have to do it. I would hope that you could understand, I must show my parents that I am grown up and that I am perfectly able to succeed at the things I set out to do."

Dulku's eyes searched over Shanti's own, and the younger girl held her head firm under the gaze. Finally, the older woman nodded.

"Very well."

"What? My love, we can't-"

"It will be okay darling." Dulku rummaged in her purse and found a small piece of card, which she held out for Shanti. "Here is a calling card for us. It contains our address and few details that will help you find us should you need us. At the very least, you must come and share your adventures with us before you leave the city."

Shanti grinned and leapt onto Dulku, throwing her arms around her in a massive hug.

"I knew you would understand!"

"Oh child, settle down before I decide you are too immature for this!" Dulku pressed the card into Shanti's hands, and Shanti tucked it into a small pocket on the front of her satchel. Shanti hugged

Darsat as well, expressing her thanks and farewells, then managed to acquire another of the wooden trolleys. She bundled her suitcase onto it and then set off to find her own way to her uncle.

As she walked, pushing the trolley ahead of herself and noting that her legs were already feeling the strain of moving the weight of her luggage, Shanti thought about how she might look from the outside. It made her quite self-conscious. Being the last one off the train does leave one awfully exposed, she thought. Shanti walked the length of the train towards the exit, the wheels of the trolley clattering and squeaking in an awful racket. She felt as though she were on display, like a stuffed bird on a mantelpiece; the pride of the house and admired by everyone but with no means to escape their eyes. Her fingers twitched in paranoia and she spun on her feet to see if anyone was watching her. Don't be so ridiculous, she said to herself, of course no one will be-

She raised a hand halfway to her mouth. At the end of the platform, standing next to the carriages, but making no move to leave as all the others had, stood a figure in a heavy overcoat. Shanti felt sure that the figure was the man who had sat so unnervingly with her last night. Surely he can't be some criminal, she told herself, quickly turning away and walking faster still towards the exit. She felt a desire to turn her head to check if the man had followed her, or indeed reacted in any way to her sighting of him, but a coldness on her neck made her more frightened of what she might discover than of her imagination.

Eventually, Shanti moved from the platform into the heart of the station. Small restaurants were opening their doors and setting out tables, smiles beaming from the proprietors and their workers. The enticing smell of bread and eggs and bacon wafted from each freshly unlatched set of shutters. Shanti's stomach gurgled and whined, as though it were a small housedog that had missed its meal, and she considered stopping for something to eat. The meal she had managed to make on the train last night had been meagre at best, a cup of tea and some thin and slightly hard biscuits.

She paused outside one such place that called itself Fulook and checked behind her. Here in the station proper, there were bustling travellers all over the paths. It was difficult to determine which ways they were all headed in the hubbub, but Shanti felt confident that her man in his overcoat would stand out from the rest of the crowd. She waited until she had counted to forty before releasing a breath she hadn't realised she was holding. Yes, I think a roll with some nice hot bacon would be just the thing to soothe my nerves, she decided as she pulled her case into the small restaurant.

THE MORNING PASSED QUICKLY in Fulook. She discovered that the trains to Gorduum ran nearly constantly. Although the platform had been drained of disembarking passengers it was soon re-flooded with embarking passengers and before Shanti had finished her extraordinarily light and crispy bread roll the trains had blasted their whistles, the conductors had bellowed their calls, and like some massive lizard or serpent each train had crept backwards out of the station, trailing clouds of steam. By the time Shanti was contentedly wiping the corners of her mouth clean of crumbs, a new set of trains began to rumble into the station and fresh waves of passengers were about to be disgorged into Gorduum.

She didn't speak in particular to anyone as she ate, though she tried to exchange greetings and pleasantries with one or two passers-by. They barely shifted their eyes to her before moving on. The waiter was very courteous, but he did begin to pick up her plates and clean the table before Shanti felt ready to leave. She supposed that it was time to move on.

Shanti managed to determine her final destination in the city after a short conversation with the young man taking orders behind the counter. It was a house near the ruins of Huaar, an ancient civilisation that had left mighty monuments of stone and literature that later cultures had used as their own foundations. In particular it was a ruined theatre that Shanti was told to seek, and the house she was looking for would be found but a street away.

Shanti wondered what it would be like to meet her uncle again after so long. Her uncle had visited them often when she was younger, and she had bubbly memories of the excitement that he always brought with him. She recalled his wiry hair and the way he would talk to the children with the same level of seriousness and wit that he spoke to other adults with. However, some years ago that had stopped. Shanti had wondered if something had happened to keep him away, or if the visits had slowed in their regularity so subtly that her child's mind had not noticed until her uncle was gone.

In recent memory her mother, his sister, always said that uncle Dunin was a rogue and untrustworthy. There was still the odd card in honour of the Festival once a year, but only occasionally. In all Shanti's years she was certain of receiving such a card only four times. And none of those were within the last four years either. Her mother was a strong woman, who ran her household, her store and her family with love and pride, but Shanti had felt confused by the way Auga would keep the cards wrapped with a thick red ribbon, bundled together on the mantel, tucked safely halfway behind a jewellery box. Settling the bill, she gathered her things and began to leave the train station.

"Watch it!" A luggage porter was shoving a trolley covered in huge leather-bound trunks along the concourse and Shanti was standing in his path. She quickly leapt to the side, heaving the trolley with her suitcase along as well. She placed a hand on it, to check that it was locked tight. The porter frowned from beneath his thick greying moustache and shook his head as he moved by. "Bloody farmers." Shanti blushed at the epithet, the skin of her neck turning hot beneath her scarf. She licked her lips and lifted her suitcase back into the correct direction then marched out of the station and into the warm morning sunlight of Gorduum.

Gorduum was old. Even before the Establishment Wars of the past, hundreds of years ago, when men had fought from horseback with swords and spears, there had been a large settlement in this harbour. Sometimes it had been the seat of power for a great empire, while other times the city had been its own country while the lands beyond the fields of light ruled themselves. Now it was not even the city of parliament, that honour going to Boldaar in the east, though Gorduum remained of central importance to the economy of the country.

The streets that Shanti found herself entering were narrow and paved with a mish-mash of cobbles and paving slabs, and some areas were even concreted. However, the numbers of people that pushed against Shanti as she walked were a never-ending tide. All kept their eyes low, watching the gaps between other pedestrians and quickly stepping to fill them. No one looked up at the astounding patterns and colours of the lights that grew along the awnings and gables of each building.

The crowd shifted around Shanti, and she found herself buffeted along and to the side of the street, struggling to keep her suitcase moving in the same direction as herself. Suddenly, there was enough space to breathe around her and she gasped in relief. Then came shouts from behind her, and the loud thunder and rattling of horses' hooves and wheels clattering in axles. She spun around and saw a large coach moving down the street directly towards her, so she yelped and leaped back towards the crowd of people swarming along the raised stone of the pavement. The driver pulled his horses sideways, barely managing to avoid smashing her suitcase, and raised a fist in the air to accompany his curses as the coach moved off down the street. Shanti put one hand to her temple and blinked, rubbing some of the shock off her face.

Now she was back in the crowd, and they were forcing her sideways again, so she grabbed her suitcase and struggled to be as close to the terminal wall as she could, allowing the river of people to wash past her until she could get her bearings without being bowled over by coaches.

She found herself pressed alongside the warped wooden board of a merchant stall. Dead rabbits and ducks hung from the wooden supports of his canvas, and a blood-stained board sat before the thick bodied man in the stall. He grinned at her, his dark eyes sparkling, probably at the thought that he had caught a customer.

"A little early morning lunch perhaps young lady?" he enquired, hefting his butcher's cleaver.

"No, thank you," she managed to reply before setting off into the swirling crowd again.

Shanti found herself feeling more confused than she had anticipated. The sun had risen further into the sky and the streets were bustling with scores of people, all busy getting on with their own tasks. A varied panoply of hats and scarves, jackets and beards moved past her vision without end. Shanti began to feel like she would see more faces, more individuals, in one morning that she could have imagined lived in the entire world. The thought made her head ache, and her throat thick. Maybe I don't really want to see more of the world than Graama, she wondered. The words clanged in her head like bells. Maybe I just need to go home as soon as I can. The thought left her stomach feeling numb.

She stood on the raised pavement next to the street. Through the crowds that thronged along the paving, a few carts and wagons made their way. Most of these were slightly run down wooden wagons, clearly tools that had seen good use through their lives but weren't going to be replaced until they had finally completely fallen apart. That said, they bore layers of paint that showed at least a veneer of aesthetic consideration. The nearest cart to her, dawdling through the crush of people behind a trudging old horse, was painted bright red, with blue decoration in the form of triangular patterns. The paint was beginning to fade and chip, but it was easy to see through the chipped areas to the paint beneath. Clearly the man seated on the wagon, with his forlorn expression and thick heavy moustache, had simply layered on the blue and red paint over what appeared to be light and dark green spirals once he had decided the paint looked too shabby.

A puffing, chugging sound caught Shanti's attention and she turned to the left, peering down the street. The sound resolved into vision, and she could just see a gleaming contraption on four wheels moving aggressively through the pedestrians like a pike through a school of minnows. As the strange device grew closer, Shanti was shocked to realise that it was pulled by no horses. Instead, she could hear the pumping pistons and hissing steam of an engine not dissimilar to the ones that powered the train by which she had just arrived in Gorduum. The pilot of the strange vehicle was wearing a thick leather cap that enveloped his entire head, and incorporated two large glass goggles over the eyes. He also appeared to be wearing large leather gloves. The vehicle was made of polished metal that gleamed under the morning light, and the wheels were huge and dark in comparison. The man didn't glance around him as he moved through the crowds, seemingly expecting them to move out of his way. Shanti was only slightly surprised to see that they did, twisting and sliding to move out of the contraption's path before it could strike them down. It must be an intimidating thing, to share one's path with a device such as that. Still, she wanted to believe she would force the driver to acknowledge her at the very least before she would turn aside for such a machine.

Taking a deep breath, she moved out once more into the swirling mass of people, trying to figure out which way would be the correct route. Perhaps I'll ask someone about that theatre, she began to think to herself. Coming up with a plan was already beginning to settle her nerves.

"Hey, watch it lady!"

Shanti turned to see another of the chugging vehicles headed straight for her, its noise masked by the other. With a yelp she dodged to the side, catching her skirts beneath one of its wheels and then managing to tug the material loose as the vehicle continued charging forward. The driver managed to pull it to a stop and then turned to lean over the side and address her.

"Watch where you're stepping you blasted ninny!" The driver was a tall man with shoulder length light brown hair and a close cropped light beard. His eyes were almost yellow, the lightest eyes that Shanti had ever seen, even though he was snarling in anger. "Unseen Eyes, you could have been crushed before I had a chance to pull the brake!"

"I'm sorry," answered Shanti automatically, then she made a tutting sound in frustration with herself.

The man snorted and then shook his head.

"I'm almost there anyway," he muttered to himself, before clambering out of the vehicle. He pulled off a pair of light brown leather gloves and tucked them into his belt. Sparing one last glare at Shanti, he moved off across the street, through the crowd.

Shanti watched him go, biting her lip. I've got to remember to be more careful. There's too many people coming and going for me to be careless. Though a flame of anger made her wish that she had pushed the man in the chest, as she might have once pushed Taanin if he was trying to trap her during their games in the forests. She took a moment to check her surroundings. One or two people scurrying along the street met her eye, but only briefly. Most passers-by simply kept walking. And next time someone thinks to blame me for walking along the street and their own lack of caution, maybe I'll be quicker to tell them off instead of apologising.

"HELLO MISS, ARE YOU ALRIGHT THERE?" The voice sounded cheerful, as though a shaggy puppy with a non-stop tail had discovered how to speak. It was the first friendly sound that Shanti had heard since arriving, other than Darsat and Dulku. Shanti shook herself out of her memories and turned to discover that the speaker was a young woman in a well-made shirt that was worn fully buttoned to her neck. A simple but clean scarf was tied and tucked around her neck, though Shanti still felt that the air hanging in the streets of Gorduum was warmer than her father's small black iron stove. She found herself wiping her forehead in sympathy just at the sight of the woman. The woman's thick black hair was pressed down by a plain woollen cap that she touched with one finger in greeting. She had a narrow face and thin lips, with the bright and sharp eyes that normally would have led Shanti to describe her as weasel faced or mouse-like. Instead, the light in her eyes and the soft smile in the corner of her mouth made Shanti feel such a description would be uncharitable.

"Hello," she ventured, unsure as to the purpose of the conversation but suddenly quite aware of how closely the young woman was standing to her. Shanti became self-conscious of her clothing, aware that she hadn't had a chance to change her clothes since at least a day earlier. She hadn't even been able to inspect her presentation in order to straighten herself up as best she could, having not been around a mirror. Suddenly she wondered if the few smiles she had gathered over the course of the morning were simply patronising amusement. She patted her sides in a futile attempt at tidying up. "I'm sorry, what did you want?"

"It's not about what I want my lady, it's about what I can do for you." With a sweeping gesture of her arm, the young woman indicated a narrow black cart with a healthy looking horse strapped to the front of it. It bore the usual two wheels at the front of the cart, and a seat where this woman presumably sat as she guided the horse through the traffic, but at the rear, behind a quite comfortable looking space for the passenger, there was only a single large wheel, sturdy though it may be. "I'm a taxi driver, and I'd be happy to take you to anyplace you need to go. Name's Keema."

"Keema? No, my name's Shanti. I'm from-" She swallowed her next words in acute embarrassment, suddenly realising that the woman wasn't declaring Shanti's name to be Keema but rather introducing herself. Her neck swum in warmth as the blush spread over her skin. "I mean, of course, that my name is Shanti."

"Not from nearby then, are you Shanti?" Keema's eyes flashed again and Shanti found something annoying about the way her bright teeth appeared in her grin.

"No. Not exactly." She considered explaining exactly how far away Graama was, but then decided against it. This woman had clearly gained some sort of advantage over her with her sudden speech and quick retorts and Shanti needed to regain some composure and a measure of control over the conversation. "Which means I'm not familiar with this role of Taxi Driver. Could you please explain yourself, I don't wish to have to call for help."

"Oh no, of course not!" From the way she raised her hands as if to defend herself, Shanti could tell

Keema meant the gesture mockingly. "It's quite simple. This cart here is called a Taxi, for reasons I'm not completely familiar with myself. I drive the horse that pulls it. Together, my horse and I will carry you through the city and deliver you to a destination of your choosing, for a nominal fee, of course."

"I see." Shanti did see. The idea made sense. It would of course be extremely difficult to house and feed one's own horse in the city. Still, in Graama if there was somewhere that you wanted to go that was further than your own feet could carry you, then it was probably far enough to warrant booking an overnight seat on a coach or train. Gorduum was going to be even more to cope with than she had considered.

"Very well, that does sound helpful. Are you familiar with the theatre of the Breed?"

"I am, it's about an hour's journey from here, assuming the crowds don't bunch too tightly."

"Good. My uncle lives there, in a street called Minter's Lane. How much would you charge to carry my suitcase and myself there?" Shanti pulled her money pouch out from where it was tied to her belt.

Keema reached forward and put her hands over Shanti's own, keeping her from opening the pouch.

"For goodness sake, don't just whip that thing out any old way." Her face was suddenly serious, without a trace of the laughter and smiles that had annoyed Shanti.

"What? Why ever not, I will need to see if I can afford whatever fee it is that you decide to charge." Shanti pulled her hands away.

"I know, I get that, but these streets are full of hungry young men with knives, and I wouldn't put it past them to slip their blades through the pouch or its string and make off with all you have. To be honest, I would be worried that they'd slip the knife between your ribs in some parts of town, but the police do tend to patrol more carefully around the central station." Keema winked. "Wouldn't want to scare off the visitors. Where else would all our money come from?"

Shanti placed the pouch back against her hip and felt backwards with her foot to check that her suitcase was still sitting on the pavement where she had left it. She nodded to herself when she struck the familiar metal bindings. She took a step backwards to rest a hand on the suitcase as well, just in case.

"To be sure, it'd be unlikely that anyone would try to run off with your whole luggage, but I can see you're taking me seriously, which is good. I'll keep it simple for you. I think an hour's journey to the old Breed would be worth about ten mola. How does that sound?"

"That sounds ridiculous," exclaimed Shanti. "I just bought an entire breakfast, including a cup of tea, for a mere three mola!"

"I'm sure, but you'll understand that I need to buy some breakfast for not only myself but the horse as well, and then there's the constant cost of repairs to the taxi to factor in." Keema pursed her lips and clicked her tongue against her teeth before scratching the skin beneath her nose. She sighed and shook her head. "Look, I think you look like a nice lady. How about I drop it to eight? Would that be acceptable?" She held out a hand, ready to shake in agreement.

Shanti considered the offer. As far as she was concerned, eight mola was an obscene amount to pay for a journey that she could probably quite happily walk on her own. However, as she thought about it, various obstacles arose in her mind.

Firstly, there was the suitcase. It was very heavy, a

fact she had noticed and considered herself very clever for avoiding by getting Taanin to carry it for her at first, and for finding a trolley while in the station later. However, she had no one to help her with it now.

Secondly, she didn't really know where she was going. For all she knew of Gorduum, she would turn left when she was supposed to turn right and then find herself lost in an oubliette of alleys and unknown faces.

Finally, an hour's ride by cart, even if the crowds of people did mean that the cart would be slowed down and moving at a speed closer to regular walking pace, did imply that the journey would take more than that on her own. She had no intention of spending her first day in this great city feeling hot, sweaty, tired and bored as she trudged to find her uncle's house. In the end, eight mola could save her a lot of time and hardship.

"Alright then," she said, grasping Keema's hand firmly in her own and shaking. "Eight it is."

"Grand!" Keema reached down to haul Shanti's trunk over to the taxi and then heaved it up into a compartment beside the passenger seat. Shanti was impressed that she managed the feat on her own, even if she did go somewhat red faced and pant for air. The muscles in the driver's arm bunched and shifted beneath the light material of her shirt, pulling it tight as the case rose through the air. Then Keema held out her hand to support Shanti as she climbed aboard, her fingers strong and worn but still delicate, before leaping into the driver's seat herself.

"Are you ready?" She barely waited for a nod before continuing. "Seeing as you're a newcomer and all, I'll throw in a bit of a tour as we go, and for nothing. How's that sound?" Again, she barely waited for

Shanti to nod before launching into her tour of the great city, cracking a short whip and guiding the horse into the morass of people that filled the streets.

"The first thing you'll want to know," began Keema as the cart edged carefully into the moving stream of pedestrians, most of whom were older men in fine suits and hats but with harried expressions on their faces. Hardly any of them even noticed the taxi as it rolled amongst them, so intent were they each on their destinations. "The first thing you'll want to know is how Gorduum began."

"Will I?" Shanti rather doubted that she cared one jot about the beginnings of this city. She lifted her eyes to the roofs of the buildings that lined the streets. Four or five stories above the street, each building decorated in pilasters and cornices, with long thin windows that shone in the bright sun. The glare off the buildings nearly blinded Shanti, but occasionally the angle was such that she was able to catch a glimpse of the life inside. Windows that hung open, with long light curtains inside that drifted out into the air. A smiling face peering down on the crowd as it hung out of another window, holding a small smoking object in one hand.

"Of course you will!" Shanti's casual response didn't seem enough to dissuade Keema from her chosen course. She pulled on the reins, turning the cart down a new boulevard to Keema's right and Shanti found herself with the sun behind her and the street illuminated as if by magic.

"About two thousand years ago," began Keema, mostly to herself. Shanti was more interested in the amazing sights that unrolled before her than in the thin woman's stories of kings, treasons, executions and angry mobs. She allowed that at least Keema was telling the bloody bits of the history of the city. If she had met someone like Taanin, quiet and obsessed with structure and bridges and how houses were built, then she imagined the talk would have become rather more boring. Keema knew how to really burrow into the good bits of a story. Shanti found herself reminded of Fellbin and the tall tales he spun every evening.

Shanti admired the boulevard that they were travelling down. It was long and wide and almost perfectly straight. She could see far off into the fuzzy distance where it began to turn, perhaps following the course of an ancient riverbed, or hill. But it was so much wider than the street that she had stepped onto from the Central Train Station. That street had been narrow and packed with people, whereas travelling along this road was a much more luxurious experience.

There was plenty of space for everyone who needed to use the lane, and even room for vendors and merchants to line the sides of the street from their storefronts or move among the walkers with their trays of merchandise. Some carried trays of baked goods, covered with a dusting of white that Shanti could only assume was sugar, while others carried carefully constructed trays containing hot coals, and sold deliciously steaming chunks of meat as they walked.

Fountains erupted through the centre of the boulevard at regular intervals, their sculptured and swirling forms covered with a veil of tinkling water spray. Some people were seated on the edges of the fountains, locked in conversation or contentedly munching on some snack or another. The smell of roasted bird that wafted over the taxi made Shanti's stomach grumble and her mouth water.

"... So clearly, the people couldn't stand for a ruler

like that! After all, where would all the bakers go? So, in response, they held a meeting at one of the theatres. Actually, do you know, I do believe it was at the Breeog's Theatre! Of course, it wasn't known as the Breeog's Theatre at this time, he wasn't to be born for probably another two hundred years, but the point is…"

Shanti smiled and lifted her face to the clear blue sky that shone in between the towering canyon-like buildings to either side. Listening to her driver babble on made for a quite pleasant journey.

As they continued down the boulevard, at a slightly increased pace now that there was more room to move, Shanti examined the narrow lanes and alleys that broke off from the main street. These were much darker and less welcoming than the street they travelled on. She could see that the buildings along those ways were closer together, with lines of laundry strung between windows; and their height, coupled with their proximity to one another, caused the pedestrians who used them to be cloaked in darkness. The few figures she could see standing around in those alleys were eerily still. There was very little movement at all, not even children playing. They were all just standing and waiting. Something about that frightened her. It reminded her of a day from when she had been very young, out in the fields around Graama with some other youths from the town. They had been clambering over fences and playing chase between the grain stalks when suddenly she had found herself at the edge of the crop, staring at a scarecrow.

The scarecrow itself had not been too scary for her, though the unfocused, painted eyes were a bit unnerving. No, what had sunk into her memory and still made her shudder was the large black raven that had been perched on the scarecrow's shoulder. It had watched her with its pure black glistening eyes as though it had been expecting her. The people in those alleys had the same expectant predatory look in their silhouettes.

"Who are they?" she whispered to herself.

"Who?" replied her driver. Shanti felt embarrassed, she hadn't intended to be heard. However, Keema soon realised who she was looking at. "Oh, the Skuggi." She snorted and flicked the reins. "They're just homeless people, they live in the alleys and beg people for food and money."

Shanti felt horrified. Bratis had always taught the people in Graama that the Masked God would watch over everyone, and that they would be taken care of by his manifestations through others. How could the god see these people live with no homes and do nothing?

"They just live with no home?"

"Yeah." Keema shook her head. "And cause trouble, from what I hear. Look, a gorgeous lady like you doesn't want to spend your time thinking about the Skuggi. Let me tell you about the Gaawalt Yadeek!"

As Keema continued her talking tour of the city, Shanti turned her eyes to the roofline again, finding that a much more pleasant sight than the figures in the dark alleys. Now she was able to make out some more of the details, including the lights that grew along the gutters and trailed down the sides of some of the buildings. She couldn't wait to see those at night, they must brighten the entire street. She glanced at the next alleyway they passed and frowned. Why didn't Gorduum simply grow some of their lights in the alleys? Surely they had the ability, they were renowned worldwide as the best place to grow lights. Shanti could see the evidence for this stretching along every building. Nowhere else could grow lights so strong, bright, and large. That was the entire reason she had been sent here.

"Hey, are you checking out the tiles?" Shanti blinked and looked forward, to find Keema had turned halfway around in her seat and was watching her. She was still smiling, but her eyes were more serious now.

"I suppose I was. I'm sorry, what were you saying about the Gaawalt?"

"Never mind all that." Keema waved a hand as though shooing away an irksome insect that was buzzing around her face. "It's not important, it's just a way for me to fill in time. I just think you need to be more careful. After all, you tried to get out your money on the street, and now you're riding around with your head in the clouds. What do you think would happen if I wasn't as honest as you must assume I am?"

Shanti opened her mouth to reply and then paused. The sound of Keema's horse's shoes ringing on the cobbles sounded extremely loud to her, cutting through the hubbub of a busy city.

"You could have taken my money," she ventured.

"Of course," Keema nodded. "But, truthfully, any taxi driver could do the same. Many people could stop you to rob you of your pouch. What about the fact that you have no idea where I'm taking you."

"I hadn't considered that." Suddenly Shanti wanted to turn and examine every detail of the boulevard they were slipping along, so that she could trace her way back to the Station if she needed to.

Keema laughed. "I can see you've got the idea now! You need to at least try to figure out where you are. This city is awfully big and smarter people than you have vanished in its depths before. You might also want to make sure I stick to the wider streets, so that I can't have an accomplice reach out and grab you. Those alleys can be treacherous." She nodded at another of the Skuggi standing in the darkness beside a small red brick statue at the entrance to an alley on their left.

"Thank you for your warnings." Shanti licked her lips. "Why are you telling me all this? Doesn't it ruin my impression of your city? Aren't you proud of Gorduum?"

"Proud?" Keema blinked twice and her brow furrowed a little. "Well, yes, I guess I am. I am proud that this is my home. But you're a nice person, you've clearly come a long way and, love it though I may, I have no illusions about the safety of my city." She turned back in her seat and stretched her shoulders.

"Now, as you were asking, the Gaawalt brought in a really famous religious festival called... Well, I forgot the name of the festival, we don't celebrate it anymore. But the festival was in honour of some other god than the Masked God. Obviously this would have been before the reformation, when everyone started following the Masked God. Actually, I tell a lie, I think it was in honour of the harvest being successfully collected. Unless it was in honour of a harvest god? In any case, that didn't last long before the betting on the games that occurred during the festival started to become more important. There was this one..."

Shanti allowed Keema's voice to wash over her. It was comforting in a way, to know that she was nearby and seemed at least nominally honest and trustworthy. However, Shanti kept her eyes on the landmarks that they passed now, and watched for how close the taxi came to the alleys and lanes that pocked the facade of the boulevard's buildings.

Keema reached a few large intersections with other wide boulevards, turning one time left, another right. Soon Shanti could see what must be the Theatre of the Breed looming over the more recent constructions of Gorduum. It was made of a much darker substance than the light tan and orange plaster that made up most of the city. There were no terracotta tiles lining the roof. Instead the external walls were covered in repeating arches. The building curved away from Shanti, so that most of it was hard to make out. She was in awe of the size of it, the way it jutted up from the surrounding rooftops like a mountain peak behind a vast forest.

"I didn't realise the theatre was so…"

"Big?" Keema switched from whatever topic she had been discussing to address Shanti's comment without even pausing for breath. "Yeah, it's a biggie alright! She looks pretty solid and imposing from back here, but you wait. As we get closer you'll begin to see the cracks and gaps where the stones have been slowly taken away to help build other things around the city. They say that back in its prime, sixty thousand people could fit in the seats without a problem and that the acoustics were so good that the actors could whisper if they wanted and the back rows would hear them."

Together that looked at the huge structure in the distance. "Well, maybe that's a bit of an exaggeration," admitted Keema. "Anyway, it's still a few minutes away, and your uncle's home should be down Minter's Lane on the right any time now."

Before long Keema was guiding the taxi across the flow of the crowd and into a slightly narrower lane. Shanti looked about warily, but this lane was wide and bright enough that she felt reasonably confident that it wasn't one of the dangerous areas that Keema had pointed out during the trip. There was a large sign nailed to one of the buildings by the corner, painted in fresh green paint. It said 'Minter's Lane'.

"You uncle lives here. I believe we agreed on eight?"

Carefully, and keeping her hands low so they would be shielded by the sides of the taxi, Shanti counted out eight mola and handed it over to Keema. The driver grinned and touched the peak of her hat as Shanti climbed out of the taxi. "Glad to see you learned a bit of caution. Good luck m'lady!"

Shanti walked along the pavement, pulling her suitcase alongside her. The entrances to these buildings looked just as lavish and impressive as the rest of Gorduum had been so far. She could see vines and fruits from lights growing over each doorway, and trailing along the walls. Again she thought about how bright the city must be once night fell. Graama was comfortable, with some light leaking out of homes and windows, from the fires and candles inside, but she was looking forward to seeing what Gorduum was like at night. The fields and dark places around her village were not places that encouraged visitors in the evenings.

Eventually she identified the building that her uncle lived in thanks to clear instructions on the note Auga had given her. She climbed the low steps outside the building and found herself standing outside a tall narrow heavy dark wooden door. With some difficulty, she managed to turn the lever and push the door open while still keeping a hand on her suitcase and pulling it inside after her. Once she bumped it across the lintel she turned and pushed a lock of hair off her face. The lobby was amazing.

Black and white square marble tiles lined the floor, each one approximately the size of a dinner plate. They formed a simple alternating pattern that stretched from wall to wall. Directly in front of her were the stairs, a flight of wooden steps that appeared to be so narrow and so high that Shanti nearly wanted to call them a ladder instead. She gulped as she considered climbing those with her suitcase. To either side of where she was standing, just inside the main entrance, were two doorways that led from the lobby. It was easy to see that they turned into small hallways that ended abruptly at what must be the ground floor apartments. Hanging from the ceiling above the centre of the lobby was a magnificent bouquet of light. Hundreds of tiny berry-lights illuminated the room with a clear pale light. One or two coloured fruits, bigger than the berries, but about half the size of Shanti's fist and in blue or red or green, had been woven into the bouquet to add a little style to the room. Besides this centrepiece, clusters of simple yellow fruits almost as big as her head were spaced along the walls. A vine curled up the staircase and around the wall to the next floor, dripping with hundreds of tiny leaves that softly illuminated the climb. She stood for long minutes, gazing at the sight and trying to imagine how such a thing could possibly be cultivated.

The walls were plastered cleanly and with a pale dusty yellow. The mouldings of the roof were a pristine white, as the tiles below. Shanti had never seen something so large and clean and impressive, and yet so empty.

Shanti tried to remember what the note said about which floor her uncle lived on. While she was thinking, a young woman made her way down the stairs. Shanti admired her dress, a sleek blue thing with thin vertical lines, and a wide-brimmed hat that tied beneath her chin. The woman had some of the longest eyelashes Shanti had even seen. They murmured pleasantries to one another as the woman walked by and left through the same heavy wooden door that Shanti had just come in. Shanti stared at the door for a moment, before shaking her head and turning back to the stairs. Exasperated with herself, Shanti had to open her suitcase and began rummaging for the note from her mother.

Along with the order from the village council, and an amount of money so large that Shanti felt her throat tighten just thinking about the coins and precious metal rods that were tucked safely deep in her case, Auga had provided Shanti with a written note that detailed business contacts, addresses, bankers to speak to, and all the other things that Shanti would need to know in order to survive in Gorduum. At the bottom of the note, as though it had been forgotten, Auga had scrawled her brother's address. Shanti mouthed a curse silently to herself as she thrust one hand through the carefully folded clothing in her suitcase, spoiling the space saving arrangement in a vain attempt to find the note. Eventually she stopped and tipped the suitcase on to its side, grimacing as her clothes spilled across the tiles. She didn't look forward to repacking everything well enough to close the case again.

"There's nothing else for it," she spoke aloud to no-one. She began pulling out pieces of clothing, squeezing along each item's length to check if the note had been stored inside, and then putting the clothes into a neat pile on the black and white tiles by her side. Skirts, stockings, blouses, dresses, shifts; they all had to go onto the pile. Shanti felt her face growing redder as she burrowed deeper into the suitcase, and she hoped that no-one else would come strolling down those stairs.

"Yes!" she shrieked as she felt a thin sheet of folder paper bend beneath her fingertips. "You sure know how to make finding you difficult." She lifted the note out of the warm jumper that her mother had forced her to pack "In case of bad weather" and lifted it to her face, tempted to kiss it. That was when she saw the man standing in the hallway that led to one of the apartments. He was holding something small to his face and then breathing out a cloud of smoke. He was also, clearly, grinning at the sight of Shanti and her possessions strewn across the lobby.

In a flash she lifted the pile of clothes and dumped it back into the case, slamming the lid shut. A few corners and flaps of cloth poked out around the lid, but she tried to hide them by sitting on the case. She felt utterly exposed and embarrassed. For some reason she held the note behind her back, though even in her own head she couldn't figure out why; she just had a strong impulse. Did she think the man was somehow going to punish her for the note? Maybe she thought he shouldn't be permitted to read it? She couldn't trace the cause of her momentary paranoia.

"I'm sorry to surprise you," said the man, walking forward and holding out a hand to shake Shanti's. Carefully, she took his hand and shook it. "My name's Voras. I live in apartment one." He used his thumb to indicate the door at the other end of the hallway he had just emerged from. "I didn't mean to shock you. I simply left my home and discovered you taking up so much of the lobby!"

"I'm sorry for that," said Shanti. She was about to continue and tell Voras about the reasons for her actions, but then she heard Keema's voice of caution in her head and changed her mind.

"That's good." Voras held the small object in his

hand to his face again. This time Shanti could see that it was a thin white stick. His face bore more lines and colour than Keema's had, and his hair was slightly longer and thicker, though just as dark as the taxi driver's had been.

"Is that like some sort of special small pipe?" Shanti asked. It was too strange to not enquire at least somewhat.

Voras grinned again, a wide grin that split his face in half. The lines on his cheeks and forehead deepened. "Sort of. We call it a cigarette, and I suppose you could say it is like we have rolled a pipe into a thin stick of paper."

"That's very clever." Shanti watched as Voras sucked on the end of his stick. The other end glowed orange.

"Indeed. Well, thank you for your time madam, but I have places to be." Voras lifted his hat in farewell and then left through the heavy wooden doors. Am I doomed to be embarrassed by everyone I meet in this city, wondered Shanti. She brought the note out from behind her back and unfolded it. Her uncle lived in apartment three. Well, if Voras was apartment one, and there are two on this floor, I must assume he is on the next floor, she decided. With that, she locked the suitcase and began the task of pulling it up one stair at a time.

The next floor contained a lobby just as clean and sparkling as the one below. As she had surmised, apartment three was indeed on this level. The lobby on this floor was different from the one below in only one way. Where the massive heavy doors had been, leading out to the street of Gorduum, here there was a wide window, with flower beds built outside it. Shanti moved closer to investigate, but was a little disappointed to find that they were only normal flowers, not lights. Their purple petals swayed in the slow breeze. Then, beyond the flowers, she saw the blue lines and wide hat of the woman who had passed her downstairs. Shanti found herself watching the woman, following her progress as she sauntered down the street until she passed out of sight. Then Shanti noticed a few of the men on the street were watching the woman also, turning their heads further than one might expect, just so they could keep her in sight. How sad, she tutted to herself. She leaned a little further forward, wondering if she could catch a final glimpse of the woman, but she had vanished into the crowd.

Taking a deep breath, and telling herself that she was just trying to delay the inevitable, Shanti walked over to apartment three, knocked on the door, and waited. She felt nervous. Her stomach was fluttering again. This whole trip had turned out to be designed to leave her ill at ease, thrust as she was into unfamiliar circumstances. The excitement of seeing such amazing sights, of finally moving beyond the expectations of Graama, was tempered strongly by a fear of the unknown that she had not realised she had. The worry about how her mother was coping alone in the store, what trouble Fellbin was causing without Shanti there to rein him in, those thoughts she had anticipated. The strangeness and desire to run home that bubbled in the back of her mind she had not. She hadn't seen Dunin in so long, not since she was a much younger girl. And her mother really did seem to think the worst of him. Surely he wouldn't be too bad though, after all, he is family.

Her uncle was taking an exceptionally long time to answer the door. She wondered if she was getting sweaty. She thought of the clean clothes that were bound up in the suitcase behind her. Should she have found the time to stop and get changed? But where would have been a suitable place to-

The door opened.

"Good afternoon Uncle Dunin," said Shanti to the short bald headed man that answered the door. He was not ugly, but he certainly had taken no pains to make himself look more attractive. He wore his facial hair in a closely cropped beard, which looked peculiar beneath his exceptionally smooth scalp. He was wearing a loose white shirt with ties dangling from the collar and loose tan pants with bare feet. Black hairs sprouted from the tops of his toes. He was holding a small piece of salami and a knife with a sparkling deep-blue glass handle. He looked over Shanti suspiciously, then gestured at her with the knife.

"Uncle eh?" He spoke out of the side of his mouth, as he still had a mouthful of salami between his teeth. "So, you'll be one of Auga's kids I imagine?" His small green eyes were watching her closely and Shanti felt surprisingly exposed.

"Yes, I'm Shanti. Auga is my mother."

"Oh, I thought you were the elder daughter. You look older than Shanti is." He chewed slowly, still watching her with a lizard-like stare.

"What do you- No, I am Shan- How old do you think I am?" Shanti spluttered, trying to make sense of what he had said. Auga and Neeran didn't have any other daughters, only Taanin and Fellbin. Who was he thinking of?

"Did you like that dress I sent you last year?" Dunin sliced another hunk of salami off the sausage in his hand and tucked it into his mouth, his eyes shifting down from Shanti's face now.

"Dress?" Shanti couldn't think of any dresses that he had sent. He hadn't sent gifts for the family in years. She even remembered the last time he had, her mother had sat in the kitchen holding the letter from him on her lap without looking at it, for hours. Taanin had spent a lot of that time sitting near her without talking either. Fellbin had been much younger, and hadn't noticed that there was anything wrong. He had spent the time running around with the carved wooden bird that Dunin had sent. The mental image of Auga sitting in the dim kitchen, and the blank expression she had worn, inspired a flash of anger in Shanti.

"You've never sent me a dress at all," she snapped.

Her uncle nodded and swallowed. "I suppose you had better come inside."

Shanti maneuvered her suitcase inside and flinched as she noticed the scraping rumble it made on her uncle's tiled floors. He was striding ahead of her, through rooms that opened onto tall bright windows that let in a surprising amount of light from the sun outside. One or two tall thin lights grew in small terracotta pots in the corners of the rooms. They passed a long low stone counter that sat beside a spacious kitchen where Dunin paused and turned around.

"Is this a social visit or something more? I'd assume that your mother wouldn't send you here for a social visit though."

"No, it's business." Shanti was finding it difficult to hold her tongue now. Her uncle was so rude! "We have a large order to fill, and we thought you wouldn't mind me staying here for a few days while I sorted it out." She didn't want to admit to him that they had also hoped that he might help her with the business dealings themselves. Something about his manner made her want to avoid giving him too much power over her situation.

"What's the business?" He placed the salami and knife down on the stone bench.

Rather than trying to explain, Shanti dug out a letter her mother had written to him and given her before she left. She handed it over. He read it quickly, his expression unreadable to her.

"Alright. I suppose I didn't have much on at the moment anyway. Come with me."

He moved out of the kitchen and down a hallway. Down the hallway were a number of doors. Her uncle indicated the first on the right, leaning against his wall and slicing another piece of salami.

"Here. This is my guest room. It'll do for you."

Shanti looked inside. There was a bed with a pale pastel yellow spread on it and lacy pillows. In fact, lace appeared to sprout like mould from beneath the mattress. The rest of the room was thankfully fairly bare, with only a dresser and a large chest of drawers to break the monotony. A framed painting of rabbits hung on the wall opposite the bed, and opposite the door to the hall was another tall thin window. Shanti dragged the case into the centre of the room. She turned to ask her uncle what was outside the window, but he was already gone.

"Oh. I see." Shanti tipped her suitcase onto the floor and opened the lid. She began pulling out clothes and moving them over to the drawers. Occasionally she would reach over and run her hands across the waves of lace that billowed from her bed. "Yuck," she said softly. When she came to the bag of money that she was entrusted with, Shanti paused. What was she going to do with this? Surely she couldn't carry it with her, but was it safe to leave it here in this room? She looked around the room carefully, trying to see it from the point of view of a dishonest person. Where would they expect her to hide money, and where else was there to put it? There were the drawers, but that was too obvious. Maybe if she hid the pouch beneath her clothes?

She lifted the white explosion of lace that dangled down the side of her bed, looking at the space beneath the bed. It was not very big, though she was surprised that it appeared to be very well cleaned. It would probably be safe to slide the pouch under here. She got up, retrieved the pouch, then knelt down again to hide it under the foot of the bed. There was a loud scraping noise as the heavy pouch moved over the wood, but Shanti gritted her teeth and continued. After all, that noise would probably just be a handy warning for her if someone did try to steal her money! She got up, dusted off her hands on the front of her dress and looked out the window. She felt a small twinge of embarrassment. No one was actually going to come into this one specific room overlooking a courtyard, why was she even worrying about it?

Once she had emptied her case and sorted her belongings, Shanti sat on the bed for a time and tried to catch her breath. So much had happened, so quickly.

Even inside the apartment, with its shade and with the windows open to allow the breeze to come through, Gorduum was hot. Shanti found herself feeling desperately like taking a nap. No, she angrily told herself. I have to make sure I know what I'm doing first. With a great effort, she got up and went over to the window, pushing open the single shutter that sat covering the window. Beyond the windowsill Shanti saw a courtyard that must lie behind the apartments. It was small, and there were watermarks staining the walls, but there were other windows opening onto the private space. In the middle of the courtyard sat a single light-tree, squat and skeletal given the poor growing conditions, but still giving off a faint green glow. Shanti stood at the window and took in the scene as she thought over the events of the morning,

Finally she had arrived in Gorduum, and it was everything and nothing that she had expected. The city was beautiful. It was grand and large and bustling. It was so very warm. The lights had been overwhelming, so huge and bright, and she was amazed to see how many there were. They grew everywhere and lit everything! Gorduum was a spectacular place to visit, and she knew she would need to be here for a few days in order to make her way through the business at hand.

But on the other hand, she had been warned about the dark alleys and money snatchers. Her uncle had greeted her as barely more than a stranger. No, thinking back on the way he had led her into his home, he would surely have treated a stranger with more decorum than he showed Shanti. He treated her like someone he was disappointed to see, and merely tolerating until he could send them on their way. But what on earth could lead a man to act that way when, in a way, this was their first meeting? The Writ instructed everyone to treat others as if they were manifestations of the Masked God, and to remember that you were allowing the god to see them through your eyes also.

She walked back to the bed thinking about how far she had come. All her life she had memories of wanting to go further than the boundaries of her small world in Graama. Now that she had, she wondered if it was worth it. The sights she had seen on the journey were wonderful, but now she was sitting inside a small drab room by herself. Had it been wise to tell Darsat and Dulku that she would find her uncle on her own? If she had allowed them to bring her here, she may at least have had someone to talk to. But, after all, she had found him on her own, hadn't she? Oughtn't she take pride in that?

She wondered if the desire to leave Graama was a genuine desire to travel and see the world, or if she just found everyone in her village boring. Certainly she suddenly found herself wondering what Fellbin and Taanin were doing at this moment, wishing that she were with them whether it be in Graama or Gorduum. The idea made her squirm with guilt. Because if she was bored by the life that she had in Graama, then that would mean that her own parents bored her, that their life bored her, that her brothers bored her. No matter how much she might think that she loved them, could she really if she was so desperate to leave them? She wished she could see her friends again right now.

But maybe it was all just nerves. Maybe she would feel better shortly. She resolved to explore the apartment and try to engage in a conversation with her uncle. And she would need to find someone who sold lights in large amounts very quickly.

Shanti felt hot and uncomfortable in the layers of her travel clothes and she desperately wanted to get changed out of them. She explored the room and found a door in the far corner. Through the door was a small dark room lined with stone and containing a bathtub resting on four feet shaped like cat's paws and made of some dark glistening metal. Shanti shook her head at the sight. She had never seen something so indulgent as this bathtub, and to find it sitting quietly in the guest room of the apartment? Surely that implied that Dunin must have one of his own to use as well! He must be finding a great deal of success in his business. Shanti found herself curious as to what his business actually was.

Smooth white handles and a pump shaped like an open fish's mouth soon delivered steaming fresh clean water into the tub, to the amazement of Shanti who had never had hot water that had not been heated over a fire. Where is the fire that heated this, she wondered. Between this tub and the lights that were so entwined with the daily life of the city, Gorduum was proving to be a most astonishing place.

Shanti peeled away the grimy clothes she had been wearing. She held them out in front of herself and shook her head. It was a travesty that she had still been wearing such drab and dirty things, especially when meeting a successful if distant relative. To be honest, she should be a little ashamed that she turned up at his door in such clothing. She threw the clothes into the corner of the room, resolving to search out and deliver them to the laundry later. In the meantime she lowered herself into the steaming water and sank deep beneath its hot soothing surface.

Shanti felt her muscles loosen and dissolve in the embrace of the heated water. Steam condensed on her face, sending rivulets of water down her cheeks and chin. It felt so good to be getting clean finally. As she lazily lifted her hands to pass them through her hair, wiping away the layer of grime that was attaching itself to each strand, she wondered about the journey to Gorduum. She hadn't expected to get this filthy, but perhaps the thick billowing clouds of smoke from the train's boiler being fired had left their trace on top of the usual sweat and dust of travel. Shanti let the thoughts mix with the water in her hand and then wash away as she let the liquid dribble away between her fingers into the tub.

On the side of the bath sat a small silver container shaped like a remarkably large scallop. Shanti lifted the lid and was delighted to find a small reserve of powder lying within. She scooped some up with two fingers of her left hand and held them close to her face. The smell of citrus fruits and something effervescent tingled in her nose. Sighing with happiness, she tipped a small handful of powder into the water and swirled her hands through the water to keep it moving. The smells alone began to calm her nerves and she felt wonderful.

Eventually the water began to grow cold and Shanti realised she would have to get out. She reached out for one of the thick white towels that was hung in easy reach and wrapped it around her body. The material was soft and comforting. If only they had made this material into my bed blankets, she thought ruefully. Moving slowly, almost asleep, Shanti got dressed in fresh clothes and then sat on the end of her bed, looking out the window into the shaded courtyard.

The idea of leaving the room and speaking to her uncle again made Shanti feel nervous. She pulled a strand of hair loose from its bun and nibbled on it. In the end she decided to wait until dinner, and pulled out a book to read in the meantime. She had brought two of her father's books with her in the end, hoping that they would help her pass the time on the train at least. She had actually expected to be too busy, and too interested in seeing the whole city to read once she arrived here in Gorduum. As it happened, the trains had been a fascinating method of traveling and she hadn't even cracked the covers on either book until now. She lay on the bizarre blanket and began to read through 'The Manors'. It was an engrossing story, about a young woman who was being pressured to marry, despite there being no suitable choices. Shanti couldn't help but consider her own life as she read. Not that she was pressured to marry, her parents were wonderful about such things, but she could certainly empathise with the idea that options were thin and not really up to expectations. All things considered, including alternatives, I have things pretty good she thought.

AFTER A FEW HOURS Shanti noticed that the light was fading. She stood and moved to the window. By sticking her head out through it, she could get a glimpse of the sky above, entrapped between four solid walls. There was still blue sky above, but the sharp angles of the shadows that cut across her neighbours' walls told her that the sun was setting. It may not be night for quite some time yet, but the room would soon be dark. She tucked a scrap of paper into the pages of her book and left it on the low bedside table her uncle had provided. Shanti undid her hair and began to brush it thoroughly. Once she was finished, she wrapped it back up into a bun, and left the room to see what was happening in the apartment.

Shanti moved back down the hallway to the living room. The setting sun had moved beyond its narrow windows and the room was growing darker and cooler by the moment. The tall thin lights in their terracotta pots were sitting at either end of the room, thin drooping leaves hanging from their miniscule branches and narrow stems. The pale blue light they emitted kept the room at a pleasant level of brightness though, and Shanti would have been comfortable seated in that room and reading for hours. Uncle Dunin was sitting at a long wooden table, so dark that Shanti nearly thought it was painted black. He had a fine porcelain dish set in front of him, and a set of sparkling cutlery laid to either side. He was making his way through a simple salad and small well-cooked piece of meat that Shanti wasn't sure was bird or beast.

"Good evening," she said.

Dunin glanced in her direction and then looked back down at his meal. He grunted at her.

"Have you left my dinner in the kitchen? I didn't even hear you making it."

"I didn't make you any." Dunin speared another mouthful of meat off his plate.

"What?" Shanti felt her mouth hang open in shock, but she couldn't think of anything more insightful to say.

Dunin looked up and met her eyes. His own were small and as green as the dark depths of an icy well. "What? You think I should feed you as well? You show up out of the blue one morning and expect me to let you stay in my house, not knowing what I might be planning with my home, and now you expect me to spend my money on taking care of you? What else do you expect from me, to dress you in the morning, or take you for walks to the park every evening?" He stabbed his next mouthful of meat as though it had personally insulted him.

Shanti tried to calm her thoughts. Her heart was beating with the speed of a galloping horse and she felt hot and dizzy. Before she could utter something she might regret, she turned and tried to walk back to the room he had allocated to her. She gnawed at her lower lip as her eyes burned and she could feel herself speeding up to a run. I can't run away from him, I mustn't, she told herself as she fled, forcing her feet to move slower in an attempt to retain some dignity. She gently closed the door behind her and made sure it was locked, before she flung herself down on the bed and began crying into the scratchy lace pillow.

How did he affect me so badly, she asked herself as she brought her thoughts to order. It was cruel of him to not make any food for me, it was rude to ignore a guest in such a way, certainly outside the expectations of the writ. Even considering that we are family, and sometimes family can be the most frustrating, surely it shouldn't be enough to send me to tears? Shanti felt somewhat disappointed in herself. She had believed she was a capable woman at her twenty years of age. After all, she had been desperate to get out of Graama for a long time, and had managed to convince her parents to let her come to Gorduum. What sort of a person would she be if she couldn't even handle a rude, bald old man? She had managed to hold her own when she met him at the front door. Maybe she was just tired. She sat up in the bed and wiped her face. Clearly the journey had been harder on her than she had expected. She had no reason to assume everyone she met would be as kind as Keema had been.

Sniffing a little, and coughing to clear her throat, Shanti resolved to be more careful. Keema had warned her to watch her surroundings. Shanti hadn't considered that such a warning would apply to family too. Well, now she knew better. She would be careful not to expect anything from anyone she met here.

Her stomach felt sore and her throat felt dry. She considered how little she had been eating during the journey so far. She also remembered the vendors she had seen walking the streets with their tantalising smells. For a moment she thought about retrieving the money pouch from beneath the end of the bed. No, she decided. It was getting late, and even if she knew that Dunin was a fool, she didn't relish the thought of having to walk past him to leave the house. She even wondered if her uncle would let her back into the house if she did. She faced a momentary vision of him explaining that he had agreed to let her stay, but not to permit her to leave. Instead she changed for bed and climbed into the peculiar sheets. Sleep came surprisingly quickly and she drifted into a broken dreamless state.

THE MORNING ARRIVED with the sounds of bustle in the streets, echoing across the building and down through the empty courtyard that her room looked over. No individual sounds were audible to her, but she could imagine the calls of the vendors out on the streets offering up their cooked breakfasts. The idea made her stomach growl. It had been so long since she had eaten a decent meal. The thought of a meal, the imagined smell of some sort of fried or roasted meat, the soft crunch of a well-made bread roll, the desire to eat something satisfying and deal with the hole in her stomach, all gave her resolve and she quickly moved through her morning ablutions, splashing some cold water from the sink in the bathroom on her face to help herself wake up.

She dressed in new clothes, a simple pale cream dress that she whipped out of the drawers, and tucked her money pouch out of sight. Remembering what Keema had told her yesterday, Shanti pulled most of the letters and money from her personal pouch and tucked them into a small pocket in the lid of her suitcase, before shoving the case beneath her bed. It wouldn't be a very safe hiding spot, but at least they wouldn't be sitting around in the open where anyone passing through could rummage through them. Then she opened the door to her room and strode out.

Dunin wasn't in the living room when she came through, for which she was thankful, but a young man was working in the kitchen, frying eggs and checking on other pots and dishes. The sight of the man caught Shanti by surprise and she stopped.

"Hello?" she asked, wondering how one was expected to address a stranger when it was oneself who was really the intruder.

"Good morning m'lady," answered the man. "You must be master's niece Miss Penpen. My name is Gunin, I do some household chores for the master of the house." Gunin didn't pause in his movements, leaning precariously across boiling pots and red hot glowing elements.

"Good morning." Shanti watched the man work for a minute before gathering her wits enough to venture a question. "Can I help you with that?"

Now Gunin did pause. He glanced over at Shanti, taking in the dress she was wearing and the neat bun her hair was gathered into. He turned back to his dishes, picking up a knife and slicing some large green leafy vegetables into smaller leaves.

"Thank you for offering m'lady, that's very kind. But no, I've got everything in order myself."

Shanti nodded to herself.

"What are we having for breakfast then?" she asked, moving towards the table to take a seat.

"Oh," exclaimed Gunin. He stood still with his back to her for a second before continuing to cut up the leaves. "I'm afraid that the master's only left orders for one meal this morning. If you don't mind waiting, I suppose I can whip something together for you?"

"No, I'll be fine on my own." Shanti felt shocked at first, with a moment of loneliness, but it was quickly replaced by rising anger. The heat began deep in her chest and rose through her throat. She coughed to clear her throat, and to ensure that when she spoke she wouldn't sound as though she were taking her anger out on this man. It wasn't his fault at all. It was, however, all the fault of her incredibly rude and frustrating uncle. She would have to consider what to say to him. Shanti rose off the seat and then headed for the front door. With her hand on the latch, she paused. She was about to enter the streets of Gorduum on her own. There would be no cheerful taxi driver who could lull her with her stories. There would not even be an angry uncle who might yell at her for getting things wrong. Suddenly she wasn't so sure about telling him off when she returned. What if he kicked her out? Surely he wouldn't kick out his family? She pushed him out her mind and thought about what lay beyond the door. She was about to find out what Gorduum was like for herself. She felt her throat grow just a little tighter, then sucked in a deep breath through her nose and pushed the door open.

The hallway, stairs and lobby of the building all shone quite cheerfully in the residual morning light that was scattering in, brighter than the light from the vines and bulbs that grew on the walls. Shanti smiled as she made her way downstairs. There was beauty to be had in Gorduum, that much was sure.

Outside, the morning was just as she had expected. Pedestrians were rushing through the streets and pocked throughout the throng were the odd cart and carriage. There was even another one of those bizarre horseless vehicles, chugging its way amongst the people like a boat in a stream. Shanti watched closely but was relieved to see that the driver did not seem to be the same dismissive pale young man from yesterday. And, not more than a few dozen meters away, a vendor was selling something hot and juicy looking. Shanti began making her way along the cobbles towards the man. One or two people arrived at him first, making their order and then whisking away with their food clutched closely so as not to bump into anyone else. Shanti smiled as she looked over the hot tray.

"Good morning," she said. The vendor flashed her a wide smile, but she could see that it barely moved his eyes. Clearly he just wanted her to order, pay and leave. "I'm sorry to be a nuisance, but what are you selling?"

"Not a worry my dear, glad to help, always glad to help. What you have here is the most delectable pheasant breast you've ever tasted, rolled in spices and roasted to perfection. Easy to eat, and easy to come back for more!"

Shanti paused to consider. These lumps of meat, while certainly appetising, didn't look particularly bird-like to her.

"Are you sure? Only, I thought they looked a little like some roast lamb, or even beef."

The vendor blinked and looked around. "No no lady, what you see is what I said. No need to get accusatory."

"No, that wasn't what I-" but it was too late. He had backed away from Shanti before turning to move off against the prevailing traffic, calling his wares to the crowd as he went.

Well that was unusual, thought Shanti. She moved out of the way as one or two people glared at her, blocking the path. He clearly broke some sort of rule with that food. Shanti wondered if it would have made her sick. Surely not; it's a big city, but someone would have found him if he was making people sick and made him stop. How could people exist together if someone was going to undermine others' well-being? What would he even get out of it if he tried such a thing, what would be the point? She resolved to simply purchase whatever the next vendor was selling and return to her uncle's apartment.

It took a little while to catch another vendor. Perhaps they had seen the first man run from Shanti and decided that she would bring them trouble? Regardless, she had to cross the street to find another vendor, a task she had to undertake with as much care as when crossing a rain-flooded stream back home by hopping from mossy rock to slippery stone. The crowd did not pause at all for her and the movement of people was from one end of the street to the other with no allowance for those crossing widthways. Although most people travelling in a single direction were clustered to one side of the street, that wasn't a perfect truth, and there were individuals moving against the current like eels. Attempting to move directly from one side to the other left Shanti feeling buffeted and beaten as she found herself bumped into and shunted aside by men and women with long grimaces on their faces. Eventually she managed to zigzag across with the currents, pausing and changing direction in order to move with the crowd as much as possible.

The vendor she had spotted was standing in the shade of a large fountain that protruded from the buildings on that side. It consisted of four or five large animals that looked like horses with long whip-like eel tails. Water spilled out of all their mouths to cascade down their smooth curved stone sides. This vendor was also selling hot food, but his meat was wrapped in a floury looking bun of bread that had been torn almost in half. This time Shanti didn't bother greeting the man or asking any questions, instead she simply said "One" and smiled as the man handed one of his greasy buns to her. She paid the required amount, surprised that he asked as much as he did but supposing that it was to do with him making his living on the streets of such a huge city, and then she began to manoeuvre her way back across the street towards her uncle's apartment.

The flavour of the meat was nothing special, nor the spices that had been used in its preparation, but the feeling of mouthfuls of fatty meat slipping down her throat into her stomach was immensely satisfying. She had gobbled the entire thing by the time she reached the doorway to her uncle's apartment and was sucking the juices off her fingers and trying to wipe her chin when she decided that she wanted another. She returned to the bustling mob and made her way back to the fountain, but by the time she arrived the vendor had moved on. Her appetite awaked by the bun, she began looking for another vendor. Instead she noticed the alleyway beside the fountain.

Shanti had missed the alley at first, because it was, of course, as dim and dark as all the other narrow alleys she had noticed during her taxi-ride through Gorduum the day before. But now she was nearer to one, she could really look inside and get a sense of what they were like. She tried not to make it too obvious that she was looking down the alley, as she was concerned that someone in the alley might mistakenly believe that she was watching them. Given the nature of the denizens of these dark places, or at least, given what Keema had told her about these

Skuggi, she was sure that such a mistake would be dangerous.

Though the mouth of the alley was a short distance away still, she could see it was lined with doorways. Shrouded figures moved about inside the alley, making way for one another given the narrow confines, but without seeming to cause one another any harm. Shanti noticed that there were vines and lights growing all along the walls of the alley, but they were dark and lifeless things. She moved a little closer, trying to get a better view of the lights so that she could see why they were dead. It was hard to see from the distance, but the plants appeared to be crumbling apart.

As she stepped closer, someone in the alley turned to stare at her, and Shanti froze. The person was an older man, his face wrinkled and his hair streaked with white. His eyes were huge and intense in the shadows, the whites seeming to shine like stars. Shanti gulped and turned back to the main street immediately.

Shanti kept walking until she found another vendor. He happened to be standing right outside a material store that was already doing a brisk morning trade. A variety of men and women of all ages were moving through the store with purpose, feeling out lengths of fabric and bossing around a trio of young assistant boys who looked out of breath and flushed, even at this hour of the morning. The proprietor stood outside the door in conversation with the vendor, who was selling some sort of long thin caramelized fruit. After a moment to ascertain that the finely dressed woman was not in the process of ordering, Shanti excused herself to the proprietor who waved her on to the vendor with a genial smile. Quickly Shanti ordered her food and paid. She thanked the fabric store owner and headed back out into the street, enjoying the sweet flavour of the fruit.

SHANTI WORKED her way through the crowded street back to Dunin's building and walked through the lobby and up the stairs. She finished the fruit quickly and licked her fingers clean. Her stomach felt pleasingly full of food and she almost wanted to go and lie down for a nap. As she walked down the hallway towards the door to her uncle's apartment, it began to open.

The tall light-haired man who had nearly driven his horseless carriage into her the day before came out, facing backwards as he said goodbye to someone still in the apartment. Shanti assumed it was her uncle, but was completely bewildered as to why this man might have been visiting with her uncle.

"...great night. I'll come to see you in three days with a new model, I think you'll be impressed. Good day!"

The man was smiling as he spoke, and it was a charming smile. As soon as he turned to face the hallway however, the smile slipped from his face and Shanti was left to face his pale eyes. The irises were so light that Shanti found it hard to tell where they blended into the whites of his eyes. The man nodded to her in acknowledgement as he moved past her and down the stairs. He didn't even recognise me, thought Shanti. Does that mean he almost runs over people often, or just that I'm a completely unremarkable person in his mind? Neither thought made her feel good. She entered the apartment before the door could be closed.

Inside the doorway she found her uncle Dunin

heading back towards a chair in the living area, soaked in the light from the morning sun outside.

"Good morning," she offered, bracing herself for some snapped retort.

"Hrmph. Yes. I suppose it is," granted her uncle, before he picked up a large folded sheet of paper covered in line upon line of spidery black writing. He pulled a set of reading glasses from his breast pocket and slipped them over his ears, nudging them up and down on his nose until he was satisfied. Then he flicked through the paper and began reading intently.

"Is that today's newspaper?" asked Shanti. She moved closer and took a seat across from Dunin. He peered at her over the top of his glasses and frowned.

"It is yes. And I'm reading it." He turned back to the pages in front of him.

"I'm sorry." Shanti looked down at her hands then up again. She spoke anyway, loudly, at the top of her uncle's head. "It's just that they don't worry much about the newspaper in Graama, as I'm sure you know. Nothing much ever happens there, and everybody knows everything about it after a single evening down the pub anyway. By the time any newspaper gets to the village, the stories are totally out of date. It would be nice to know what the news is in a city as big as Gorduum."

"Indeed." Dunin looked over his glasses at Shanti again, and for the first time she felt like he was really seeing her. He took in her hair, pulled back in a bun to keep it from getting in her way. He noticed the colour of her eyes, she was sure. Eventually he put the paper to one side and sighed. "Yes, I remember how little excitement there was in Graama. It was always 'Tugan's wife was seen hanging around the blacksmith's shed' or 'You'll never guess what I saw young Faamin doing yesterday'. Tedious stuff."

"Yes, especially as I'm only just twenty now, so half the time they were talking about me."

Dunin laughed at that, just once, and very quietly, but Shanti was encouraged.

"Recently, everyone has been talking about how they think that I should begin courting Buan. He's a nice enough boy, but he has never shown any desire to get out of the village."

Dunin nodded.

"I think I'll have set quite a few tongues wagging now though. I went to the pub with Fabrin a couple of days ago, and he is certainly a popular young man among the girls." Shanti found herself giggling, imagining for the first time how jealous some of the other girls around her age would be at this very moment. "But I don't think he really wants to go anywhere either."

"It's important for you to head out of Graama?"

"Yes. It always has been."

"Why?"

"I don't really know." Shanti leaned back a little in her chair, looking out the window at the buildings on the other side of the street. Just the glimpse of unfamiliar architecture made her feel light and airy. "Ever since I was young, I've wanted to see more of the world. To know what else is out there. I've always thought that Graama is a comfortable place to live, but it can't be everything that there is."

"It certainly isn't." agreed Dunin. "So why haven't you come to Gorduum before now? You could have written."

"I have so much to do, I don't have time to even think about writing a letter. I run the store most days, and I chase after Fellbin so much of the time, and my father needs all the help he can get keeping the house in order. I have been trying to spend more time with

Sudru, learning how to take care of the lights, but..."
She trailed off, shaking her head. "There's always another shift at the store. My mother has always said
I'm not really ready to come out here. She's been pro-
tecting me, I think."

Dunin's face darkened and his brow furrowed.
"Dammit Auga. Didn't you learn enough from your
childhood? Why wouldn't you be wise enough to let
your own children alone?" He sounded frustrated
and angry, but Shanti was shocked to notice how it
sounded as though he was addressing her mother in
the room. And how it sounded as though he cared for
her mother, and was upset that she was getting a bad
deal. Before she could ask any questions, he continued. "Would you like a cup of tea?"

"Yes please."

Dunin stood and moved off to make them a pot.
As he left he brought over the paper and left it over
the arm of Shanti's chair. "Have a bit of a look
through," he suggested as he left the room. So she
picked up the paper to see what was written on it.

The paper was an awkward thing to read. To begin
with, it was printed on very large sheets of paper, so
Shanti had to hold her arms wide in order to actually
be able to see a page in one go. If she tried to hold her
hands at a comfortable angle, the paper twisted and
crumpled, creasing the articles in the middle. Secondly, the writing was very small, and printed in row
after row of minute type. She had to squint in order
to make out some of the words, and sometimes what
appeared to be a bewildering sentence of one article
turned out to actually be the title of another, although
that was difficult to be sure of as well. Finally, the
print was of a low grade ink, on cheap reams of paper,
that had been rushed out the door that morning, so

she found her fingers stained with the ink very quickly, and she had to be careful as she manoeuvred the paper around not to leave horrible thick smudges across the articles and render them illegible. Still, it was a thrill to be reading about the important issues of the day in one of the great cities of the world.

The front page was largely taken up by a story about a war that was being waged overseas. Shanti didn't even realise that there was a war going on, she hadn't heard any mention of such a thing back in Graama. At first she wondered if perhaps the war was between two other nations and not her own. As best she could make out from what was written here, both sides were stuck-up prideful fools who were going to leave more destruction than progress when they finally made peace. Near the beginning of the article she recognised the name of one country, supposedly the wronged party, who had been rebuffed at all their attempts to encourage civilization in the lands around one of their mines. Then later on she found the article mentioned the other country. It turned out to be true that her own country was not involved. Shanti began to assume the second country must be the lands around the mine. They acted as though an offer of help from the first country was an insult.

A narrow column to the side of the front page bore the stark headline "More Lights Dying". Shanti allowed her eyes to drift over the words, only picking out some of the keywords as she went. Someone was concerned that a large number of the light plants were withering in various locations across the city. Shanti's mind flashed to the alley she had been standing outside of only a few minutes earlier, and the flaking dried out remains of the lights that had once covered its walls. The article referred to the phenomenon as a blight.

Towards the bottom of the third page was a small headline that read "River Bodies Found." As Shanti began to read this one, she found herself horrified, and a little ill. A body had been found in the main river of the city. Such a thing was terrible when it was accidental, but the newspaper described the body as having suffered severe and intentional wounds. Shanti offered a small prayer to the Masked God to watch for the awful person who could have done this. The paper said it was a similar crime to one a few months earlier, which made her blood run cold.

Dunin returned from the kitchen carrying a large tray that bore a pale white porcelain teapot, steaming from the spout and decorated with simple light blue swirls and geometric figures. Two thin cups and saucers rested on the plate as well, beside a small jug of milk and a bowl of sugar.

"This is lovely, thank you," said Shanti, as her uncle lowered the tray carefully onto a small table that sat in front of the large soft lounging chairs they were using.

"Yes, they are, aren't they?" Dunin looked down on his tea set with a pride that Shanti thought she had only ever seen before in the eyes of parents, watching their children win a race or say their first words. "I bought these while I was travelling in the Vakaluk Valleys." He turned his gaze to her with a lazy smile on his face, partially hidden by his close cropped black beard. "You are familiar with the Vakaluk Valleys I assume?" He raised one eyebrow as he lifted the teapot to pour Shanti a cup. She nearly snorted in surprise. The movement reminded her so much of her mother. Suddenly the family resemblance between this man and the woman she knew so well was made starkly clear. She picked up the cup and inhaled the scent deeply before answering him.

"No, actually, I haven't heard of that place in particular." She lifted the cup to her lips and sipped, noting the slight shake of her uncle's head at her response. Clearly he thought less of her for not knowing where he had collected this item. Given that he was at least conversing with her at all though, she would accept the slight dip in her fortunes. "However, I would be very interested to hear you tell me about it. Where is it?"

Dunin sat himself into his own plush chair and straightened his back, then ran a hand across his chin, stroking his beard. He sighed and took a sip of his tea. He smacked his lips and then spooned a small amount of sugar into the cup and stirred it briskly. "I suppose I could tell you. But I really find your lack of knowledge about such an important place to be quite disappointing."

"You understand that I have lived in Graama my whole life, don't you sir?" Shanti tried to take the complaint out of her tone, worried that she might set him back to his earlier condescending attitude.

"Of course, of course." Dunin waved her concerns aside and took another sip of his tea. This time he smiled and leaned back into his chair. "But you understand that coming from a small provincial village like Graama cannot be considered an excuse for not understanding the real world, don't you?" Again, he arched an eyebrow. Shanti was beginning to hate that eyebrow, both from his sudden application of it and from years of repeated exposure to her mother's brow and its doubting unspoken questions. She wondered what would happen should she attempt to steal into her uncle's room at night and shave the blasted thing off while he slept. The thought amused her greatly, though she tried not to show it on her face.

"I don't understand. I read every book that I could find amongst the homes, pubs and schools at Graama. I spoke to as many people as I could."

"As did I at your age. And I must admit, I may not have known about the Vakaluk Valley until I was somewhat near your age now. But the important difference is, I knew enough to know that I had to leave."

"I've left." Shanti was confused. She took another sip of her tea and enjoyed the sensation of the warm liquid slipping down her throat and filling her belly.

"No, no you haven't." Dunin gestured with the small silver sugar spoon for emphasis, waving it about like a tiny metal magic wand. "You are on a journey outside Graama, and for that I will give you some credit." He nodded, as if that alone would suffice as a reward for her daring to climb aboard a train. "But you didn't do it of your own choice, did you? It wasn't your idea to book a ticket and come stay with me?" He tilted his head a little to the left as he looked at his niece. "You could have done so at any time if you really wanted to leave. Just got on a coach, bought a train ticket, and come to find me. You didn't have to wait for someone else to send you here." He sniffed and nodded. "You do get some credit for coming at all," he repeated. "But you will be going back, won't you?"

Shanti sniffed a little and ran her tongue across her teeth, but did not answer him. He was right, but some part of her wanted to argue anyway. She tried to think about the fact that she would be returning to Graama and found it difficult. Already she wanted to spend much more time in Gorduum, exploring the strange buildings and customs that she had barely glimpsed so far.

"I suppose I will," she allowed.

"Of course you will," her uncle insisted. "Almost nobody ever has the stomach or stamina to leave Graama. Everyone just stays there, because everyone else in their family has stayed there. None of them have any dreams."

Shanti frowned, very aware that it was not a lack of dreams or courage that prevented her from leaving Graama, but a love of her family and duty to ensure that they were well provided for. She covered her expression by taking a sip of her tea. It was beginning to cool down, so she topped it up a little from the teapot to add some heat. She was thinking of her mother, Auga.

Shanti's mother had been young when she had had Shanti, but most of the women in Graama had their children young. It was a fairly natural progression of life in such a town. Children grew up together and played together. They got to know each other thoroughly as they grew up surrounded by friends and family. Eventually they fell in love and got married. There weren't many options around, so most people knew quite early on who they would end up with, and why put off something that you wanted to happen anyway? And once they were married, why not have children?

Shanti studied her uncle. He really thought that the people in Graama were missing something. But Auga didn't seem to be missing anything at all. She spent her days with a smile on her face and laughter bubbling in the air wherever she went. Many of her days were hard, staying up all night worrying over stock, supplies, and orders. Working with Neeran to maintain the house, to raise the children, and all the other little tasks that needed constant vigilance in order for a household to continue. Shanti was very aware of the difficulty that Auga had chosen for her life by getting married young and having a family, and taking over the store. Shanti's mother was bound to the village irrevocably.

But Shanti remembered the look in her mother's eyes as she watched Taanin, Shanti and Fellbin playing in their youth. There was always a shine, a glint, a sparkle as the children ran screaming around the streets. There was a glow that Auga had about her, even when she was bustling through the store with loads of stock in her arms and the children playing on top of the counter. Sitting at home while her husband prepared dinner. Shanti thought there was certainly happiness there. His claim that Auga was missing out on something was bewildering.

But then, Shanti agreed with her uncle in so many other ways! She absolutely wanted to get out of Graama, to see what amazing sights the world had in store. She was still curious about this Vakaluk Valley that Dunin had mentioned, although their conversation had been side-tracked. And there was no way that she wanted to live the same life as her mother. All through her childhood and as she grew into an adult, she had been aware of the path that was generally followed amongst her peers, and she knew it wasn't the path for her. Why else had she been so keen and impatient to head out to Gorduum for this order? And now, here she was! But then why did she feel so angry towards her uncle? Why wasn't she simply nodding?

"How did you get out?" she asked.

"It's not much of a story." Dunin topped up his own teacup. "When I was not much younger than you are now, I simply left. I packed up the few meagre possessions I could, took all the money I had been able to earn running errands and doing odd chores, bought a ticket and left."

"Where was the ticket to?"

"I can barely remember." He scrunched up his face as he thought. "I think it was just a coach ticket to the next town, or maybe a few stops down the line at first. It didn't matter, I was out. And then I started picking up jobs there, earning my way, earning a living, and saving up more money for tickets to go further and further away."

"How far did you get?" Shanti was beginning to feel inspired by the idea of travelling for no reason other than to be moving, despite her earlier anger towards this man.

"Well…" Dunin held up his cup of tea and nodded towards it. "I don't mean to brag…" He allowed the sentence to trail off, a sheen of pride spilling over his face and his chest filling with importance.

"Oh of course, the Vakaluk Valley." Shanti nodded. "Is that very far away from Gorduum or Graama?" She sipped at her tea, not looking at her uncle but smiling at the thought of his pomposity being deflated. She took pleasure in the idea that he might think she believed Graama and Gorduum were very near each other also, despite having just spent two days on trains to travel between the two places.

She looked back, carefully positioning an expression of polite curiosity on her face, just in time to catch the last of his splutters.

"Of course it is! The Valley is right at the southern end of Brukoluk. You do know about the continent of Brukoluk, at least I would hope?"

Shanti did. Brukoluk was where so many of the fantastic and imaginative adventure stories that she had spent much of her childhood reading were set. It was supposed to be a jungle-filled and hot place, though some stories had described vast flat plains that howled with cold winds, and massive snowy mountains. She had grown up in awe of the place, and inspired by the brave men and women in the stories that travelled through it, facing down natural disasters and wild beasts alike.

"The Valley is in Brukoluk? My goodness, weren't you afraid?" As soon as the words escaped her lips, Shanti realised her mistake. Just as she feared, Dunin's chest swelled again and he began to expound on the journey that had taken him to the valley. Still, despite his silly ego, Shanti could not help but be enthralled by his stories. Dunin had travelled the long way, working from village to village, town to town; always trading and doing enough jobs to travel further. As the tale grew longer, it sounded as though he had spent most of his career working on assignments from a friend who ran some sort of trading company, but the route he took in these assignments was circuitous and frequently dangerous.

He talked of being stalked in the evening by gigantic cats, like the ones that yowled and scrabbled in the alleys of the village, hunting the rats and vermin that plagued the gutters; though these predators were bigger than a man, and far less thin and ugly. He captured the shine of their coat, and the way their eyes flashed in the reflection of the sun's last dying rays of an evening. Shanti felt a shiver of cool fear trace down her neck at the thought. Dunin was once saved by a local farmer who charged the cats with his hoe, scattering them back into the trees.

"I would never have believed such powerful beasts would be scared by such a simplistic display!" Shanti laughed.

"I know! I was just as shocked as the animals, I'd wager!"

Dunin had stayed with the farmer, and paid him well in coin and in some of the goods he was travelling with.

"I wouldn't mind seeing that man again before I die," mused Dunin. "Take some treasures back to him and his wife from Gorduum. Just to see their faces."

Eventually, Dunin's stories led to him wandering through the Vakaluk Valley, a particularly rainy jungle, full of rivers and small villages amongst the huge twisted tree trunks. It was here that he finally made contact with the people his friend had sent him to find, explaining to them about some of the paths through the mountains he had used, and which towns had the best supplies for a merchant caravan, or goods to trade for. Then he had travelled a little further to a foreign port, boarded a large ship and enjoyed an uneventful cruise back to Gorduum

"And this is where I've stayed for the following ten or twelve years." Dunin finished the last of the tea from the pot as he wrapped up his tale, then looked around the room. Midday light was pouring in through the windows. "Did you have any other questions?"

"Just one more, and then I will need to get ready for some meetings this afternoon."

"Meetings? What meetings?"

Shanti explained. She was going to go out into Gorduum and look for some merchants who might sell her lights for the festival. She would appreciate some advice from Dunin about where to begin her afternoon.

"You are just going to wander around the town and hope that you can speak with merchants selling bulk lights?"

"Is that unusual? What have I done wrong?"

Dunin pinched the brow of his nose. "I suppose I could come with you, see if I can get you into anyone's offices today at least."

Shanti was delighted! This was such a welcome turnaround from the way he had been treating her earlier! "That would be very much appreciated."

"I'm sure." Dunin scratched his chin. "If we get lucky and someone agrees to see you, then you'll have to go in alone. I do have errands to run and I imagine that you'd be stuck in any meetings for a while."

Shanti's stomach clenched into a round, hard ball of worry. "You'll introduce me but not stay with me?"

"Well, what of it? You weren't expecting to have me with you at all a moment ago."

It was true, but Shanti knew there was a difference between knocking on someone's door by yourself and being introduced by a businessman and then left alone. She was much more likely to be left to try and discuss her business with someone important, with no experience of what such a conversation should look like. If she went knocking by herself, at least there would be no expectation on her. At least she would be dealing with the lower level members of whatever organisation she approached!

"What was your question?" Dunin's voice cut through the fog of nerves that was beginning to fill Shanti's head at the realisation of what she would have to do now and she had to blink twice before she could focus on her uncle's face. He was standing behind the chair he had been seated in, leaning on the back with both hands.

"I'm sorry?"

"Your question. You said you had one more?"

"Oh." Shanti trawled through the sudden chaos in her mind to try and recall what her question had been. It was like searching through the clean laundry for a single needle that had been left in an item of clothing, full of colour and madness but almost impossible to complete. Then she remembered. "Yes! I was just wondering what sort of lights those places have? I know that Graama only has a few proper lights, mostly on the town hall and the tavern, but there Sudru has been making plans to grow a few street vines along the main road now. And the council have been expanding her greenhouse, and encouraging her to take on an apprentice. They want to expand the lights in the village however they can." She didn't mention that she had been trying to make herself into a suitable candidate for the apprenticeship. She was sure that her uncle would see it as simply another sign of her lack of will to leave Graama.

"Most of the places I went are much like Graama in that regard." Dunin sniffed. "Gorduum is lucky. The climate here is so perfect for lights that I don't think the world would have turned out quite the same without them. Certainly this city wouldn't exist." He picked up the tray with the tea making equipment and began to walk it back to the kitchen. "There's a few places large enough to have bought some street vines, a few towns that have tried to build their own greenhouses and nurseries, the odd well to do business or council that has some large brilliant coloured bulb as a nod to their importance." At the door to the kitchen he turned and smiled at Shanti. "But there's nowhere with fields of light like Gorduum."

SHANTI GOT CHANGED into her finest blue dress. This was the one that her mother had given her nearly two years ago, as a festival present. Auga had held it up against her daughter and there had been the suggestion of a tear in the corner of her eye. Shanti had felt so grown up, so responsible, and all for the gift of a beautiful deep blue dress. She hoped that her mother's trust in her was justified, now that she was preparing to go and spend a large amount of money on something so important for the village and also for the reputation of her parents as good reliable storekeepers.

Feeling it was appropriate, she put on a heavy necklace as well. The metal shone, a series of large flat drops that spread across her shoulders and chest. She looked in the mirror and decided that it would work well for her.

Finally, she dug out the pouch of money and bank notes, ready to pay her way.

She returned to the living space, where her uncle was waiting.

He was dressed exactly as he had been before; clean black trousers held by thin black suspenders over his shoulders, and a reasonably clean white shirt, though it was crumpled more than Shanti thought appropriate for a business meeting. He had picked up a long brown coat and a simple round hat that he would clearly put on after they left the apartment. He noticed the money pouch that Shanti was carrying.

"Are you just planning to carry that around in your hands?" he asked.

"I hadn't really thought about it," answered Shanti, thinking of the warning that Keema had given her. "I don't have enough room in my satchel for all of it."

"All of it? Let me have a look." Dunin pulled the pouch open and looked inside. Shanti noticed that he kept his hands at the lip of the pouch and never inside. He pointed as he counted, then whistled softly. "I suppose that people say it is best to negotiate from a position of strength. The council have sent you well armed." He looked up at Shanti's face, his eyes serious. "But that is far too much money to be safely carrying through the streets. Or even carrying into an office! If they know how much you have, they will be sure to ask for all of it if they can. Best to get a contract from them in person, and then meet the payment of that contract at delivery."

"Oh." Shanti felt silly. She didn't like the way that this was making her look like an uneducated countrywoman. "I'll put them away then."

"That's probably the best idea."

They left the apartment together, Dunin setting a brisk pace as they moved down the stairs and out of the building. Without pausing at all, he strode into the chaotic turmoil of the river of pedestrians. Shanti had to dive after him and eventually she realised that she would have to hold onto him or risk becoming separated and possibly lost. With some level of displeasure, she hung her arm onto his elbow. She was still buffeted by passers-by, but at least now she felt confident that she would not be left behind by her uncle. He gave the back of her hand a brief pat, and the patronising gesture made her feel immensely frustrated. She hoped that he wasn't getting the impression that she was completely incapable of taking charge!

As they walked towards the south, Dunin began to speak to her about Gorduum and the buildings and statues that they were passing. At the end of the street, centred in a particularly large intersection where six streets burst onto one another, there stood a massive archway made of stone and covered in detailed carvings. Even at a distance, the figures stood out to Shanti. Some were dressed in armour and carried long spears. Others had flowing robes around them, and those figures floated above the first ones.

"It's a victory monument. One of the ancient generals led an army into Brukoluk and conquered many people. When he returned, so proud of himself, he built this archway."

"It's amazing," said Shanti, her eyes drinking in the beautiful statues.

"It is. But we still find it hard to trade with the continent even now, hundreds of years later. The people are unwilling to send us ivory and fruits, even for the most verdant lights." Dunin shook his head. "I think it would have been easier to negotiate."

Shanti was surprised, and glanced at her uncle's face as they passed the massive archway. The crowds split around and through it, the curved roof passing far above their heads.

For a while, Shanti was sure that her uncle intended for them both to walk the entire distance to the lights traders. As she had no experience of Gorduum, this worried Shanti for a multitude of reasons. First, she had no idea how far away such a walk might be. Although Dunin had told her stories of his adventures, and he clearly had a portion of bravery and daring in his personality to enable such things, from the sight of his stomach pressing against the buttons of his shirt, he quite enjoyed his comforts now, and she doubted that he would lead her on an hours long trek if it was not necessary.

Secondly, she didn't know the streets and turns of this place. She had been quite comfortable walking along the wide busy boulevard, as it was clearly a main road and she imagined that people would be able to direct her to it. As well as that, she felt sure that she would be able to recognise her uncle's apartment as she passed by, so all she would have to do is return to this street. The magnificent archway was a very useful landmark in that regard. But as they continued, Shanti was unsure which of the streets they had turned down, and shortly Dunin began to take more and more turns. Shanti was quickly becoming disoriented.

"How much further?" she asked, hoping to get her bearings.

"Not far."

"Good. Do you have any advice for me, for when I'm negotiating and discussing the order?"

"Sorry? When you're-" Dunin missed a step as he glanced over to her, then realisation smoothed his face. "Oh I see. How far to the lights merchants." He sniffed and narrowed his eyes. "Yes, I will give you some advice for your meeting, but we still have quite a way to go before we will speak to anyone. I meant that we were nearly at the ferries."

IT TURNED out that Gorduum contained within it the wide and slowly moving Naatat River. Shanti hadn't seen any sight of it on her way into the city, and so when they turned right at the top of a broad white flight of stairs that led down to the river's edge, Shanti found her breath snatched away. The water spread out in either direction in a deep green-brown, like liquid glass, with ripples and waves cresting and washing by each other across the surface. The opposite bank looked to be a few hundred meters away, and pale buildings lined the shore like the sheep she remembered from the farms back home, pushing at the fences while they waited for food, their wool tangling and intermingling so that you almost couldn't tell where one stopped and the next began. So it was with the buildings, covered in washing lines, balconies, small dark irregular holes of windows peppered through their walls. Overhead, a clear blue sky and a distant autumn sun shone down brightly on the city.

At the bottom of the stairs, occasional waves from the river washed over a broad stone platform that was set mere centimetres above the surface. Tied to large dark stone cleats was a motley navy of ferry boats; captains gathered on the stone dock, conversing loudly and enthusiastically. Pipes poked from dark beards, women slapped one another on the back with an alarming regularity, and laughter erupted like summer thunder. Scurrying around their masters were the young men and women who were training as apprentice ferry-hands.

Dunin walked past the first four boats and headed for a wide man with a huge bristly beard and spikes of thick hair thrusting out from beneath a leather cap.

"Dunin, you old fraud!" bellowed the man as he caught sight of Shanti's uncle. "What brings you down to our besodden neighbourhood today?"

Dunin smiled and reached out to shake the man's hand. Shanti followed carefully, lifting her skirts to keep them from dragging in the film of water that was sliding across the dock and stepping carefully so that she didn't slip.

"Good morning Varlin! Just a simple trip today if you would be so kind. We would like to head upriver to the light merchant offices."

"Only that far? It seems hardly worth my time." Varlin stuck his hands in his pockets and narrowed his eyes a little.

"Really, you're going to turn into a tough negotiator now?"

"I'm always a tough negotiator." The smile that peeked through his beard was as sly as a cat that was stalking a mouse.

"I don't really have time for this. Shanti, do you have twelve mola?"

Shanti was not expecting her name to be brought up. She stepped forward quickly.

"Yes, I think so."

"We'll pay twelve, alright?" He held out a hand to shake. Varlin's eyes widened a little.

"Sure. That'll do nicely!" He reached out and shook Dunin's hand again.

"Pay the man Shanti, and let's get on board."

Shanti's internal thoughts growled about how presumptuous her uncle was being, spending her own money as though it was water. And so much more than the taxi ride had cost! Was this a remotely reasonable price? However, she cautiously retrieved her personal money from her satchel and handed over twelve mola to the ferryman. He gripped her hand after taking the money. "Thank you very much young lady. I hope you know this old thief well?"

Shanti wondered if the man was trying to warn her about her uncle. After all, he didn't know that they were family, maybe he thought she was a prospective business partner. Maybe this was a truly outrageous price for the ferry journey and he thinks I have no head for money? She considered the pair of them from the outside. Or maybe he thinks that we are courting? She shuddered.

They walked across a simple plank onto the ferry. It was quite long, with a low wooden roof that covered most of the craft. Varlin stepped up onto the sides of the boat easily, striding over the top of it as he pulled ropes away and the boat began to bob in the river water.

. . .

THE TRIP along the Naatat was one of the more delightful experiences Shanti had been through since she left Graama with Darsat and Dulku. The sight of the pale orange buildings of Gorduum sliding past her along the distant banks to either side left her with a new sense of just how large Gorduum actually was. It had taken nearly twenty minutes to walk from her uncle's apartment to the ferries and now, another twenty minutes had passed and there was no sign of an end to this huge cosmopolis.

Although she wasn't sure about Varlin, he appeared to be following through honestly with the job. Shanti wondered if this level of suspicion was normal and natural, especially in newcomers to such an overwhelming place, or whether her conversation with the cautious taxi driver Keema and her unexpectedly harsh meeting with Dunin had soured her on the idea of trusting people. Bratis would certainly have told her that hidden eyes would be keeping watch over her even here, and that she should have comfort in that. She was worried that it had been so easy for her to forget. She did keep watching the shoreline, wondering if a boat would come rushing out to overtake them and relieve her of her money. She couldn't decide whether such a dreadful circumstance would be the fault of her uncle or the ferryman. She tried to put it from her head and enjoy the sun from her low and comfortable seat near the rear of the ferry.

Varlin knelt nearby, resting his elbow on one raised leg and keeping his other hand on the tiller, steering the ferry against the current of the river. It was a narrow craft, and Shanti wondered how easily he was able to actually see ahead of them and guide them safely. Four youths sat towards the front of the ferry, each with a long oar that they dug into the water with trained regularity. The two closest were the focus of Shanti's attention.

The boy on the left looked a few years younger than herself, but he must have spent a long time rowing already in his life. His shoulders were broad and strong beneath a very light white shirt that he didn't bother to tie closed, revealing the shining muscles of his chest every time he leaned forward over the oar. His hair was just long enough to fall across his face as he rowed too, causing him to flick his head and toss it back from time to time. Shanti found the movement delightful, like a small puppy or kitten batting at a toy.

On the right sat a young woman with long hair bound up in a single thick plait. She looked as though she was newer to the trade, and certainly older than the boy. She wore a shirt and waistcoat, and voluminous trousers, all of which were better tailored than her rowing partner's. Shanti assumed that the woman would find cheaper clothes to wear as she continued in her job, as the river water and exercise damaged the clothing.

In the distance, Shanti began to see more boats in the river. They had always been present, oars skipping through the river, but now she saw bigger vessels, some with sails and some with entire banks of oars. They were all coming and going from one set of docks that appeared to bustle with tiny figures from this distance, exactly as the giant anthill in Taanin's fields had looked when she was a young girl. She found the hectic movements of the tiny black dots just as hypnotising here as he had in the fields.

As they approached, Shanti began to be impressed at just how large some of the boats were.

"I keep thinking that I will get used to this place,

and then it shows me something strange and new," she murmured.

"Aye," nodded Varlin. "I've lived here most of my life, after sailing upriver from the coast with my wife as a young lad, but it still manages to press me with its awe."

"What are all these huge ships?"

The ferryman laughed. "They are bigger than this ferry indeed, but most of 'em will only travel down to the coast. Then they'll shift their cargo at harbour and the really massive merchant ships will carry them to other countries."

"What do they carry?"

"What else? They carry lights; potted, planted, and tended by on board lights-keepers and expert gardeners. The river mirrors the stars in the sky here at night."

"The fields did that when I arrived on the trains."

"Yes, the farms and orchards can be pretty too." Varlin's tone made it clear that he was willing to grant them a measure of beauty, but that they were clearly of no real competition to the lights as they travelled by river.

"So, this is where people trade in the lights?" Shanti asked, not expecting much of a reply. Varlin nodded.

As they pulled closer to the docks and piers that jutted into the water, Shanti looked up and admired the buildings. In the streets around Dunin's apartment, lights grew in carefully cultivated lines along the walls, providing illumination for passers-by. Some shops and stores had clearly invested in particular bloom and fruits to help them stand out from their neighbours. Even that had been a riot of colour and money in comparison to the brief glimmers that grew in Graama. But here, every building was covered in vines and foliage, a massive thick curtain and canopy of lights. Even in the middle of the afternoon, the buildings glowed. Shanti had to squint in order to look at their destination. The lights were glorious.

SHANTI AND DUNIN got off Varlin's ferry at a dock that looked very much like the low stone dock that they had left. As they walked away, Dunin tromping through the film of water that moved slowly across its surface and Shanti lifting the hem of her dress a centimetre or two to try and avoid it, she could hear the heavily bearded man yelling at the youths to get the ferry tied up.

"Why is he tying up?" she asked her uncle. "Why isn't he just turning around?"

Dunin snorted softly. "He isn't going to row all the way back to where we came from for free! No, he'll tie up here and wait for someone to take back the way he came. If he's still here when we are done then we might even get him to take us back."

Shanti tutted and mentally berated herself. That was a pretty obvious reason and she felt silly for not having thought of it. Then she had a moment of clarity that worried her. "Where did we come from exactly?" She tried to ask the question casually, without allowing the fear that had suddenly struck her to fill her tone. She had just realised that she didn't know what to say to a ferry in order to go back to where she had come from. In this massive city, that could mean that she would be lost forever.

She thought of the taxi-drivers like Keema that thronged the streets. Maybe not lost forever, she admitted to herself, but it would certainly be quite an inconvenience.

"That is a good point," replied Dunin. "I should

have told you the neighbourhood earlier, especially as I won't be able to be with you the whole afternoon." He reached over and squeezed her shoulder. "When you're done, you just make your way back here to the docks, which shouldn't be too difficult, and ask to be taken to the Arfa district. It should be easy enough to find my apartment again from there."

"Oh, thank you." Shanti felt relieved.

They walked together up another flight of stairs, where each step was very long but also incredibly low. It was almost a ramp, especially where the edges of the steps had been worn away over decades of use by workers. Shanti watched the workers now, walking in pairs mostly, and holding long thick poles of wood between them. The poles passed through sets of handles on the sides of large pots that held a variety of light seedlings, bushes and young shoots. It was like watching a noble be carried through the city streets in a sedan chair, only the passenger was a large amount of rich dark dirt and various shapes of glowing light.

At the top of the staircase the path continued as a street that led between two towering buildings with almost no windows. The building on the left was covered in dense green leaves, thousands of small dark teardrop-shaped leaves. Speckled through this covering were star shaped blooms that glowed a dull red. It was stunning.

Shanti found herself slowing and staring at the wall, but stepped back up to her uncle when he paused to see why she had fallen behind. He glanced at the wall.

"Yes, it's very nice isn't it? We may as well start with them as anywhere."

"There aren't many blooms though. Will they be able to fulfil my order do you think?"

Dunin laughed once. "That is the main office and greenhouse for the Oibaa Company. They are one of the most prestigious and ancient of the light-growing families!"

"But then why…" Shanti trailed off, confused by the disparity between what he said and the lack of lights actually growing on their walls. It wasn't that she thought these red blooms weren't pretty, they were. She walked closer, reaching out one hand to lift the red petals and feel the softness of them in her fingers. It was just that they were so few. Was a company that kept so few lights on display really the best option for her?

"It is the wrong time of year of course."

That was true. As the days grew colder, it would become much more difficult to keep flowering lights blossoming. But there were so many other varieties of light that Oibaa could have grown on these walls. Back in Graama, Shanti had heard Sudru talking about one variety of creeping vinelight that actually shone brighter in the darkest months. Why hadn't they trained some of those thin vines through this wall? She looked up to the roof four stories above her.

"Trust me, they're worth asking." Dunin led her away to the corner of the building and they stepped out onto a main thoroughfare.

Shanti had thought that the street outside her uncle's apartment was busy. She had considered it to be full of people and movement, reminding her of nothing so much as a stream after the spring thaw, full of rushing white capped water and swarming with young fish leaping. However, it was a calm pond in comparison to the main street in the lightsellers' quarter. Even Dunin, who had strode forward so confidently in his own neighbourhood, had to pause to consider a plan of attack.

"Let's try Oibaa first" he said, raising his voice to be heard above the hubbub of the street. They turned left and found a flight of stone stairs beneath wide doors that led into the Oibaa offices only a few meters away. Shanti placed her hand on Dunin's elbow again and they climbed the stairs together and pushed open the doors.

Inside, the lobby was broad and bright. Instinct made Shanti look up to the roof, expecting to find a large oculus or window that was allowing so much light to suffuse through the space and reflect off the well-polished white marble surfaces. There she saw a chandelier made out of a growing light tree, which she realised was not at all surprising. The branches spread out like a child's drawing of a spider web, and were covered in wide thick leaves that shone with an intensely white light.

"I told you," said Dunin with a smile as he noticed the direction of her attention. "They are worth your time."

As they walked into the lobby, Shanti noticed some rather large men standing to either side of the doors. They weren't making themselves obvious, but it was hard to miss the large wooden truncheons hanging from loops on the side of their belts. Their faces were pleasant, although they were not smiling, but Shanti was disturbed by the way their well-tailored suits were pushed and distorted by muscles beneath. Clearly, the Oibaa Company would not tolerate any trouble in their office.

In front of them were line after line of desks, each containing a studious looking clerk. Various people were sitting at rows of plush seats in front of the desks. Dunin walked straight past the people sitting in the chairs and stood at one of the desks. Shanti stepped quickly to follow, although she felt awkward moving past other people who were waiting. She tried to look forward, at the back of her uncle's neck, so that she wouldn't accidentally catch the eye of someone who she was skipping in the queue.

She caught up with Dunin just in time to hear him say "- to place a large order please."

"Do you have an appointment with any particular dealer?" The woman behind the desk did not seem perturbed that some man had simply strode past all the other clients in the room, though she did seem quite put out to have to speak with someone at all. She wore thin-rimmed small circular spectacles, and wore her long hair pulled back into a tight tail that fell halfway down her back.

"No, but we were hoping there might be room to see someone this afternoon?"

"Let me check. Take a seat, Mr…"

"Call for Shanti Penpen," answered Dunin, gesturing at her. The woman nodded, stood up and walked away without another word.

Shanti realised that she was standing at the desk alone, watching the women disappear across the wide stone floor. She turned to see that her uncle had made himself comfortable in a chair not far from the desk. She joined him.

"So, all these people," she began, waving a hand at the occupants of the other chairs. "They already went to a desk?"

"Of course. Why, how would you expect to meet with someone?"

"I suppose I had imagined that we would go in to talk to them immediately, and everyone would have waited in a queue until it was their turn." After all, that was how they served people in her family store. Customers came in and came to the counter, she served them, and then served the next person waiting.

"They're too busy for that. Can you imagine all these people waiting in one line? No, instead they all talk to the clerks and arrange meetings and whatever else they need."

Shanti sat silently for a moment, studying the huge lobby.

"So, how should I begin this meeting? Do I just hand over the order sheet and ask how much?"

"We haven't got a meeting yet."

"What do you mean?"

"That girl is checking if they have any dealers with an opening this afternoon. You'll have to come back and chat with the dealer then. I'm just helping get you through the doors. But no, I wouldn't just hand over the list. I'd get them to show you their stock first, then ask how much for some of the simpler lights that might suit the order. Once you get an idea of that, you can decide whether you want a full quote."

Shanti made mental notes of her uncle's suggestions, like a checklist in her mind that she would hopefully remember during the meetings.

"And don't decide on anyone today. Get all your quotes together, and then choose the best. It might not be the cheapest you choose, mind," Dunin jabbed a finger in the air to emphasise his point. "But choose tomorrow."

THE CLERK DIDN'T RETURN for a long time. Dunin had sat for a while, but pretty quickly had risen again to walk around chatting to the other businesspeople who were waiting in the seats. He began to talk with them, in low tones to avoid the massive echo of the large marble room. Shanti didn't feel like talking to even more strangers, and so she remained in her seat, looking at the architecture of the room.

Eventually the young woman came sauntering back from a distant doorway. Shanti didn't notice her until she was quite close, as there were similarly dressed clerks moving backwards and forwards throughout the maze of rich wooden desks. But then the clerk called her name, and Shanti stood to go over. Dunin managed to excuse himself from his conversation and get to the desk moments before his niece.

"Thank you for waiting," began the clerk, without a trace of emotion in her voice. She may as well have been reading a list of furniture out loud. "We do have a short opening in an hour and a half with Mr Lufuf. If you would return then and let one of the clerks know your name and his, they will escort you to his office."

"Perfect, thank you very much." Dunin bowed slightly, his smile wide and cheerful. Shanti was surprised to see how utterly charming he was trying to be. The smiles, the tone of voice. All of it was a far cry from the taciturn frown that had greeted her. Even now that he was treating her more kindly, his manner with the clerk was even kinder. As they left the Oibaa office, she questioned him about it.

"You felt that this was a fairly painless exercise at getting a meeting, don't you?" he replied.

"Yes." It was true. Shanti didn't really understand why she had needed his help at all, if this was that level of difficulty that was involved in business meetings.

"You are right, it was. But part of that was my

choice of clerk. I looked for the one that seemed the least busy at the time we walked in. To know that, I had to gauge how high her paperwork was piled, and whether it was a neat stack of incoming forms to complete or file, or if it was the dishevelled pile of work that had become overdue. I had to determine her mood, from the briefest glimpse of her face and posture."

"She looked pretty grumpy to me." They passed out of the great doors and back into the hectic noise of the main street. Dunin extended his elbow again as they descended the stairs.

"That's because you haven't seen just how grouchy people in her position can get! This is often a thankless job, and if you get the wrong run of forms it can be mentally draining." He looked up and down the street and then led Shanti to the left, following the traffic on their side of the street. "By being very kind and grateful, I am oiling the machinery that allows us to get to our meeting before the end of the day. That woman arranged a meeting for us that will be very important, but she could just as easily have lost our names, or declared that there were no meeting times available, or any other of a huge number of impediments."

Shanti realised that it was true, the woman could have left them waiting for any length of time if she wanted. However, she didn't know if Dunin's skill at convincing a clerk to get them a meeting was really as valuable as she had believed it would be on her journey into Gorduum. Now that she had seen how he operated, she was fairly sure she could do it herself.

FURTHER ALONG THE street there was a sign sticking

straight out of the wall above the door to the next company that Dunin said they should look into. It said Aregak Lights.

This lobby was much less impressive than the previous one. Shanti was still amazed at the size of the room, but it was made of more familiar wood, with simple potted lights in convenient spaces around the room. She also realised that she was acclimatising to the new things she found in Gorduum with alarming speed, as the lobby might have contained the entire tavern from Graama easily. Dunin led the way over well-polished floors covered in expensive deep red rugs, woven with intricate gold patterns. He reached a wide desk where four clerks were sitting, filing paperwork and filling in forms. There were chairs for waiting in, just like at Oibaa, but no-one was sitting in them at the moment.

"Good afternoon," beamed Dunin, leaning forward at the counter in front of a young man wearing a close-cropped beard and with spiky hair. "My name is Dunin Penpen and I am here to see if we can have a meeting with-"

"Wait a moment Pavaan," yelped a voice from further down the desks. An older woman was standing from her seat and pointing at Dunin with a trembling finger. "I know that man!"

"I'm sorry, I don't-" sputtered Dunin, the smile slipping off his face faster than a frog sliding beneath a pond surface when a crow flew by.

"Yes, I'm sure it's you!" The woman's voice was raised and faces were turning to watch. Shanti saw doors behind the desks opening, and curious faces peeking out. "You were in here last year with your scams and schemes! Well, we didn't fall for it then and we aren't falling for it now!" She began to storm forward, lifting her shawl over her shoulder to allow her more room to stride and leading the way with her accusatory finger. Dunin flung up his hands in defence, though she was still separated from him by quite a distance.

"Madam, I can assure you that I don't-"

"Morda, what is going on out here?" The woman who came down the hallway was dressed very finely, her clothes fitting her perfectly. Her hair was bound back in a tight arrangement of coiled plaits, but it did not pull at her face, which looked relaxed and dignified. Her hair was already mostly white, though streaks of the original dark colour were still visible, giving her a stately impression. Though she walked at a sensible pace, and her voice was pitched with a volume and emotion that were clearly designed to not offend potential customers, the frown in her eyes showed that she was very upset by the commotion.

"I'm very sorry ma'am, but this is Dunin Penpen, that same crook who came to our offices last year. I believe he managed to convince you to meet with him then, but I thought we couldn't have him back here, peddling spider webs and dew again!" The clerk bowed her head slightly and stepped back, worried that she may have overstepped her mark.

The authoritative woman glided to a halt on the far side of the desk and peered at Dunin, who cleared his throat and smiled, nervously running a hand through his beard as though to make himself more presentable. The woman straightened and reached out to put a hand on Morda's shoulder.

"I do believe you are correct Morda." Dunin opened his mouth, but the woman sliced one hand through the air and cut him off. "You were not welcome here one year ago sir, and you are not welcome here still. Please leave immediately, or I will send for someone to escort you out."

Shanti could tell from the way that the woman spoke that anyone who came to escort them out would do so in a most unpleasant fashion. She lifted her skirts and spun around to leave.

Once outside she paused to catch her breath and process what had just happened. She turned to look back and wait for Dunin to come out of the building, but found that her uncle was right beside her, her face darkened in anger or embarrassment.

"What was all that about?" she exclaimed.

Dunin groaned and tutted his tongue. He ran both hands over his scalp, looked up into the sky then back down and into Shanti's eyes.

"Okay, I'll explain that one." He muttered. He beckoned for her to walk with him and began to head further down the street, though he spoke as he went.

"It's quite simple really, they didn't want to invest in a venture that I brought to their attention last year. To be quite honest, I'd forgotten that I went to them entirely, until that damnable woman began to shout at me."

"Were you deceiving them? Was it a con?" Shanti was surprised at just how easily the words fell from her mouth. This was her uncle! But she was becoming more and more aware that she didn't really know him, and that her mother must have some good reasons for feeling so angry at her own brother. Dunin didn't become angry at the accusations either, which made Shanti think there must be some element of truth to them. She wondered if anyone knew what was happening in his life. Maybe she was meant to be the hidden eyes that would see him now, and provide a way for him to become better.

"No." He replied simply, though his grimace showed that there was more to be told about this story. "It's just that..." He took a deep breath and stopped walking. Shanti looked at the building they were outside of. Again, a simple sign was set above the doorway, nothing as impressive as the offices of Oibaa had been. However, this sign was painted with careful calligraphy and the name Artee flowed as beautifully across the wood as the best lights vine across the side of a building. Dunin paused at steps and scratched his chin. "Do you understand what I do for my work?"

"I don't think I do," admitted Shanti carefully.

"I didn't think so. Has your mother ever even tried to explain?"

"Not that I can remember."

Dunin shook his head. "No matter. What I do is, I find people who have business ideas but lack money to complete them. I give them money to follow their plans, and when the business is profitable, they pay me a share in the profits."

"That sounds reasonable."

"It is very reasonable! Many many people all over the country make their livings this way! And some-times, I will act as a go-between for other people to invest in projects too. After all, if I want the business to succeed, so that I can get my share of the profit, it is often worth getting others to invest also. Clearly I took an idea to that company, and they didn't think it was as good an idea as I had."

"Clearly."

Dunin nodded, and turned to go into the new busi-ness. Shanti followed, but slowly, thinking through what he had said. It sounded like a very reasonable thing to do for a living. After all, the best ideas weren't always going to come to people who could enact them. Someone would need to provide money. She won-dered where he had got the money to begin doing this.

She also wondered what happened when a business wasn't successful. Did Dunin just lose his money? Or what if the business looked good, but actually the person just took the investment money and vanished?

Dunin opened the door and held it for her. She smiled at him as she walked through, but it was little more than a rearranging of her facial muscles. There was no feeling in it.

What if the person ran off with the money, and had a channel to send some back to Dunin? What if that was even more profitable than just running a successful business? Shanti felt as though there was a stone in the pit of her stomach, churning over the suspicion that boiled through her brain when she considered her uncle. He had allowed her to stay, he had agreed to help get her into some meetings. Why did she keep thinking the absolute worst of him?

"Good afternoon," Dunin greeted a young male clerk at the front desk. The boy wore thin eyeliner, and had carefully arranged the curls and tufts of his black hair. His shirt collar was pressed sharp and his waistcoat was exactly the right degree of tight to show the strength of his shoulders even while sitting at the desk.

Dunin and the boy had a quick conversation, asking for a meeting with a dealer. This was the quickest interaction so far, with the young man pencilling down Shanti's name in a space for an hour's time.

As they left, Shanti began to feel nervous about returning to these companies on her own.

"When are you leaving for your other appointments?" she asked her uncle. She wondered if he would manage to stay for at least one of her meetings with a dealer.

"I can try one more place," he answered, pointing down the street a little further. "Then I will have to take my leave, as my meetings are quite important. You'll be fine though, now that they are expecting you; and even if these places don't work out, I should have more time to spare tomorrow. We'll get your order sorted."

The sign outside the final business that Dunin was leading Shanti to said Aiskuu. It was painted neatly and formally on a well-made panel that hung from a simple sturdy iron framework leaning out from the brick wall. Everything about the building's facade, from the well painted doorframe and window sills to the simple stone statues of lions that sat stoically to either side of the entryway, said that this was a well-run establishment. However, the entrance was at the end of the block of buildings, and an alleyway neighboured it. Shadow spilled from the alley and she found herself walking slower as they approached Aiskuu.

"Are you sure that this is a good company?" she asked her uncle.

He paused and turned towards her, though he looked up at the sky as he moved. He shaded his eyes with a hand and muttered softly to himself. "...be enough time, if they have space quickly," was all Shanti was able to hear before he looked at her and spoke at a more normal volume. "What do you mean? These are perfectly good traders."

"I'm sure that they have been. But, well, what about..." Shanti tried to gesture discreetly at the alleyway. Now that they were closer, she was able to see the thin black lines of light vines that had previously grown around the corner and over the door and windows of this business. They spun out and spread across the bricks like veins, but to see them black and lifeless was shocking to Shanti. She was used to lights bringing brightness into the world, colour and safety. These thin brittle twigs, snapping off like burnt branches were unsettling. It was too much.

"Oh. Yes, the blight is causing severe problems all over." Dunin frowned and stroked his beard. "Well, we will meet with them, but keep your eyes open for any lights that look ill. They will have done every-thing they can to keep the blight out of their green-houses, but you never know when tragedy can strike." And with that, he offered his arm to his niece.

Feeling nervous, but glad that he had taken her concerns seriously, she placed one hand on his elbow, and they entered Aiskuu.

"Dunin!" came a woman's voice as soon as they stepped inside. "It's wonderful to see you! Where have you been?"

The speaker was dressed in deep blues that made it look as though she had wrapped herself in the night sky. She wore a thin vine of lights as a sash, the tiny leaves appearing as though stars in her clothing. Wearing lights, thought Shanti to herself. That's amazing! I wonder how she keeps them alive. As the woman strode closer, arms outstretched to greet Dunin, Shanti realised that there couldn't be any way of keeping the vine alive after it was borne for almost any length of time. She must dispose of the vine at the end of the day. The realisation left Shanti feeling both impressed and shocked by the sheer outra-geousness of the waste. But it does make her look amazing, she thought.

"Good afternoon Zala. My, that outfit is absolutely incredible." Dunin met the woman with his own outstretched hands and they both gripped tight and smiled into each other's faces.

"Thank you so much," Zala replied, and released his hands so that she could step back and spin around. "I love it." Once she had finished spinning and turned back to Dunin, she crossed her arms and pursed her lips. "So, what finally brings you back to these dusty rooms?"

"My niece," Dunin said, bowing slightly and indicating Shanti. Zala looked over Shanti with a professional eye, but at least there was no overt judgement in her gaze. Zala held out a hand.

"It's a pleasure to meet you my dear," she said, and they shook hands politely.

"And you," replied Shanti. Zala's eyes flickered slightly, whether in amusement or familiarity Shanti was unsure, but then all focus returned to her uncle.

The pair linked elbows and walked back beyond the desks and counters and into a small office, painted with light cream colours and featuring ornamented mouldings around the edges of the ceiling. Shanti followed, unsure of whether she should or not, and sat in a chair next to Dunin in the office. As the pleasantries rolled off of the others' tongues, she glanced around the room and noted several small holes in the mouldings.

When there was a lull in the conversation, she leaned forward with her question prepared. "What are these holes for?"

"We're very proud of those actually," smiled Zala. "They are light holes. Instead of training the vines up a wall and into position, it is possible to grow them through small tunnels so that they grow only where you desire them. This room once held a wonderful crown of lights in those curls and crevices." Zala's head rose as she spoke, and her shoulders shifted back.

"So why are there none growing now?" Shanti's question lay in the room like a dead fish, immediately noticeable and obviously it must be dealt with but no one wanted to touch it. Zala cleared her throat.

"We are off season."

"Yes Shanti, you must take the seasons into account," rushed Dunin, clutching his hands together and rubbing his left thumb with the thumb and fingers of the right. "Everyone knows that the seasons can be very difficult for many lights, conditions must be kept pristine for optimum growth. Isn't that right Zala?"

"Exactly so, my dear." Zala nodded sharply.

"Of course, I don't know why I didn't think of it," Shanti offered. "I remember how much Sudru complained and moaned when the mayor or some shopkeeper wanted to keep the same light in their window through summer to autumn."

"Just so, just so," nodded Dunin again.

The conversation was muted for a moment, but soon Zala and Dunin were joking and laughing again. At one stage Shanti was surprised to see Dunin lay his hand on the desk and Zala reach over to touch his fingers, just briefly. Even so, the familiarity of it surprised her. Finally the impromptu meeting drew to a close, with Dunin apologetically drawing attention to his prior engagements.

"I really am very sorry, it has been so good to speak with you again. And I haven't even asked about little Reetak! How is he doing?" Dunin was half standing, half crouching over his chair. Zala stood and rushed around to walk with him out of the office.

"Reetak is fine, he is fine! He's begun hanging around with some other boys and playing ball in the streets in the afternoons, such a delight!"

Shanti followed them out through the lobby and past the desks.

"It is such a shame that we can't speak long," her uncle was saying, "But I really must leave now if I'm to make it to my other meetings."

"I quite understand, really I do," Zala assured him. "I know how busy the life of a scoundrel such as yourself must be." But she spoke with such a wide smile that Shanti assumed that the insult must be a fond joke.

Eventually, after more apologies and reassurances, Shanti and Dunin were standing outside the doorway to Aiskuu, abandoned by the whirlwind inside to the humdrum seeming commotion of the streets. Dunin looked to the sky, where the sun was definitely sitting lower than Shanti had expected. Shadows were beginning to stretch quite far.

Dunin sighed deeply.

"Okay Shanti," he said, somewhat distractedly. "I'm sorry to leave you now, but we got three appointments set up with brokers. Go back through the offices in the same order we just saw them and you should be fine. They know who you are now."

"Did I get an appointment though?" Throughout the cavalcade of quips and laughter, she hadn't noticed Dunin actually ask Zala about Shanti's order.

"Oh yes," he replied, waving aside the question with his hand. "Zala will see you when you return, don't worry about that."

Shanti nodded.

"Thank you for your help," she said, although she still wasn't sure if she couldn't have got largely the same amount of attention from most of the offices if she had simply arrived by herself. At least he did show her to the district, and showed her how to use the ferryboats. Without that she may have taken longer to arrive.

"You're welcome. Remember, let them sell themselves to you, and don't react to their quotes. Tell them what you want but not what you have. And under no circumstances agree to a deal without thinking on it overnight!"

Shanti smiled, hoping her uncle took it as an expression of her thanks for his advice. In reality, all she could think of was the way his eyes sharpened and the way he pointed to the sky as he made his points. He looked and moved so much like her mother that the resemblance was uncanny. Furthermore, her mother had looked like this while giving an almost identical speech regarding negotiations with some of the more duplicitous members of Graama, ensuring the young Shanti would not be fooled or swindled when she first started working in the store.

Dunin looked her in the eye, searching for something. She didn't know what it was that he hoped to find, but he seemed satisfied and then nodded once.

"I think you'll be fine," he said with confidence. He reached out with both hands and held her shoulders. There was even the hint of a smile in the corner of his mouth. "Well, I'll see you at my apartment later on!"

And with that, he spun on his heels and set off into the crowd. Within moments he was lost to sight in the swirling tide of pedestrians and Shanti found herself alone.

WAITING in the lobby of Oibaa felt less overwhelming now that Shanti felt purposeful about her presence.

Previously she had been following Dunin, with no real understanding of what it was he was going to do. But now she knew that she was going to be speaking to a broker, she knew what she wanted. The feeling held her neck high and straight.

Before long, her name was called and a young clerk bustled along to guide her to an office in the distance. They walked side by side up a wide flight of stone stairs, the pale surface gleaming under lights that grew in coils above the bannisters. At the top of the stairs was a broad and bright hallway with many doors, and the clerk gestured Shanti into one with a smile wide enough to reveal every tooth in his mouth.

Inside, Shanti found herself facing a middle aged man that reminded her very much of Dunin, although he had thick black hair, worn loose and long. However, he wore his hair firmly brushed back from his face and his clothing was stiffer than Dunin's. The collar stood firm and close around the man's neck, and the edges and folds of his sleeves were almost like folded paper, so sharp did they seem.

"Good afternoon," said the man as he stood to welcome Shanti into the office. "My name is Ortan. What can I help you with today?" His handshake was firm and professional.

Shanti sat in the chair by his desk and explained that she had been sent by the village in order to procure lights for their upcoming festival. She tried not to give away how much money she had been sent with, and instead focused on describing the way the village would be decorated, and the feeling that such a display needed to inspire in her family and friends. The burden of ensuring that the festival was an exciting day for them all weighed upon her. As she spoke, Ortan leaned forward in his seat. Shanti found herself thinking of the cat that lived next door at home. Something about its eyes when he licked cream from a saucer.

"I think we can help you with this," he said, standing up again. "Come with me."

They left the office together, Ortan taking care to walk with Shanti rather than leading the way. As they walked he made small talk, asking her about her family back in the village, and her childhood. Soon they approached a large vaulted metal doorway.

"This is our Greenhouse," he said, with pride in his voice. With a grunt of effort, he turned the massive metal handles on the door and began to swing it open, as slowly as a cow chewing in a field.

Beyond the door was a scene like nothing Shanti had ever imagined. Lights grew in thick tangles of vines in every hue, from pale and bright to deep and solid. Light fruits blazed in bunches, piercing the vista with their concentrated knots of light, echoed in the leaves that spread or spiked from vines and branches. There were species Shanti had never heard of before, with trunks of normal wood, or branches likewise. There was one fascinating tree that grew straight and branchless for nearly 3 meters before erupting into a canopy of vines that collapsed to the ground like a dress, and none of it shone except for clusters of small berry sized light fruits at the end of each branch.

Shanti found herself squinting, and lifting a hand to shield her eyes from the sea of light. There was no escape, no shadows at all in this growing space. Through tightly squeezed eyelids, Shanti was able to see that in the distance above them hung huge glass panels that created a barrier to the outside world, trapping the sun's heat and nourishment inside. Oibaa knew how to grow lights.

Ortan handed over a pair of simple round spectacles with darkened glass in the lenses. Shanti slipped them on and looked around. The world became dimmer and darker, though the colour and light still washed over her.

"These are very good!" she said, as Ortan extended a hand and led her forward into the brilliant jungle.

"Yes they are!" he smiled.

The path wound in slow curves around the trunks of the larger light trees, and wove past the small stone walls keeping the light gardens in check. Demure white wooden signs, none larger than Shanti's palm, labelled various light-beds and identified different species and varieties of light. Past the foliage, Shanti's spectacles allowed her to just make out thick fluted columns that soared to the roof and supported its arches upon curling carved stone that looked like the spiral at the end of a vine. Beneath her feet tiny square pieces of stone and glass in mosaics covered the path, depicting human figures dancing and twirling among white clouds.

Before Shanti was ready, Ortan led her back through the massive vault doors to the offices and the mundane world. Shanti turned to look over her shoulder for one last look at the brightness that vanished as the door swung shut. She sighed and handed her spectacles back. "It's truly magnificent."

"Thank you very much," beamed Ortan, his teeth seeming to shine as bright as the lights they had just left behind. He guided Shanti back to his office. "We work extremely hard in order to get the most powerful lights, with the strongest shine. And of course, it is the off season. Keeping that much foliage alive and prospering takes an awfully large effort!"

"Yes, I can easily imagine."

They sat down. Ortan leaned forward across his desk, with one hand around the other, resting on his elbows. His smile still stretched wide as he asked "So, what were you looking for?"

Shanti found herself feeling quite on display as she reached into her satchel for the list that she had been given. She managed to keep herself from handing it over, somehow feeling that would be completely giving over control of the meeting to this man. She didn't want to feel browbeaten into a deal that was no good. Instead, she held onto the list and read most of the entries out to him, discussing as much of the finer points as she could. She noted that time was limited, but that she also had a clear list of species, sizes, and colours that the village council were interested in.

"... asked for the smallest white blossoms that we could conceivably have in a line on either side of the main path to the village inn, so that they outline the way in for visitors and participants. But I thought that perhaps a vine might be easier to train that way, with some stakes or hoops to support it? Or even if there is a moss or lichen, would stones work for such a purpose?"

Shanti could tell this had been the correct way to proceed. Ortan showed no sign that he was surprised or taken aback by her choice to read the list to him, then sat back into his chair as she began. Soon he had pulled out a thin pencil that he used to begin making notes on a small pad that he pulled close from the side of the desk. He nodded as Shanti spoke, adding his own comments from time to time.

"Yes, I would agree with you, the broader leafed varieties would suit that much more, they tend towards a more diffuse light. Going with a narrow leaf, or even a blossom, in orange could create more of a point of light, which could be a distraction for viewers."

Eventually, she came to the end of the list. She felt breathless, as though she had run a race against the children from the streets back home, with the slightly damp forehead and neck to go with it, but her heart was racing with the flush of success.

"I think we can work through most of this," nodded Ortan, looking at his notes with a stern face. Then he raised his eyes and the smile flashed up again. "Of course, it is the off season. Some of these may not be available."

Shanti raised a hand and waved it, as though his comments were of no consequence. The thrill of running this meeting properly was making her confidence explode. "I am sure that I can trust you to make appropriate decisions in such cases."

Ortan smiled again, then stood. "Please wait here while I consult with some others. We should be able to give you at least a rough estimate of costs within a few minutes. While I'm gone, shall I send you through a cup of tea or some refreshments?"

"Actually, a lemon and ginger tea would be wonderful, if you have such a thing?"

"Of course." Ortan dipped his head and slipped out of the room.

Shanti felt wonderful. This was what she wanted to be doing, talking about money and important decisions that would affect her whole village. And she was able to do it! Ortan hadn't laughed at, or even acted amused by the way she had run things. Clearly he was used to different levels of expertise, but Shanti had fit in. The door opened and a young clerk came in with a cup of tea steaming on a saucer.

"Here you are ma'am," said the young woman, before leaving almost too quickly for Shanti to thank her. She leaned back in the chair and sipped at the tea. It was warm and delicious. Shanti allowed the aroma from the cup to rise up and breathe through her nose as she relaxed. This was all going to work out fine.

AFTER A FEW MORE MINUTES, as Shanti neared the end of her tea, Ortan walked back in through the door. He sat back at the desk and opened his notebook, smoothing the pages down with both hands and then running one hand through his hair to keep it out of his eyes.

"Okay, we should have most of this stock ready to go," he began. "There are a few species that we don't have at the moment, or at least," and here he winked at Shanti. "We have some but they are too young for travel or cutting still."

"That makes sense."

"So, here is a list of costs based on what you told me. I've totalled the product at the bottom of the page. However, that doesn't include transport costs." He pushed the notebook over towards Shanti, spinning it as he did. "We do have some transport options we can offer to help you with, but often people prefer to speak to their own contacts for that. We are completely happy either way."

Shanti looked down at the dark numbers scratched onto the white paper with his pencil. Ortan had circled the total in a flourish, at the bottom of a column of smaller, neatly arranged numbers. The room began to retreat, the walls shifting and racing away from Shanti. Sounds became muffled, and she was suddenly very aware of her own breathing. It sounded too harsh, as though she had picked up a cold or a sore throat. She tried to slow it down, to breathe easier. That number couldn't be right.

"I'm just looking over the individual costs," she heard herself offer, moving a finger down the column.

"Certainly," she heard Ortan reply, as though from the far side of a curtain.

No, these were all correct. The list included everything that they had discussed from her list, and the costs were lined up correctly. They were just so much more than Shanti had ever imagined they could possibly be! She was reasonably certain that there was nowhere near this much money available to her for the order, although she would have to investigate some of the bank notes that she had been provided with. If she had this much money available to her, she could probably buy the entire village!

"Okay, well that all seems to be in order. May I take this page with me to consider overnight?" She could hear Dunins's firm instructions ringing in her ears.

Ortan nodded, then reached out to slowly tear the page out along the spine. He folded it in half, creasing the edge, and handed it over to her.

"Thank you very much for coming to see Oibaa for your light needs. We hope that you decide to confirm this order with us in the near future." He spoke with seeming sincerity. Shanti smiled and thanked him, and then rose, making her way back out of the office and through the lobby to leave the building.

She waited until she had begun to walk away from the offices before letting herself slump slightly and lean against a wall. One of the other meetings she was going to had better be able to provide much better prices than that! After feeling so confident, she was beginning to worry again.

Gathering herself together, Shanti patted the pocket on the outside of her satchel where she had placed the folded quote from Oibaa for safe keeping. She was fairly certain that she would never even remove it from that pocket again, but one never knew.

Shanti stood tall on the path, lifting her chin and breathing deeply. The smell of the city and the river filled her lungs. The darkening light of the afternoon matched the scent of bodies and moisture in her mind. But further down the street lay the offices of Artee, and she hoped that things would go better there. With her newfound experience at negotiating keeping her blood pumping and her cheeks flushed, Shanti strode down the street.

ARTEE WAS JUST as it had been a little over an hour earlier, though the afternoon light brought a red tinge to the well-crafted letters on their sign. After Shanti entered she found that there was a different boy at the desks now, even younger than the previous boy had been. A few wisps of new beard curled by his ears. However, he knew his job well enough, and when she gave her name and asked for her meeting with a dealer, the boy quickly passed on the message and delivered Shanti to an office through a door behind his desks.

This office was not as large and airy as the last she had been in. Instead of large stone walls and curved white designs lining the corners of wall and ceiling, she found wooden panels, buffed to a shine and featuring golden inlay that lightened the overall effect. It still looked expensive, but she hoped that wood was cheaper than stone overall.

The man sitting at his desk rose to greet Shanti and ushered her to a seat. His smile was more genuine than the others that she had seen today. He was almost entirely bald, with only a narrow band of black curls that stretched around the back of his head from ear to ear, and he pulled a handkerchief from his jacket pocket to dab away some sweat from the top of his head before he sat down again.

"Good afternoon my dear, my name is Orlin. I understand you have an order that you are looking for a quote of?" He squinted a little as he spoke.

"Yes thank you." Shanti retrieved the notes and went through them again with Orlin. This time she felt much more comfortable, having done it already not long ago. Orlin took notes in much the same manner as Ortan had, asking similar questions. When Shanti finished, he leant back on his chair and frowned, tapping his lips with the pencil as he studied his notes.

The buttons on his shirt were pulled quite tight against his belly as he sat in this position and Shanti cleared her throat and adjusted her gaze. He blinked and looked back up at her, sitting forward as he did so. She was fairly sure that he was simply startled to realise that she was still there, and that he had no idea of the way he had been sitting. She wondered what sort of dream world he had found himself in.

"You seem unhappy?" she asked carefully.

"Oh, no no no!" Orlin dropped the paper and reached out, as if he thought that Shanti was about to run out of the office and he might be able to grasp onto her and stop her. "I'm sorry if my expression became concerned! I was just contemplating what our orchards and gardens are like at the moment. I fear we may not be able to fulfil all of your expectations."

"Oh, I thought that you might be able to make some suggestions of other species that could replace the ones you can't provide, for a similar effect?"

"Oh, I see." Orlin frowned again. "I… certainly, I think… I think that I could manage that. Shall we take a tour of the greenhouses, and see what we can find?" He stood, straightening his pale brown jacket and extending a hand to help Shanti rise from her chair.

"That sounds perfect," she smiled.

The greenhouses were well built and carefully maintained, but Shanti found that she was unable to look over them without comparison to the massive stone and glass structures she had experienced in Oibaa. Here the houses were built of iron and glass, with each one existing as a smaller individual structure that housed a small variety of similar lights. As they got close enough to begin peeking through the doorways of each greenhouse, Shanti realised that they were truly huge structures in their own right, and it was simply that Oibaa had converted the entirety of the building into a greenhouse. These were nearly two stories tall, and tens of meters long. Lightskeepers worked in each, potting small young plants, pruning dead vines and branches.

Orlin began pointing out houses that contained the plants that she had on her list, and Shanti found herself excited to begin imagining what the village council had in store. She was impressed at the broad flat crimson leaves that were intended to place above each doorway along the main street. Those lights grew leaves so thin that they would lift and wave softly if the wind was of a respectable level. And despite that effect, the light that they gave off was strong and clear.

There were various thin vines that the council intended to outline window frames, some of pale blue and others a chilly green. She found herself drawn to a species that grew a deep yellow and was tempted to add it to that part of the order. She herself felt that the colours complimented, but she was worried that there was more than she knew in the decision of which colours to include, and as such she didn't feel that she could make such a change without discussion.

Orlin spoke apologetically as he pointed out the nearly empty greenhouses that would have contained some of the plants Shanti was tasked with ordering.

"As you can see, it has been a good year and we have sold much of our stock." He smiled but his eyes were lifted with a faint anxiety. "We would love to provide you with these lights, but…" He trailed off as they both peeked inside the greenhouse.

It was surprisingly dark inside, a fact that made Shanti reassess what she had been seeing in all the other greenhouses. They had been clear and easy to see through due to the combined glow from the various lights growing within. However, here the beds were almost utterly empty, full of rich dark soil that was being turned by a team of young children under the supervision of an older lightskeeper. The lightskeeper turned to the doorway and waved slightly at the visitors. Shanti waved back at her.

Along the sides of the greenhouse were row upon row of trays, each containing a small container of soil with a single spike sticking up from it. These were clearly new shoots of the lights for this greenhouse. Some of the shoots were beginning to pull aside as they grew and stretched higher.

"I suppose I ought to congratulate you on your success at least," joked Shanti.

Orlin bowed his head and grinned. "Thank you very much my dear."

"So, do you think you could suggest any alternatives?"

Orlin drew his handkerchief and wiped his forehead again. "I, uh, unfortunately am not the most familiar..." he began to explain in a voice that trailed off into softness.

"You looking for alternatives, eh?" The voice that cut across Shanti's hearing was deep and rough. Shanti turned to find the lightskeeper from inside the greenhouse walking over towards them.

"Yes, I am. I have quite a specific list that I-"

"Let's see then."

Shanti was too flustered by the brusque way that the newcomer was speaking to her, but Orlin recovered quickly, pulling his notes out. He began to point out the items that he was unable to provide but the lightskeeper shushed him and read it to herself, murmuring slightly as she did.

"Simple enough," she declared when she reached the end "I could find you some pretty good replacements for most of these. Got a pencil on you?" This question was directed to Orlin. He patted his pockets and then handed one over. The keeper made some extra notations and then handed it back to Orlin. He ran a finger across the page and smiled.

"I can update your quote with these options if you like?" he suggested and handed the paper over. Shanti looked at the new names noted alongside his handwriting.

"How reliable are you?" she asked, without looking up. A silence greeted her question, making her raise her eyes. They met the lightskeeper's own gaze, eyes like stones staring back at her. "Oh. Uh, I suppose you must know your job pretty well."

"I do."

"This is reliable then, I'm sure."

After a little more conversation, Shanti and Orlin returned to his office in order to write up a quote for the lights she needed. Shanti shook hands with the lightskeeper as she left, and before she knew it, found herself standing outside the building with another possible order ready to be confirmed and filled as soon as she was happy to do so. At least this felt like a much more reasonable price, she thought to herself. The amounts asked were less than half the costs of Oibaa, and Shanti thought it was very unlikely that she would accept that quote.

However, Artee didn't have nearly as many of the lights that had been asked for and, regardless of the stern expertise of the woman that worked in the greenhouse, Shanti wasn't sure that it would be reasonable to return with so many replacements and alternatives.

Feeling a little less sure of the outcome, even though she had felt more in control of the meeting, Shanti tucked the new piece of paper into her satchel and headed off down the street towards Aiskuu.

THE WALK WAS PLEASANT, although the air was beginning to feel quite chilly and Shanti wished she had a thicker shawl to pull around her shoulders. After the heat that had greeted her arrival in Gorduum, this breeze was unexpected. The crowds were as heavy as ever and crossing the road was difficult once she saw the sign for her final meeting.

She paused and stood outside, taking in the building and its surroundings again.

The darkness of the alleyway concerned her. Those dead lights curling around the bricks to the main road were encroaching upon Aiskuu in a way that made her stomach curdle. The sight of dead lights at all was something that she found surprisingly upsetting. She had seen dead lights before of course, because lights grew and flowered and then died. But usually the plant itself would continue, merely wilting and losing leaves. Usually there was some new growth of light, or at least a shoot such as the ones she had just seen in the greenhouse.

But here, the branches were dead. They were dried and flaking, pale and dusty versions of themselves, visions of unusual decay.

With a heavy sigh, she walked up to the door and entered.

Shanti received an enthusiastic welcome inside Aiskuu. Zala came back to speak to her personally, though the sincerity of her conversation never quite reached her eyes. Shanti went through the same motions again, with Zala offering similar excuses and apologies as Orlin had. Of course, this was due to the season having only recently ended, and the new growths still being too young to take cuttings from or replant. Once Zala had written down an offer, she politely but firmly began to encourage Shanti to leave. However, the cracked branches from the alley were tangled at the back of Shanti's mind and she found that she didn't want to leave the office without seeing the greenhouses of the company.

"I was wondering if you had time to take me through your greenhouses?"

"It is very late, and I'm sure you can appreciate the delicacy of lights while they are so young."

"I can, but I just feel that I couldn't risk selecting a supplier without being sure that the colours and sizes were truly 'just so'." Shanti felt a tightness in her throat as she spoke, but consoled herself by thinking that it wasn't a lie. She truly would feel troubled if she accepted this supplier and discovered that their lights didn't match the expectations that the council had expressed. She didn't have to tell Zala that she was chiefly concerned that whatever disease had affected the streetlights outside could have insinuated itself into the Aiskuu greenhouses.

Zala grimaced and almost rolled her eyes. Shanti was surprised to see such a display of rude behaviour at the request of a customer. She wondered if it was because Dunin had introduced them. After all, if Zala was familiar and comfortable with him, maybe that meant she was willing to let her guard down a little with Shanti. That would probably work in Shanti's favour in the long run. People who were friendly with one another were often more willing to take a lower cut in order to put together a deal that works.

"Fine, I'll take you through. Just-" Zala paused and waved a hand in Shanti's direction while making a low grunting noise. "Can you just… be careful?" And then she turned and headed out of the office, barely waiting to see if Shanti was following.

On the other hand, though Shanti, maybe having Dunin introduce her was actually a problem? Now this woman wouldn't see her as a proper business person with a real deal to negotiate. Maybe Zala just thought Shanti was Dunin's silly farm girl niece, in the city to feel important but really just a rube to pat on the head and pass on. As they walked down a short hallway and through a few doors, locked but opened quickly via a key hanging at Zala's side, Shanti began to consider how she must look to the world outside her own head. Who's to say that she really wasn't just a farm girl rube in the big city? Maybe she really was being patted on the head by all these businesses.

She pushed her shoulders back and lifted her chin. No matter. She still had a job to do, and other people's possible opinions of her couldn't be allowed to get in the way of that.

Eventually Zala pushed open a set of dark wooden double doors that creaked heavily as they moved. The scene that lay beyond was full of light and shadow.

At first it was hard for Shanti to understand what she was looking at, even though she had just seen other greenhouses less than an hour earlier. There was the same eruption of light that she had experienced in the other greenhouses, but here it was shaped and directed. Whereas at the others she had worn glasses, or shielded her eyes, in order to manage with the volume of light that was pouring towards them, here the walls of the greenhouses were thicker and more solid. The light bloomed out of their roofs, which Shanti could only assume must be glass, or even open to the elements, in order to receive the nourishment of the sun. But there were only a few support beams and panels on the distant roof to reflect that light, and so what Shanti saw was mostly darkness with only beams and lines drawn in light criss-crossing her vision.

Shanti began to walk into the room but Zala stopped her with a hand out as a barrier.

"Sorry, but we have decided to take some precautions recently."

The older woman pointed to Shanti's right, where a bucket sat with some stiff bristled brushes similar to the sort that Shanti had seen people brushing down horses with.

"What's this?"

"We have some scholars who assist us in our work, helping us develop new strains of light, or better fertilisers."

"That makes sense. But..." Shanti found she didn't want to finish the question.

"Well, they have told us that this solution will help

ensure that nothing dangerous enters the green-houses without our knowing about it." Zala's face was drawn and suddenly Shanti realised how much older than herself the woman must be. The reluctance to show the greenhouses wasn't anything positive or negative about Shanti, but a reflection of the difficulties the company must have been having with them.

"What sorts of things could enter the greenhouses?" She asked as she sat down on a small wooden bench by the bucket, dipped in the brush and began scrubbing the soles of her shoes, as instructed by Zala.

Zala groaned. "Oh, you know, it's just about precautions." She rubbed her forehead and then pinched the bridge of her nose, then sat down to scrub her own shoes. "Look, I'm sure you noticed the dead lights in the alley next to our office?"

Shanti nodded, without meeting the other woman's eyes.

"Well, that's some sort of blight that's been growing across the whole city."

"I'd heard," murmured Shanti. Dunin had mentioned it before they came in before, and there had been that headline in the newspaper.

"So you can't blame us for all this." Zala took in the bucket and brushes. "Obviously if we were to find blight in our greenhouses..." She couldn't continue the sentence.

"It would be devastating." Shanti finished for her. The other woman simply nodded.

"Come on. I'll show you around."

They moved closer and Shanti discovered that Aiskuu was keeping its greenhouses carefully monitored. A worker stood at each doorway, clearly more concerned with keeping people out of the greenhouse than tending the lights within. They nodded at Zala as she and Shanti approached, but they did not move aside.

"We'd just like to have a look inside," said Zala, and Shanti was surprised that the tone of voice clearly communicated that this was a request, not a command. Shanti had assumed that Zala was in charge of this company, surely she could simply tell these workers what to do?

The worker at the door opened her mouth as though she was going to say something, and then closed it again. She leaned over to the door, but didn't open it. Instead, she pulled on a small handle set into a panel on the door and Shanti made a small noise of surprise as the panel moved sideways to reveal a hole in the door. Zala motioned her closer and they looked through the hole into the greenhouse.

Shanti was unimpressed by the lights beyond the door. She peered through as carefully as she could, craning her neck to try and get multiple angles of view of the lights beyond, but it was almost impossible to get a good view from such a restricted vantage point. Maybe it was the huge displays that she had been lucky to see at the previous companies, but these greenhouses were almost barren in comparison. She was barely squinting, so soft was the light that she was looking at.

"So, we can't actually go in to have a look around?" she asked.

"No," was Zala's clipped reply, as though she had to restrain herself from further explanation.

"Earlier in the day we might have," offered the worker who was still standing nearby and watching. "Then we would have had time to do a good prep clean and swap your shoes for our boots, all of that sort of work." She smiled ruefully. "But it takes ages, and I want to go home soon."

"I see." Shanti looked back into the hole. The lights within were alluring colours, she supposed. This was a greenhouse of fern lights, uncoiling like tails or chandeliers, in many hues.

Just as she stepped back, as the worker slid the panel closed again, Shanti thought she saw a grey branch sticking up from the lower left of the garden beds. It looked like it was made of ash, with fine lines tracing all over it, as though a spider web had sliced through it. But maybe it was just a shadow. Maybe it was the remains of a light from last season.

Zala began to lead them away from the greenhouses. Shanti felt as though she should mention the branch, or ask more about the precautions that they were taking. But she couldn't. They entered Zala's office and the older woman waited for the younger to sit first.

"So," she said, leaning back and pushing a hand through her hair, pulling a thick wavy bunch forward over her shoulder. "Shall I write you up a quote?" She sounded resigned.

Maybe her attitude had nothing to do with Dunin, realised Shanti. *Maybe she is just tired of trying to survive in the face of the blight?*

"Yes, thank you," replied Shanti. She noted the blink as Zala realised what she had said, and felt a laugh begin to rise from her stomach. She managed to turn it into a clearing of her throat by the time it emerged. She thought *I would say no!* With the knowledge that she was going to think on all her quotes overnight, Shanti knew that it wouldn't hurt to get this one as well. But she also knew that she did not feel inclined to accept the offer.

Zala finished writing her prices down and slid the

paper across to Shanti. "Here you are." She smiled, as bright and fragile as rose petals made of ice. "I hope we see you back here soon."

"That would make me happy too," smiled Shanti, before rising and leaving.

SHANTI BEGAN WALKING against the mob of pedestrians back towards the steps above the river. She was looking forward to finding a riverboat that would get her back to her uncle's apartment. As she walked, she found herself no longer distracted by the scale and noise of the Gorduum. Whereas earlier she had been looking to the sky, watching the clouds pass over the distant rooftops and gigantic buildings, now she was looking at the corners around her. Looking into the alleys and doorways as she passed, watching where buildings meet pavement or path. And she was discovering that Gorduum was not as glorious as she had initially thought.

There were more people sitting in those corners than she had noticed earlier. Most of those people looked tired, slumped down on the spot, and wrapped in layers of worn out clothes. Rubbish blew between the feet of passers-by and gathered in the same corners. Old newspapers, leaves and twigs, bits of broken bottle.

And down many of the darker alleyways, Shanti could see old dead light vines and branches. It was "the end of the season" she had heard so often. It's not the right season just now, they said. And yet, these lights looked more dead than that could explain. She wondered how long lights would still be growing in Gorduum.

Shanti walked down the long low stairs back to the Naatat. Light was draining from the sky rapidly now, and the clouds were beginning to turn red and yellow, like the autumn trees near Graama. The sheer number of pedestrians was still much more than Shanti was used to, though there was beginning to be a shift in their direction. More of her fellow travellers were turning towards the river, or away from the light trader offices at least.

At the bottom of the stairs, the ferry-pilots were much quieter than they had been earlier in the day. Each had a queue of people lined up by them, engaged in quick conversation as prices and destinations were haggled over and agreed to. The boats were filling up, and some were already untying and heading out into the choppy water of the river. Boats and ships of all sizes were moving up and down the river, leaving waves of wake behind them that criss-crossed and leapt with white curls.

Shanti was looking for Varlin, feeling that a semi-familiar face would ensure she felt confident about getting back to her uncle's. The river water appeared thick and black in the encroaching evening air.

But, after walking up and down the dock for ten minutes, she realised that Varlin wasn't here. She wondered whether it would be worth waiting. Other pilots were heading into the dock as she watched. Clearly this was an area that was known for picking up fares in the evenings. However, she could see similar locations dotted along the opposite riverside, at such a distance that the boats and people were small coloured dots, barely bigger than ants. The chances that he would come back to this exact spot must have been low. Eventually she resolved that she would simply have to find a new pilot to get home.

Walking along the row of boats again, Shanti looked more closely at the pilots, and at the passengers who were already settling themselves into the ferries. First was a man too oily and greasy for her liking, with matted hair that stuck down on his skull. Then came a tall and clean pilot with a nice smile, but the glares of the men in fine suits seated on his boat made Shanti keep walking. After four or five similar decisions, Shanti found a pilot who had just shaken hands with a young man in a heavily starched shirt and then helped him climb aboard. She was shorter than Shanti, but built like a barrel, much wider than tall. She had shoulder length curls of black hair, and a soft face with bright brown eyes that met hers with a friendly sparkle. She hefted a long heavy wooden pole as she looked Shanti up and down.

"Want a lift do ya?"

"Yes please, I need to get to Arfa district. Is that close to these others?" Shanti indicated the four or five others already seated.

The lady sniffed and tilted her head as she considered this. "It's close enough. That'll be five."

Five. Shanti recalled paying more than double that for herself and Dunin earlier. She pursed her lips at the memory, anger flushing her cheeks that her uncle would take advantage of her for one of his colleagues.

"Oh, not good enough for you?" asked the pilot. "Well my young lady, I can tell you-"

"No, no, it is definitely good enough." Shanti explained, reaching for her satchel. "You just made me think of something that happened earlier today."

"Oh." The pilot leaned back a little, mollified by the explanation, but making no apology for her reaction.

Shanti handed over the money and then accepted the support of the pilot's long staff as she got into the boat. She sat down and settled her skirts close around her. The young clerk who had got on before her was sitting to her right, and around them sat an older man wearing a very tall hat and absent-mindedly stroking his thick white moustache; a middle aged woman with one hand holding the back of her child's clothes, a young boy with spiky hair and a grubby face who was leaning dangerously far over the sides of the boat; and a middle aged man wearing heavy work clothes whose eyes were drooping as though he were about to go to sleep.

The pilot had a crew of two and not long after Shanti sat down it appeared that she was ready to get moving. With plenty of shouted obscenities and threats, the crew and the pilot got the ferry untied and moved out into the river, where they began to turn with the current and head back downriver towards where Shanti had set out earlier that afternoon.

Varlin had used four crew, each on a long oar, whereas this ferry only had the two. Shanti wondered if that might have been a legitimate reason for the higher price he had charged. She also wondered if this ferry was able to move as quickly as his had done. At least for her purposes, it moved fast enough. The current helped carry them.

BEFORE LONG, Shanti found herself moving back along the same streets that she and her uncle had come up earlier that afternoon. As the light of the sun in the sky bled away, the vines and lights that grew over every doorway began to reveal their strength and colour. Though each path was illuminated by the growths on the walls, Shanti found that Gorduum had attained a shadow that wouldn't be pushed aside by their efforts.

As she walked, she noticed people sitting down in

dusty doorways, or in the lee of stairways or fountains, sheltering themselves from the breeze. They pulled dark and worn cloaks and blankets around their shoulders and stared at nothing. Shanti was pretty sure these were more of the Skuggi that Keema had told her about earlier. Quite a few were slowly heading towards the darker alleys, where the lights were dying most. She assumed that was where the blight was heaviest. Then she wondered if the rumour that these people had anything to do with the blight could be true. She looked around at her fellow pedestrians and noticed that she wasn't the only one glancing at the wanderers in the alleys. There were some pitying expressions, but many more were glaring or frowning. Maybe these Skuggi really were causing the blight somehow. She resolved to ask her uncle more about it when she got back to the apartment.

She was glad most of the lights were alive and thriving, as they ensured that the boulevard was still lit well. She was beginning to feel anxious, wondering if she stood out as a foreigner to the city, an easy mark for the sorts of people who might take advantage of the shadows in the night. She offered a silent prayer to the Masked God to ensure its eyes were upon her. Thankfully, she realised that she was on the correct street to return to the apartment. She had to focus herself in order to continue walking, and not break into a run. Tall iron light posts ran in regular intervals down the centre of the street, roots and trunks spiralling around the metal that had been shaped to mimic the living forms that grew around it. They plunged into rich dark soil below each post, sheltered by a carefully constructed iron cage that would allow for sun, water and rudimentary tending by Gorduum's gardeners. Far above, the huge broad leaves of streetlights spread out and shone with a harsh orange glow. These were hardy lights, survivors of even quite rough weather and treatment. They could be encouraged to grow well all year, and as such were fantastically useful for just this purpose.

As she climbed the stairs, faster than she was proud of, she heard voices from her uncle's floor. She reached the top and turned to see her uncle in conversation with the man who had been leaving the house that morning again, the one who had nearly run her down the day before. Shanti was struck by his long hair and the way it caught the light from the white and pale blue blooms in the ceiling. It shimmered, like the Naatat River.

Dunin was smiling, but it was the same smile that Shanti had been blessed with during the majority of this trip. It revealed his teeth, bright and white in his dark face, but the smile did not reach his eyes. There was no sparkle to them. Dunin turned and noticed Shanti approaching.

"Ah, my niece has returned from her business in the lights district," he said, loud enough for her to hear clearly as she approached down the corridor. "It would probably be best if we spoke more in three days, as we discussed previously." He placed a hand on the younger man's arm, gently but clearly guiding him away from the door.

"Yes, but you don't understand," urged the man. His eyes skittered around the hall, darting across Shanti and back to Dunin. "I can have the new model to you by then, but I am in need of backers tomorrow. If I don't have some suitable old men at hand when I attend the Innovation Society Gala, with their respect and money and names to lend to my own, then no-one will pay any attention to me. It won't matter what models I bring you!"

Dunin closed his eyes and lifted his hands in a calming gesture. "I will see if I can find someone to come with you," he assured the man. "But for now, it is late. The streets are dark. I wouldn't want you to be at risk."

Dunin began to make progress with the man, ushering him towards the staircase, passing where Shanti was waiting for space to clear so that she could enter the apartment.

"I know where the gala is being held. If I can contact someone who agrees, they will meet you there. That is the best I can do!" he exclaimed as the man began to object. "Now. Good night!"

Finally, the younger man turned and began to leave. Shanti was watching as he turned for one last backwards glance, his yellow eyes meeting hers. They shone like the sun.

"Who is he?" asked Shanti as her uncle entered the apartment behind her.

"An investment," groaned Dunin, squeezing the bridge of his nose and cracking his knuckles. He swung the door shut. "But I am beginning to think that he may have been a poor choice."

"He was here earlier wasn't he? Why did he come back?"

Dunin looked surprised. "Yes he was. How did you know?"

"He was leaving when I came back after getting some breakfast this morning." Shanti sat down at the table while her uncle walked into the kitchen to speak to Gunin who was wearing an apron that clearly saw plenty of use. Dunin murmured to the lad who then turned to fetch a large kettle which he filled with water from a large jar on the kitchen bench. He set the kettle on the stovetop and checked on the food inside.

"I didn't realise you had a lad when I arrived," said Shanti. "He wasn't here then was he?"

"No, I can't afford to have him in all the time, so he lives with his family and comes in on certain days for cooking and cleaning and all that." Dunin waved a hand to encompass all the tasks that a lad might be asked to undertake. "As for that man at the door." He sat down opposite Shanti. "His name is Gaibaan, and he's a bit of an inventor.

I first met him about a year ago at an evening hosted by one of my best contacts, an older woman with plenty of money and from a good family. She never ended up marrying, and I don't believe she has children, so she spends her money entertaining her friends. Luckily, she finds new inventions and research and art and business to be entertaining.

So, when she hosts an evening, everyone with a new opportunity that can arrange an invitation will be there. Gaibaan was there, sharing his ideas about creating new vehicles from steam engines."

"Like the one I saw him riding around in yesterday," said Shanti. "I've seen one or two of those things in the streets. Does that mean he has been successful with his vehicles?"

"A little," admitted Dunin. "But we have already seen such devices in trains, and so he is not the only one who has worked on smaller, personal versions. I think he has spent a lot of his money there, without much return."

"I thought he said just now that he wanted to go to this party to find people to give him money? But you say he spent his money? Did he have his own money?"

"Yes, he is the last son of a very famous family. I believe his mother may still be alive, but he has shown no signs of marriage, and he is already spending a huge amount of the family fortune. I don't know if he has been cut off, or given an allowance, or if," and here his voice fell to a murmur, "or if they simply have no more."

"He doesn't sound like he is worth being in business with then. Why are you meeting him?" Shanti was confused.

"He does have some intriguing ideas. His latest thought is a way of passing energy along wires. He seems to think that it will revolutionise the world, but he has yet to give me a really useful working prototype." Dunin sighed and leaned back in his chair. "I have invested quite a bit of money in this research already, and promised to help him look for more." He grimaced and ran his fingers through his hair. "Maybe you have point. Maybe it is time to cut my losses."

The lad brought over a tray with tea making supplies, and then stood beside the table while Dunin spooned some leaves into the pot and set it to steep. "Thank you Gunin."

"So this meeting in a few days, is for him to show you a prototype?"

"So he says. If I can't see a way for it to make money, I will have to cut him off. Luckily his family name is no longer the tool it once was, so I shouldn't risk my reputation with any of the other well off families in Gorduum."

He poured a cup of tea for Shanti while his lad continued making dinner in the kitchen. They spoke more casually then they had before, with Dunin asking about how her meetings with the lights dealers had gone. He even expressed admiration for how well she had checked the actual stock of lights, and looked over the quotes she had received. He thought they were reasonable for what was being offered.

Over dinner he finally asked about her family back in Graama. Shanti tried to be open, after all, this was his own sister and nephews that he was asking about, but she found that she didn't want to tell him too much. It was no longer his place, it was hers, and she wanted to keep it as sheltered as she could.

SHANTI WOKE up feeling rested and ready for the day ahead. She had successfully got in some quotes, and all the options were reasonable. She would be able to arrange the delivery soon.

She rose and washed her face in the small private room next to her own, then got dressed in clothes that would be easy to move around in.

The conversation with her uncle last night had been much closer to what she had expected on her way to Gorduum. She had memories of him from when she was young, and he had always come across exciting and fun. To be honest, if anyone had asked her what her uncle looked like right up until she had arrived at his apartment a few days earlier, her description would have revolved around a distant smile in a darkly bearded face, and the feeling of excitement that a visiting family member brings. It had been hard to deal with this surly and closed-off man in his place.

But the way he had asked about her brothers, and shared genuine concern for her father's broken ankle, made her feel more like her old self. They had eaten dinner as they spoke, and then her uncle's lad had said his farewells and set off home for the evening. Before turning in themselves, Dunin had suggested that Shanti not return to the lights district for at least a day.

"You have plenty of time to return with the stock," he had reasoned. "And if you wait a day and try to act as though you are not convinced, there's a slim chance that they will lower the price, or add some other incentive."

Shanti moved through to the dining room, where Dunin was already up and eating a simple breakfast of bread and cheese that he had prepared himself. There was a plate, with a knife and butter bell, placed on the other side of the table to himself. Shanti sat down at it and began to butter her own roll.

"I think I will go to the University today," she said.

Dunin nodded and chewed.

"The sweet older couple that brought me into Gorduum work there. I thought I might try to see them for lunch, and explore the city a little."

"Certainly."

Shanti was confused and chewed on her own roll as she pondered his reaction to her. Did he not feel more comfortable after their conversation last night? Maybe he was just really bad at mornings.

"What will you do today?"

Dunin grunted and Shanti could see his tongue moving behind his lips to extract some piece of food from his teeth. "I promised Gaibaan that I would try and find him some nominal supporters for the gala tonight. I'll have to spend most of the day knocking on doors now."

Maybe that was the reason for his black mood.

"Well, maybe one of them will agree early on and you will regain the rest of your day?"

"I can dream."

There was a moment of silence.

"I felt like there were a lot of dead lights in the

streets as I walked home," began Shanti carefully. She didn't want to imply that Gorduum was in any way disappointing. She hadn't been able to tell if Dunin was in love with his new home, or if he was aware of its flaws? She didn't want to seem ungrateful.

"Yes, the blight has been spreading."

"I couldn't tell if it had made its way into Aiskuu, but I am worried that it had. I wouldn't want to carry something like that back to Graama."

"That would be terrible. There's no way your local gardeners and lightskeepers would be able to properly contain it, especially considering that it is not even properly contained here."

"That's what I thought." Shanti finished her roll and gathered her dishes. As she walked them into the kitchen bench, she asked "Where did it come from? Shall I leave these for the lad?"

Dunin nodded, and began gathering his own dishes, clearing the table. "No one is really sure. I suppose that's why it has been so difficult to control." He placed his dishes next to the pile Shanti had left. "Some keepers have said that it is a parasite, an insect that is eating away at the roots of the lights, or perhaps a disease that is killing them off."

"We've had things like that in our crops before," said Shanti. "But don't diseases usually only affect one species alone? Or maybe some of the related plants. It seems to me that there are too many species of lights for a disease to affect them all."

"I tend to agree. But, the argument goes that they are all more related than common people like you and I generally assume. After all, we have been breeding these lights for generations, and although their outward appearance is so different, they come from the same stock."

"I suppose that makes sense."

"Some, but I am not knowledgeable enough to truly judge it. There are a few more superstitious ideas that one hears raised from time to time."

"Oh?" Shanti wondered what Dunin meant by superstitious.

"Yes. First of all, there is a group of people who are convinced that the blight has been laid upon Gorduum as punishment by the Masked God."

"What? Punishment for what?" The very idea horrified Shanti. The Masked God did not punish!

"Well, the group splinters when you ask about that. Some think that society has not been upholding the expectations of the Temple. I think a lot of them believe lights allow people to head out into Gorduum later in the evening than people may have in the past. And of course, this must lead to decadence. After all," and here he smirked, raising a knowing eyebrow at Shanti. "Only naughty things happen after dark, and decent folk would clearly want to avoid such situations."

Shanti felt her cheeks flush. Dunin ignored this and continued.

"But then there are others who think that the government has not been dealing in the right way with foreign countries, or that one business or another has taken advantage of the common folk, or whatever."

Shanti could see the logic here. The Masked God could possibly manifest in order to force such groups to cease their behaviour.

"Surely the Masked God wouldn't create such a punishment though? One that is so indiscriminate and harms all, not just those who have acted wrongly? Doesn't that go against what the Temple teaches us about the Masked God?"

Dunin pursed his lips. "I suppose it depends on how you read the writ. Some think the Masked God is within all, and uses otherwise flawed people to its ends. They might argue that the punishment is deserved but affecting more than the actual target due to the flawed nature of the people enacting it." He picked up a piece of fruit from the bowl on the kitchen bench, taking a bite through the pale yellow skin. "I think I tend to agree with you, that doesn't sound like the Masked God that I was taught about when I was young."

Shanti found herself wondering whether Dunin even believed in the Masked God at all.

"Then there are those who think it is due to various elements of society. Some think that the rich are no longer contributing their taxes and charity enough to tend all the lights in the city."

"But even the lights companies are affected."

"Yes, exactly. Some think it is the influence of foreigners, bringing in new gardening techniques, or new lights varieties that compete with the local species more viciously."

That sounded plausible to Shanti. "So, have people tried isolating the lights, or tracking who works with the lights in each area?"

"They have, and I haven't seen anyone seriously defending that point of view. It's quite common though." He took another bite of the fruit, wiping some juice from his fingers as it ran down his hand. "Honestly, some people might look at you funny for coming here from outside Gorduum. Maybe that's foreign enough to upset the lights?"

"I would never!" Shanti was shocked at the implication that she was someone responsible for such a thing. She had only been in Gorduum a few days!

"Of course not. At least, not intentionally. But that doesn't matter to them. Finally, and I think this is actually the most common thought amongst the general population, many people think that the various beggars and street urchins are causing the damage. The Skuggi. They may not think that the damage is intentional, but they certainly think that it is the poor that are causing it."

Shanti remembered the people she had passed by on the way home last night. They had sheltered in dark spaces, exactly the sort of places where the lights were dying first. They wore worn out clothes, and who's to say they weren't carrying some sort of dirt or parasite to the lights while they huddled in their alcoves? "I can imagine that," she said slowly.

"Well, I think it's ridiculous." Dunin finished his fruit and left the stone on the bench. "The one thing that those people want is a way to get some money and to get themselves inside and warm instead of staying out on the streets. But with the lights dying, more and more jobs are becoming tenuous."

He walked across to the window of the dining room and leaned out onto the sill. Shanti followed. Below them the river of pedestrians was already thick and moving fast, street vendors like rocks in the current, causing eddies and swirls that moved down the flow. "There are less guards needed by traders and merchants, less men to carry fertiliser through the streets, less labourers to prune and weed the light-beds. And all of them find themselves, as the jobs dry up, closer and closer to joining those already on the street. I don't know how many of the Skuggi out there were employed only months ago, but I think it would be a lot." He turned to his niece, and Shanti was surprised by the light in his eyes. Finally she had found something that Dunin was truly engaged in. "Why would people work towards their own destruction like that? Besides," he turned back to the window. "The first blight strikes came before the streets began to fill."

Dunin didn't have much to say after that, and he made his way to his office to do whatever it was that he spent his days doing. Shanti went back to her room and prepared to go out. She made sure she was dressed appropriately for walking and gathered just enough money to get through the day. She carefully hid the rest back in her pouch beneath the bed.

As she walked out, she knocked on the open office door and leaned in to let her uncle know that she was going out.

"I'm going to find the University today and have an explore of some of the city."

"Enjoy," muttered Dunin as he dug through a pile of papers on his desk.

THE STREETS WERE BUSTLING and noisy, and Shanti was beginning to find the movement of the people around her enjoyable. She stood for a moment outside the door to the apartments and breathed in the smells and sounds of the city around here, the voices that babbled like a rushing river in the forests near her home, the scent of cooked meat and dirt and the crush of people. It was still overwhelming and new, but she could see why it excited some people. She began to wonder if she would be able to survive here, like her uncle did. How did someone like her find work, find a place to live? What could she offer?

As she lowered her gaze from the slash of blue sky and sharp white threads of cloud that were visible between the buildings, she began to notice the dark shadows that still gathered in the corners of the street, even on such a brilliant morning. People were still huddled in the lee of some buildings, and now that she knew they were there she was also able to see how the pedestrians reacted to them. Most walked on without noticing, but some threw angry glares in their direction. Just as she moved forward to find a driver who could carry her where she wanted to go, she did see one young woman dig through a purse for a few coins, tossing them onto a blanket next to one of the poor people. He touched his forehead in acknowledgement as she moved away. The Skuggi had lived here, had been working here, and now they huddled in the shadows of others. Why did she think she would be any different?

"Well look at what the dogs are fighting over!"

The voice cut through the hubbub of the street and caught Shanti's attention immediately. A sharp familiar smile beneath thick black hair was seated in a cart at the side of the street nearby.

"Keema?" Shanti recalled the driver's name easily, shocked at how glad she felt to see this woman who was a stranger to her.

"Well, I'm not the Breed reborn!" Keema laughed easily. She climbed down from her driver's seat and leaned against the black wood of the cart, crossing her arms. "Fancy seeing you here, right where I dropped you off, and early in the morning when people are about to head out on their day's errands." Her eyes shone and Shanti smiled in return.

"It does seem extraordinary that I would bump into you."

"Oh surely, because a busy entrepreneur like myself would never arrange to be in a likely position to meet up with a newcomer with probable need of my services in this city."

Shanti felt flustered, unsure what to say or do. Did Keema mean that she had been waiting for her? Why would she waste her time doing that?

"Oh, I'm sorry, I didn't realise that-"

Keema laughed again, a loud and joyful rattle of laughter. Shanti felt relieved that she hadn't offended her.

"You don't have to worry about some mere driver!" Keema began climbing up onto her cart again. "Come on then. Where shall I take you today?"

Shanti lifted a foot onto the metal step then pushed herself up and into the small cab of the cart, arranging her skirts around her legs and then looked around. Keema had turned on her seat, leaning on the wooden wall that divided her from the passenger's space. She watched Shanti closely, the attention making Shanti avert her own eyes.

"I was hoping to go and visit some friends at the University. Would that be okay?"

"Of course it is." Keema turned and picked up the reins to her horse, flicking them to get it moving, and then the cart moved out into the crowd.

"So, who do you know over there?"

Shanti explained who Darsat and Dulku were, describing the way they had explored the statue in Graama so thoroughly, and shared their ideas about what it all meant. The night at the pub, deciding to come to Gorduum. Through it all, Keema asked a few questions and offered many witty comments. She grew quiet when Shanti was talking about Fabrin and Buan, and she certainly didn't turn around as much when Shanti mentioned her stolen kisses with each of the boys from back home.

"So, you're spoilt for choice it sounds like?" Keema said in a flat voice.

"I suppose you could describe it that way," conceded Shanti. She leaned forward, reaching out to place a hand on Keema's shoulder. "But they are both so small in their visions. Buan can't imagine anything other than a life on the farm, raising a family. And Fabrin wants to be a great artist, but being the greatest in the village would suit his pride well enough." For some reason she wanted to be sure that Keema didn't think that Shanti was eager to run back to Graama. "I want more than them." She gestured around them at the tall yellow and cream coloured buildings, the bright red tiles that lined most roofs. "This is all so amazing to me. I want to see more."

Here, Keema did turn around, lifting Shanti's hand off her shoulder, but not letting it go either. "I'm glad to hear it. Gorduum is a wonderful place to live. It is so wide, full of surprises and new things to see at every corner." Keema looked so different when she didn't have a smirk in the corner of her mouth. Shanti tried to smile herself, feeling that she needed to lighten the mood.

"Speaking of evenings at the pub, I myself enjoy spending time playing darts at the Bare Faced Con," said Keema as she turned back to the street. "Maybe I'll show you it some time."

"What's that?"

"Oh, just a pub that a lot of taxi drivers spend time in. There's a good crowd, and always someone ready to put a wager on a few darts."

Shanti could hear the satisfaction in her driver's voice.

"I would love that," she smiled.

"Yeah? How about we go for a bit of early lunch and game now then?" Keema flicked the reins in her hands.

"Oh, I'm not sure," began Shanti. "I was really hoping to see my friends, and-"

"Were they expecting you at a particular time?"

"Well, no," admitted Shanti.

"Then we have time for a nice drink and a quick

game of darts!" Keema turned around to look at Shanti again. "It'd be my honest privilege."

"How can I say no to that," laughed Shanti.

"Exactly," grinned Keema.

THE PUB WAS ONLY a short distance away. Shanti saw it in the distance easily, with high tables on the footpath outside its large windows. A variety of men and women leaned on the tables already, though it was still early in the day, drinking from tall glasses of ale. Some nodded at Keema as she pulled her cart in nearby and hitched her horse up securely.

"Come on," said the driver, holding up a hand for Shanti to hold as she stepped down. "I'll get the first round."

Inside, the pub reminded Shanti of being a child and hiding under her blankets playing games with her brothers. There was the same warm pressing feeling to the space, the same comforting dimness. Patrons sat in booths around the walls, chatting in soft murmurs to one another.

"So, this is the Bare Faced Con huh?" said Shanti, looking around.

"Oh, no, this is the Cross Eyed Seamstress."

"What?"

"No, the Bare Faced Con is on the other side of the river, closer to my place. This is just the closest one I could think of to take you to. Not bad though, right?"

Keema led Shanti by the hand up to a counter.

"We'll have a couple of glasses of the Meeru, alright?" she said to the young boy cleaning glasses behind it. He nodded and began pouring the drinks.

Keema turned back to Shanti.

"So, how are you finding my city then?"

"It's been pretty good actually. I was a bit worried at first, because it was so huge, and you did make me concerned about being robbed, but since then things have improved." Shanti began explaining to Keema about her reason for coming to the city, and how she had managed to get three meetings with lights dealers unscathed. Their drinks arrived and Keema led the way to a darts board at the far end of the room.

"Sounds like I didn't need to give you any warnings, you've been knocking about like a professional," laughed Keema.

"Yes," agreed Shanti, lifting her head slightly. "I am rather impressive."

"No kidding," said Keema, pushing her shoulder gently and smiling. "So what's the place I dropped you off? Didn't you say it was a family member you were staying with?"

"Yes, my uncle. He's my mother's brother."

"Uncle's often are."

Shanti bit her lip as Keema gathered up the darts and explained how to score points.

"Nice job," Shanti said as Keema began to throw the darts into the board with startling accuracy. "My uncle has been quite difficult to get my head around." She explained how he had been such a fun visitor when she was a child, but now he had been so grouchy to her at first.

"Do you need me to come up and have a word with him?" Keema narrowed her eyes, fingers curling around the last dart.

"No no, that's silly! He has got better. I'm not really sure why." Shanti watched Keema throw her last dart and calculate her points, then fetch the darts and hand them over. "I think that he liked me more after I said that I was trying to leave Graama."

"Alright then," Keema nodded. "So long as I don't have to show him who's boss." She sniffed and stepped back, gesturing at the darts board. "Is leaving your village a really big deal for you, huh?"

"Oh yes. I've been wanting to leave for years, but there is always some reason that I'm needed at home, some reason to stay. Don't you feel the same?"

"I haven't thought about it before. This city is pretty big, with a lot to see."

Shanti nodded but didn't know what to say.

"I suppose I wouldn't mind seeing what else was out there though," added Keema.

Then it was Shanti's turn to laugh, as she stepped up to throw the darts. The first one sailed wide on the right, clanked into a metal fastening near the board, and bounced back towards the women before stabbing into the carpet near their feet.

"Unseen eyes," swore Keema. "You really haven't tried this before at all, have you? Here, let me help."

Keema stepped up behind Shanti and took her throwing arm in her hand. Shanti felt her mouth open slightly at the feeling of the other woman's fingers pressing around her wrist. Keema placed her other hand on Shanti's side. Shanti could feel her breath brushing the back of her neck.

"You just need to stand like this," began Keema, pressing against Shanti's side to turn her slightly. "And then you just..."

Keema moved Shanti's arm back and forward once or twice, a slow movement like a dance. Shanti felt a shiver slip down her spine.

"And you just throw it here." Keema paused, holding Shanti still, with their right arms stretched out in front of them both. The position meant that Shanti could feel Keema's whole body pressed against her from behind. She swallowed.

"I see. I'll give that a go." For some reason she thought of Fabrin, and the way he had felt standing so close to her after walking her home from the Tired Rabbit the other night.

Keema nodded and stepped back, clearing her throat. "I'm sure you'll do great. You've got a wonderful teacher!"

Shanti smiled, pulled her arm back, and threw, trying to follow Keema's direction.

The dart flew forward and stuck resolutely into the board. It was nowhere near the centre, but Shanti was just pleased that the dart hadn't come arcing back to try and stab her or Keema. She squealed and clutched her hands to her chest, spinning around to grin at her companion. Keema had her hands held up in victory and stepped forward to hug Shanti for a moment, before they both stepped apart again.

"You see! You're a natural!"

AFTER A SECOND DRINK, a lot of laughs, and more than a few games of darts, Shanti told Keema that she really did want to visit Darsat and Dulku at the University. Keema reached over and touched the back of Shanti's hand, shaking her head.

"I wish it were easier to say no to you, I'm having a really good time here," she said. However, she returned their empty glasses to the bar and then led Shanti back out and onto the cart.

As they made their way back into the street, Keema described the neighbourhoods that they were passing through. She pointed out particular markets down side streets, where the crowd was somehow even thicker and stalls crowded the walls. At one intersection stood a gigantic block of stone that was covered in carvings, a single ribbon of figures that marched higher and higher until Shanti could not make them out. At the top stood a tool bronze statue, glinting in the early light. On the lower areas, nearer to the crowd, she could see densely carved depictions of people walking side by side. The effect was a series of lines, with heads like bubbles floating along the surface of a stream. Shanti recognised the traditional form of the Masked God and its servants. She even picked out her favourite story from temple writ, where the Masked God appeared as a gruesome beast that defended a weary traveller from wolves.

As they travelled, Shanti found her attention drawn back to her driver, over and over again. What was the feeling that had come over her in the pub, playing darts and talking with her? It had been so warm and relaxing. Shanti wasn't sure when she had last felt so comfortable. Her cheeks felt warmer as she studied Keema's face in glimpses as the other woman turned to speak.

It's just that no one has been this kind to me here, she decided. Everyone has been so distant or grouchy, and I have needed someone who will treat me as a friend. Yes, she is the first friend I have made outside Graama. This conclusion settled Shanti and she sat back in her seat to enjoy the rest of the journey, watching the passing buildings during the brief intervals when she wasn't watching Keema.

The University wasn't much further past this intersection. Keema pointed it out when the bell tower became visible. It was a much more organically designed building than most of the apartments and halls of Gorduum, with curved twisting stonework wrapping around the four sides of the tower. Even the roof that crowned the tower curved in a wave unlike the tiled surface of the roofs around it. Beneath the tower Shanti could make out more buildings that looked largely similar to the others on the street, but with flags and crests above most of the windows and with much larger doors.

"It looks very big!" she exclaimed.

"Yeah, it's a big building," agreed Keema. "And they think that shows how big their brains are. But there's plenty of idiots that find a way inside those walls so that they won't struggle to survive outside them."

As they drew closer, Keema steered her cart into a wide passage that led to a courtyard inside the walls, away from the street. A couple of guards watched her enter, but from the way that they sat on their chairs and waved, Shanti assumed they were there to keep the peace rather than restrict who could come in. Other carts were in the courtyard, some with passengers getting aboard or disembarking, others tied up to hitching posts as they were unloaded with boxes of Shanti didn't know what. One or two were just tied up and left alone.

Keema manoeuvered her cart into a space to the left of the entrance passage and then jumped down and began tying it up. Shanti admired the way Keema's shirt pulled taut as the driver quickly completed the task. It made her look strong and purposeful. Shanti realised she was smiling and rubbed her face, bringing her expression back to neutral.

"Thank you very much for the ride," said Shanti. "What do I owe you?" Shanti wondered how the fare would account for their time spent at the pub.

"Owe me?" Keema looked momentarily confused, but quickly regained her usual smiling confidence. "Oh no! This is on the house. I'm showing my new friend the city today!"

"That's very kind!" Shanti found herself feeling bubbly, and for multiple reasons. For one, she was able to save money. Much as she didn't want to admit it, her small town instincts were horrified that so much money had left her hands for simple tasks such as cooking or travelling. Secondly, it was nice to hear someone describe her as a friend, even if it was only a potential friendship truly. Thirdly, it made her heart beat faster to watch Keema smile at her and say that she wanted to spend more time with her. "But I haven't even told my friends that I am coming, and I don't know how they would feel about accommodating an extra person whom they have never met."

"Shall we find out then?" declared Keema, scooping Shanti's arm into her own and leading them into the University.

THEY WALKED through a pair of mighty wooden doors that were held open by a large statue. Shanti was sure that a work of art like that was not intended as a doorstop. It was a life size general, wearing detailed armour and with a large spear at his side.

"Can't think of a better use for a guy like that," joked Keema when Shanti mentioned it.

The corridors were surprisingly narrow, and each wall was covered in drawings or papers full of scratched writing. Some prints were there also. A very scraggly looking light had been grown along one corner of the ceiling, but its hairy stem and small leaves did not cast a very strong light.

"Do you know where you're going?" asked Shanti.

"Not at all," exclaimed Keema, without slowing her stride.

"Then where are we going?" Shanti tried to slow down, pulling at Keema's arm with her elbow.

Keema stopped with her. "I figure we follow the

hall until we find a desk or office where we can ask for directions."

Shanti felt like an intruder, walking through these halls when she didn't have a proper destination in mind. Frowning, she looked at the doors that lined the hall, until she spotted one that looked larger than the others. She led Keema to it and knocked, then carefully pushed it open.

Inside was a large room full of chairs around a long massive table. A few people were seated at the table, though they weren't seated together. They looked up as the two women entered.

"Good morning," stammered Shanti, a cold feeling in her stomach causing her voice to be slighter than usual. "I was wondering if you know Darsat?"

The people at the table looked at one another.

"I believe he is a professor of astronomy?"

Again, there was an unvoiced shrug in response from the people in the room. After an awkward pause, where Shanti began to wish she hadn't come into the room, an old woman at the far end of the table spoke.

"I don't know that professor, but the astronomy department is in the next building."

"Thank you. How do I get there?"

"Keep going down this hall until you reach the Atrium. You should see signs leading you through a small garden to the Ulini building. Someone in there might be able to help."

"You've been very kind, thank you." Shanti led Keema back into the hallway and released a deep breath that she didn't even know she had been holding.

"Wow, you really don't like making waves, huh?" asked Keema.

Shanti grimaced. "I just worry that I will say something wrong."

Keema patted her shoulder. "You'll be alright. You've got me here to say the wrong things before you can." The women smiled at each other.

Just as the older women at the table had said, further down the hallway was a wide open hall. Shanti and Keema assumed it must be the Atrium. At least six other hallways opened into it, and the polished wooden walls and floors gleamed. There were clear pathways worn into the wood where hundreds of feet must have walked over the years. The entire space was lit from above by a huge glass dome, supported by heavy looking iron beams and lattice. There were surprisingly few lights in the room, sitting in some small pots set far apart around the octagonal walls. Hanging on the broad wooden panels around the walls were large painted portraits with small plaques set beneath them.

Shanti leaned closer to the one on their left as they entered the Atrium. It named the man in the portrait and gave a set of dates and a title. The man was Darbrit, and the dates given were over one hundred years earlier. His title was Deputy Head of Economic Prediction. Shanti leaned back to get a better view of the whole portrait. The painting was huge, nearly as tall as she was but portraying only his head and shoulders. The artist had done an amazing job of conveying Darbrit's eyes, they shone as though alive. However, the creases around his eyes, the set of his mouth, all showed a man who would have been a grumpy person to interact with.

"Seems like a party animal to me," said Keema from next to her. "Come on, let's see if they can help."

Keema was pointing to three glass windows set into the walls around the large Atrium. Behind each pane sat an older person wearing a severe uniform. All three had grey hair, bound up into buns behind their heads, both the men and the woman, and spectacles sitting on their noses while they read from documents, or wrote furiously onto others. The nearest was about four meters to their right.

Shanti was surprised to find that the woman behind the glass didn't even glance up or acknowledge them once they arrived. She kept reading and reading until Shanti opened her mouth to say "excuse me", but the woman lifted one finger into the air before any breath could leave Shanti's mouth. The interjection died in her throat. Shanti could tell Keema stiffened in annoyance at the dismissive gesture.

"Yes, what?" snapped the woman.

"Um." Shanti was taken aback. She hadn't expected someone to be so hostile to her, without even hearing what she had come to ask for. "I was wondering if you could let us know which way to go for the Ulini building?"

The woman sighed. "Why do I always get the ridiculously easy questions?" she muttered, making no attempt to hide her disdain.

"Now look here-" began Keema, pointing one finger forward like a knife.

"We don't have time for that, I have to answer everyone else's questions too, not just your minor little troubles." The woman waved a hand out at the otherwise empty Atrium. "The Ulini building is right through there, as you should have been able to tell by the signs." She pointed to a hallway further around the wall.

Shanti took Keema by the shoulder and began leading her towards the hallways indicated by the woman. Keema walked backwards and kept her eyes on the woman behind the window, anger making her face seem to glow like some avenging spirit. However, when Shanti shook her head Keema frowned and withdrew back into herself, clearly using all her effort to avoid yelling at the clerk behind the glass.

"Thank you for your help," called Shanti as they moved away.

As the woman had said, each hallway had a set of wooden signs hung alongside the entrance, made of a much paler wood than the panels of the wall. The signs consisted of a list, and the names of destinations that could be reached down each hallway were written one to a line.

"That woman," growled Keema as they entered the hallway. "That woman should be fired."

"She was a nuisance, but we won't have to talk to hear again."

"Hmmmm." Keema didn't seem to think that this was sufficient punishment.

At first, Shanti wondered if the horrible woman sitting behind her little glass panel had lied to them. Perhaps she got a little thrill from causing chaos for the people she was supposedly helping? The corridor stretched on much much farther than Shanti could have imagined, it's length disguised by turns and corners ready to leap upon them like wolves in a forest.

"This is ridiculous," she said angrily.

"It is," agreed Keema, patting Shanti on the arm. "But the whole University is like this. I've come in once before, making deliveries for someone. It's all tiny hallways and hundreds of offices and workrooms." She leaned over with her head and bumped Shanti on the shoulder with it. "We'll find your friend eventually."

They turned to the right and suddenly found a

long window set into the wall beside them. It was not very high, but it stretched on and on for the length of the corridor. Behind the window was a tall long room that was clearly designed for carrying out some sort of work. Huge broad leaves of the brightest lights were resting on fine wire meshes strung across the ceiling, illuminating every surface of the room so that Shanti couldn't see any shadows. Metal surfaces gleamed, and the few people working at the benches were all wearing long white coats and heavy gloves.

Shanti gasped and had to resist the urge to duck down and hide out of sight below the window.

"What's the matter?" asked Keema.

"I know him," hissed Shanti, lengthening her stride to try and get past this eternal window before he turned and noticed her.

Inside the room, arms flailing as he tried to get his point across to another young man, was Gaibaan. Shanti recognised him instantly, even though he was wearing the same white coat as the others over the top of his regular clothes. His skin and hair looked even more pure under the brilliant lights, as smooth and enticing as a chocolate dessert.

"That man who seems to be shouting. He's an investor with my uncle, or an inventor, or something anyway. I can't let him see me!"

"Why not? Did you insult him?"

Shanti blinked and slowed down, but she didn't stop walking. "No."

"Did you ruin one of his deals with your uncle?"

"No. He seems to be doing that himself at the moment actually."

Keema narrowed her eyes. "Would this man even recognise you?"

Shanti thought about the three times she had walked past Gaibaan, close enough to reach out and grab him by the shoulders. Once he had nearly hit her with his strange machine, and blamed her for it as well. Only a day later he had stormed past her in a narrow hallway without even the tiniest flicker of recognition. And he had been so worked up when she came back to her uncle's apartment that she couldn't imagine that he was aware of almost anything else happening around him.

"Possibly not," she conceded grudgingly

Keema rolled her eyes. "I get it. Well, let's take a peek at what's going on in there, assuage your curiosity."

"I couldn't," squeaked Shanti, but Keema had stopped and pulled Shanti around to look through the window with her.

Able to pause and truly examine the room now, the women saw that its walls were lined with huge sets of drawers, although the drawers themselves were incredibly wide and short, as though they had been sat on by some huge beast. Diagrams and paintings of strangely shaped insects and bugs were pinned to notice boards around the room. On a bench near them, closer than Gaibaan and the target of his ire, a pair of women younger than Shanti were hunched over one of the metal benches, with their hands buried in two small wooden boxes.

As Keema and Shanti watched, the women pulled out massive black beetles, with strange antlers and knobbly legs. Shanti was fascinated. She had never seen bugs like this at all! The women moved these fist-sized insects over to a large board and Shanti realised that the board was already half covered with other insects that looked remarkably similar. Their smooth shiny carapaces reflected the light that poured down from above.

"Well, those are pretty gross." said Keema, though

there was laughter in her voice as she said it. "I'd hate to find something like that inching its way over my foot in the dark of the night!"

"I think they're amazing," breathed Shanti.

It appeared that all the insects were dead, as they only moved when the women moved them, positioning legs and antennae and then holding them in place with long, dreadfully thin pins. After stepping back to admire their work, the women returned to the box.

Behind them, Gaibaan was still waving his arms about while he spoke to the other man. He had begun to pace backwards and forwards, like a cat stuck at a cupboard door knowing there is a mouse cowering behind it. He reached one table in his pacing, and picked up a small pot with a tiny blue light growing up out of it. He pointed at its leaves, and Shanti wondered what he was trying to get the man in the white coat to understand.

"I think we've seen enough," she said to Keema. "I really don't think it would be a good idea if he were to see us."

"If you say so." Keema allowed herself to be drawn onwards down the corridor, though a board covered in butterflies in a panoply of colours and sizes did attract her gaze before they finally left the long window behind.

Not much further down the hallway, the women found themselves walking into a large open space with no roof. The passage moved past on one side of a garden, full of beautiful flowers and large bushes that had been carefully pruned and shaped into living statues. Stone pillars held up the roof over them in colonnades, and the sky beamed down beside them onto the garden. They stopped and admired the foliage before moving on down the covered passage.

At the end of the colonnade was another set of large doors, with a sign above them. It contained just one word: Ulini.

As they entered, Shanti was drained to realise that beyond this door was yet another long dim hallway full of office doorways. Was she going to have to knock on every single door before she found her friend?

Luckily Keema solved the dilemma for her, knocking on the first door they found and swinging it open before waiting for a voice from inside to invite them in.

"We are looking for Darsat, can you tell us which office he is in?"

The old woman sitting at her desk and sipping from a hot steaming mug nearly choked on whatever it was she was drinking, but placed the mug down and patted her own chest as she recovered. After Keema repeated the question, the woman smiled and explained that Darsat was exactly twelve doors further down the hall, on the same side. Shanti apologised for the intrusion and they left again.

SHANTI STOOD and examined the door. Darsat's name was exquisitely painted onto a wooden plate set beneath a frosted glass window that let the light from within the office out into the hall. Iron curls held the glass in place.

"Well? Aren't you going to knock?"

Shanti shook her head. All her experience with Darsat had been in her home village, and she had felt confident and knowledgeable while she spoke with him, even when he was discussing the orbits of distant stars. He had a knack for conversation, and she had thoroughly enjoyed their time. However, now she felt uprooted. She had discovered how little she knew about the world, in this city that teemed with people. She was adrift in the rapids, and although she had begun to learn how to guide her canoe through the river without striking the rocks, she still knew that there was more going on beneath the surface that she would struggle to deal with. She reached out and took Keema's hand.

"You'll be fine. Nothing about you has changed, nothing about him has changed. So you're in a new place, so what?"

Shanti bit her lip but nodded. "Okay." She felt Keema squeeze her hand and was grateful for the understanding and support that her new companion was able to show, even when they had known each other for such a short time. She knocked.

"I thought that I heard voices outside the door," came Darsat's familiar voice. "Please come in."

The old professor was seated in a luxurious green chair in front of a bookshelf that filled an entire wall. His desk sat on the other side of the room, covered in books and paper. He peered up at the newcomers and then smiled broadly. "Why, it is my new friend Shanti, from the village! How delightful to see you here! And who is your friend?"

"This is Keema, she's been kind enough to show me around Gorduum a little."

"I'm delighted to meet you my dear." Darsat stood up from his chair, placing the thick book he had been reading down on a small table next to it. He placed it down open, with the pages spread against the table and the spine of the book creaking. The huge smile still stretching his cheeks, he shook Keema's hand enthusiastically.

"When Shanti said she had a friend at the University, I hadn't imagined someone so distinguished," said Keema. "I wondered if she had met some enthusiastic student in a cafe or gallery."

Darsat laughed loud. "Ah, but I am still a student of so many things as well! Come, sit down. Would you like tea?"

Darsat invited the women to sit down and then left the office to collect tea making supplies. While he was gone, Shanti examined the towering bookshelf that took up most of the space on his wall. The books were huge and leather-bound tomes, with long complicated names that used technical words and old language. Many were titled as questions, or as "A study of..." and Shanti wondered exactly what knowledge was contained within them. They looked so old and worn, so well-read, that she was nervous about the idea of touching them though. She was certain that they would begin to crumble beneath her fingers as soon as she began to turn a page.

"You like books?" asked Keema from her simple seat by the desk.

Shanti glanced over her shoulder at Keema but then turned her attention back to the shelves. "I guess so. My father has some." She thought of her father, back at home with his single small shelf, and his treasured novels. "He loves rereading them, and encourages us to read them also."

"I've never been into reading. I don't see the point." Keema was looking around the whole room, examining the mouldings in the corners, and the doorway.

"You don't see the point of reading?" Shanti was surprised, but also distracted by the memory of her father lying in bed with his broken ankle. She found that she missed him deeply, though she had not been gone long. It was the sight of these shelves she decided. She could only imagine the joy that would have suffused his face if he had been here, and she wished that she could have brought him with her, just for that sight. Maybe another day, another time, she would get such a chance.

"No, I mean, if you have friends and family, there's plenty to do. I prefer to play darts at the pub when I have time to be sitting around."

Shanti smiled. "Yes, that was a fun way to pass the time." She imagined trying to set up a dartboard in their home in Graama somehow. There was nowhere to put it, and her mother would certainly be annoyed at standing up to try and play a game. And her father! He would never stop fussing about holes left in the wall. Just imagining them felt warm and bright, but still gave Shanti an ache in her chest. Did the Tired Rabbit have darts? She had never noticed. "Maybe I'll ask my father to play a game next time we are together." There was a tug on her heart as she spoke, thinking of home. "But reading lets one travel to distant places, distant towns and countries. By reading, one can have adventures that would never be possible at home, learn about things that would never arise in normal life." She pointed at the shelves behind her again. "I mean, just look at the knowledge that Darsat has gathered in one space. Can you imagine what ideas there must be on those pages? Aren't you curious?"

Keema shrugged. "Yeah, I suppose?"

Shanti felt confused. The way Keema was dismissing what Shanti was saying hurt her, and she didn't know why. Surely it was okay if her new friend didn't like reading? Thankfully, Darsat returned to the room at that moment, pushing the door open with his legs and awkwardly sliding through the gap sideways like a cat or dog nosing their way into a kitchen. He had to do so due to the large tray he was manoeuvring, trying not to spill the teapot and jug that it bore. He managed to set the things down on his desk, shuffling the tray to move aside various papers as he did so.

The three of them chatted as he prepared the tea, with Darsat asking Shanti how she was settling into Gorduum. Shanti spoke about the strange welcome that she had received from Dunin, but reassured them both that he was warming up to her. Keema shared some funny stories about strange passengers that she had taken around the city, causing Darsat to nearly choke on a mouthful of his hot tea. He spluttered and coughed, his face darkening before he finally had to spit the liquid into a bin that was tucked under the corner of his desk.

Finally, once the tea was drunk and stories had been shared, Shanti asked if he would be able to come for a walk with them and tell her about the buildings and history and art of the University.

Darsat nodded enthusiastically and stood.

"That sounds like a wonderful idea! I had no meetings this afternoon, and I can read my books at any time." He placed a hand on Keema's shoulder, taking her into his plans. "Let us show this young woman how wonderful our city is!"

He was ready to leave in moments, and the trio set off back through the hallways they had come from. After they left the garden space, Shanti began to feel a little worried. "Do we not need to turn down any of these other halls?" she asked, hopeful that their path would divert soon.

"No no, we must go back to the Atrium where you met our wonderfully brusque administration staff." He laughed. "They make my job so much more entertaining than the students do. At least they fight back!"

Moments later, Shanti saw that they were approaching the long window with the insects behind it again. She immediately noticed that Gaibaan was still there, although he was speaking to someone new. The newcomer wasn't wearing the same long white coat that everyone else had been, and it was their distinctive clothes that made Shanti slow her pace even further. Dark brow, hard eyes, and a heavy overcoat. The man standing beyond the window, speaking with Gaibaan, was the same one who had sat brooding in front of her on the train into Gorduum. What on earth was he doing here?

He was standing close to Gaibaan, their heads huddled within centimetres of each other, and their jaws moved minutely as they spoke. From the tension in their shoulders, Shanti thought that the conversation was delicate or somehow otherwise important.

"What has caught your eye in there?"

Shanti jumped and nearly lost her footing. Darsat's voice had erupted right next to her ear, and the shock left her panting. She hadn't even realised that she had turned her head to look into the window. Now she turned back to her companions and found Darsat smiling knowingly and Keema frowning.

"I just. Well, you see, when we came past before, the creatures they had on display…" Shanti found her voice faltering.

"It's quite alright my dear. I am sure the subject of entomology is fascinating to us all."

"Entomology?"

"The study of insects. It's actually a very important field!" Darsat continued to expand as they walked on. Shanti snuck one more peek into the workspace and saw that Gaibaan and his conversational partner had moved over to one wall, where a huge glass case was set up. Inside the case was a pile of twigs, leaves and soil. Shanti thought she could see movement in the case, but they moved on too fast for her to be sure.

"With Gorduum the size that it is, it is absolutely vital for the nearby farms to grow plenty of food. Where else would it come from? And, of course, it is difficult to determine whether land should be used for food crops and such things, or lights. Some people seem to think that the money they make from lights would be enough to make up for the fact that people would starve." There was an edge in Darsat's voice. Shanti wondered if he knew anyone who had been affected by such thoughts. "So, as you can see, the farmers come in quite regularly, in order to test their crops to ensure that there is no disease hidden in their roots and seeds."

"Like the blight on the lights?"

"Something like that," agreed Darsat. "However, that has not been isolated yet. We find the dead lights, but we have yet to find one with a clear cause for its dying."

"There's plenty of outraged people on the street," chipped in Keema. "I hear them, all day every day. Pointing at the Skuggi, saying that they are punishing the rest of the city for their misfortunes, whether intentional or not."

"I don't think it can all be sabotage, if indeed any of it is." The old man sniffed and scratched the white hair at his chin. "Although I can't say that I approve of those layabouts clogging up the streets."

"Why do they come to this room?"

"Often the reason that crops or lights are suffering is due to some sort of small insect. So long as we can find the insect, we can develop a way to kill it, or at least learn how to protect our goods."

Shanti found herself thinking of Buan as they

kept walking. He was such a kind and gentle man, and he was totally obsessed with the family farm. She considered one of these farmers. Making their long trip all the way into this city, and into the depths of the University building, all in order to check that a disease wasn't destroying their crops. It reminded her just how much time and energy must be spent in caring for crops, and in managing resources to get the most out of the little plot of land that you or your family owned.

She considered how long Buan had stayed in Graama instead of travelling back to his home and returning to all these chores. She knew that he wasn't simply avoiding the work. He was such a serious and responsible man, he would never shirk from work he needed to complete. All of this just made it even more clear how much he must have valued being around her, even for only a little longer.

Shanti remembered the way she had kissed him before she had left. She felt a thin coil of shame begin to gather in her stomach. He didn't deserve to be confused, and he was a wonderful match for somebody in Graama. But, despite gaining this sudden insight into how valuable he would be for somebody, she was beginning to feel that he really couldn't be for her.

The idea that she would marry him, and return to his farm, and help him tend crops, plant seeds, gather harvest… It just made her blood run cold. Seeing the buildings and noise of Gorduum had revealed a world that stretched beyond her horizons, and she couldn't contemplate hiding from it once this errand was done. She was surprised to discover that she did think of it as just an errand now.

Without meaning to, she had shifted in her mind from being on a dramatic adventure to a simple errand, as though a journey along a tropical jungle river to a distant temple had somehow turned into taking some flour to the neighbour's house. And yet it was true. She would complete this errand for the village, and then she would want to head back out to find still more distant horizons. Whether or not she would be free to was another matter. Could everyone cope without me, she wondered.

"You're very quiet all of a sudden." Keema's voice slid into Shanti's reverie like a hawk in the breeze.

"Am I? I suppose so. I was just thinking about home."

"Is that all?"

"No, I suppose not. There was a boy there, named Buan. I mentioned him on the ride to the University, remember? He's a farmer and I guess I was just realising how much work goes into that. I'd never really thought about it."

"Farming's an important job," nodded Keema, running a hand forward across her head, pulling dark spikes of her hair low enough to shade her eyes. She was looking down, instead of directly at Shanti. "How long have you known Buan anyway?"

"Oh, since we were children." Shanti laughed. "I'm pretty sure he wants to marry me. Like I told you, I kissed him before getting on the train to come to Gorduum! But that was just the excitement of the trip."

Keema nodded again, her lips level and no sign of her smirk appearing on her face.

"I wonder if he knew that," murmured Darsat, coughing into his hand. Shanti felt the coil in her stomach thicken.

They moved on through the halls back to the Atrium, where Darsat guided them through a new exit on the farther wall. The horrible woman was still sitting behind her glass window, and Shanti had to concentrate very hard to avoid making a rude gesture at her. There was a gasp from the clerk and Shanti snapped her eyes sideways just in time to see that Keema had not tried to avoid the temptation at all. Keema grinned at Shanti's shock.

BEYOND THE ATRIUM, the hallway twisted and turned a few times before coming out into a courtyard that was clearly near the main street again. Shanti could see the usual crowded streets through the tall iron gates, though they must have been locked as none of the crowd was even attempting to come in. The courtyard was wide and cobbled with broad light-coloured stones. On three sides the heights of the University buildings leaned over them, making Shanti feel like an insect herself, exposed beneath the gaze of curious children that might choose to destroy her without a second thought. She shook her head and cleared her throat. What a silly fancy to take hold of her mind. She straightened her shoulders as she walked with Darsat across the courtyard to a truly impressive entrance on the far side.

A wide flight of stone steps narrowed as they ascended to a huge set of doors, flanked by statues and gigantic round stone pots that each held a tall thin tree of light. Heavy fruit shone deep red on each tree, even in the midday sun, and contrasted against the trees' small thick leaves that were so green as to be almost black. Tall narrow windows reflected the sunlight.

"What's this then?" asked Keema.

"This is the University Gallery!" exclaimed Darsat, clear pride dripping from his voice. He spread an arm at it as if to emphasise how amazing it was. Shanti had to admit, the spire that climbed into the sky above the entrance, the pillars and structures that surrounded its windows and levels, all contributed to a very impressive and overwhelming first experience.

"In fact it is just one of our many galleries, but most of the others are devoted to one faculty or another. As such they can be quite small or esoteric or even both at once! This is the main Gallery, and it houses some of our most spectacular collections."

They walked into a monstrous space that shone with reflections and polished stone. The silence was a tangible thing, a presence that sat on their shoulders and leaned against them, making even their hushed breathing seem overwhelmingly loud. There were a few other people walking carefully through the galleries, the occasional clack of a poorly placed footstep echoing and ringing for far longer than Shanti would have believed possible. However, despite the awe that pressed down upon her, Shanti found herself loving this place immediately. Keema clutched her hand and grinned, and Shanti found herself beaming in return.

They quickly passed from one hall into another, pausing at various paintings for a close inspection. Art students sat on portable stools in front of many artworks, sketching compositions and mimicking the colour palettes in their books. Some enthusiasts were standing so close to the artworks that Shanti almost expected to see one of them lean forward and kiss the surface of a painting. And the thought of standing so close confused her, as the paintings were gigantic! Many walls were taken up by a single huge piece, but even when multiple paintings were sitting side by side on a wall they were massive things. The portraits of the rich and famous were life-size, if not bigger, and there were some beautiful portrayals of the Masked God's visitations.

In one hall the paintings were all focused on mountain landscapes. Shanti thought they were beautiful, but then Darsat began to explain that these were not fanciful visions, invented by the artists, but records of adventures and expeditions to far off places. The artists had accompanied one traveller or another for all sorts of reasons, and these paintings were some of the record of it all. "These are from a land we know as Kukchar Prada. The people there are very serious, and their warriors used to be renowned, but there is little contact any more. Some trading I think."

Shanti wanted to go there. She stood before one of the paintings, showing a range of mountains that stretched into a misty sunrise in the distance, and peered at the plains beneath, wishing that she could see through the painted fog to find the people who lived there. What were they like? What did they do with their days?

"The landscape is very dim," she noted.

"Oh yeah," said Keema, who was leaning down beside her to examine the painting. "Not even a single point of light. Maybe they were trying to emphasise the sunrise? It's stunning."

"I hear that in Kukchar Prada there are no lights at all."

Even though she kept being told of these places without lights, the idea still stunned Shanti and she straightened up. She looked at Keema who wore a gobsmacked expression. Shanti imagined her own face had looked similar the first time she heard someone say this, muscles loose and her mouth hanging open.

"No lights?" Shanti felt light headed. How was so much of the world surviving without such an essential resource?

"How would they…" Keema waved a hand around, trying to find a single example to complete her question, but clearly conveying that she wanted to include anything and everything. How would people function without lights? "How would they anything?!"

Darsat chuckled. "Well, there are some places where there are not many lights at all. You only had a few in your village, did you not Shanti?"

Shanti grudgingly agreed. "But not having a lot of lights is different to having none!"

"In some ways. But, they function as you do, as did the other lands I told you about in our chats. Candles and fires mostly. They have oil lamps in many places I believe."

"You said there is only a little trade." Keema spoke slowly, carefully constructing her thoughts as she spoke them. "But surely, they would give anything for our lights if they don't have any?"

"They don't feel as though they are missing out on a lot," Darsat shrugged. "And it is extremely difficult to transport lights so far, or to encourage the seeds to grow in such a different climate and landscape."

Dazed, Shanti walked up behind one of the people copying the paintings. The young woman was sitting on a well-padded leather bench, with a broad book of thick art paper open on a small easel in front of her. She drew with soft chalks and pastels, wide sweeping strokes and then detailing in small sketches and dots. Although she wasn't managing to create a perfect copy of the jungle valley in the landscape on the wall before her, Shanti thought the drawing was beautiful.

"That's amazing," she said.

"Thank you," answered the woman, though she did not turn her gaze from the painting. "I think I've managed to capture the shadows really well. The trick was to use purple instead of black."

Shanti looked at the jungle painting in surprise. "It looks black in those shadows to me."

"Yes, it does, and that's the trick of it. Here, look at this." The woman carefully turned a page in her book, showing another drawing of the same scene. This one looked almost completely black.

"I can't really see anything," apologised Shanti.

"Exactly," smiled the woman, finally turning to address her admirer. She blinked as she took in Shanti, and then her smile grew wider. "The black sucks out all the colour completely. But the purple captures the shadows much better. I don't think I've seen you here before? I would have remembered."

The woman stood up from the bench and stepped closer to Shanti, reaching out to shake hands.

"No, I'm visiting with my friends here." Shanti pointed out Darsat and Keema who were standing nearby. Darsat appeared to be explaining something about a painting of a wide stone road that passed through a tall imposing forest. Keema may have been listening to him, but she was certainly watching Shanti with piercing eyes.

"Your friends are they?" asked the woman. She smirked. "Then why does that girl look so angry with you?"

"She's not angry," began Shanti, but then she realised that Keema did seem to be angry. What has happened, she wondered. Has Darsat said something terrible? Surely not, he had been nothing but kind so far.

"You probably need some time away from someone in that mood," said the artist. "I know a delicious restaurant just ten minutes from here, very popular with the students. Would you like to come and share a drink with me?" The right corner of her mouth rose in a grin and she smoothed down the sides of her dress. Shanti swallowed.

"I can't, I really need to spend my afternoon with my professor friend. I owe him so much. And I am sure she isn't really angry."

The woman pursed her lips then nodded. "Alright. Well, it was gratifying to meet you. And thank you for the kind words about my piece."

They shook hands again, and then Shanti walked back over to the others.

"Are you alright Keema?" she asked quietly. "You looked a bit angry. Did Darsat say something?"

Keema shook her head but didn't say anything.

The tour continued. Keema began to seem less interested as they walked, sighing deeply. She would follow Shanti up to an artwork but then begin talking softly and trying to stand next to Shanti. Shanti had to shush her and brush her aside, and Keema began to follow more sullenly, with her arms folded and her eyes on the floor.

Then they entered a room full of paintings that made Shanti gasp. The paintings reminded her of her train ride into Gorduum. They were made up of hundreds of points of colour, arranged on the canvas in galaxies and constellations that made pictures. However, these were not pictures like the figures in the constellations that Shanti had discussed with Darsat. They weren't star figures, a few imaginary lines close enough to be able to connect together into a recognisable shape. These points were packed in clouds that appeared from a distance like regular paintings. Shanti was enamoured with one that depicted a crowd of people in a marketplace. As she walked closer, it was harder and harder to see each stall, each figure wrapped in its clothing. Instead she found herself staring at tiny individual blobs of paint, small lumps that dotted the canvas. She wanted to reach out and stroke the surface of the painting, to see how each bump felt.

"This is weird," Keema said from behind her. "Why didn't they just paint it normally?"

"This is the more experimental end of the gallery," answered Darsat.

"You aren't kidding."

Shanti felt a little let down. Keema had been so interesting and optimistic, and Shanti had been happy at the idea that they would spend more time together today after this visit. But now she was finding that even an exciting person like Keema had their limitations. They all had a limit to their horizon that didn't match Shanti's own.

"What's next?" she asked brightly.

The next hall was separated into two halves. On the wall to their left were a series of traditional artworks that focused on design and geometry more than figures. They were built of simple shapes in strong colours, and they reminded Shanti of her childhood. These were similar to the designs that were strung across the street during festivals, the patterns that decorated the hems of the dresses in Graama worn by older women. One design matched exactly the edging of the Temple ceiling in Graama.

The other side of the hall bore some other sort of artwork.

"What are these?" Shanti breathed. She heard Keema snort, but ignored her.

"Quite experimental artists. You don't have to complain," he said as Keema began to open her mouth. "Most of these are not exactly admired. But they are experimental, and the University does try to encourage new ideas."

Shanti walked forward to examine the artworks.

They fascinated her. One appeared to be some sort of portrait, but it was entirely made of straight edges. The eyes looked like diamonds, the limbs like broken glass. She could readily understand how many people would turn their nose up at such a distortion of the human form, and yet… She could not look away.

She found that she was reminded of her conversations with Fabrin during the last night at the pub in Graama. Listening to him talk about how he wanted to do something different, to make people think about what it was that they were looking at. She just knew that he would be thrilled to be here with her right now. She remembered the feeling of his arms around her as he kissed her after walking her home. Suddenly she ached for him to be standing with her in the University, and the feeling shocked her. She turned around and tried to hide her face.

"Are you okay?" Keema was by her side within a second.

"I'm fine, truly."

"What happened?"

"I was just thinking about someone I know back home. I think he'd really be fascinated by all of these." She wiped a tear away from the corner of her eye.

Keema stepped back. "He would, would he?" She bit her lower lip. "I bet you wish he was here right now, not us."

"Yes." Shanti nodded, then shook her head fiercely. "No, not instead of you." She sniffed and blinked to clear the moisture from her eyes. She reached out for Keema's hands, but the other woman turned and stuck them into her pockets. "I just wish I could see how his eyes would light up if he were here. He is obsessed with craftsmanship and experimentation. I think he would love to see what people can do.

But I don't want you to go, I am glad that you are here with me."

Keema nodded and shrugged. "Okay."

"Would this be that nice young man we spoke to on our last night there?" asked Darsat, who was standing at a polite distance and trying not to intrude.

"Fabrin, yes, the leather worker."

"He was a charming young man." Darsat scratched his cheek. "Lots of good ideas. And he had taken quite a shine to you, if I am right?"

"I… I suppose so," said Shanti. She knew he had, he had made his feelings and intentions very clear. But she found that she felt awkward addressing this in front of Keema.

They walked through some more galleries, but conversation was stilted and forced. Darsat continued to explain the ideas behind some of the more unusual artworks, but Shanti was only half listening. Most of the time she kept her attention on Keema, who had been acting more and more like a young child. She refused to pay attention and wandered off into strange corners, poking at the artworks when she should not have touched them, and loudly complaining that one piece or another was boring or too weird. Shanti was angry, but more at herself. She was the one who had brought Keema along, and now one of her only friends in the new place was bored and wanted to leave. The anger made her guilty as well. It was difficult not to snap at Keema, or to respond to her childish behaviour by shouting.

Eventually they made their way in a loop back to the beginning and Darsat began to lead them back to his office. He inquired as to what they had enjoyed about the galleries, and Shanti tried to give him her attention. But it was so difficult. Even the sun shone less brightly as they crossed the courtyard.

WHEN THEY REACHED THE ATRIUM, Keema suddenly turned aside. "Actually, I've used up quite a lot of my day here, and that won't be good for business. I think I'm just going to head out right now."

"Are you sure?" Shanti was nonplussed. Why would Keema leave her so suddenly like this? "I was wondering whether you might show me that other pub. The Fair Faced Don, was it? And I will need a ride back to my uncle's."

"There'll be plenty of other taxis around," said Keema. "And you'll probably want some alone time with your friend. After all, you keep talking about how you enjoy time one on one with the people you care about. I'll just get in the way." She nodded at Darsat. "So I'll see you around. I know where you live now anyway." The dark woman turned to leave, flashing a hint of the smile she had been beaming earlier in the day as she did so.

"But what if I want to find you first, how can I do that?" Shanti asked, but Keema didn't appear to notice. Hands buried deep in her pockets, she strode rapidly out of the Atrium and was gone.

"Having some trouble there?" asked Darsat.

"It would seem so," said Shanti. She clutched her hands together, wringing her fingers. "But I don't know why!"

Darsat smiled and offered Shanti his elbow as they made their way into the hall that would lead back to his office. "Being young is difficult. I am glad that I spent so little time there!"

Shanti laughed.

Darsat offered Shanti another cup of tea when

they reached his office, but she declined and didn't sit down.

"I don't know why Keema decided to suddenly rush away, but actually I didn't want to distract you from your work too much anyway. Now I know where to find you, I can always come by again if I want. I will leave you my uncle's address also."

"Yes, that would be wonderful. My door is open anytime!" Darsat gave her a small piece of paper and a pencil so that she could write down the address. "Sometimes I am supposed to be lecturing, but you will always be able to wait here until I return from such a thing."

"You're very kind." Shanti hugged the old man and left the address on his desk. "I will see you again soon I'm sure."

Shanti was on her way out of the University, still deep in thought trying to figure out how she had upset Keema so badly, when a voice interrupted her from behind.

"I'm sorry, what did you say?" she asked as she turned around. Her throat clenched as she realised that Gaibaan was jogging down the corridor towards her.

"I said, don't I know you?" He caught up to her and stood almost a meter away. He extended a hand. "My name is Gaibaan Setet. You strike me as familiar, where have we met?"

Tucked under his other arm was a long narrow wooden box.

"Uh." Shanti wasn't sure how to respond to this, but manners took over. She reached out to shake his hand, suddenly exceptionally aware of how clammy her palm felt. "My name is Shanti Penpen. Actually, I do know a little about you."

"I thought so!" Gaibaan smiled and Shanti was

amazed at how the movement made his face shine. "What have you heard? Only good things I hope!" He laughed.

"Well…" Shanti was trying to figure out the best response. She wanted to punish him for the way he had treated her previously, to make him realise that she was not someone he could just ignore. But at the same time, it was mortifying to have him still not recognise her at all, despite nearly hitting her with his strange vehicle, and having to squeeze past him in the hall outside her uncle's apartment. And then there was Dunin. How would their business dealings continue if she embarrassed Gaibaan now? Would he take offence and dump her uncle? Gaibaan needed the support of Dunin more than vice versa by the sound of things, but Shanti found that she wasn't sure enough to risk being too forthright here. "I think I saw you outside my uncle's apartment last night? He said you were a business partner?" she left the questioning tone in her voice, trying to undersell how well she knew him. It made her stomach curdle.

"Really?" Gaibaan cupped his chin in one hand as he pondered her statement and then smiled again. "Oh yes, Penpen! Of course! I do think I recall seeing you as I left. You had on that blue shawl, didn't you?"

"Yes I did."

"That's right, I did see you! Oh." Gaibaan's face fell as he recalled his behaviour in the hallway. "Oh my, I must have been quite a sight last night." He grinned apologetically. "I do apologise, I was a bit upset with some plans that weren't coming out how I had expected." Shanti was surprised to see that he sounded genuinely sorry.

"It's okay really, I didn't think anything of it," she lied.

"All that is in the past now anyway," went on

Gaibaan. "Today is a new day, and things appear much brighter!" He patted the narrow wooden box under his arm. "Suddenly the future is glowing!" His eyes were glowing too. Something had changed since last night, his joy and optimism were leaking out of every pore. Shanti found she couldn't help but smile in response.

"Dunin was looking for someone to be my sponsor at a gala this evening, did he tell you that?"

Shanti decided to shake her head and see what else this young man had to say.

"I was hoping for someone who could help me meet other well off people and gain some funding for my new projects. They are very clever new projects," he confided, leaning closer to Shanti and lowering his voice. "I'm going to change this city, and then the world, you watch and see."

Shanti felt blood rise in her cheeks at his proximity, flushing her face. Her stomach trembled again.

"But enough talk, would you like to see them?"

"I suppose I could."

"Fantastic! Then you will join me for the gala!"

"What?"

"The Innovation Society Gala tonight! Dunin was looking for a sponsor, but I can still bring a companion with me regardless. I would be honoured if you would join me for the gala."

Shanti felt her mouth open and close a few times before she regained control of it. "Tonight?"

"Yes!"

"I don't think that- I mean, I have nothing to wear and my uncle is probably expecting me."

Gaibaan tilted his head slightly to the right and narrowed his pale eyes, though his demeanour stayed jubilant.

"Well, if you're sure?" He let the question hang in

the air, giving Shanti plenty of opportunity to change her mind. "That's fine. I know where to find you now anyway, perhaps I'll see you again before you know it!"

Shanti's stomach felt as though it had been plunged into an ice filled stream.

"Maybe you will," she managed to say as Gaibaan shook her hand again and moved off. Shanti watched him leave down the corridor, striding with purpose and with a high head. Now he was so different to the angry man she had first encountered on the street, and the frantic one who had besieged her uncle. How could one person be so different at different times? It was as though she had met two men who looked the same, who shared memories and goals, but who were nevertheless entirely separate men. She kept watching as he walked away. She couldn't figure out whether to be pleased or saddened that he had accepted her excuse so quickly. Did she want to go to the gala, to see the high life of the city? Or did she want to find out more about this man?

Shanti walked out of the University, through the courtyard full of carts and people, and then stood under the arch that led back into the main street. She watched the people walking by for a while. She wasn't quite sure what she should do next. Keema had been her ride home, but she had vanished. There was no trace of her at all in the courtyard, and when Shanti had asked one older man who was grooming some of the tied up horses, he didn't have any memory of Keema. He wasn't able to give any idea how quickly she had left. Shanti didn't feel as panicked as she would have only a day or two earlier. Gorduum was still large and complicated, but she felt as though she could navigate it in broad terms at least. She saw two carts that looked very similar to

Keema's moving along the street, passengers sitting in the back.

She decided that she could always call the attention of one of the taxis, but as she hadn't been able to truly explore Gorduum yet, she would take the opportunity to see what she wandering through its streets would uncover. So long as she headed towards the Breeog's Theatre, she would be heading in approximately the correct direction.

SHE ENJOYED MOVING through Gorduum at her own pace. The faces that she saw were mostly serious and stern, clearly people with destinations in mind and errands to fulfil, but occasionally she caught a smile from a stranger and was pleased to return it. A small child sitting on their father's shoulders waved enthusiastically as they passed in the opposite direction and Shanti laughed and waved in return. The buildings were well kept in this district, and the streets were not too narrow. There was enough room for everyone to move along. Occasionally Shanti paused to look down side streets and into courtyards, of which there were many. These smaller spaces were often full of stalls, people sitting at seats and smoking pipes as they conversed in the afternoon sun, strings of laundry criss-crossing the air above them. It made Gorduum feel even more alive to Shanti.

However, she found some more areas where the lights were being affected by the blight. Not many, and only small patches, but the grey and dried out vines that were beginning to flake off from the walls were hard to mistake.

Mostly they appeared near the very thin alleys that separated some of the more business-like buildings, spaces that had clearly been left to allow deliveries and similar unseemly aspects of trade to occur. Shanti slowed and looked down some of them. With the lights in the alleys dead or dying, the narrow spaces became exceptionally dark and dangerous. Piles of rubbish and old boxes filled them, and made them appear threatening. Anything could be hiding in those dark spaces. Shanti shuddered more than once, as if cold water were dripping down the back of her neck and down her spine.

After passing a few of these alleys, she noticed movement in the next. A small bundle of old rags was shifting in one spot, and she wondered if it was a stray cat or dog, but then the rags shifted and she saw the tired face of a middle aged woman appear. Skuggi. The woman was looking down, and didn't re-cover her face with her shawl immediately, so Shanti was able to observe her for some time.

How could people imagine that this woman was responsible for the blight? The idea was suddenly absurd to Shanti. What would this woman be able to do that could kill the lights? Why would this woman even want to do such a thing? She felt a huge amount of sympathy for the woman and began rummaging for her purse in her satchel so that she could give the Skuggi woman some money. She stepped forward into the gloom of the alley.

Almost instantly other shapes rose up from the boxes and Shanti found herself confronted by five or six other faces, all looking just as exhausted as the first woman or more.

"Whatdya want?" snapped one older woman whose grey curls were beginning to peek out from beneath the hood that she had pulled across her head.

"Get out," snarled a man whose face was as whorled and tough as old wood.

"I just - I, I…" stammered Shanti as she took a step

back towards the main street. The passers-by were so far away, and suddenly the noise and hubbub of the street was dulled and distant. She managed to lift a hand, with the glint of a coin held between her fingers. An arm darted around from behind her and snatched the coin away, causing her to yelp in surprise. A young man was standing right beside her. Clearly she had walked past his spot before any of the inhabitants of this dark alley had moved.

"Got any more?" he said, his teeth and eyes sparkling in the gloom as he stepped closer.

"No!" yelled Shanti, and she reached out and tugged him out of her way, tripping him in the same way she would have one of her brothers when they played chase in the woods. She pulled him off balance so that he fell between herself and the others who were moving towards her, a tactic she had learned from those games with her brothers, good for slowing down someone who was chasing you. She darted out of the alleyway as quickly as she could, moving rapidly to the middle of the street before turning to risk seeing whether they were chasing her. She saw them huddled at the mouth of the alley, but held back by the glares and temper of the pedestrians in the street.

"Causing more trouble, eh?" came an angry voice from the crowd, and passers-by began to slow and stare at the Skuggi. They raised their arms in a gesture of mollification and quickly vanished back into the dark alley. Shanti caught one last glimpse of the woman she had first seen, lifting a baby up to rearrange the blanket that was wrapped around them both, before the shadows swallowed them up. Shanti was left standing alone in the midst of the street, a scrap of rags still held in her hand.

With her heart still pounding in her ears, Shanti

looked for a taxi and tried to get its attention as soon as she saw one. She had to ignore a few angry faces as the taxi stopped beside her in the middle of the street instead of to one side of the pedestrians, but she didn't feel safe moving to the sides herself. She wanted to stay as far as she could from those alleys.

She explained to the young woman driver that her uncle lived on Minter's Lane and then sat back in the seat, trying to calm her breathing. She held up the rag that she was still holding onto. Clearly, in her panic, she had clawed at the clothing of the man nearest her and torn some of it off. She held it between both hands and gave a small tug, finding that the threads came apart easily. Then, as she was holding it, she noticed an exquisitely tiny insect crawl off the cloth and onto her finger. Her initial impulse was to flick it away, but she managed to restrain her instincts and peer closer at the insect. It was incredibly tiny, and looked as though it was made of glass. She looked at the cloth and noticed there were more. It was extremely hard to see them if you weren't looking for them, or if they stopped moving. She found it impossible to count the number of these insects on the cloth, but there were at least ten. Curious, but unable to think of anything else that she could find out about them while she was in the cart, she bundled the rag up into one hand and leaned back to stare at the sky as they travelled.

Shanti didn't quite sleep during the ride back to her uncle's apartment, but she allowed her mind to wander. She thought about how she had upset the only friend that she had made so far. She wondered whether she had succeeded in her task of completing an order for her village. She tried to decide whether she was angry about the way the people in the alleyway had treated her, or whether she was sad that they were stuck there. Was she frightened of them?

Eventually she made it to the apartment. Dunin was not at home, but his lad was busy cleaning the kitchen and preparing a meal for the evening.

"Good afternoon," she said as she came in, and the lad made a brief bow of his head to acknowledge her but quickly returned to his chores.

SHANTI SPENT the rest of the afternoon having a bath and sitting in her room. She had found some books in the living room and began reading one of her uncle's novels. It was a scary one, about a man living in a remote rural place with an entire household of servants, but the ghost of a woman he had loved kept trying to break into the house.

She roused herself when her uncle returned. She explained to him which lights dealer she had decided to work with and asked him for his opinion on the decision. He agreed with her choice and the reasoning behind it, and she felt confident that she would be able to return to their offices in the morning and place her order happily.

Then, just as the lad was setting the table for dinner, there was a knock at the door.

"Get that, would you?" asked Dunin, not looking up from his newspaper. Shanti wondered if he meant the request of her for a moment, but the lad quickly moved over to open the door.

"It's for you sir. Gaibaan."

Shanti felt her throat clench as the pale young man walked inside the apartment, beaming his smile into every corner.

"Good evening friends!" he declared.

"Gaibaan," sighed Dunin. "Why are you here

again? I thought I said you could come back in two days to show me a prototype?"

"Did you find me someone for the gala?"

"No." Dunin looked as though he was about to offer an explanation, taking a breath and opening his mouth, but then snapping it shut again.

"That is frustrating," said Gaibaan, but there was no rancour in his voice. He looked at Shanti. "Have you thought again about my request?"

Dunin looked at his niece and raised his eyebrows. "What's this about?"

"I bumped into Gaibaan here while I was visiting my friend at the University," admitted Shanti. "He asked if I would accompany him to the gala."

"Oh he did, did he?" Dunin narrowed his eyes.

"Yes, I did! And who could blame me, asking for the company of such a beautiful young lady." Gaibaan was smiling, but his gaze was directed at Dunin. They stared at each other for a quiet second, with a tension rising in the room. Shanti broke the moment.

"I haven't reconsidered. I still don't think I should."

Gaibaan returned his yellow eyes to her. "Well, take a moment now. I am here, I can take you with me, and it will be a lot of fun." He lifted a hand. "Of course, if you are sure, I will move on."

"Why wouldn't you go?" asked Dunin grudgingly. Shanti could tell that he wasn't thrilled about the idea of her spending more time with Gaibaan, his body language made that clear. He was hunched over in his chair, and he hadn't stood to greet the other man as he entered. She wondered then why he was suggesting that she reconsider the idea at all.

"I didn't think it was appropriate, for one thing," she began to explain slowly, watching him carefully for any hint or sign of what he was thinking.

He waved one hand in the air. "It would be appropriate enough. You aren't in Gorduum very often, and you would like to experience as much of it as you are able to, I'll be bound. The Innovation Society Gala will be a very entertaining affair, and I'm sure you would find it enjoyable." The words forced their way out of his mouth like hedgehogs forcing their way through a hedge.

"I don't have anything to wear though," Shanti could feel her own defences beginning to sway. The idea of a large party in Gorduum was beginning to sound exciting. But she wasn't lying, what could she wear?

"Oh, I'm sure that whatever you have brought along will be acceptable!" Gaibaan exclaimed, his eyes gleaming. "Why don't you go and see if you have anything, I'll wait for you and your final decision here." He pulled out a chair and sat down next to Dunin, turning halfway in the seat and leaning in close to the older man. "I can chat with your uncle while you look."

Dunin grimaced but nodded. Shanti made her decision and raced back down the hallway to her room and began to search frantically through the drawers where she had put her belongings when she arrived.

That's too green, it would clash with the clothes Gaibaan is wearing, she thought to herself as she dug through the clothing. Does that matter? Maybe that would emphasise to him that she did not really see a connection there? This one is too blue, it would make me look too dark. She couldn't imagine how well lit or dim the gala would be and so was unsure if the deeper colour would simply conceal her or not. Finally she decided on a yellow dress that she decided would emphasise the colour of his eyes. Not that I'm really going in order to bring out his fashion choices, her thoughts burst over one another.

She changed and looked at herself in the mirror in the bathroom. Yes, it wasn't the most elaborate or high quality dress in the world, but she felt that she was dressed appropriately for a formal evening. Hopefully she wouldn't have to stand next to too many people in expensive high quality clothing. That might be too much for her.

She walked slowly back down to the living room, hoping to catch the men's eyes and prepared to bask in a moment of impressed silence. The occasional bit of admiration was good for anyone's ego after all. And so it was most deflating when she stood for a full count of twenty in the entrance to the living room without so much as a glance from either of them. Gaibaan was leaning close to Dunin, muttering intently and making short stabbing gestures with his fingers, even though the men were only ten or twenty centimetres apart. She coughed.

"Look at you!" exclaimed Dunin, leaping to his feet and walking over towards her. Behind him, Gaibaan frowned in his chair but then took in a deep breath and Shanti watched as he forced a smile to cross over his face. She was having second or even third thoughts about this evening's plan already.

"That is a splendid dress. I think you will have a great time." Dunin smiled as he took both of Shanti's hands and she was surprised to realise that he looked genuinely happy. As best she could remember, this was the most caring that he had ever appeared to her during this visit. She felt more like she had when she was much younger, with her exciting uncle coming to Graama to visit. She couldn't stop a smile from spreading across her own face, and she leaned forward to hug Dunin. He squeezed her shoulders and then stood apart from her. "You really do look lovely," he repeated.

Gaibaan walked up to stand next to Dunin. "Certainly you do. That dress is a wonderful choice." He sounded sincere, but that frown from only moments earlier remained foremost in Shanti's mind. "Shall we go?"

They couldn't walk out of the door immediately, they had to make some arrangements for when Shanti would return, gather a shawl to keep warm in the night air, amongst other things. But, before she knew it, they were walking out of the apartment and heading for the stairs. Gaibaan offered her his hand and she found herself taking it as they descended. There was a flutter in her chest as she did so.

As they left the building, Shanti scanned the street for Gaibaan's carriage. She was expecting something quite well decorated, as her uncle had told her that he came from a well off family. However, she could not see one. Although the streets were quieter now, there were still enough pedestrians that she began to wonder if she had missed it somehow or if he had left it further from the apartment for some reason. Then Gaibaan led her over to a strange contraption that, nevertheless, quickly jogged a memory in her mind. She gasped and covered her mouth.

"It is quite special isn't it," said Gaibaan, mistaking her momentary shock for delight. "It's one of very few models built in Gorduum and I doubt that there are any to be found anywhere else in the entire world." His chest swelled with pride as he patted the wall of his automobile. It was exactly the one that he had nearly struck Shanti with only days earlier, and then blamed her for the incident. Of course he would be travelling in this, she thought. Why am I surprised?

"How does it travel without horses?" she asked, stepping closer but not sure whether she trusted him enough to climb aboard. The memory of his snarling face glaring down at her from this very contraption was definitely making her wonder about the wisdom of this decision. How could this man, who looked so stunning and could apply such charm and brightness, have been so uncaring and cruel to a perfect stranger? It was so utterly outside the way people were instructed to by the writ. She considered her uncle's comments and realised that he didn't think much of Gaibaan but also thought that she could handle him long enough to enjoy the evening.

Steeling herself, she took Gaibaan's offered hand and pushed herself up and into the passenger seat of the automobile. She realised she was more worried about his anger being revealed again, than the physical threat and proximity of the automobile.

"It's extremely clever. Have you ever seen a windmill turning cogs and gears in order to grind grain?"

Shanti nodded.

"Well, it is like that, only instead of relying on the wind to provide motion, we burn fuel that forces movement into a piston, and we use that to power the movement instead."

"That sounds clever."

"Thank you, I made a variety of modifications to the engine myself, to improve efficiency." Gaibaan swelled again, like a sparrow who had found a half-eaten bread roll that no other bird had yet claimed. He walked to the rear of the automobile and there was a loud clattering noise. While he performed whatever operations it was that got the engine started, Shanti looked across the street.

Everywhere she could see the Skuggi encroaching on the normal street, picking through the gutters for scraps and approaching passers-by for charity. She could see the well-dressed inhabitants of Gorduum flinching aside. The lights growing up their metal posts through the middle of the street illuminated it well, but the vines that clung to the buildings around her were dimmer than they should be, and the shadows were thickest near the alleys. There was a strange rhythmic roar from behind her and then Gaibaan was swinging himself up into the driver's seat. He took hold of a long lever, like a tiller on a river boat, released another, and they began to rattle forward along the cobbled street.

The path before them was lit by a deep orange light, more like the light from candles and fireplaces, but steadier. Shanti leaned forward to try and figure out where the light was coming from, and eventually realised it was originating from two boxes at the front of the automobile. But there had been no light when she approached the automobile.

"How do you fit lights into such small boxes?" she asked. "There's not nearly enough room for soil."

Gaibaan chuckled. "You will be amazed! Most people don't pay enough attention to notice. There are no lights there, at least, not as you would recognise them."

"What do you mean?"

"There are no living lights, nothing that requires tending or pruning, no soil to maintain at all."

"But then, how..." Shanti was confused, and leaned forward further, risking tumbling off her seat.

"It is my own invention, and in fact it is what I am attending the gala for. I want more supporters to help me create prototypes and working models and to begin production and sale of these."

"But what is it?"

"I call it an electric light!"

"Electric? I thought you said it wasn't a light?"

"Not a light as you think of. It is a small glass globe, and I have devised a way of passing electrical current through a wire in a way that creates illumination! Once the engine begins, as well as providing motion to the wheels, it is powering a generator to produce electrical current!"

Shanti tried to imagine what Gaibaan was telling her, but couldn't.

"I want to see."

"I will make sure you can once we arrive."

As they continued to make their way through the quiet night streets of Gorduum, Gaibaan explained more about his various projects and inventions. Shanti began to be genuinely impressed. Here was a man utterly consumed by the quest to create things, especially things that would improve the lives of those around him. He was working on ways to improve the water supply to Gorduum, he wanted to make transport cheaper and faster so that products would cost less and people could travel more. He wanted to find ways for the University to be funded more, so that research and investigation could grow and spread further.

Shanti found herself caught up in his words, imagining a world where everyone was taken care of and provided for. As the automobile juddered over the cobbled streets towards their destination, Shanti watched the dark figures of Skuggi huddled near the alleys in the shadows. She reached over and placed her hand on Gaibaan's forearm.

BEFORE LONG, they were pulling up to a courtyard, through large iron gates. Other carts and carriages were lined up along the small space, with various grooms and drivers taking care of their horses and equipment. Many were still dropping passengers off at the foot of a wide low staircase that led to the main doors. Large drooping orange lights had been placed at intervals up the sides of the stairs, their massive pots still resting on platforms that were clearly designed to allow porters to move them when needed.

"Here we are," said Gaibaan, guiding the automobile to one of the side areas.

"We aren't going to the stairs?" asked Shanti.

"No, I wouldn't trust any of these servants to take this vehicle safely across a field." His eyes grew hard for a moment, then relaxed again. "So we will have to walk over."

Shanti wasn't sure if this was some sort of insult or not. She could see that no one else was walking themselves across the courtyard to the stairs, but Gaibaan would be suffering the same slight if it was perceived as such. And the reason that they had to was because he was the only one in the yard who was driving such a new machine, such exciting new technology. She let herself place a hand in his elbow as they walked. They walked up the stairs and through the doors, entering a world or shining lights and dazzling reflections.

Although they had walked up a flight of stairs in order to enter, Shanti was intrigued to discover that they immediately had to descend a short flight of stairs again. Beneath them was a wide atrium, with dark stone floors and surrounded by glistening polished wood. Lights and glass were intertwined around the walls, leaving the crowd bathed in a panoply of colour that shifted and danced across them. Two large doorways led out to the left and right, but it looked like there was a bar at the far end of the atrium.

As they descended the stairs and began to walk across the floor, various faces turned and smiled at them. One of two older people, men and women alike, acknowledged Gaibaan by name, and Shanti drew more than a few inquiring glances. She drew closer to her evening companion as they moved through the crowd.

"How are you doing?" asked Gaibaan, leaning to speak to her, but keeping his gaze forward and manoeuvring her through the crowd.

"Very well," murmured Shanti in reply. She allowed herself to look up and around the room, examining the dresses and clothes that were on display, trusting in Gaibaan to keep her from colliding with anyone.

She was impressed by the most elaborate and colourful outfits being worn, dresses with huge feathered trims and boas, suits in brilliant colours and designs. However, she was very pleased to see that she was not unusually dressed. There were many like her, in clothing that was well made and attractive, but not at the level of a worn piece of art. Soon they were standing by the bar, waiting for the attention of the young woman in the crisp uniform behind it.

"What would you like?"

"I don't usually drink," answered Shanti.

"I'll choose something for you then." Gaibaan smiled as the woman made her way back to them. He ordered a small glass of a strong whiskey for himself, and some particular wine by name. When their drinks arrived he picked up the wine and handed it to Shanti.

"This shouldn't be too strong, as you're not used to it, but it is a very fruity wine. Hopefully you like it."

She took the glass by the long stem and took a sip. He was right, it was very fruity and tart, though it left a strange aftertaste in her mouth. They both turned back to the crowd as they sipped at their drinks.

"What happens now?" she asked.

"Nothing much. Lots of mingling and conversation and making connections." Gaibaan looked more serious, and he was lifting himself higher on the balls of his feet, his eyes flicking as they scanned across the people milling before them.

"Are you looking for anyone in particular? Perhaps if you described them I could help?"

"No," chuckled Gaibaan. "I am looking for no one person in particular, but for everyone in general." He turned back to her. "There's many possible contacts for me to make here, but I don't know which would be most appropriate until I see them and give it a try."

Shanti took another sip. It really was quite good wine. She stood next to Gaibaan for a while longer, unsure what else she should do. As she watched, she realised that there was music echoing across the atrium, and lots of the crowd were moving towards the doorway on their left.

"I'm just going to see where they are all going," she said.

"Fair enough. I'll come too."

As they reached the doorway the sound of music grew louder. Through the gap they were able to see a band playing familiar dances. In front of the musicians, beneath a huge chandelier, couples spun across a dancefloor. Light vines were woven through the glass droplets dangling above, and the swirling result made the entire scene look like a dream. Shanti breathed out slowly, feeling tension leaving her shoulders as she took it all in.

"Oh," she breathed. "Can we dance?"

In reply, Gaibaan took her hand and walked ahead of her, pulling her into the whirling dancers. A gentle tug on her arm spun her to him and he placed his other hand on her hip. She became very aware of how close their bodies were, and how his hand felt on her side.

"Do you know how to luzo?" he asked, his voice low and his breath on her ear. She tried to keep her hand steady on his shoulder.

"I've had a few tries, mostly when I was younger. This seems a little more intimidating." She tried to imply that it was the setting and the crowd that were making her nervous. She could feel his body, centimetres from her own. She was very conscious of each breath she took, and how it brought their bodies closer. She wasn't sure whether or not he was convinced by her explanation.

"You will be fine, just listen to my instructions. No one will mind if we make a few mistakes, and we can stick to the side rather than the centre." Gaibaan lifted his head slightly, listening to the beat of the music. "And stepping back with your left foot on the four… one, two, three, FOUR."

He moved against her, his hands directing her and his voice murmuring directions as they began to circle the floor. Shanti felt herself begin to let go, focusing only on where she placed her feet and the rhythm of the music in the air. After they had circled the small area of floor around them three or four times, she found that even that level of awareness was melting away and all that remained was a sense of lightness and happiness, an awareness of Gaibaan standing near to her. She spun and circled and danced, pausing to clap as the musicians paused between dances but then leaning in to the experience once more.

Eventually, Gaibaan wound her to a halt, standing beside her, holding onto one hand. She found that she was breathing heavily, but not tired. His chest rose and fell deeply, and he puffed his cheeks once to catch his breath after the exertion. Shanti giggled. Maybe village life was good for her. Her blood pulsed and she felt as though her eyes would be glowing. She grinned at him.

"That was amazing, thank you!"

"You are very welcome," he replied, bowing slightly. "Come on, there will be speeches and dinner in the other room."

THEY MOVED BACK through the crowded doorway into the atrium and across to the other door. In this new space Shanti found herself looking at row upon row of pristine white tablecloths draped over tables, shining cutlery arrayed in disciplined ranks along each. Centrepieces of pale white and blue flowers were emphasised by a single strong deep blue light that grew from the middle of each. People were beginning to find their places at the tables, and a podium was set up at the front of the room, far to the right of the doorway Shanti and Gaibaan had just entered through.

"Where do we sit?"

"I have an invitation, so I should have a place setting, and they should have provided me with a space for my partner..." Gaibaan trailed off as he replied to her, searching the tables for a sign of where he should go. Shanti didn't even know where he would begin looking, there were so many tables arrayed across the room that the thought of finding one specific seat amongst it all was incomprehensible. Gaibaan pulled a folded card from his pocket and looked at it.

"Over there," he said, beginning to walk alongside the tables. "They are all marked, subtly, with symbols and numbers." He pointed out the small tasteful plaques as they passed. "Ours should be symbolised with a bunch of grapes, and then we can check the chair backs for a number."

As it turned out, he was correct, and they managed to find their seats without too much trouble. Shanti was seated opposite him, and the seats around them were beginning to fill up. Gaibaan smiled at her and asked if she needed anything.

"Another glass of that wine would be very agreeable," she replied, blushing.

"Your wish is my command," grinned Gaibaan, rising and heading off through the guests.

Shanti placed her hands on her lap and looked around, taking in the surroundings.

Guests continued to pour in through the doors, murmuring and muttering as they figured out where their seats were. Shanti's neighbours all turned out to be older than her, close to Dunin's age. Some of them looked her over as they arrived, but very few actually spoke to her, and even then it was mostly cursory greetings.

Not willing to simply sit in her seat like a decoration with no will of her own, Shanti leaned over to an older woman on her left. The woman had bright white hair, cut short, and she was wearing a striking red dress.

"Good evening," began Shanti. "Have you been having a good night?"

"Certainly." The woman turned her gaze on Shanti but did not smile. "It has been a very enjoyable evening, as it is every year. I haven't noticed you here before." It was barely even a question, more of an accusation, as though Shanti had no right to be at the table.

"I'm here with a-" Shanti's voice caught for a moment as she considered how to describe Gaibaan. "Friend," she finished. "He is a very clever inventor."

"Indeed. As are we all my dear." The woman was not impressed. "What makes him so clever?"

"Well, he drives an automobile."

The woman sniffed, but said nothing derogatory, and Shanti thought that perhaps that signified a measure of success.

"And he has developed something he calls electric lights in order to illuminate the street as he drives it at night."

This had an effect, and Shanti was pleased. The woman jerked slightly and her eyes widened. She turned away from Shanti to whisper into the ear of a bald old man seated on her other side. He jumped as well, then stared at Shanti. The woman turned back to her.

"Are you telling me that that young upstart Gaibaan will be here, at this table?" Her voice was slightly higher than before.

"Um." Shanti didn't know how to respond to that. She knew that he certainly hadn't made a good impression at first on her, but she felt more positively inclined towards him now that he had shown her how well he could dance. "Gaibaan is sitting there," she pointed at his seat. "But I don't know what you mean by upstart? He's been very nice to me."

She considered.

"Tonight," she added, in the interests of honesty.

"I'm certain he has, a good looking young woman is inclined to receive compliments," said the woman. "But I cannot bear the thought of having to endure his mad proposals and desperate attempts to swindle money out of us. Come Lobit," she addressed the bald man as she rose out of her seat. "We will need to find somewhere else to sit for the speeches."

Shanti was stunned and watched as the two stood and made their way towards a far corner of the room. She turned back to the others at the table and was just in time to notice all of their eyes jump away from her, trying to pretend they hadn't been watching and listening. She wondered if any of them would leave now also.

Moments later, Gaibaan returned and settled into his seat, placing a second glass of the fruity wine in front of Shanti.

"Have you made any new friends?" he joked.

"Well, I did speak to a woman sitting here," she said, gesturing at the now empty seat. "But she and her husband Lobit decided that they needed to find new seats." She didn't want to explain why they reached that decision, but she didn't know how best to cover it up. She supposed she could have claimed that no one had sat there to start with, but the thought of directly lying to anyone made her feel uncomfortable. She hated the idea that the Masked God's hidden eyes would be watching her deceit.

"Lobit? Was he a short bald man?" Gaibaan leaned forward across the table, his eyes boring into Shanti. She was taken aback by the rapid intensity of his expression.

"...Yes?"

"Dammit!" He pushed himself back in his chair, hitting the table with a fist and making the cutlery jump. Glasses rattled, and he nearly hit someone walking behind him with the sudden movement of his chair.

"Watch out," snapped the passer-by.

"Oh shove off you boring mole," growled Gaibaan

without even looking around. The man glared at the back of Gaibaan's head, but did move on.

"I don't understand, why are you so upset?" asked Shanti, trying to calm Gaibaan and very aware of the attention that the rest of the table was directing at them.

"I've spoken to him many times before, I thought he would be a supporter. But that cursed wife of his controls the purse strings and she won't even give me the time of day!" He shook his head, his lips twisted in something like a frown or a sneer.

"I'm sorry that you won't get to talk to them," said Shanti. "But maybe some of the others here will be just as good conversation?"

"It's not conversation that I need," he snarled, mostly to himself.

Shanti didn't respond to this. Suddenly she was reminded of the look she had seen on his face when he nearly ran her down in the street. She sipped at her wine, noticing the way it bit at her tongue. Maybe this evening had been a gigantic mistake. Gaibaan remained slumped in his seat, sipping at a dark brown liquid in a short glass. She wondered what he was drinking.

A MAN in a very well-tailored suit walked up to the podium and stood quietly, waiting for attention. The hubbub of conversation that had been filling the dining hall subsided. Shanti hadn't even noticed it was there until it left. He began to speak, his deep loud voice carrying to every corner of the hall. He thanked everyone for coming to the gala, to celebrate the wonders and successes of the year, and to socialise with people that they may not have seen since the previous year. He noted those who had passed on and asked for a moment of silence in their memory.

It was at that moment that Gaibaan leaned over to one of his neighbours and began whispering into their ear. The woman Gaibaan had chosen tried to shush him and lean away, but he simply allowed his voice to rise louder, calling attention from the rest of the table.

"... sure that you would agree, if only you'd come to a demonstration of my prototypes."

"Shhhhhhhhh," came the sound from others around the table. Shanti felt her cheeks beginning to grow red.

"Oh tell the Masked God on me if you're so worried," snapped Gaibaan. He continued to try and speak to the woman.

The rest of the speech passed slowly for Shanti, as she found it hard to concentrate on what the man at the podium was talking about, and sometimes she simply didn't understand what he was referring to. She was mostly distracted by the way Gaibaan completely ignored everything that was going on and kept trying to convince everyone else at the table to give him money. Shanti felt incredibly embarrassed but didn't know how to stop him.

"I can see that you are unimpressed by your companion tonight," said a warm voice to her right. Shanti turned to see an older man with an extensive moustache, thick and furry as a bear's arm, that traced a path over his lip and along his jawline to pass over his ears and mix with the hair on his head. He winked.

"Didn't know what you were getting in for I'd wager. Thought a pretty young man would take you for a night of dancing, didn't you?"

"Sort of," admitted Shanti. "I didn't know about

this part of things." She gestured at the dining hall and podium, as servants began to walk along the tables and deposit small delicate plates containing starters for the guests.

"Oh this is just some pomp for those of us who think we're important," chuckled the man. "My name is Zareet."

"I'm Shanti."

"It's a pleasure to meet you." He shook her hand firmly. They both listened to the speeches continue. It appeared that the first man was now announcing a variety of people that were in the running for some form of medal or trophy as a reward for the exciting things they had done during the last year. Shanti found it difficult to follow, but much of the crowd were familiar with the names as there were rounds of enthusiastic applause after most of them. Interesting, some received much more tepid applause, and one name received a burst of conversation before the audience realised how impolite that was and launched into fitful clapping.

Zareet leaned back over to her. "Would you prefer to return to the dancing?"

"Are the musicians still there?" Shanti asked in surprise. She had assumed that all the guests for the gala would have moved into the dining hall by now.

"I would imagine so. There's often a large group that simply come for the dancing and stay there."

Shanti was tempted. "I should probably stay here with Gaibaan," she said finally. "And it would be nice to have something to eat."

Zareet smiled and nodded, then turned his attention back to the speakers at the podium. Someone was thanking others for something now.

Shanti ate her starters, a range of crisp onion pieces, heavily seasoned chicken, and fried pastries filled with delicious pieces of vegetables. She tried to ask Gaibaan if he was enjoying his, but he was leaning over his neighbour in order to try and converse with the next person around the table.

Shanti tried to follow the speeches as they continued, but simply did not know enough about the various people being mentioned to make sense of it all. It sounded as though those who received rewards and acknowledgements were generally well-liked by the reactions of the audience. But she wasn't clear what they had each done. It sounded like one woman had developed a new method for creating tea sets, a material that looked fine but was easier to produce and hardier than traditional ceramics. Alongside that was a man who had invested a great deal of money into building new water pumps and fountains in various locations of the city. She tried to ask Zareet to help her identify the people, or to understand what they had done, but by the time he managed to explain about one person, two more had been mentioned or come forward to speak. Eventually he shrugged sorrowfully and said "I think there's too much to say, I'm sorry."

The main meal came and Shanti ate it, once again trying to engage with Gaibaan. By this point he was out of his seat and walking around the table, leaning down onto the shoulders of everyone else there. Each of them grimaced as he approached, but he didn't seem to notice.

Shanti used her flat bread to scoop up some rice, dipping it in the rich yellow sauce. Again, it was delicious.

"This is wonderful."

"Mmmmm," agreed Zareet from beside her, his mouth stuffed full.

Shanti finished and watched as Gaibaan began to

walk off towards other tables. His expression was that of a fox, creeping through the farmyard towards the chickens. She wondered who he was hunting.

"You know, I think I will go and see if there is more dancing to be had," she said to Zareet as she raised herself from her chair.

"An excellent idea!" he replied. "Have a wonderful evening!"

The musicians were still playing, and there was still a crowd in the dancing hall, spinning across the floor. However, these dancers were very enthusiastic, and Shanti realised that she did not know any of the steps that were on display. It was more entertaining to watch the dancers and enjoy the music than to sit lonely at a dinner table while strangers gave speeches, and so she stayed where she was. If she was lucky, some kind soul would ask her to dance and teach her a few simple steps.

The evening passed slowly, and Shanti did manage to get noticed twice, led forward onto the floor and spun through a dance. Neither occasion was particularly memorable. The first partner was kind, and had hair that tumbled in dark waves around his face, but he tried to show her steps that were far too difficult for her. She found herself stumbling and tripping regularly, until the music ceased and he led her back to the side of the room. He was sweet enough about it, but he didn't return to dance with her again.

The second invitation was from a somewhat plain looking man, but Shanti was keen to try another dance. Unfortunately, his attempts at conversation revolved around his interest in architectural styles in Gorduum, and even if she had been interested in arches and supports, she wasn't familiar enough to know what examples he was referring to. This didn't give him pause in those explanations however. Shanti was glad when the dance ended.

The night wore on.

EVENTUALLY THE MUSICIANS completed a song and did not start another. They began to pack away their instruments, and the crowd began to leave the hall. Shanti wondered how late it was, then realised that she would have to find Gaibaan or she could end up lost in strange streets in the middle of the night. She began to push as hard as she dared through the crowd towards the dining hall. This was made more difficult as the diners were all moving out towards the doors and street as well, so Shanti felt as though she were swimming upstream through rapids.

After deploying her elbows in a distinctly impolite manner, Shanti made it through the throng to the table she had been at for dinner. It was empty now, each seat as barren as a meadow immediately after a hawk has struck and taken a rabbit in its talons. Shanti felt a cold pressure spread across her shoulders. She turned slowly, examining the guests battling against each other demurely as they pushed towards the exit. She couldn't make out the soft brown hair or yellow eyes of Gaibaan anywhere. She sank into one of the chairs at the table.

All right Shanti, she thought to herself, mentally grabbing herself by the shoulders. You can figure out how to deal with this. It's not that big a problem. Obviously there will be drivers outside in the street, just look at the number of people leaving the gala. It would be bizarre of them to not take advantage. But to be safe, it might be worth seeing if I can find any familiar faces first. As the plan grew stronger in her mind, Shanti pulled her shawl tighter around her shoulders and prepared to stand and approach the crowd.

A hand landed on her shoulder and she nearly yelped. She turned and saw Gaibaan, looking calm and smiling. She was a little put out by that. She had expected, should she have found him, that he would look worried or frazzled, as though he had been searching for her and was beginning to panic that he had lost her. But clearly, such worries were not affecting him.

"There you are!" He held her hand to help her fully to her feet. "I wondered where you had gone, but I figured this was where you'd return to. Where did you go?"

"I decided to go and keep dancing. You looked busy." Shanti wondered if it was worth pointing out that he should have offered to go dancing with her. Or at least stayed near her and talked to her during the dinner.

"I was, indeed I was!" Gaibaan rubbed his hands together. "It took some time, but I think I've found a few new contacts who can give me some support for further developing commercial versions of my electric lights. Of course, they all want to see prototypes and demonstrations, but I can arrange that easily enough." He blinked and looked back at Shanti. "Dancing you say? What a splendid way to pass the time. Was it good?"

"It was amazing," lied Shanti. "But now I am quite tired. Can you take me home?"

"Of course."

Gaibaan was true to his word, leading Shanti out through the dwindling crowd and helping her into his automobile. It started with a jolt and then Gaibaan was guiding it out into the dark streets of Gorduum and towards Dunin's apartment. There was a silence as they moved along the streets, though it was punctuated by the rattle and grumble of the automobile's engine and its wheels on the cobbles. Shanti worried that the homes along these streets would be woken by the noise, but there were no sudden glows of unveiled lights in any windows. Gaibaan made one or two attempts to ask her about her family, or her work back in Graama. Shanti answered in short phrases, one word if possible. She just wanted to get back to her bed.

Thankfully they were soon there, and Gaibaan helped her down. He began to walk with her to the doors and Shanti placed a hand on his upper arm to hold him back.

"Thank you for a memorable night," she began, politely. "I'll be fine from here."

"Oh, I couldn't let you walk through the apartments alone," smiled Gaibaan. "Please allow me to make sure you get home safely."

Shanti pursed her lips but nodded.

They walked in silence through the doors, across the lobby and up the stairs. Shanti unlocked her uncle's door and then turned to say a final farewell to Gaibaan. She had decided that, intriguing though he may be, pretty and unusual as his eyes were, she would prefer not to spend any more time with him. Her initial impressions of an angry and self-obsessed young man were clearly correct. He could be charming when he wanted, but his true desires and the focus of his attention was never going to be her.

When she turned, Gaibaan was moving closer to her, his arms reaching out to embrace her. Shanti's eyes widened and she began to lift her arms to push him away. His lips closed in, and his eyes were closed. She turned her face and felt his kiss land on her left cheek. He stepped back, confusion in his eyes. She tried to smile "Thank you for taking me to the gala, it was completely outside my usual experience."

She pushed the door open behind her and slipped through as fast as she could. The door slammed shut and she leaned back on it, breathing deeply. She waited until she heard Gaibaan's footsteps retreat down the hall, and for the grumble of the automobile's engine to reach her through the still night air before she straightened up and made her way to her room. As she prepared for bed, her thoughts raced. She knew she couldn't spend much more personal time with Gaibaan, he was just not a kind enough person to invest in. There was something hidden and angry and clutching about him that she could not ignore.

And, although she had been drawn to his looks at first, that feeling had vanished as she stood watching the dancers. But now she wondered if that would cause a problem for her uncle. She considered the way he had grimaced when Gaibaan had walked in that evening. Hopefully it would not be too difficult for him to cease his business dealings with the younger man.

In the morning, Shanti ate the breakfast that Dunin's lad Gunin had prepared for them and talked with her uncle about her evening out.

"Sounds like he is as much of a bore as I might have expected," said Dunin. "I'm sorry about that. But I did think you would enjoy the meal and the dancing, was I right?"

"Yes, I did enjoy those parts, thank you."

After breakfast Dunin moved to the living room to read the newspaper. Shanti came to sit opposite him, pulling the bundle of rags that she had torn from the alley dweller out of her satchel while the lad prepared tea.

"I'll have to go back to the lights district and let them know I've reached a decision."

"Mmm." Dunin didn't look up.

"Do you think that I should go and speak to each of them?" Shanti felt nervous about going into such professional spaces only to explain that she wouldn't be using that person's services. Would the dealer's take offence and have her thrown out?

"No. If you really feel you need to, you could go in and leave a message with one of the clerks." Dunin still didn't look up, but Shanti was glad that he engaged with her now. They had come a long way in a few days.

"That's a relief." She turned the rags in her hands, searching for more of the tiny insects that she had seen before. They were harder to find, which surprised her. She would have expected that such bugs would survive more than one evening in her satchel. She still felt that they were familiar.

"I think these might be some type of aphid." she remarked. Dunin looked up.

"What are?"

"These." She moved closer, holding the rag so that her uncle could examine it more closely.

"They're tiny, they could be anything. Where did you get this?"

"I tore it off one of the Skuggi while I pushed him away."

"What?" Dunin looked appalled. "By the God, how would I explain such things to your mother!?" His face paled.

"I'm okay, it was my own fault." Shanti remembered the woman with the baby. "I'm sure they didn't intend to scare me, I just got a shock."

"Nevertheless, maybe I should ask the lad to accompany you on some of your errands. The streets are getting worse." He reached out and fingered the coarse material. "But if this came from one of them... These are probably just lice."

Shanti nodded, but didn't say anything. They didn't look like lice to her.

"I mean, why would any other bugs be living on people?" Dunin laughed. "Are they aphids? Do you think sap runs through their veins rather than blood?" He grinned at his joke. Shanti chuckled half-heartedly.

I'm sure that they aren't lice, she thought to herself. And they're aren't aphids either, but they seem somehow similar.

OUTSIDE THE APARTMENT, dressed for a day of business, Shanti called a taxi with ease now. However, instead of asking it to take her to the lights district, or to the ferry dock of the Naatat, she instructed the driver to take her back to the University. He nodded his grizzled head and they set off. Once they arrived, Shanti paid him and set off through the narrow corridors, looking for the laboratory that she had seen Gaibaan in.

Standing outside the laboratory, looking through the windows, Shanti paused. She wasn't sure why she had come here. Why not just assume that the bugs are lice, she asked herself. Wouldn't that be okay? Why did she feel the need to prove that they were something else? And that was another point to consider, how could she be sure that they even were something else? They looked extremely odd and they were so small. Perhaps she was just wrong? But something in her core wouldn't allow her to pass over these strange little bugs. She wanted confirmation.

She walked to the end of the hallway and found a door, where she knocked. Shortly after, a middle aged woman wearing a long white coat opened the door.

"Yes, can I help you?" The woman was short and peered up at Shanti through a pair of small glasses. Her hair was pulled back into a tight bun, but wisps poked out.

"Yes, I was wondering if I could speak to some sort of insect expert? Are you one?"

"Of sorts," smiled the woman. "Come in and have a seat."

Shanti found that the room was very well insulated once she was inside. The long window out into the hallway was much harder to see through from this side, and the air was still and warm. There was a strange hum, almost too quiet to be sure of. She found she was tilting her head, trying to pinpoint the source of the low noise.

"It's some of the farms near the walls," said the woman, answering the unspoken question. She guided Shanti to a tall stool next to a high workbench near the door they had come through. "My name is Meeza, what is yours?"

"Shanti."

"What a pleasant name," Meeza smiled. "Now, why do you need to talk to someone about bugs?" She sat on the next stool.

In response, Shanti pulled the rags out of her satchel again. She unfolded the cloth and spread it out on the workbench, looking closely until she found another of the tiny translucent insects. There were far far fewer than there had been when she first noticed them.

"Here," she said, pointing at the insect. Meeza leaned closer, pulling her glasses further down her nose. "I found this piece of cloth and it has some strange insects on it. My uncle said that they were probably just lice, but I thought they looked similar to aphids, in some ways."

Meeza made a noncommittal noise in response, reaching out to move the cloth a little.

Then she sat up and her eyes drove into Shanti.

"Where did you find this?"

Shanti was taken aback by Meeza's question. "It was just out in the streets?"

"But which streets?" Meeza leaned closer to Shanti, managing to somehow make her shorter frame feel intimidating. Shanti leaned backwards, despite being taller than the other woman.

"Just outside here actually, near an alley."

"Near here," muttered Meeza, turning back to the cloth. "I suppose that is possible, though..." The woman trailed off, still examining the cloth.

"They do seem to share some features with aphids, though of course they are not aphids," she finally said. "They are something extremely rare. We received a specimen of them about a year ago, and we've been trying to breed them since then."

"Why would you breed them?"

"Because we need more to study, and it is extremely difficult to retrieve them from their natural habitat. It's almost a six month journey to the heart of Jorkalah. Very dangerous.

And yet, here you are walking into our laboratory with some on a random cloth. I can only hope that these are some that have somehow managed to escape. If they are out in the wild... Here, I'll show you."

Meeza stood and led Shanti over to the far side of the laboratory, where there were dozens of large glass containers, mostly containing thick bundles of branches and leaves. One of the smaller cases on the right held less foliage than the others. Meeza pointed at it.

"Have a look in here."

Shanti peered through the glass. It took quite some time, but eventually she managed to spot one of the insects creeping along a thin green leaf. It was extremely difficult to be sure, given the size and colouring, but it did seem to be another of the same insects she had found on her cloth.

"It does look the same."

"It does, doesn't it? They have been extremely hard to breed, and we are trying to keep them very carefully quarantined."

"Why?"

"They are potentially a severe crop pest. We received our first specimens from some farmers who were losing swathes of their crops. Thankfully they didn't survive long in the new climate, but more kept showing up. We knew we had to find a more secure solution.

If our specimens escaped and got into the farms, then we could be exposing many more farmers to this pest than already are at risk. IT could lead to starvation, or at least a very difficult situation. This is why we have collected some at all, in order to find a way to kill them in the wild and protect our food." Meeza reached out and took the cloth from Shanti's hands. "And yet, despite all that risk and worry, you found some on some random pieces of cloth outside."

Shanti watched as Meeza retrieved some glass containers from beneath the workbench that the enclosure was sitting on. The older woman placed the cloth carefully inside and then attached a lid, with a thin layer of some sort of thick oil between the box and the lid.

"I can only hope that these are some that escaped while we were transporting them to the University." Shanti could hear the scepticism in Meeza's voice, and after a moment's introspection Shanti thought she knew why. If these insects were so dangerous and worrying, then surely they would have been transported with just as much caution as they were housed in the University.

"Thank you for bringing it in. Here, I'll decontaminate you on the way out."

"Oh," Shanti was surprised to be hurried out of the laboratory.

"I'm sorry, but I have a lot of work to do, especially now that you have brought me this. It really offers some worrying questions about what we are doing here."

"I suppose you must be busy. Well, thank you for sharing so much of what you know."

"It is my pleasure."

"What does decontaminating involve?" Shanti wondered aloud as they returned towards the door she had entered by, and was turned to a small enclosure next to it. A thick curtain hung on the side and Meeza motioned for Shanti to step inside. Then the older lady pulled the curtain closed.

"It's a powder that kills bugs. It makes sure that none of these things are still on your person after you leave here. Would you take your dress off and hang it on the hook just outside the curtain?" Shanti blinked but slowly did as she was instructed. She stood in her underclothes behind the curtain, feeling remarkably exposed.

"Now what?"

"Now I dose you," answered Meeza. As her voice

wound around the thick material of the curtain, a small cloud of white powder burst over the top and descended upon Shanti. A second followed it quickly.

"Why don't you just use that to kill these insects I brought in?" coughed Shanti. "Dust the fields?"

"Oh, you wouldn't want this stuff on our food!"

"But you've just covered me in it?" Shanti tried not to let the panic into her voice, but it was hard to avoid a certain tightness.

"You'll be okay, I'll get you to dust off the excess with this brush and you'll be right as rain in a few minutes." Her hand poked past the curtain, holding a brush with thick soft white bristles and waving it back and forth. Shanti took it and ran it across her skin and underclothes. It did a good job of brushing away the powder, leaving her skin slightly pale, but feeling relatively clean. "And it'll wipe out any other bugs that you may have been harbouring." Shanti could hear the smile in Meeza's voice as she insinuated that Shanti was covered in bugs. "You can get dressed again now."

As Shanti did, Meeza continued talking, thinking out loud. "I'm really curious about the bugs you brought in. We've found that these things die quite easily, and take an inordinate amount of work to get to breed, and so we have a very limited supply at any one time. It's the only reason our crops haven't been wiped out yet. But they keep showing up in the fields, which is very distressing. But you said you found these yesterday?"

Shanti agreed.

"And there's still quite a few on that rag," pondered Meeza, though Shanti found herself surprised that Meeza considered the number of insects remaining to count as 'quite a few'. "Either they are surviving longer than I might have expected in the streets, which is worrying, or they are breeding much easier and there are more of them, which is also very concerning!"

"Hopefully it is some that escaped the transport," said Shanti as she pushed the curtain aside and walked out of the enclosure.

"Even so."

THE NOT-APHIDS TOOK up most of Shanti's mind as she left the University and caught another taxi cart to take her to the lights markets. She barely noticed the crowd moving around her, or the colour of the sky. Something about these little insects burrowed into her brain and worried her. They could be so dangerous and yet they were just out in the streets? She remembered one year when the harvest at Graama had been poor, and the difficulties that had followed. Luckily the village would always look out for one another, and no-one was left truly broke or hungry.

The thought of people starving made her think of the hungry and poor Skuggi who were living in the alleys. She had found the insects on a rag that had come from one of them. And they had surrounded her in that alley before she had grabbed this rag. She still couldn't decide whether that should leave her feeling uncomfortable or not. Her thoughts turned to the woman and her baby and she felt sure that they wouldn't have hurt her.

But these bugs came from them. Maybe Dunin's rumour mongers were right, maybe the Skuggi were sabotaging the lights? The idea was outlandish, why would anybody deliberately kill lights? It would just make one's own circumstances harder. And why? The blight just made it even harder for people to get jobs, and surely that was the worst outcome for the Skuggi?

She looked for them as the cart moved on, the huddles of dingy rags at the mouths to alleys, and always accompanied by the dim and dying dead lights that were flaking away from the corners of the buildings around them. She began to see it as so many of the inhabitants of Gorduum must see it, angry people who have been ignored by the rest of society lashing out and striking at that same society in any way that they can. She shook her head. I don't want to fall into that trap, she told herself. Dunin said that the blight came first. I have to remember that.

Finally the cart deposited her in the familiar street where she had come a few days earlier to meet with the lights brokers. As she walked along the street towards the offices, she wondered if her decision was the correct one. She had sat up into the night, checking numbers, and she had weighed the consequences of this choice carefully. It was terrifying to think that the success of the annual Graama festival would now entirely hinge upon how well she made this decision. Maybe she should change her mind? She still had time to. She was walking along the street from the opposite direction today, and so the first office she saw was Aiskuu.

The lions still guarded the entrance, and the simple sign looked the same. But something looked different. Shanti stood facing the entrance for a few minutes while she tried to figure out what the problem was, what had changed. Then she realised. The lights that had been growing around the corner of the building had been sick when she last came, but they were worse now. She had thought that the thin vines were dead when she came last, but she hadn't been conscious of small leaves higher up, and young shoots trying to outrun the blight. Now, only a couple of days later, even those small touches were black.

Shanti thought of Zala sitting inside. The woman had been intimidating and daunting for Shanti to interact with, but by the time she had left there had been a connection of sorts. Shanti liked her. And that was the only reason she had stopped at this door, the only reason she was half considering opening the door to make her order, the fact that Shanti liked the woman she had spoken to. Even though she had decided to return to Artee for her order, the sight of Aiskuu's offices had made her pause and reconsider. But those dead lights kept her from changing her mind.

Just as she was about to leave, a sudden thought gripped her. Shanti walked to the left, approaching the mouth of the alley. The act made her pulse quicken and she felt sweat bead on her forehead. Memories of dark figures rising up around her pressed forward, making it harder to breathe. However, the crowd was busy in the street around her and she wasn't going to actually enter the alley. She swallowed hard and forced herself on. She got close enough to examine some of the dead vines.

It only took a moment to be sure, to find not-aphids on them. Identical to the ones she had just delivered to the University. So many that they were in constant motion, and easy to spot.

The discovery left Shanti confused and scared. How had these things escaped? They must be the reason for the blight that was devastating the lights of Gorduum, but Meeza had said that they didn't breed well and that they died quickly. So how were they causing such a massive problem in Gorduum? Would it spread? Why hadn't anyone else noticed that these bugs were the problem?

However, that became clearer as she watched. There were fewer bugs on the vines that had been dead the longest, and the few that were there were dying in swathes before her. In a tiny, nearly imperceptible but constant stream, the minute insects fell off the vine to the ground. There were clusters on the lights that had been alive when she last came, but now that those were dead, even there the insects were falling like sand in an hourglass. Shanti moved a little closer, and could quickly see that the lights that had been dead longest didn't have any noticeable bugs left on them.

So, clearly they were dying fast enough that no-one had managed to capture them, or notice them in such a way as to realise what they were. Perhaps they were nearly all dead every time someone came to investigate a dead light? But if that was the case, how could they be breeding fast enough to spread around the city? And surely they should be spreading out from central locations, as the bugs moved on, not hitting patches all across Gorduum in no pattern? It was bewildering.

Shanti backed away and slowly made her way to Artee. She still had a job to do, but now she wondered what she should do about her discovery.

Shanti made her order at Artee and left deep in thought. The broker had been very pleased to take her order and confirm the details, offering her tea and chocolates which was very kind. She sipped at her cup but found it hard to stay focused on the conversation. Something about the insects was worrying her. She was quite certain that these insects must be the cause of the blight, but they appeared to die in large numbers. They slipped from the lights she had seen them on in huge numbers, falling like dust. To her mind, such a short life cycle would limit their spread to short destructive bursts but little else, as Meeza had said was happening in some farms. If they died so quickly, it would be extremely hard for them to spread through Gorduum. So, in that case, how were they appearing in other locations around the city?

The discussion in the comfortable office continued, focusing on where she would like her stock delivered, and by when, and then signing various contracts that made guarantees about all those details. Shanti kept trying to clear the fog in her head, to bring herself to focus on this task. It was vital for her village that she get this right! And yet, she found herself getting more and more tense about the blight in the city. If the insects were so short lived, that must mean that someone was bringing them to locations of lights deliberately and allowing them to spread. There was no other way for them to move between the infected areas in the times that her uncle and others had been talking about. But how could anyone think that such a thing was acceptable? What motivation could they have?

Papers signed, deposits paid, and her satchel stuffed with documents that she would need to keep very safe, Shanti left the brokers and stood in the street wondering what she should do next. The crowd drifted around her like snow in the winter air, softly spinning and moving without leaving any impression upon her. Finally she turned towards the Naatat ferry docks and began to walk towards them. She floated through the crowd like a cloud on a still summer day, moving slowly towards her destination, where she paid for a ferry and leaned back in her seat, watching the sky over the city on her way back to her uncle's.

Outside the apartment, she looked both ways down the street, scanning the passers-by for a familiar cart. She stayed at the edge of the road for minutes, hoping that she would see that smile she was searching for, a friendly face that she could talk to and confide in. She felt like her head would explode with the thoughts and worries that were filling it, and there was only one person that she could think of who might help her relax. But there was nothing. Eventually, feeling empty but unsurprised, Shanti turned inside and headed up the stairs.

Gaibaan was standing in the hall outside the apartment.

"What are you doing here?" Shanti squeaked, and then immediately slapped her left hand over her mouth in embarrassment.

"It's a pleasure to see you," smirked Gaibaan, straightening from where he was leaning his back against the wall and walking towards her. "I was hoping I wouldn't have to wait long."

"I didn't see your automobile," stammered Shanti, still trying to get her thoughts in order. This was the last thing she had expected.

"No, I don't use it all the time. The fuel is quite costly to obtain, and so I have to ration the use sometimes." Gaibaan frowned at the admission, but brightened again almost immediately. He had reached Shanti and leaned forward to kiss her on the cheek, placing a hand on her shoulder as he did. "How has your day been?"

It was possibly the first time Shanti recalled him simply enquiring about herself. "It has been good. I returned to the lights brokers and placed the order for my village."

"Capital!" Gaibaan took her by the hand and began to walk back to the apartment door. Shanti felt as though he was pulling her. He asked no further questions about her day.

As she followed in his wake, Shanti found her attention drawn to the lights in the corners of the hallway ceiling. They seemed dimmer than usual though it was hard to be sure, with daylight streaming in the large window at the end of the corridor.

At the door, Gaibaan stood to the side and waited for Shanti to unlock the door. She did so but then turned to speak with him. She did not open the door. He made no move to go past her.

"What are you doing this evening?" he smiled.

"I didn't have any plans."

"I was wondering if you would come to have dinner with me at my home?" His pale eyes glowed in the dim light like a cat's.

"I'm not sure that would be entirely appropriate," Shanti began. She was hoping that the risk to a young person's reputation would be a polite enough way to avoid the invitation. The idea of being alone with this presumptuous self-centred man made her feel nauseous.

"I can see your point. Would it help if I asked you to bring a chaperone? I would not be offended," he interjected, heading off her excuses before she could even speak them aloud.

"I suppose." Shanti trailed off. She wasn't sure how she was going to politely refuse the dinner, but she desperately wished that she could.

"It's settled then," he grinned. He pulled a small piece of cardboard out of his jacket pocket. Written on it in simple but fine calligraphy, was his name and titles, with an address. A coat of arms took up much of the right hand side of the card. "Here is my card. If you give this to your chaperone or a taxi driver, they should bring you to my home. I might recommend you bring your uncle! I will expect you both by five o'clock." He leaned in again to kiss her cheek and then walked down the hall, whistling as he went.

After he had descended the stairs, Shanti moved back down the hall and tried to stretch up as high as she could to look closely at the ceiling lights. They were definitely beginning to look a little grey. As she watched, a tiny translucent insect came scuttling around from the back of the vine, raced along it for a stretch and then ducked back into the hidden space again. They were here, in her uncle's building. Shanti took a deep breath, suddenly desperately aware that she had brought a rag full of these insects into this building. The guilt balled up in her stomach as she returned to the apartment and went inside.

THE REMAINDER of the day passed without incident. Dunin returned and was polite in conversation with her, and the lad came in to clean the home and collect some laundry. Shanti told Dunin about Gaibaan's invitation, though he had delivered it as more of an instruction she realised.

Dunin sighed. "I suppose it would not do to insult the man completely by simply not showing up," he groaned.

"I am not sure. I know that I would prefer not to spend any more time with this man."

"He is a trouble-maker, but he is a sometimes profitable trouble-maker." Dunin pursed his lips and sipped at a fresh cup of tea delivered by the lad. "We can go for a simple dinner. Perhaps after a cold and awkward evening, he will let go of any position you hold in his thoughts."

"I can but hope," she replied before thanking Gunin for her tea.

The lad helped them prepare for the evening, selecting suitable clothing and giving them advice on accessories. Soon it was time to go. Together they walked down the stairs and out into the street. Shanti was keenly aware of the shadows in the hall, even as Dunin blinked and narrowed his eyes in order to see better. He grunted in displeasure but spoke no concerns about the hall's illumination. Shanti risked a glance upwards and saw one distinctly grey and flaking leaf. She dropped her gaze immediately, the knot in her stomach pulling still tighter. Maybe it was no specific person spreading the blight, but many people who did not know what they were carrying. After all, she had not realised what the bugs on the rags were when she had brought them into these hallways. The idea did not assuage her tense stomach.

Outside, Dunin stepped forward and hailed a passing cart with no passengers. As it pulled to a stop before him, Shanti groaned as she saw who the driver was. Keema made eye contact with Shanti and her face drew taut. Despite the uncomfortable meeting, Shanti did feel glad to see Keema again. She wondered what she should say.

"Good evening!" Dunin spoke with a brightness that Shanti knew was unfelt. "We are on our way to dinner with a young man who has taken a shine to my sweet niece here! Would you please take us to this address?"

Keema flicked her eyes down to the card that Dunin held out, then nodded once. Her lips were set in a horizontal line. Dunin gave the card back to Shanti as he helped her climb up into the passenger seats, then sat down next to her. He leaned over so close that their shoulders were pressed together and then whispered from the corner of his mouth, "My, we found a grumpy one here."

Keema drove in silence through the busy evening streets, and so Dunin began trying to fill the cart with conversation himself. He asked Shanti about her experience of Gorduum so far, what had stood out. She felt very self-conscious answering his questions while Keema sat in front of them. She knew the other woman would be able to hear her every word, though she made a fantastic show of ignoring them completely.

"I've been particularly lucky to meet a wonderful young woman while I've been here," she told her uncle. "She showed me much of Gorduum, and helped me feel less lost from the first time I walked out into the streets."

"That is lucky. Will you see her before you leave?"

"I would like to," said Shanti, staring at the back of Keema's ears. "Unfortunately when we were looking through the University art gallery she did not enjoy the art works that I did, and seemed to take the difference of opinion personally. I have always wanted to see new things and go to new places, and so I loved the strangest artworks, whereas I think she was insulted that I might not appreciate this city as she does. I haven't seen her since the day before yesterday."

"You have no way to contact her?"

"No, she kept finding me. She once said that she often enjoys meeting her friends at a pub called the Bare Faced Con, so I was hoping to find that place and see if that allowed me to track her down."

"Oh." Dunin sniffed and rubbed his mouth. "Well, I'm sorry about that. It's always difficult to have a falling out and no way to resolve things. Even if you aren't to remain friends, I always find it is best to clear the air before heading your separate ways." He patted Shanti's knee, in an attempt to comfort her. "I'm sure things will work out."

"I just want her to know that I would never intentionally upset her. I need her to know that she doesn't have to like the same things I do, I still treasured her company. She was already one of my closest friends, though we had just met."

"It will work out," Dunin repeated with a hopeful smile, though his eyes betrayed his doubts.

In front of them, Keema's head never moved an inch.

Blackness was spreading through the sky like spilled ink and a chill breeze was blowing along the street when they arrived at what must have been Gaibaan's home. The house was part of a circus, a large circular plaza, with a huge green garden taking up much of the centre. A fountain, and a series of small ponds occupied the garden, and tall metal light posts stood at regular intervals within it, the vines criss-crossing around each thin metal pole and clustering their pink fruit at the top. Most of the space was well tended short grass, with gravel paths winding through it, surrounded by criss-crossing metal arcs lower than a person's knee. Flower bushes and short fruit trees grew in small beds alongside the paths.

The homes were all much larger than anything Shanti had seen so far in Gorduum, and gave the impression of space, even from outside. That alone was impressive. While Dunin's apartment had been a single tall building divided into several homes, this was a smaller building that was clearly entirely made up of a single residence.

Shanti and her uncle climbed down at the gate that matched the address on the card, and Dunin paid Keema. Shanti looked at her friend, but found she was unable to read the expression on the woman's face. Whereas Keema had been so happy and bubbly before, now she was silent. One improvement was that there was no longer the same anger or tightness that had been on her face when they first climbed aboard. Shanti wondered if perhaps her comments had struck home.

Keema collected her fee and nodded to Dunin. "Have a diverting evening sir. Ma'am." Her deep eyes flickered to Shanti and she grimaced. She leaned towards them slightly and said "I like this city myself, but I've said before that I wouldn't mind seeing what's outside it. Maybe you might think of other reasons your friend could have been upset." Then she flicked her reins and led the cart off down the street again. Shanti watched her until she turned a corner and was gone.

"Are you coming?" asked Dunin, opening the tall metal gate that protected a very small garden courtyard before the actual front door of the home. Shanti nodded and followed.

They thudded the large brass knocker on the door. Shanti was impressed at the loud banging that echoed through the house and returned to them. It made the home sound absolutely enormous. Eventually footsteps began to make themselves known in the vast echo, their click and clack rising in volume as their owner approached and the door was opened. A large stern matron answered, wearing a tightly buttoned formal dress. The matron bid them a good evening and welcomed them into the house. She led them to a small guest room and installed them into very well cushioned chairs, looking out a window at the garden in the middle of the circus. As night drew in the view was very pretty. Shortly the matron returned with two small glasses of port, giving one to Shanti and one to her uncle.

"At least he treats us well," smiled Dunin after the matron had left again.

"Yes!" agreed Shanti enthusiastically. She was still not thrilled about being here, in this man's home, but the port was sweet and strong and left her feeling very relaxed about the whole situation.

"And the matron seems to know her job very well." Dunin sipped his glass of port and watched the doorway. "I wonder how he can afford to employ her when he has so many debts, and is asking for so many sponsors?"

Then, Gaibaan joined them. He walked in with a smile, striding across to shake hands with Dunin immediately. He brushed his hands on the sides of his trousers as he crossed the room, taking Dunin's hand in his own and enveloping it with his other.

"Dunin, sir, I am so glad that you agreed to chaperone this delightful woman to dinner with me! I am absolutely overjoyed to have you!" The younger man pumped their hands up and down furiously.

"Yes, I must admit that I'm curious to see your home, after all our work with one another," answered Dunin, manoeuvring his hand back out of the over-eager grip.

"And Shanti!" Gaibaan moved over to her and spread his arms wide, catching her in a hug and kissing her on both cheeks. "I knew you would join me. I feel the connection too!" He let her go and then offered them both his elbows. "Shall I give you a tour while Mrs Shada ensures that our meal is served in the dining hall correctly?"

Without waiting for their response, he whisked them out of the room and down a well-lit hall.

Gaibaan led them to a wide flight of stairs. Looking up, Shanti could see that his home encompassed at least three floors. At the first floor, he led them down a hallway and showed off a library, and his office. There were papers and notes strewn through his offices, and some small metal boxes and balls of glass sitting on the desk.

"Your prototypes sir!" He declared, leading Dunin over to the desk. "They aren't quite put together yet, there's just a few connections and adjustments I need to make, but I will bring them to you tomorrow, just as we agreed."

Dunin sighed and nodded. "Yes. I'm sure they will be very impressive then." He picked up a thick cord that dangled from the metal box. "It comes with its own vines, just like regular lights I see."

"Yes. Ha ha. Very droll." Gaibaan was smiling, but his tone was much less enthused.

Dunin looked up. Above them, illuminating the busy workspace, was a light dangling from its fixtures, winding through the chain, and then growing spread out on a broad and intricate wire frame to create a concave disc looking down on them. "I see you favour the yellow for your own work, rather than one of these electrics?" said Dunin. Shanti noticed a crease of anger appear and vanish in Gaibaan's forehead.

"Obviously it is difficult to have them installed into a house just now, but I have plans." His voice was flat. He blinked and sniffed, his smile re-establishing itself between his cheeks. "However, I do have these plans that I can show you!" And so saying he began to dig through the piles of paper on his desk, pulling out sketches, diagrams, sheets of tiny cramped writing. He pushed each one into Dunin's hands, muttering to himself as he did.

Suddenly the dinner came into focus for Shanti. This was all an excuse for Gaibaan to get Dunin deeper into whatever dealings were happening here. It was the same as the dance the night before. While Gaibaan might find Shanti interesting on some level, it was not enough to overcome the way he saw her as a tool, or a lever, to apply to others in order to achieve even more investment in his plans. With a jolt she realised that he had even suggested that she bring a chaperone, and that it be her uncle. He knew that she was uncomfortable around him, but he found a way to use that in order to create an opportunity for himself. Shanti felt nauseated and unclean, used by this scheming man.

"I'm just going to find a bathroom," she said. She felt an urgent need to wash her hands and face. Not to mention a need to get away from this man and the way he made her feel like an object for him to use.

"Certainly, there is one down the hall. Feel free to have a bit of an explore. Some of my ancestors decorated the rooms in fascinating fashion." Gaibaan didn't even look around at her. Dunin's eyes grew wider and he pleaded silently with his expression at Shanti. She shook her head slightly. Then Gaibaan stood straight and spun around. He jabbed a finger at Shanti.

"Don't go upstairs!" he snapped, his eyes flashing. He paused, then chuckled nervously, rolling his finger back into his hand and lowering his arm. "I mean, please don't go further upstairs. That is where my personal rooms are, and they are private." He smiled and Shanti stepped backwards.

"Thank you, I won't." She held on until she had passed through the door and back into the hallway before lifting her skirts and fleeing as fast as she dared.

THE BATHROOM WAS NOT FAR down the hall and Shanti was relieved to shelter inside its cool surfaces. A mirror stood above a basin to one side, with brass taps curving up and over the porcelain curve. She looked at herself in it, considering the colour of her dress, and the quick style she had managed to pull her hair into with the help of the lad before leaving her uncle's. She felt that she looked good. What a pity that it was wasted on this self-centred man.

Shanti considered Gaibaan's eyes, his long hair, and the way his hands had felt as he held her close. It was true, she could feel her breath catch and her pulse quicken, but she could not condone the way he passed her aside so often when he had a chance to advance his business interests.

Without meaning to, she found herself thinking of the way Fabrin had held her. The way his smile creased into his cheeks. The way his eyes had burned as he had looked at her before kissing her, the night before she had discovered she was coming to Gorduum. Why did she think that she needed to avoid upsetting Gaibaan when she knew that there were other, kinder, people that were truly interested in her and her life? For the first time since arriving in Gorduum, Shanti felt as though she wanted to go home, for herself.

She freshened herself up, and then returned to the hallway. At first she looked to the right, in the direction of the office where she had left her uncle dealing with Gaibaan's desperate enthusiasm. Then, she looked to the left. There the hallway continued, with doors that beckoned her curiosity. So, smiling as she did so, she walked left.

The doors revealed quite unexceptional spaces. Each was lit by a similar lights-hanging as had illuminated the office, and mostly they looked like storerooms, closets, or workspaces. Clothing lay on one bench within reach of a selection of threads on spindles and a pillow bristling with needles. Clearly a repair space. Another room contained brooms, buckets, brushes and all manner of cleaning items, kept out of the way but easy to hand. Shanti realised as she explored that the house, although spectacular, must no longer have a proper space for the servants to occupy. That was why their workspaces were next door to the master's office. She wondered if this was due to a lack of money. Dunin had said that Gaibaan had been spending his inheritance on various projects for years. Perhaps he could no longer afford many servants and had to clean and repair for himself, like so many others would? The thought pleased her.

On the other hand, if he didn't have servants, was it really better to keep this equipment where guests might walk in on it, even if that did mean they were easier for him to retrieve? It was true that he did not entertain guests very often, so perhaps it was not a concern of his. But what could he be doing with the old servant's spaces that forced him to move these things here? Where would they have been in a house like this?

The downstairs had contained proper entertaining spaces, and they had walked past a large dining room as they had embarked on their host's tour. So would that mean this second floor was the original servant's space?

Shanti looked into the last room and found herself in a large bedroom, though the lights had been shaded and there was a clear layer of dust in it. Cobwebs were beginning to grow down from the corners of the room. One thin strand of web hung from the wardrobe in a long drooping loop that reached to the light hanging in the centre of the room. She looked at the ornate moulding at the top and bottom of each wall. The huge bed was still impeccably made up in rich blankets and laced pillows, though faded from lack of use. Clearly this had been a bedroom for one of the house's family. This was not a servant's room. Upstairs then? But Gaibaan had said that was his personal quarters? Would he have swapped his living space on this second floor in order to live in the old servant's quarters? That was ludicrous, surely?

Shanti began to walk back down the hallway, pacing slowly as she tried to figure out what Gaibaan was doing here. She strolled barely faster than a snail, creeping to a stop just outside the office door. She listened to the voices within.

"... was talking to Rarvit, and you know how often he supports many many engaging young people with their ideas, and he will certainly be investing in the electrics, and-"

"I believe you Gaibaan, I am sure you have found many investors, I just don't see why that means you are still trying to sell things to me?"

"Obviously you should look at investing further yourself! Or perhaps, now that you know I have the support of such a successful investor, you can spread that word and get others to join in with him. They can be confident of a strong return, knowing that Rarvit is investing."

"They would see it that way. Did you say that he has already invested? Did he write up an agreement for you already, since the gala?"

"Of course, it is far too soon to have an agreement that is actually written up, but he…"

Shanti stopped listening. They were still going, and so she had time.

She edged up to the side of the doorframe and peeked around it. Inside she could see the two men sitting by the desk, new papers being bundled from one space to another while Gaibaan held them up as though they would convince Dunin with their mere presence. However, neither of the men was looking towards the door. Breathing quickly, but trying to keep control of herself, she stepped past the open doorway and then spun her back against the hall wall. She held her breath and looked upwards. After a short count it became clear that no-one was about to come out into the hallway and find her. And so, she turned and walked as quickly as she could to the stairs.

She moved up the stairs cautiously, hoping that she was not about to bump into the matron of the house. She crossed her fingers as she climbed, pleading with the universe that the matron would be busy preparing dinner and not coming upstairs. She realised that they had been on the second floor for quite a while now. Dinner couldn't be too far off. Right at that moment, she heard footsteps on the flights below her. Eyes widening, she darted up the remaining stairs, pulling open the door and jumping through, before swinging it shut and leaning against it, holding the handle to avoid a loud click that might echo down the stairs.

She breathed, counting in her head, until she was sure that the matron was not continuing up the stairs. Whether or not that woman came upstairs,

Shanti wouldn't have long to explore before the men noticed she had been gone too long. She turned to see what the top floor held in store.

The hallway behind her looked almost identical to the floor below, though the floor had no rugs or carpet covering its bare wooden planks. There were no paintings on the walls, but at least the floor was well swept. Shanti began to walk down the hall so that she could investigate what lay behind each of the doors.

She only had to open one door for her stomach to twist in shock and fright. Behind the first door she opened on the left, she found a small cramped room that must have once been a servant's room. She could see the discolouring on the floor that showed where a small bed and chest must have sat at one point. But now the room was filled with glass boxes, stacked on top of each other like bizarre bricks. A narrow path led through the boxes. The boxes hummed with noise and activity, as they were utterly filled with the same not-aphids that she had found on the rags and vines in the streets.

The bugs were identical for sure, and they teemed within each box. There were small tubes that allowed the insects to crawl from one box to another. As she followed the thin gap that wound in between them Shanti found a hatch in one box that would have allowed her to open it up, reach in, and take out a hand covered in the tiny insects. She spun on the spot in the centre of the room, her mouth hanging open. As she began to take in what she was seeing, to consider what it might mean to find this huge enclosure of horribly destructive insects, she wondered about the rest of the upstairs.

She left the small room, and stalked across the hallway to open another door. The same sight greeted her, a wall built of see-through glass boxes like bricks and swarming with tiny insects that would devour any lights that they came across, sucking the life and light from their vines and leaves, until they crumbled like ash. Instantly she shut the door and moved to the next. Yet another room of the same, filled with insects in their enclosures.

How had he done it? How were they breeding? The woman at the University had been so clear in explaining that they had been unable to get the insects to breed. A professional lab, full of scientists and experts, that was unable to keep their numbers of these insects up. Yet somehow a single young man was able to house swarms of them!

And these were not eating lights! There were no lights in the glass enclosures, just regular branches and leaves, covered in a shifting sea of tiny bugs. They were pock marked with holes where the bugs were eating them, but the foliage wasn't turning into dried up grey flakes. Was that something to do with his success?

She opened one last door and found a room similar to the others. The only exception was that here there was one large central glass enclosure. Within it sat a creature that Shanti found repellent. It was almost as long as her foot, and its bulk was a soft pale apricot-coloured blob that pulsed and shifted. At one end she could make out the vestigial body and head, the legs twisting uselessly in the air. It was a queen.

As she watched, she saw more bugs bringing it sustenance, and carrying away tiny pods of translucent goo that she assumed must be eggs. In this room there were some lights, contained within the enclosures, in small pots. The twisted bushes were being drained in exactly the manner that she had seen in the streets. The blight was caused by these insects draining something from the lights in order to feed their queen. That was why these things were so disastrous to the lights in Gorduum, they were workers trying to feed the queen. That was why they were dying so quickly, they were not meant to survive. They were meant to live in a hive, like the one that Gaibaan had created in his own home.

Shanti shook her head. It was one thing to have believed that the blight was a disease that was affecting lights in Gorduum. It was quite another to discover that someone had clearly deliberately released these things in order to cause the blight in the first place. For a moment Shanti wondered what in the world could have possessed him to do such a thing, but then she realised that his electric lights would become far more valuable in a world where the lights were no longer growing. Could he truly be so ruthless?

By the door Shanti found a set of boxes and gloves, clearly designed for extracting insects and carrying them away. Yes, he could be.

Next to these items was a box that looked familiar. Shanti leaned down to investigate it more closely and recognised it after a few moments. It was the box that he had been carrying out of the University when he bumped into her in the hallways. He had been carrying it after meeting with someone in the insect lab. Near the door was a small enclosure that contained another of the unsettling queen's, though this one was much smaller. Had he intercepted a queen that some farmer had found and brought into Gorduum? If he could keep them from making this connection, he would keep control over the blight for longer.

Shanti hurried back out of the rooms and reached the door at the top of the stairs. Placing one hand against its surface and twisting the handle extremely slowly, she slid it open a tiny crack. Through the opening she was able to peer out to the staircase and determine that there was nobody there. She slipped through and gently pushed the door closed behind her. Step by step she moved down until she was able to move back into the hallway towards the office where she hoped Gaibaan and Dunin were still in discussion.

She turned into the room just as Gaibaan turned towards the doorway, spotting her instantly.

"Ah there you are!" He beamed and spread his arms wide, as though he were about to embrace her. "Mrs Shada has just been in to inform us that dinner is waiting. Shall we?" He swept forward, gathering her up as he went, with Dunin trailing behind.

SHANTI TRIED to let her uncle know that something was wrong as they walked downstairs and into the dining room, but Gaibaan clutched her hand onto his elbow and she was unable to say anything for fear of how he might react. When their host was not looking, Shanti attempted to make a face, twisting her eyebrows or lips, anything that might communicate her fear to Dunin, but nothing worked.

Within moments she was sitting at the dining table, with a large clean white plate laid before her, and silver dishes sitting beneath their large curved covers along the table in front of her. Gaibaan sat at the head of the table to her left and her uncle sat to the right. She stared at the large serving dishes, the curved reflections of herself and her uncle appearing warped and bloated on their surface. Shanti wondered how she could get herself and her uncle out of this house.

As the matron came by to lift the lids on the

serving dishes, Shanti inspected the food that was revealed. Although it steamed with fresh heat and the sauces glistened in an appetising manner, Shanti found that all she could imagine was the shining flesh of the queen lying in its glass case somewhere above her head, ruining what little appetite she may have had.

Fried triangular appetisers were placed carefully on the plate before her, and small silver bowls of green and deep red sauce placed alongside. Shanti couldn't imagine actually eating anything right now. Then, an idea came to her. She picked up the large samosa and dipped the corner into the green sauce, then took a middling bite. She was impressed, it actually tasted very good. For a moment she considered eating more, but looking across the table at Gaibaan as he stuffed the food into his mouth gave her renewed courage. The man had no shame whatsoever, he wasn't feeling at all guilty, while a massive society-damaging plague of insects were happily breeding and living only meters above their heads. Resolved, she began to groan and roll her eyes.

"Are you alright?" Dunin asked. Gaibaan barely glanced in her direction.

Shanti shook her head in response.

"What's the matter," said her uncle.

She tried to mime a reply, motioning her hands around her stomach and clutching at her head. When his face remained a mask of confusion, she sighed internally, then opened her mouth to say "I don't feel very well." She allowed a small piece of the well chewed food to fall from her mouth, hearing a wet splat as the morsel hit the table next to her plate.

Dunin stood immediately, placing a hand on her back between her shoulder blades. Gaibaan frowned and took a sip from his wide glass of red wine.

"Did something in the meal upset your stomach?" he asked.

Shanti shook her head. She had sudden visions of an angry Gaibaan taking out a punishment on Mrs Shada. She didn't want to be responsible for that.

"Do you want to go back to the bathroom?" asked Dunin.

"No," gasped Shanti. "I think-" Here she paused for effect, gulping in a huge mouthful of air. "I think we might need to go home."

"But-" Dunin looked up at their host, who was gently swirling the wine in his glass as he watched them. He pursed his lips and shrugged.

"If Shanti is unwell, then perhaps you should." He sipped more wine. "It is a shame that you would miss the meal, Mrs Shada is a very fine cook." He stood and walked around to the other side of Shanti. "If you feel that unwell, I will walk you to the street." There was the tiniest hint of a question in his voice, but he helped Shanti to her feet immediately anyway. Of course, thought Shanti. I didn't need to worry about upsetting him. He's already had enough time to try and get Dunin more engaged with his schemes.

Once outside Gaibaan stood with them until they had managed to summon a taxi. He shook Dunin's hand and gave the other man a hearty farewell, then embraced Shanti and kissed her cheek. She tried to cough to avoid it, but he came in anyway.

"I hope to see you again soon," he said with a smile, but without a single word in regards to her feeling unwell. He waited for them to climb on board their taxi before turning and heading back into his house. Shanti found her gaze drawn to the windows on the upper floor. They were dark, but it was impossible to figure out whether that darkness was caused by the night currently wrapping around them, her limited perspective from the street below, or whether it was caused by Gaibaan's efforts to hide the insect enclosures. Would she have noticed that darkness earlier, before she knew what was contained in those rooms?

As the taxi began to move forward, Dunin turned to Shanti and asked "What is all this about? There's no way you are really sick, is there?"

"Do you think he could tell?"

"I think so." Shanti grimaced at her uncle's comment. "But I don't think it matters. He got what he wanted out of the evening." Now it was Dunin's turn to grimace.

"Yes, I did notice that."

"So, I don't think he is offended. You had already shown that you weren't as keen on him as he thought, but he got a business meeting out of things."

"Good." She didn't want him as an enemy. Someone who would go to the lengths that he already had could be more dangerous than she wanted to contemplate.

"So, again, what was all this about?"

"You will not believe what I found on the top floor of that house." And she explained, from her decision to slip past the office doorway all the way up until her return. As she described the rooms and rooms of insects, he blinked and then his mouth fell open.

"Are you sure?" he asked, though there was no real doubt in the question, just shock at the very revelation itself.

"Absolutely," said Shanti, before explaining how one room had lights ready for feeding to the queen. By the time she had finished, Dunin was slumped back in the seat, staring up into the dark night sky.

"What do you think?" she asked.

"What do I think?" Dunin answered vaguely, as though he still didn't know the answer to that question himself. He slowly straightened and looked around them, before lifting one hand to squeeze the bridge of his nose. "You know, I think we should go and pay a visit to an old friend of mine. I think she would be very very interested to find out what you know."

He leaned forward and tapped the driver on the shoulder before giving a new set of directions. There was a moment of haggling as a new price needed to be negotiated, but Dunin didn't put up much of a fight. From the glinting smile on the face of the driver as they turned away, Shanti assumed that her uncle was paying far too much. She was glad to see this evidence that he believed her and took her concerns seriously.

The streets were quiet. Dunin's hand stayed at his chin, stroking and pulling at his beard. Shanti breathed the cool air deeply, watching the stars move against the solid shadows of the buildings that towered on either side. The corners of buildings chipped away at the midnight blue sky, shadowing and revealing their pin point lights above. In the darkness of the streets and alleys around her, Shanti knew that people were cowering and suffering. All because of one man with an obsession. Was he unable to see what he was doing? Did he think that it was a price worth paying for his invention to become part of the world? She couldn't countenance the thought. How could anything be worth such sabotage?

SHANTI SHOOK HERSELF AWAKE. She had fallen asleep on her uncle's shoulder. She sat up and wiped the crust from the corner of her mouth, and felt the bones in her neck and spine click and creak into position. She stretched her arms and shivered.

"Perfect timing," said Dunin. "We're here."

The house beside them looked pretty much the same as the one they had just left. It was tall and of a piece with the other houses in the block. Unlike Gaibaan's home, this one didn't face onto a broad circus with pools and gardens filling it. This plaza was rectangular, and covered in cobblestone. Statues guarded the four corners.

"Where is this?"

"This is the home of my old friend Zala. You met her, at Aiskuu?"

"Yes, I recall." Shanti did recall, and now felt very aware that she had confirmed an order with a different company earlier that same day. She had stood outside this woman's workplace and made a conscious decision not to work with her. *I wonder if she saw me?* Shanti tried to remember if there were many windows on the facade of Aiskuu's offices.

They walked through another large iron gate and approached the door to the house. All was dark. The house's lights must be shaded. *How late is it?* Shanti thought to herself. She had lost track of the evening by sleeping in the taxi.

Dunin lifted the brass knocker and swung it heavily down, the thud echoing across the plaza in the darkness. Somewhere a dog began barking. *Who could be watching over us now,* Shanti wondered. *There were no eyes for the Masked God to see through.* Shanti felt lonelier than she had in a long time. A smirking face came to her mind, and she wished that face was alongside her now.

They waited and then Dunin knocked again. Just as he was lifting the knocker a third time they heard footsteps approaching. The door opened slightly, revealing the narrow suspicious eyes of a tall thin woman who was clutching her thick dressing gown around herself.

"What do you want at this time of night?" she snapped. "Who are you?"

"A reasonable question," replied Dunin. "My name is Dunin Penpen, and this is my niece Shanti. She has discovered something that I know my old friend Zala will be extremely interested in hearing about. Could you please wake her?"

"Are you kidding, at this time of night?" The tall woman looked out over their heads. "Is this a trick? I warn you, if you try anything I will grab the sword off the wall next to me!"

"I am extremely sorry to have disturbed you," said Shanti, placing a hand on her uncle's chest to shift him aside as she stepped forward. "I didn't know what else to do. I have found out something extremely distressing and my uncle suggested that Zala might be just the person I need to talk to. Please, I know it is the middle of the night, but it is that important, and that urgent."

The woman sniffed and squinted down at Shanti. She pulled her dressing gown tighter. "I'll see what I can do. Come in and take a seat in the front room. But don't touch anything or make any noise!"

"Thank you," said Shanti, leading the way into the house.

She and Dunin sat silently in the front room for nearly half an hour before Zala joined them. In that time, the matron returned and grudgingly agreed to bring them some water while they waited. As they sipped their drinks, Shanti decided to question her uncle.

"Why have we come to Zala?"

"What do you mean?"

"Why did you think that she would be the appropriate person to tell? I mean, she will surely be upset by this news, if she believes me, but then what?"

"Zala is not a person to be crossed in this city. She has strings tied to many important people, and she will know what to do."

Shanti looked over the detailed stitching in the heavy curtains that were drawn across the front window as they waited. The intricate embroidery must have been extremely valuable, but Shanti could see where the stitching was beginning to pull apart. This house was going through hard times.

Then, there was a noise behind her and she turned to see Zala standing in the doorway. The woman wore her hair loose in a tumble around her shoulders, but she had taken the time to get dressed in blue. She remained in the doorway and crossed her arms, with her head tilted slightly sideways as she examined her late-night guests.

"I see. It is an old acquaintance," Dunin winced at the description, a stark contrast to the way he was greeted days earlier in the offices of Aiskuu. "Bringing along with him a woman who has not taken up an order with my business. These are the people who decided to rouse me from my bed, just as I had fallen asleep. How lucky I am."

"I'm sorry about the order-" began Shanti, but Zala held up one hand to stop her.

"Business is business. What I don't understand is why you are here, in my house, at this time of night."

Shanti bit her lips together and looked at Dunin. She found he was looking back at her. He raised his eyebrows and nodded his head at Zala.

"Uh…" Shanti made a noise while her mind raced, trying to figure out how she should explain what she had found out. "I guess the first thing to say would be, how much has the blight caused problems for your business?"

"Are you some sort of fool?" was all Zala said as an answer, her voice flat.

Shanti cleared her throat. "Well, what would you say if I said I had found out what was causing it."

"That's great. It really is." Zala walked further into the room and sat in one of the chairs. "But why tell me? Why not go to University, or the council? They can apply whatever formula is needed to strengthen the lights or end the disease better than a single lights trader can. And why in the world would you come to me now instead of in the morning?"

"What if I had found that it was caused by one person? Deliberately?"

Silence filled the room as Zala looked back at Shanti. Though the other woman's gaze was intense, Shanti steeled herself to meet it without flinching.

"I would say that I think you should tell me more."

After five minutes the matron was summoned to stoke the stove in the kitchen and prepare tea. The conversation continued deep into the night.

Dawn was beginning to lighten the sky as the cart rattled across the stones in the circus. Birds were disturbed by the noise, and began to flutter out of the trees in the garden. The water in the fountains trickled and tinkled with little else to drown them out.

Dunin motioned the driver to stop much further from the house than they had disembarked the previous night. Shanti and Zala got down and looked around the streets. A second cart entered the circus from a wide street behind them. It pulled to a stop behind their cart as Dunin was climbing down. Two very large men climbed out of the second taxi and walked over to join the trio. Both carts moved off, awkwardly turning in the lane so that they could return the way they came as instructed, rather than continuing forward along the street.

"Thank you for coming so quickly Gartan, Kargin," said Zala, shaking each of the men by the hand. "I'm sure you appreciate that a certain amount of discretion will be required by this work."

The smaller of the two men nodded. These two looked remarkably similar to Shanti's eyes, like twins or mirror images of one another. Each had extraordinarily wide shoulders and they wore pale cream coloured shirts that pulled tight against their muscles as they moved. Each had a bald head and a thick black moustache. However, one of them was taller than her, and the other was noticeably shorter.

Shanti was reasonably sure that the shorter one had been standing near the glasshouses in Aiskuu a day or two earlier. Perhaps he served as a guard quite often. From the way he stood, the set of his eyes, and the way he moved along the cobbled street, she could tell that he was dangerous. She began to reassess what she thought she knew about Zala.

The five of them walked quietly along the street until they reached the gate to Gaibaan's house.

Here they watched as Gartan and Kargin hunched over the gate and did something that sounded conspicuously loud to Shanti. She was not able to see their hands, and they shielded one another from outside eyes, but she heard a clicking and jangling of loose metal before the gate swung open with a creak that went on and on. Shanti cringed, but followed the two men inside.

Motioning the others to follow slowly, the taller of the men ignored the front door and began looking through the windows for a way in. When that didn't seem successful, he pointed at the door and the shorter man moved up to bend over that entrance. Again, Shanti heard metallic noises before the door swung open and the man gestured for the others to follow. This meant that all five of them were standing in the front hall of someone else's house, having broken in without the owner's knowledge.

"Alright," whispered Zala. "Which way to these insects?"

Shanti pointed at the far end of the hall, through a doorway that would lead past the dining room that she had managed to trick her way out of only hours earlier. Beyond that dining room were the stairs that Gaibaan had taken them up on his tour of the house.

"The stairs are back there. It's the third floor, pretty much every room up there was filled with them. But be careful, I think he sleeps up there."

Zala nodded and turned to her two men with a raised eyebrow. They nodded too, but the shorter one stepped in and spoke softly. "I think we should all stay close. It would be easy for one person waiting down here to be found and to give the game away. Better that we all know where each other is."

"You heard Gartan," said Zala. "We stick together."

As a group, they moved down the hallway to the stairs, stepping lightly and carefully, easing across floorboards and avoiding the sides of the rooms so that they would not bump into any shelves or ornaments. Gartan took the lead as they began to climb the stairs, and Kargin waited for the other three to follow before beginning to edge up the stairs sideways, keeping an eye on where they had come from.

They paused at the second floor while Gartan listened for movement in its rooms. Then he slunk down the hallway a short way, investigating the nearest rooms before returning and shaking his head.

"Should be fine. Keep going." He took the lead again to the third floor.

Shanti's heart was beating like a drum in a parade. The sound was pounding in her ears so loud that she was sure everyone else could hear, sure in fact that the noise would wake Gaibaan and bring him running upon them. Her mouth was bone dry, and swallowing was becoming difficult.

Gartan turned the handle slowly and pushed the door gently into darkness. He moved into the hallway. Dunin moved after him, and held out a hand for Shanti. She took it and followed.

The lights that grew along the corners of the hallway ceiling were still glowing, though darker than Shanti remembered. Usually these sort of lights provided a decent light at all times. Seeing as people generally didn't sleep in hallways there was no need to cover them at night. But she found that they outlined Gartan's form as he moved forward rather than illuminating him.

Kargin and Zala followed them into the hallway and shut the door to the stairs behind them. Kargin rolled his shoulders and reached into a pocket to pull out something small. He spread his arms a little and rolled his head around on his neck, loosening it. Gartan opened the first door.

It was exactly as Shanti had described.

SHE RELEASED A SIGH OF RELIEF. She hadn't realised the concern that had been clenching her shoulders. Concern that, somehow, Gaibaan may have realised what she had found out and managed to hide the insects in the time she was gone. She knew that the idea was inconceivable, because of the sheer size of the hive and boxes, but it had been a worry in the back of her mind. Now she was vindicated.

Zala followed Gartan in and stood in the middle of the room, turning slowly to take in the piles of glass containers that filled the space. Her eyes met Shanti's and she shook her head slowly, her eyes and mouth wide in shock.

"It's not that I doubted you," she breathed. "But the scale of this…" She licked her lips, still shaking her head. She rubbed one eye with her hand, as if trying to ensure that what she saw was truly real. "And you feel certain that these insects are responsible for the blight?"

"It's not the only room," was Shanti's answer, beckoning the others back into the hall and pointing at the door that had concealed the queen she had found earlier. The group moved over and opened this door.

This time there was a sharp intake of breath from Dunin as the room was revealed. He whistled quietly.

"Look at all these potted lights," he whispered.

"They are for feeding the queen, see here?" Shanti showed them where some of the lights had been placed inside the enclosure and how the insects were sucking nutrients out of it, swelling their abdomen like little glowing pouches. Then, they waddled back to the huge and gross queen, before disgorging the light into her mouth.

"And here you can see the transport boxes. Clearly he has been taking these workers, as they are the ones that attack the lights, and placing them at various locations in Gorduum."

Zala nodded. "You are absolutely right. Okay, Kargin, if you can gather up some of these insects we will go to the council and-"

A scream pierced the quiet, making Shanti shriek and Dunin leap sideways into a tall light in its pot, knocking it over and causing him to trip and fall to the ground on his back. A figure burst from the hallway, metal flashing in the dim light as it shouted and flailed around. Kargin was closest to the door and it was he who bore the brunt of the sudden attack. Shanti was flattened against a wall, both hands pressed to her abdomen as she tried to see what was happening.

Kargin and the intruder were struggling, arms around each other's shoulders. Their heads banged against her other, making Shanti wince at the hollow sound that their skulls made. Gartan circled the pair, reaching forward and withdrawing, frustration clearly showing on his face. Zala was on the opposite side of the struggle, also trying to find a way to help but finding none.

There were no voices now, only the heavy sound of bodies twisting and smacking into the floor as they tumbled around each other. Panting and grunting were the only sounds that left their lips. There was a louder grunt than the others, followed by slow rattling exhalation. One of the figures slipped to the floor and ceased moving. The first figure stood, swaying, and turned to examine the others in the room.

Shanti saw, as his face turned into the limited light, that it was Gaibaan. His eyes shone like the full moon. In his hand, glinting as the light caught its edge, she could see now that he was holding a long thin knife. Fury twisted his lips and he lifted the blade to point it at Gartan. Gaibaan backed away slowly so that he could see all of them and no-one was left behind him. The blade was darkened and dripping.

"What in the unknown name are you people doing in here!?" Gaibaan bellowed.

Zala lifted her hands wide, palms facing him. "Please sir, be calm-"

"Why should I be calm? You have invaded my property madam, and I would be entirely justified in dealing with you all in exactly the manner I have dealt with your companion there!" He pointed one foot at the still body of Kargin. A black shadow was growing from beneath where the bald man lay sprawled. Shanti felt her breath coming in swift, shallow bursts. There was a ceramic clonk as Dunin tried to turn and lift himself up from where he was sprawled across the floor.

"You stay right there!" snarled Gaibaan. While his attention was on the vulnerable man, Gartan began to move towards Gaibaan's back, but the slender man spun back, jabbing the knife towards him.

"Oh no you don't! Move over there by the girl!" Gartan moved extremely slowly but came over to stand next to Shanti. Now Gaibaan's eyes met hers.

"You." Shanti had never heard such a small and simple word spoken with such a level of anger and hatred. The syllable burned into her ears and buried itself in her chest. "I should have known. You were so ingrateful for all the things I tried to do for you." He laughed bitterly. "You four will stay in this room while I decide what to do with you." He moved backwards to the door. "Because, as you have surely figured out by now, I can't exactly take you for punishment with the authorities, can I? Wouldn't want them finding the queen."

He stepped out of the doorway and pulled it swiftly shut with a bang. Gartan leapt forward, but couldn't get a grip on the handle before they heard the loud click of a lock sliding into place. Gartan stepped back and placed both hands over his face.

Zala stepped over to him, placing both hands on his shoulders and leaning against him. Shanti could tell that the woman was whispering to Gartan, but she decided she would leave them to their privacy. Without looking at what lay in the middle of the room, she moved to help her uncle out of the tangle of pottery that he was still lying on.

"Are you okay?" she asked, as he took the hand she had offered and pulled himself to his feet.

"Ah…" said Dunin with a concerned light in his eyes. "It hurts a bit…" He turned to show his back to Shanti, wincing as shards of pottery shifted and fell. She sucked air between her teeth.

Somehow, Dunin had fallen right on top of the pots that broke beneath him as he fell, and their ceramic shards had left many slices and cuts across his back. There were wedges and slivers of pale red pottery stuck in some of the wounds. Blood flowed freely down her uncle's back, soaking his clothes.

"It looks bad, but hopefully they are not deep," Shanti said, trying to keep her uncle calm.

He made a noise in the back of his throat to acknowledge what she said, though he did not look convinced.

"Zala?" called Shanti. The other woman came over and groaned.

"What did you do, you fool?" she said, carefully plucking the pieces of pottery out of him, not pausing as he groaned and moaned. "Do we have any fabric to bind this?"

"I'll look," said Shanti. "But there are only shallow cuts, so won't he be okay?"

"He would be okay normally, I'm sure. But we don't know how long that madman will keep us in here, and if we can't stem the bleeding it could be worse than usual."

Shanti quickly found that there was nothing suitable for binding the wounds in the room with them and so tore a wide strip off the bottom of her dress. Together she and Zala wound it around Dunin and got him to sit down and hold it in place.

"Okay," said Zala once Shanti's uncle was settled. "Gartan is pretty upset about his brother, but he thinks he can pick the lock from this side."

"Should I say something...?" Shanti wasn't sure exactly how to ask the question, or what she meant by it. She didn't really know the short man, but what had happened to his brother... Zala shook her head.

"No, maybe later you can talk to him. For now, you need to stay here and watch over your uncle. We are going to see if we can track down that bastard and deal with him."

"Okay."

Shanti sat with her uncle and watched as the other two worked on the door for a minute or two, before it thunked and they were able to pull it open. The hallway beyond was overflowing with shadow. Zala turned back to Shanti and Dunin.

"We will be back soon." And with that, they were through the door and gone, closing it behind them.

TIME DRAGGED ON. Shanti could see morning light beginning to peek around the edges of the curtains drawn behind the glass containers of insects. The room remained dim with no way to open the curtains. She wondered how she had ended up here. She had thought that coming to Gorduum would be an adventure, but only that she would see sights that she had never dreamed of seeing, and meeting people with experiences so far beyond her own. She hadn't imagined that adventure could be so life threatening.

It had been difficult for her to leave, knowing that her family would have to manage without her there to clean up after them, to take care of the store, to talk to the neighbours and calm them down after one prank or another. She found herself thinking of Taanin, working in his fields and oblivious to the world around him. Would he even remember to eat if she didn't return to remind him?

She had wanted to reconnect with her uncle, and she had managed to do that. She had met some wonderful people. She suddenly found herself longing to be with one of them in particular, a feeling that surprised her initially. There was nothing more that she wanted then to have someone to hold her in this moment of dread and there was only one smiling face that she knew would comfort her now. Shanti wondered if Keema knew what this feeling was. She wanted to talk to her, to ask her. She felt her cheeks flush at the thought.

Perhaps she should have left well enough alone and stayed in Graama. She pondered the idea. Stay working in her mother's store. Spend time with Buan and Fabrin, before eventually having to choose one of them to settle down with. No. She shook her head slightly at the thought. I couldn't have stayed. I wish I wasn't in this room right now, but I needed to see what was beyond the forest. Did Keema want to see what lay outside Gorduum?

A floorboard in the hallway creaked.

"Do you think... they are... back... already?" gasped Dunin. He was having difficulty breathing, but Shanti tried not to dwell on the possible depth of his injuries. She couldn't afford to focus on them right now, there were other more urgent matters to be worried about.

Shanti looked at the door.

"No."

She stood and took a deep breath.

She wanted to go home and see her family.

She needed to know that her father was recovering. She knew her mother needed help to run the shop. There was a freedom in being able to return to her home, to ensure that her people were well and safe. If she knew she was able to do that then she knew she would be able to explore even further into the world. But first she would need to find a way home.

Shanti began to move towards the door, sliding her feet more than stepping, so that there was no click of her shoes on the floor.

She wanted to find Darsat and Dulku and have them show her more sights in Gorduum, this beautiful, gigantic place; full of buildings and art and people.

She pulled her arms back and twisted them from side to side, feeling the muscles in her back and shoulders stretch and loosen from the anxious tightness they had contracted into.

She wanted to see so much more, to bring lights to her whole village, to go exploring into far away countries.

She was standing right behind the door now, positioned so that she would be behind when it opened, but not close enough for it to strike her if it opened quickly. She lifted her arms.

When it opened, the door did open swiftly, but there was no other movement. Quickly, Shanti lifted a foot and kicked the door back hard. There was a shout and bang as the door hit whoever was standing on the other side. Not waiting to give them time to recover, she lunged around the door and dove onto the figure that was staggering back from the impact. They fell down underneath her and she called upon all the wrestling matches she had found herself subjected to with her brothers when they were younger.

She pushed the figure's arms down, keeping his hands away from her. She twisted her legs around his, keeping him from kicking free. Now, close to the figure, she could finally see if she was attacking their captor, or whether she had hurt Gartan.

Pale yellow eyes glared at her and she felt determination strengthen her muscles.

"You caught me by surprise," growled Gaibaan. "But I am stronger than you."

To prove his point, he began to strain against her grip, and he was right. She found that she was unable to hold him completely still. The point of his knife began to scratch at her arm. His mouth spread into a thin smile.

Now what, she asked herself. Where are the others? What will happen to me, or to Dunin? How could such a simple errand as collecting an order of lights end up this way? How did I beat Fellbin when he was at his most energetic? She scoured her memories, fear making them flash through her mind in bursts.

Wrestling with Fellbin in the dusty fields during summer, trying to tip water from the watering can down each other's backs, shrieking in laughter. She even thought of matches with Taanin, tickling the sides of her stomach when she was younger. Gaibaan's arms pushed against her again and Shanti grunted with the effort of keeping him still. The point of his knife was a hot spot on her arm now, but she tried to put it out of her mind.

The fear in her stomach and anger in her head burned like an oven, red and deep. She remembered a time she had felt the same burning emotion, watching Ban laugh about his captured rabbit. And then she knew what to do.

With her right hand she had been holding Gaibaan's knifeless hand. Shanti shifted her grip and, just as he began to take advantage of the movement, she dug in with her nails. Just as the boy in the forest had, Gaibaan screamed. Exactly as she had done those many years ago, she lunged forward with the top of her head and was rewarded with a sharp crack. There was a clatter as the knife dropped from his spasming hand and Shanti launched herself off him to snatch it up. She spun, holding it in front of her, and saw him twisting on the ground, clutching at his face as blood ran between his fingers.

"Zala!" Shanti yelled as loud as she could. "Come back now!"

Shanti floated in dreams and the colourful madness of her memories. She saw visions of the city, dripping with darkness and shadow. A giant insect strode through her uncle's apartment, cracking the walls with its carapace as it forced its way through them. The statue near Graama pushed itself up and out of the earth, standing towering over the forest, while Fellbin stood beside her, smiling, white light pouring out from between his teeth.

She felt her body twist and turn, sweating in panic, and then returning to a fitful rest. It took a full day and night of sleep before Shanti began to come back from the jumbled memories and to feel aware of herself again. She swam out of the depths of sleep to find herself wrapped in the uncomfortable lace of her uncle's guest bed. Shanti lay and stared at the ceiling, trying to unpick the threads of what had happened. Eventually she sat up, stretching and groaning as her muscles complained.

She rose and cleaned her face, pausing to stare at herself in the mirror. She studied the eyes that stared back at her. Memories pushed to the forefront of her mind.

Gartan had bounded through the door at the top of stairs within an instant of her call, quickly securing Gaibaan and making sure he could do no more harm. Zala was holding the matron firmly with one arm twisted behind her back. The woman appeared surprised and bewildered by all that was happening around her, not any rush to cause any trouble.

Zala had taken Gaibaan away, letting Shanti and Dunin know that she would deal with him. Shanti hadn't asked exactly what that meant would happen to the vicious pale man, but she was happy enough to let Zala arrange a suitable punishment. Dunin had been helped to his feet and Zala had sent both Shanti and her uncle to a doctor whom she was familiar with. Dunin would need rest and plenty of attention, but Zala had promised to ensure he would receive it.

Shanti closed her eyes and pushed the memories of the room to the back of her mind once more. Then, she left her room and moved into the dining room of the apartment.

Dunin was sitting with both hands around a steaming mug, staring out a distant window.

"Good morning," murmured Shanti, sitting beside him.

"Glad to see you made it back to us," he answered.

"What time is it?" Shanti stretched, feeling the pain and tension in her shoulders ease.

"It's been a whole day." Dunin sipped at his mug. "Zala has arranged for Kargin's funeral to be today."

Shanti felt the surprise wash past her, without sinking in. Of course. He would need to be remembered soon. Waiting longer could only be harder on his family. She wondered what his family were like, having met him so briefly. What were they going through at this moment? They probably weren't sitting with a warm cup of tea to start their day. She felt a tear move down her cheek.

"I didn't even know him," she began, unsure how to finish the sentence.

"I didn't know him well myself," said Dunin. "But he was always someone Zala referred to when there was a difficult situation. Maybe a debtor wasn't paying, or a delivery was suspiciously lacking." He smiled. "Kargin was someone who fixed problems."

"Should we attend?"

"I think we owe it to him."

Gunin helped the two of them dress. Neither of them felt much like speaking. Shanti had worn her nicest clothes to the gala and they were not in a condition to wear again so soon. So she had to put on a deep red dress that was less well cut and made of a rougher material. Gunin made impressed noises though, and helped her pull her hair into something more attractive than her usual plait. She was pleasantly surprised at how well Dunin scrubbed up when he wanted to as well. His waistcoat was embroidered in a soft cream thread, and he had found a hat that was not faded or threadbare.

He took her arm as they left.

"Are you doing okay?"

"I can't complain really," said Shanti. She was very aware of their destination. "Is it normal that Zala be the one to arrange his funeral?"

"I believe Gartan should have been the one, as his closest relative. But, obviously, that was impossible."

The taxi took them to a nearby Temple quickly. The sun wasn't even at noon yet. Shanti looked around at the streets, clogged with people scurrying on their errands. She didn't know how the city could continue as normal. The driver spoke cheerfully with her uncle, and Shanti found she was staring at the man as he spoke. How could he be so happy? How could all these people continue as though nothing important had happened? The source of the blight had been uncovered, a man had died. Surely everyone should be celebrating or mourning, not this... this... normal day.

The driver shared some gossip that had flooded the streets the previous day about a fire in the rich end of town. Apparently it had been brought under control quite quickly, luckily saving the neighbouring houses, but completely devouring every stick of the original structure. He said that he thought it was the Skuggi, moving on from their attempts to destroy the livelihood of Gorduum. Dunin snapped at the man to keep such thoughts to himself.

They arrived at the temple before much more could be said, and Dunin paid for the trip then took Shanti's arm again as they walked into the Temple.

Shanti felt comforted by the familiar shapes and symbols that surrounded her. Although the domed ceiling in the round hall was much larger than Bratis' hall back in Graama, that only heightened the feeling she had of being a small child again, stepping into a place of safety and kindness. She moved with her uncle to kneel on some very wide plump cushions near the sides of the hall. Older people were settling into the seats and benches that circled the space, grumbling as they adjusted themselves into semi-comfortable positions.

Shanti felt a familiar knot of guilt begin to tangle itself in her stomach. She knew that she should have spent more of her time in Gorduum trying to find a Temple herself, or thinking of how to bring the Masked God's compassion to those around her. This one was so close to her uncle's apartment, she probably could have come in each morning to start her day. But she reminded herself that she had achieved a great many things in her time in the city, not least managing to disarm and injure a terrible violent man long enough to rescue some friends who would have suffered immensely otherwise. She put the knot aside for now.

In the middle of the hall, surrounded by many veiled attendees, the priest spoke softly to Gartan while holding the short man's hands in his own. Zala was standing nearby, but with her hands held together in front of her and her eyes down. She was wearing a veil too.

"Was Zala related to Kargin?" asked Shanti.

"Not that I am aware of," replied Dunin. "But I know that she has always tried to do the best she can by her workers. I am sure she has taken this very hard."

The ceremony followed the same patterns as a funeral back in Graama would have. Family shared their joyful memories of Kargin, through sniffs and tears. When wails rose from the attendees, all would pause to let the pain pass through them. After the formal speaking, the attendees were encouraged to come forward and share their condolences with the family individually. The family stood in a line, and attendees spoke to them as they left the Temple.

Zala took a position at the end of the line, not

quite declaring herself family, but certainly close enough to be approached by any who felt it appropriate. Shanti saw that only about half of the attendees went to her.

Dunin strode over to her quickly, embracing her in a tight hug that went on longer than Shanti would have expected. The pair spoke quietly to one another without turning to face each other, their hands clutching one another tightly. Shanti remained at a distance, so as not to intrude. I am glad they have someone to speak to about what has happened, she thought to herself. It would be terrible to have to try and keep this all in your own head.

Shanti moved forward and coughed softly as she touched her uncle on the shoulder. "I am going to go. I would like to try to see Dulku again before I leave Gorduum."

Dunin barely nodded before Shanti turned and left the Temple.

SHANTI WAS able to get a taxi to the address on the card that Dulku had given her when she arrived in the city. As it moved through the streets she looked back on her first day in Gorduum. She had been so unsure about the streets, so wide-eyed about the buildings and people. And yet here she was navigating through them all without a second thought. She had come a long way in a short time.

Dulku's house was bigger than an apartment, but smaller than the rich homes Shanti had found herself inside more recently. Each level in the building appeared to be a complete and luxurious home. Dulku and Darsat lived on the second floor. Dulku herself opened the door, her hair bound up in a simple scarf. She smiled broadly when she saw Shanti.

"Why Shanti, how delightful to see you! Darsat was telling me that you have visited him recently-"

Shanti fell forward into the woman's arms, bursting into tears.

Dulku bustled her inside and listened while Shanti unleashed all the fear and tension that had been building upon her during her time in Gorduum. The words tumbled out of her in no sensible order, beginning with the horror of what had happened in Gaibaan's house, but then jumping to the time that he had nearly run her down, and then her fear of being lost on the river, or when Keema left her at the University, and how her own uncle had turned out to be so distant at first, and more and more. The older woman patted Shanti on the shoulder as the initial tide ebbed and Shanti found that she was able to lift herself upright again. She sniffed and wiped her face with the back of her hand.

"I'm so sorry, I have completely overwhelmed you," she began, but Dulku shushed her quickly.

"No matter, no matter! It sounds as though you have been caught up in quite a bit more adventure than you were maybe expecting! Would you like some tea?"

Shanti nodded and then remained in the sitting room while Dulku left to prepare the drinks. Shanti relished the quiet, the escape from all her cares. I wish I had come here sooner, she thought.

Dulku returned with hot drinks, and then asked Shanti to go through everything that had happened since leaving the train when she arrived in Gorduum. This time, the story took much longer and was explained in order, and Dulku was able to pause Shanti and ask questions. Shanti could see by her intermittent slow nods that this was much more comprehensible to Dulku. She was grateful to the woman for allowing her to explode when she arrived, it felt good to expel all those thoughts and words.

"I just feel like I should have done more. I should have realised what was happening."

"No love," answered Dulku. "It sounds to me as though things could have been much worse without you."

Before they had even managed to finish off the pot of tea, Shanti found herself yawning over and over. She covered her mouth with her hand and apologised, and then rubbed her eyes.

"I think you might need to go and get some rest," said Dulku as she gathered up the cups.

"No," Shanti shook her head. "I slept for over a day yesterday! And I haven't even managed to ask how you have been this week-" she broke off as she yawned again. Dulku laughed.

"That's as may be, but look at you! I'd be surprised if you didn't sleep all the way home in the taxi!"

Shanti found she was too tired to argue, and so made her farewells, promising to return to visit both Dulku and Darsat as soon as she returned to Gorduum. She hoped it would be soon.

In the taxi home, Shanti felt her head falling backwards towards the soft cushion seats, and her eyelids felt as heavy as boulders, but she refused to allow herself to fall asleep. She was concerned that being asleep in a taxi would make her far too easy pickings for any duplicitous types. And so she fought her instincts all the way back to Dunin's apartment.

With a head full of wool, she carefully lifted each foot up the steps one by one, until she managed to go back into the apartment. Neither Dunin nor the lad were there, so she went to her room and collapsed face down into the bed. Sleep crashed on top of her.

. . .

MORNING ARRIVED before Shanti was ready for it and she lifted her head with difficulty. Sunlight was slipping through the window. She sat up on the edge of her bed and squeezed the heels of her palms into her eyes then sighed.

With arms that felt as heavy as thick metal chains, Shanti moved around the room and gathered her belongings back into her suitcase. She was confused to discover that, somehow, they wouldn't all fit, and she had to stuff clothing down far harder than she recalled having to do when she was packing to leave. But, soon, she was packed and the room looked as though she had never been there. She stood in the middle of it and examined it. What would she leave behind in this city, in this apartment, with these people she had met? What would remain of her here? Would anyone think of her?

She pulled the suitcase down to the kitchen where Dunin sat with a mug of tea once more. He saw her walk in, took in the suitcase, and then stood. He walked over and hugged Shanti. She returned the hug, and smiled as he stepped back, with hands on her shoulders.

"You did well," he said. He opened his mouth to say more but then frowned, unsure what else to add. "Don't wait so long before you visit again," he ended with.

"I won't," said Shanti, leaning over to kiss his cheek. "Thank you."

She spent the taxi ride to the train station going over her contracts and bank notes. She did so carefully, using the lip of the satchel to conceal her papers from the casual eyes of passers-by. She wanted to stay in Gorduum. She had realised that there was something very important that she had left unresolved so far. However, she could not disappoint her whole village over it. The contracts she had made said that the lights would be delivered to the railway station today, and she would need to escort them back safely to Graama, though her heart hurt at the thought of leaving things unsaid in Gorduum.

The contract saw her able to access another area of the station that she had not seen when she arrived. Beyond the broad flat grey platforms for the passenger trains, steaming like monstrous metal serpents beneath the broad curve of the vast ceiling, was a small, dirtier area. It was a field of gravel covered in rails and carriages, teeming with greasy workers in rough clothing, and carrying heavy metal pieces of equipment. A guide took her over to where nearly fifteen large carts, each drawn by two massive horses, had been driven through a pair of gigantic metal gates and up to a train car that was simply a set of wooden walls around an empty space. It was as though someone had removed all the seats and a wall of one of the passenger cars she had ridden in on the way to Gorduum.

The greasy workers were shifting boxes and pots of lights into the space.

"Careful now please," Shanti called out as one pair nearly dropped the box that they had held between them. The workers glared back at her, but she ignored the look. It is worth being disliked for a moment rather than disappointing everyone back home, she told herself.

Shanti tracked down the representative of the company and exchanged contracts with him. They both read through the terms and checked that the delivery was correct, then signed the forms and gave them back. Shanti handed over the money and bank notes that she had been entrusted with. The representative took these and locked them in a very weighty looking chest that was placed onto a cart between two wide men. They were dressed very much in the same way Kargin had been and Shanti found she was on the verge of crying without warning. She turned away and took a deep breath.

"Are you alright ma'am?" asked the representative.

"Yes. Yes, certainly," she replied, without looking back. She stood straighter and watched the delivery being moved into the cargo car. "I was taken by surprise. But I will be alright now."

A thought struck her and she walked forward, helping pick up one of the smaller boxes. A wide bed of light blue lights created a lush blanket inside the box.

"Good morning," she said to the worker lifting the other end of the box. The worker nodded, as if agreeing to Shanti's statement was a favour she would fulfil, but that required no reply in return.

"I just wondered," asked Shanti between gasps of air as they lugged the box over to the car. "If you know. Where I can find. The Bare Faced Con?"

'Sure enough," answered the worker, and after they had loaded the box safely, she explained the directions to Shanti, who noted them down carefully.

SHANTI BREATHED DEEPLY as the train left Gorduum later that bright cold morning. Far behind her, in the cargo carriages, boxes and boxes of carefully packed lights would be shifting in their soil-filled pots, gently sliding and wobbling as the train rattled along the tracks. Outside the window she watched the fields of light farms roll past, looking more like regular farms and fields of crops now under daylight then the galaxies and stars that she had admired as she arrived in the dark of night.

She leaned back in the cushioned seat and absent-mindedly scratched at the scab that had formed near the wrist of her left arm. She flinched and shifted a little as a bruise twinged near the base of her spine.

For now, she was glad of the lack of conversation and company. She could rest and relax and look forward to returning to familiar people and familiar ways of life. To small buildings that housed friendly people who she knew and who cared for her. She felt like she was in need of the time to replenish her energies.

But then.

Then she would return to the trains and their passage to the wider world. She had never expected it to contain so much, and now she had whet her appetite and knew she could never be satisfied without following its trails as far as she could go.

First, she would deliver the lights to the village council and dance with Buan at the festival. She would sit with her father and tell him about the things she had seen. She would describe the art and buildings of the great city to Fabrin. She might even help Fellbin play some tricks on others in the village.

But then she would return to Gorduum. She would find the Bare-Faced Con and wait for someone to play darts with. And if that went well, then maybe, together, they would see the world.

THE END

ABOUT THE AUTHOR

Aaron Dick is a teacher living north of Auckland in New Zealand with his wife, their two daughters, and a small menagerie of household animals.

He grew up as a voracious reader of science-fiction and fantasy, often to the annoyance of his unheeded family. Becoming an author was a childhood dream, alongside being a palaeontologist, or a rock star.

His stories have featured in a collection of New Zealand short stories inspired by Grimm's' Fairy Tales and in the gothic art and lifestyle magazine Nocturne.

www.ingramcontent.com/pod-product-compliance
Lightning Source LLC
Chambersburg PA
CBHW051541030726

47592CB00001B/87